The Yesterday Girl

The Yesterday Girl
Springfield, OR 97478
gladeyepress.com

Published by GladEye Press March 2022

Cover photography by S.K. Nelson
Editing and layout by J.V. Bolkan

ISBN: 9781951289034

Library of Congress Control Number: 2021924953

Interior text is set primarily in Garamond, an old style typeface inspired by the famed French printer Claude Garamond in the 16th century.

For my grandchildren,
who light up my life in unexpected ways,
and seem to like me just the way I am.

"If you travel back into your own past, that destination becomes your future, and your former present becomes the past, which can't now be changed by your new future."

— Professor Hulk, *The Avengers: Endgame*

"It is a wise father that knows his own child."

—*William Shakespeare*

Prologue

8 May 1971

"Push!" the nurse shrieked.

"I can't," Jaz howled in retort like some wild, angry caged animal.

"Yes YOU CAN," the nurse repeated in a voice dialed up to 11. The doctor wasn't there and it was clear that although she knew the procedure, she was clearly panicked without the assistance of the physician. Hovering somewhere down between her legs, all Jaz could see was the nurse's head, no neck, just a bobbling cranium with a pair of eyes opened wide like two giant cantaloupes floating on an asymmetrical moon face, but she could feel her plastic gloved fingers digging hard into her thighs. "Pussssshhhh," the voice shrieked from the head.

God this hurt. In all of her 17 years, she had never experienced pain like this. But she wanted this thing, this baby out of her, right now, so she did what she was told and pushed. In fact, she pushed so hard that when it rocketed from her vagina, her body shot back against the spongy hospital pillow like a bullet. Her eyes stung from the sweat dripping from her hair, but she opened them just long enough to see the nurse, still down there, but now holding this red, gooey creature covered in plasmatic gook and slippery afterbirth. "It's a boy," she said coolly, as if she hadn't been freaking out just mere seconds ago. Standing up, she whisked the little alien off to another part of the room. The hospital room became a miasma of activity—other nurses flooding in, along with the doc who apparently had finally decided to show up.

Doctor Weber strolled over to the bedside. "What's wrong with him?" Jaz asked.

"Not a thing. He's just fine," he said with a self-satisfied smile, presumably taking credit as if he'd done any of the work.

Jaz didn't tell him that she had meant what was wrong with her husband? Where was he? He was nowhere to be found, but she didn't bother to correct him.

When the screaming started and they'd wheeled her off to the delivery room, Adam had decided this might be a good time to slip out for a quick toke. Jaz wouldn't notice if he was there or not. The screaming made him feel edgy. He didn't like it. Besides, he'd be back in time for the birth, he reasoned. He tapped one Converse-covered foot to the muzak as he rode the elevator down the three floors to the hospital lobby, and then breezily exited through the automatic doors. Woosh . . . out into the fresh air. It was hot up there and the sterile, unidentifiable hospital odors made him feel dizzy; not in a good way. He walked around the back of the building searching for a secluded alcove to light up. Slipping behind a big metal green dumpster, he pulled the fat doobie he'd been hankering for all day long out of his shirt pocket. He lit up and took a long, lazy hit and held it in for 10 full seconds, letting the sweet, earthy taste and pleasant properties take hold. If only he could smoke pot every day, all day. Oh yeah, well, he kind of did, he thought, but now with this kid coming, it could potentially screw up his whole routine.

The last month or so had been bad. Jasmine had been a total bitch, constantly nagging him about smoking too much weed. "Why don't you go look for a job?" She didn't seem to understand that jobs for 18-year old high school dropouts weren't exactly that easy to come by. Sure, he could get a job in fast food, but why should he when he could make more money selling dope? He leaned against the dumpster and took another deep drag allowing the soothing calm to wash over him. No worries. No screaming. No bad smells. Ahhh, just mellow.

"Dude," someone said. Startled, Adam turned in the direction of the voice. An orderly in green scrubs was making his way toward him. He quickly snuffed the joint out with his finger and tried not to act stoned. "Hey," he nodded. The orderly, a burly, guy, probably 6 foot, looked mean. He thought he was busted for sure. "Whatcha doin' back here little dude?" the guy asked. Adam stammered a weak reply: "uh, wife's having a baby . . . upstairs . . . thought I'd come down for a smoke before she popped." The orderly smiled then and said, "That's cool." He pressed in behind the dumpster next to him. "Smells like some good shit," he said.

"Primo," Adam said nodding and pulling the joint back out from his jacket pocket. "Try some?"

"Fuck yeah," the orderly answered enthusiastically.

Adam couldn't remember how long he stood out by the dumpster getting high; it could have been a few minutes; could have been an hour. All he knew was that he'd seized his mellow.

The doctor and another set of nurses began working on Jaz; delivering the afterbirth, another messy endeavor, and then snipping and sewing down there like a couple of gleeful little tailors. Mercifully, they had finally given her some drugs so she couldn't feel the pain anymore. She could hear the baby making bird-like squawking noises from across the room. With the birthing agony over, she could focus now on what had just happened. Was he okay? Did he have the correct number of fingers and toes? Despite the last nine months spent watching her growing belly and anguishing over the fact that she was pregnant at 17, she still hoped the baby would be healthy. Plus, it wasn't exactly an accident, this pregnancy. It was the inevitable conclusion to a summer of frenetic teenage lovemaking—in fields and orchards, in the backseat of the car; in Adam's bedroom listening to Gregg Allman after passing a joint around, when his parents were away. She remembered clearly the night he had told her he was moving. He rolled off her and was lying on his back looking up at the stars on the blanket they had spread out in the dirt in the orchard adjacent to her house.

"We're moving," he said.

"What?" Jaz said as she fumbled with the clasps on her bra. "What do you mean, you're moving?"

"We're moving," Adam repeated, taking a drag from the cigarette he'd just lit, "to fuckin' Iowa man." The dispassionate way he said it made Jasmine pause. Didn't he care about their relationship? Was he just going to leave her here, drowning alone in this stupid cesspool of a small town? It wasn't fair.

And so, it began in earnest. Unspoken between them but carried out with the zeal of two impulsive and horny kids, not so much in love with one another, but desperate to escape from what they both perceived as unsatisfactory home lives. The plan, though ill-conceived, seemed like it was the one thing that could force the hand of both sets of parents. And it had worked as well as any plan that's deeply flawed from the beginning can be expected to work. Jaz told Adam she was pregnant. They broke the news to their parents, who in their heart of hearts knew that teenager marriages rarely succeed, but a mutual inplicit desire for grandchildren persueded them to reluctantly consent to the marriage.

The nine months leading up to now had been tumultuous, to say the least. Between Jaz riding a hormonal roller-coaster of emotions which only pregnancy can produce, and Adam being Adam, carrying on as if nothing in his life had changed or ever would, life had been a tsunami of slammed doors and angry fits and starts and hurt feelings, dramatic apologies, and make-up sex. He'd started and quit or was fired from five different jobs, crashed their VW, emptied their meager bank account to buy pot, sold their waterbed—twice, and gotten a misdemeanor for growing a single marijuana plant that he'd foolishly left outside their duplex to get some sun. Jaz had quickly assessed that this would be her life.

Back in her room, she pulled the flimsy hospital sheet up around her neck, turned on her side, and wept into her pillow. After the delivery, she had held her son for all of five minutes, just long enough to check his fingers and toes and make sure they totaled twenty, before they whisked him away, ostensibly to be bathed and swaddled. After stitching her up, they gave her a mild sedative and wheeled her back to her room. Outside the window, it was getting dark, and Adam never showed up.

1

2 August 2019/30 November 1971

Breathing in and out slowly, evenly, she closed her eyes and waited for it. A swirling kaleidoscope of sunsets and landscapes. Kittens and puppies. Spring blooms. Fall foliage and pumpkin patches, flora and fauna and forests and snow angels. Summer magic. A memory box of humanity rushing past, followed by a flash of brilliant light, juxtaposed by a composition as dark as pitch—spinning and spiraling and vanishing as she began the stealth descent through the deepest and most disconcerting part of the journey—plunging headlong through the lens that would momentarily deposit her, unceremoniously, into the light and time at the end of it.

Once her feet were planted securely on terra firma, Imogen opened her eyes and looked around at her surroundings. A clear, blue sky and the sun, directly above her, beat down hot against her bare face and arms. Luckily, she was dressed appropriately for the elements in jeans and a cool cotton T-shirt. Although it seemed uncharacteristically warm for late November, when she bent down and began rummaging through her backpack, it was deeply reassuring to find a warm down parka, a flannel shirt, and an extra pair of heavy wool socks packed inside. Although it was warm now, she'd surely need it tonight when the temperature would likely dip into the teens.

Part of prepping for any trip through time required that she assemble the 21st century versions of items she might need, to which they transformed into the period-specific articles apropos to where she was going. How this worked never ceased to fill her with wonder and amazement—one minute you're staring into a completely still, inanimate, two-dimensional photograph and the next thing you know you've been magically transported inside the moving, vibrant, three-dimensional reality depicted in the picture.

Imogen rose from her kneeling position, and noting a stand of old growth Douglas firs bordering the trail and majestic Mount St. Helens looming in the distance, she breathed in the rich pungent scent of the forest and trees. Although the area where she had arrived was now clear of anyone, farther down the trail she could hear detached voices and laughter echoing up from other hikers, and presumably whomever had taken the picture she had just entered. The date stamped on the photo was November 30, 1971. And on the back, the caption read: "Spirit Lake trail-head near Mount St. Helens in Washington State." It was the area Adam Curry had last been seen before completely disappearing off the map.

In her research, Imogen had read that for many years prior to the volcanic eruption in 1980, Spirit Lake was a popular tourist destination. There were six camps on the shore of the lake as well as a number of resorts that catered to visitors, including Mount St. Helens Lodge, which was occupied by Harry R. Truman, who would become one of the volcano's most vocal victims, famously saying, "If the mountain goes, I'm going with it!"

Her client, Sean Curry, vaguely remembered his mom showing him an old photograph once of the man he believed to be his father, standing outside of a rustic grocery store, flashing a smile and a peace sign, his large backpack on the porch at his feet. But over a course of many moves, the picture had long disappeared. And when his mother died last year, most of Sean's remembrances of his dad died along with her. However, he did recall that the lost photo had a date stamp printed on it, which had allowed Imogen to find a similar photo with a date close to the original.

Imogen lifted the heavy pack, foisted it up and onto her thin shoulders, and headed down the trail toward the cabins and camps by the lake to see what information she could gather and to pick up a few more provisions, well, probably goodies, for the upcoming hike. As she rounded the final turn, a magnificent, crystal-clear mountain lake came into view. But clear was an understatement, its luminous turquoise color seemed surreal and unworldly, like it couldn't possibly be real.

Up ahead, a gathering of people mingled outside a sturdy, log-built structure, likely the community store. Although it possibly wasn't nearly as busy as during the summer months, there were still quite a few people milling about on the porch drinking sodas and eating candy bars, perhaps squeezing in one last hike in the warm weather before the rain and snow returned. Like many of these types of camp stores, a large community message board attached to the front featured layers of fliers and paper plates and scraps of papers with messages for so-and-so to meet Jason at cabin #4 or where to meet a hiking party at a certain time for a rendezvous. Imogen scanned the board looking for any messages or notices for or about Adam Curry, but seeing none, headed up the steps, leaned her backpack against the wall—one of several others already there, and entered the store through the squeaky screen door.

Taking a basket and hanging the handles over her arm, Imogen browsed the shelves, picking out a few extra provisions for the trail—disposable salt and pepper shakers, candy bars, a couple bags of chips, a bottle of rum to fill up the flask she'd noticed in her pack. After making her purchases, she returned to the porch and struck up a conversation with a couple—a young woman about Imogen's age wearing overalls and hiking boots with a red bandanna tied around her hair—and her scruffy bearded partner.

"Where you headed?" the girl asked as Imogen began stowing the stuff she'd purchased inside her pack.

"Not sure yet," Imogen said. "I'm looking for someone who passed through here recently, but I don't know which direction he was headed."

"What's his name?" the bearded guy asked.

"Curry, Adam Curry," Imogen said. She wished she had a description of him, but Sean's recollection of him from the photograph was hazy at best.

The girl cocked her head to one side. "Hmmm, doesn't ring a bell," she said. Her partner nodded agreement, but then added, "there might be someone who can help you though."

Interested, Imogen stopped what she was doing to ask, "Who might that be?" she inquired.

"His name is Gil. He's the boat rental guy. Seems like he always knows who's coming through, not the day hikers so much, but the ones that are packing in. You might ask him."

"I'll do that," Imogen said. "Where can I find him?"

The guy pointed to a small, shabby looking shop/house with peeling paint, just beyond the store next to the docks. Imogen thanked them both and finished packing up. She filled her flask with rum, for the cold nights, she rationalized.

As Imogen approached, she observed an elderly gentleman sitting on the porch. His wardrobe comprised faded coveralls and a pair of well-worn boots; and on his head, one of those iconic yellow fisherman hats like you'd see in a Gorton's Seafood commercial. She also noticed his aged hands, creased permanently by many years of boat oil and grease, she surmised, as he whittled away at something resembling a fish from a small piece of wood.

"You must be Gil?" Imogen asked in a chirpy manner, extending her hand to the man.

"That I am," Gil said, taking her hand for a quick shake before releasing it to spit chew out one corner of his mouth. "What kin I do for ye?" he asked in a grumpy sort of gravelly, old timer voice one completely expected to hear coming from him.

"I'm looking for a hiker that came this way recently," Imogen said. "I'm sorry, but I don't know exactly when, but his name is Adam Curry."

The old man stopped cutting into the wood, leaned back in his chair and stared across the water, seemingly lost in cavernous thought. He sat that way for a good minute or so before leaning forward again and pronouncing, "Nope, never heard of him."

Imogen was surprised. It had sure taken him a while to come up with an answer. "Well all right then, thanks for your time," she said. As she turned and began to walk away, she heard him say,

"Not many hikers leavin' out for the backcountry this late in the year, but I did see one about a week ago; don't know if his name was Adam Curry or not, but he was headin' up the direction of Windy Ridge. That's all I know." When she stopped and turned back around, Gil was looking down, fully engrossed in his whittling as if he hadn't spoken to her at all.

"Thanks," Imogen called out.

Well, good, she thought. It was a start, and at least she could be confident that when she began this trek, at least she would be heading in the right direction. After getting everything properly stowed, she was ready to get going, and leaving the store and the lake and Gil behind, she headed up the sloped trail toward Windy Ridge.

She had to admit that she had been looking forward to some alone time to escape with her own thoughts. Even with the heavy pack she felt light in step, unburdened. So much had happened recently. During an investigation that had taken her back to the turn of the 20th century, she met Simon and fell in love. But someone was trying hard to keep them apart. That person turned out to be another time traveler from her own time named Teddy Diamond, who had kidnapped Simon's mother against her will and cruelly abandoned her in 1884, alone and pregnant with his son. When they figured out who Teddy was and Imogen was preparing to chase him back to the 21st century to confront him, Simon impulsively grabbed ahold of her at the very last minute. Without knowing whether or not a person from the past could survive time travel, astonishingly Simon was pulled through intact from 1913 to the present, they could only assume, because he had been conceived in the future.

That was three months ago. It hadn't been easy for Simon to adjust to so many new things and ideas that had changed or come about in the century between his previous life and this one. There were the inventions: the microwave oven, hair dryers, airplanes, television, radio, computers, batteries, cell phones, video games, vacuum cleaners, aerosol cans, movie cameras, medicine, to name only a few—and historical events and movements and revolutions and wars and beliefs about civil rights, a women's right to vote, abortion; two world wars, the atomic bomb, Vietnam, Albert Einstein, the Great Depression, feminism, Black Panthers, Mohammad Ali, prohibition, the holocaust, Marxism, Communism, Hitler, hippies, LSD, the Beatles, landing on the moon, 9/11—he had a lot of catching up to do.

And when the thoughts and questions became too overwhelming for him, Simon had taken up gardening and building miniature furniture. He read a lot. Imogen wasn't surprised that he was confused. She couldn't imagine how it must feel to not know about any of these things—having skipped right past all of it and landing somewhere on the other side of the century. Still, it was exhausting for her as well and she wearied of answering his endless stream of questions about everything.

Imogen had taken time off from her private investigation business to assist him in acclimating to his new life, but he was needy and clingy, so unlike the self-assured man she'd met in 1913. She tried to show him how to use the mouse to search on the computer for information on his own, but he was frustrated by the technology. "It's too soon," he had said, tossing his arms in the air in frustration and knocking the chair away from the desk. "I can't process all of this and learn how to operate your confounding machines at the same time!"

Eventually, she had gone out to the local thrift shop and purchased a set of dusty encyclopedias, a stack of old *LIFE* magazines, and various other ephemera that he could pore over and catch up on at his own speed. And then, if that wasn't enough to deal with, there was also the unsettling knowledge of the circumstances surrounding his birth—that his biological father had abandoned his mother in the past, but also dealing with Teddy's mother, Simon's grandmother, Mimi Pinky. About a month ago, Mimi had come by the house when Imogen was out and had spoken to Simon. During their conversation, she alluded to a ghastly unnatural mother/son bond she and Teddy evidently shared. When Imogen arrived home, Simon was visibly upset. It was too much for anyone to have to go through.

And yet, as much as she wanted to help Simon, getting away, although it seemed selfish, was exactly what Imogen needed to get centered and tend to her own neglected mental well-being. As she walked along the trail, she had ample time to not only revisit the disclosures that affected Simon, but also mull over the surprises Teddy had dropped on her as well. Before he had vanished into a photograph of Bikini Atoll—an island where the US was testing nuclear bombs in the 1950s, and a beach he was unlikely to ever return from—he confessed that to prevent Imogen's parents from revealing his secrets he was the one responsible for destroying their photographic portals and imprisoning them in the past. And though it was semi-satisfying to finally learn the "why" of her parents' disappearance, she still had no clue where or *when* her father was. Teddy had tossed out a small crumb of information about her mother's whereabouts—San Francisco—the burning question again was when? When was she in San Francisco? Pinpointing it was analogous to searching for a needle in a haystack.

Imogen was still a good distance from reaching the ridge when the sun began to set. Without the warmth of the sun, the temperature began to drop, and it was getting colder by the minute. It was time to stop and make camp before dark. Glancing around at her surroundings, Imogen spied a nice semi-flat area just off the trail there, tucked away between a pair of trees. Although modern hiking gear from REI would have been fancier, probably lighter too, and a bit more manageable, Imogen discovered that surprisingly she didn't mind going old school. She had everything she needed—a bedroll, a cook kit with a metal pot, a cup and spoon, a flint for fire-starting, a buck knife and little red axe, a pup tent that tied up nicely between the two trees, a few odds and ends, as well as some basic foodstuff. When it was all said and done, it really was all about getting back into nature again, walking through a magical forest gate and leaving the busy behind, basking in the warmth of the sun on her shoulders, her boots kicking up trail dust and pine needles as she hiked, breathing in that unmistakable damp mossy forest smell that she loved so much, and listening to the screeches and warbles of hawks and blue jays and other birds from high in the canopy of trees above.

After setting up the tent and using the flint to build a fire, Imogen cooked up some hearty beans and stew, which she ate all of, washing it down with a nice cup of hot chocolate. Her belly full, she felt spectacularly calm and relaxed, but also super tired from the all-day trek. Leaning against the tree she stared up at a magnificent sky filled with a billion bright stars. In the mountains, far away from the light pollution of the city it was like being inside an enormous planetarium, but better. As she allowed her mind to free float across the night sky, Imogen didn't hear the sound of someone shuffling up the trail until the person was standing practically in front of her. Startled, she lurched forward, spilling hot chocolate on her parka. A man, who appeared to be in his mid-forties had stopped in front of her and was staring directly into the fire without speaking. Imogen slowly grasped the handle of the axe hidden behind her although noting that despite the heavy pack on his back, he seemed lost and out of place in his black, lightweight raincoat, loafers, dark suit, and pressed white-collar shirt.

"Pardon me," he said as politely as if they were meeting for a bourbon and soda at some fancy restaurant rather than on some shadowy, dusty trail. "May I join you?"

Imogen felt like maybe she should be afraid. Something about his close-set, piercing eyes and weird attire screamed serial killer, but at the same time, his body language was that of just another weary hiker, looking to warm up beside a nice fire.

"Sure," Imogen said, her hand still holding onto the axe tightly but flashing him her best, most confident, I-am-not-afraid-of-you-just-because-I'm-a-woman-alone smile. The man nodded without speaking, unhooked his pack and leaned it against an adjacent tree, plopped down cross-legged opposite Imogen, and immediately thrust his hands directly over the fire and began rubbing them together to get warm. He then reached into his pocket and pulled out a dented pack of cigarettes. "You mind?" he asked.

Imogen shook her head no. Fumbling around in his pant's pocket he withdrew a book of matches, which he used to light his cigarette before bringing it to his lips and taking a long drag. "Oh dear, where are my manners?" he spoke, half to himself, half to Imogen. "Would you like a smoke?" He held the pack out to Imogen. She didn't smoke . . . well that wasn't entirely true. Sometimes she did have a smoke socially when she was drinking at a party or something. She thought about saying no, but then, on impulse, decided that it might not be such a bad idea to bond a little with this stranger over a cigarette.

"Okay," she said, reaching out and taking one from the pack. She leaned in toward the fire, intending to light it, but the man quickly struck another match from the book and lit it for her. If anything, he was well-mannered, Imogen thought. They sat smoking in silence for a bit and she watched with fascination as he took another drag from the cigarette and blew out a couple of perfectly symmetrical smoke rings. Imogen was impressed. In high school when she used to smoke with her boyfriend Dylan he could blow rings, but she could never quite master the technique, cool as it was. They were both mesmerized by the swirling rings, watching them swirl and float until they lost their shape and dissipated into the air when he blurted, "People are going to remember my name."

Imogen forced herself not to laugh. What a perfectly peculiar thing to say. But okay, she'd play along.

"So, what's your name?" she asked him.

"Cooper, D.B.," he said confidently, thrusting his hand out for her to shake. Imogen was tempted to say something, but that wasn't what she was here for. Instead, she smiled and shook the man's hand.

"It's a pleasure to meet you, Mr. Cooper."

"Call me D.B.," he said, grinning back.

There were benefits to being from the future. She knew the story, no, the legend of D.B. Cooper, the man who had hijacked a Boeing 727, extorted $200,000 in ransom money, and parachuted to an uncertain fate. From the accounts she'd read, it explained his calm and courteous comportment. But more importantly, she could relax now with the knowledge that he was no serial killer.

"So D.B., can you teach me how to blow those smoke rings?" she asked.

"Only if you have some bourbon stashed in your camp gear?" he said laughing.

"Well, it's not bourbon, but I packed in a flask of rum," she said, "for the cold nights."

D.B.'s eye's widened with delight and he smiled broadly. "That'll do sister!"

As the night deepened, the flask passing back and forth between them, they talked about Vietnam, deconstructed Watergate and Nixon, smoked cigarettes, and Imogen finally blew her first mostly successful smoke ring. At some point, she had fallen asleep and when she awoke the next morning, a low bank of fog had rolled in, the fire had become a few dying embers, and D.B. Cooper was gone. She unzipped her sleeping bag and as much as she dreaded it, wriggled out from inside the warm depths. Brrr, it was chilly, but she had to pee. On the way to the bushes behind the tent, she stumbled, stubbing her big toe on a rock that she hadn't remember being there before. "Oww, damn it!" she yelped, hopping on one foot while she pulled her toe up to see if it was injured. It wasn't. Stupid rock. When she looked down though, she noticed something that looked like green paper sticking out from beneath it. Leaning down she pushed the rock aside revealing five, crisp $100-dollar bills. She took a deep, knowing breath and shrugged. D.B. Cooper's money would be worth a fortune in her time. Too bad she couldn't take it with her. She unrolled the bills and tucked inside was an empty matchbook with the handwritten words: FOR THE RUM. Happy Trails Imogen Oliver, D.B. Cooper.

After a strong cup of black coffee, a hard-boiled egg, and a couple of bacon strips, Imogen broke camp, and with her pack securely cinched, she was back on the trail in no time. She wondered if she'd catch up with D.B., but as morning turned into afternoon, so far, she had seen no sign of him, or anyone else for that matter. Around 12:30 she decided it might be a good idea to break for lunch before starting up the incline. She'd need some energy. Windy Ridge was the perfect place. True to its name, it was windy as hell, but the 360-degree panoramic view of Mount St. Helens, Mount Adams, Mount Rainier, Mount Hood, and Spirit Lake below was beyond spectacular. Gil had indicated that someone, hopefully Adam Curry was heading in this direction about a week ago. She hoped that by staying on this trail she'd have the good fortune of catching up to him eventually. She had enough provisions to last about a week, but if she couldn't locate him before then, she'd have no choice but to abandon her search.

As she ate her bologna and cheese sandwich and took in the spectacular vista, a thought popped into her head, what if something horrible happened down there while she was safely up here? Clearly, she had been watching too many apocalyptic graphic novel-based TV shows lately. She would have to live off the land, certainly, but she would be safe because everyone knew zombies can't climb. Simon had been less than impressed by the whole zombie genre. "Scientifically speaking," he had said, "It makes no plausible sense. If they are dead, how can their brains continue to function, and why in the world would they be hungry?" He was right, of course, but it was still great fun to watch and imagine. He was far more impressed by literature and art that had outlived its creators. He was amazed that *The Phantom of the Opera* and Bram Stoker's *Dracula* had withstood the test of time and continued to be sources of endless theatrical productions and movie remakes; that some of his favorite books, which were newly published when he had read them, were still entertaining audiences today. In a way, he said, it gave him a sense of renewed hope for humanity.

Hope, or at the very least, information about his dad, was something Imogen wanted to bring back to Sean Curry. Sean had contacted her about a month ago. Having exhausted all traditional efforts to find his dad, he was ready to give up on the search entirely, but after running across an ad for an investigative service called Dead Relatives, Inc., he decided to give it one more shot. "I'm not quite sure why, but it spoke to me," he had said to Imogen. Hearing Sean say that Imogen could scarcely contain her delight. She knew the name would pay off! She had chosen the name Dead Relatives because it sounded unusual and intriguing, but specifically because it encapsulated the kind of detective work she did, although her clients weren't privy to her unconventional methods. Although she also employed traditional detective processes—internet research, databases, and the like—having the ability to walk directly into a photograph and become part of the scene, completely equipped by the universe with period-specific attire, was not something your average private detective could do. It was still a big fat mystery why or how she could do this but combining two of her passions—photography and history with helping people—it wasn't a terrible way to make a living.

In his mid-forties and wearing a suit and tie, Sean was handsome, fit, and projected a youthful vibe. In fact, with his clean-shaven face, chiseled jaw, impeccably coiffed head of hair, and expensive Italian loafers he looked like he'd walked straight out of *GQ* magazine. Imogen wasn't accustomed to seeing men so well turned out. Simon would love him! Simon adored that dapper look. In fact, it was like pulling teeth to get him out of his beloved trousers and vest and into some comfortable shorts and a T-shirt; at least when he was out getting dirty in the garden.

When Sean introduced himself as the CAO of a software company, it made complete sense to her then—he was an accountant! After some gentle nudging from Imogen about how she would need to know the full story before she looked into finding his father, he loosened his tie, leaned back in his chair, and slowly began to relax and open up a bit.

"From the stories my mom told me about my father, along with the fact that he'd walked out on her the day I was born, I decided very early on that I wanted to be everything he was *not*,"

Sean began. "He had long hair, he smoked pot, he couldn't hold a job, he was in a band, he wrote poetry. I decided I wanted none of that. I followed the straight and narrow. I was a good student." He paused, taking a deep breath in, before talking about his mom.

"My mother raised me herself," he said, "and she worked very hard to put me through college. I worked at accounting jobs for a few years, did people's taxes, but when I was asked by a friend to come on board with his startup company, my career took off. All of a sudden, I was making tons of money. I met Margaret and we got married. Everything was perfect."

He paused again and Imogen took the opportunity to jump in with a question. "Kids?" she asked.

"No, he said. "Maggie couldn't conceive, but it was okay, my life felt full and complete with only her."

"And then what happened?" Imogen probed.

"When I turned 40 something happened," he said, "my thinking . . . I don't know how to explain it; but it began to shift."

"Shift?" Imogen asked, "How so?"

"I guess if I'm honest it was the stirrings of a full-blown midlife crisis. I thought I, of all people, would be immune to that sort of thing, but I couldn't stop having these completely uncharacteristic thoughts about wanting to escape; to quit my job and get lost somewhere, like he had, like Adam, dad. I felt reckless and out of control and I had an affair and Maggie left me."

"I'm sorry," Imogen said. "That must have been devastating for you."

Sean seemed on the verge of tears then, but he held it together, likely out of force of habit, Imogen surmised. She waited for him to gather his thoughts without pressure until he was ready to continue.

"After the divorce, I decided to take a trip to Brazil. I needed to clear my head. I went on a long hike, sort of like walkabout, I guess you could say," he said, snickering softly.

"And it helped?" Imogen asked him.

Sean nodded. "Yeah, sure, it did help some. I did a lot of

soul searching about myself and about my father. My mother had once noted that behind the veneer of lies, there was a genuine sweetness about him; a truth that he wanted to live, but for some reason couldn't. I thought about who I was, wondered if I was just like him. Was it nature vs. nurture? I wasn't sure, but I realized that I needed to find him somehow, see if he had some answers. If only I knew where to start. After about six months of roaming around, I figured it was time to come home and deal with things." Sean snickered again before continuing, "The irony in all this was that apparently he had done the exact same thing I was doing. He went on an extended walkabout too, only he never came back."

Sean's mother had received one letter from Adam, dated November 24, 1971 with the photo of him standing in front of the Spirit Lake store. He had written that he was sorry for leaving, and that maybe someday he'd want to come back, but he needed to find something first. He didn't say what that something was. After jotting down the details about when and where his dad had last been seen, Imogen promised Sean she would do her best to come back with answers—perhaps not the answers he wanted, perhaps even with news that he wasn't alive—either way, she'd do her level best to help him come to terms with a loss he'd been grieving over, literally, since the day he was born.

Sean had been correct about hiking and thinking, they went hand in hand. Walking the trail, you fell into a certain rhythmic pace, and lulled by the steady movement of your feet on the ground it put you into an almost meditative state, allowing your mind to wander off in different directions. Walking today gave Imogen ample time to think as well, which at times was a good thing, other times, not so much.

As she walked, she cogitated on a lot of stuff. It was a curse to be a woman who thinks too much. But being alone like this gave her permission, and time, to let the thoughts flow without distraction, specifically interruptions from Simon. She loved him, and Imogen would never, ever tell anyone this, but there were times when she missed Fletcher, a lot. Before Simon, they had been lovers, but also good friends. After these past exhausting months with Simon, she sometimes yearned for the stress-free company that Fletcher afforded. Theirs was a comfortable relationship. There were no awkward silences between them. They could hike or read together or watch TV in silence. With the sexual tension removed from the mix they were able to simply enjoy one another's company without pretense. It was something that she had taken for granted at the time, but now sorely missed.

Geez, what was wrong with her anyway? Imogen wondered. She wasn't some fickle female, or was she? There was something to be said for finding someone you were comfortable with though; someone that you didn't have to pretend with. And after the red-hot passion faded, what were you left with anyhow if not compatibility and somebody you could talk to and have fun with? With everything that had transpired over the last few months with Simon, there had been little time for either passion or stimulating conversation between them. It had been all about his adjusting to this time, and while she understood the circumstances, it felt a little like everything was *always* all about him. Granted, he came from a time when a man's concerns far outweighed those of a woman's, but it made it difficult for Imogen, and infuriating. She felt like all of her feelings and concerns had been relegated to the back burner. It didn't seem fair, and as much as she loved and adored Simon, she was feeling quite put upon. Her patience was wearing thin. She could do this for a while, she figured, but for how long? A lifetime? She didn't know.

Fletcher, on the other hand, being a progressive-minded man, understood that it didn't have to and shouldn't always be about him. There was an equal balance that seemed to be lacking in her relationship with Simon. Of course, she would never say anything. And besides, Fletcher was no longer in the picture anyhow. A month or so after she'd come back with Simon, he'd decided to return to Idaho, and for all Imogen knew, had reunited with his former fiancé. And if he had found her or somebody new, good for him, she thought. He deserved better. He deserved someone who could love him absolutely.

As Imogen walked and allowed her mind to wander, the afternoon flew by. Since Windy Ridge, the trail had switched back a few times as the climb was becoming steeper. Imogen was feeling fatigued. It would be getting dark soon. This was it though. She would camp one more night, and if she found no sign of Curry by about noon tomorrow, she was heading home. The trail here was quite open and exposed but she noticed a stand of trees up ahead in the distance. She'd find a more secluded spot there.

Hoisting the pack back onto her shoulders after a 15-minute break, she resumed her uphill trudge. As she rounded the curve, a pillar of white, billowing smoke came into view and with it a whiff of burning fir. She hadn't noticed it before, but it was visible here in the clearing. She continued on for another two-tenths of a mile or so until she came to a fork that veered off to the left of the trail. It appeared that the smoke was coming from that direction. She realized now that she had a decision to make. Should she stick to the trail or follow the smoke? And where there was smoke there was fire and where there was fire there were likely people. Potentially, it could be her friend D.B.; it could be Adam Curry, or the other possibility, that it could be someone dangerous, was cause for hesitation.

Well, she'd have to stop soon anyway and make camp, she thought, which would require starting her own fire for warmth, so whoever was up there would certainly take notice of her one way or the other. The best course of action that she could see was to simply follow the smoke and see where it led; she'd deal with the consequences when she got there. She had her knife and axe in her pack. It was reassuring to know that she could always get back through her photo portal if she was in any real danger, but as she got closer to the source of the fire, she'd be ready, just in case.

This trail led deeper into a forest of old growth trees. Large threads of dense moss hung down in clumps from the tree branches like spooky lime-green spider webs, and the canopy of large trees had nearly squeezed out any light from the sky above. The smoky smell of the fire became more pronounced as Imogen walked cautiously along, wary of making any noise. Just up ahead she saw something large and dark looming in a clearing—a miner's shack maybe? Quietly, she slid her backpack from her shoulders and leaned it up against a tree, pulling from it her buck knife and the axe. Leaving her pack, she stealthily moved toward the direction of the light. As she drew closer, the clearing opened up wide and she could see the source of the smoke. It was pouring out of the stone chimney of a small wooden cabin perched on top of a bluff overlooking what looked like the end of the world. And then BOOM, just like that, out went the lights.

Imogen opened her eyes. Everything was blurry, and the back of her head hurt like hell. Gradually, the small room she was inhabiting came into view. The only light source was a fire burning in the fireplace, the rest of the room was hidden in shadows. Despite the dimness, she could barely make out the shape of another person sitting across the room from her, tied to a chair. That's when she realized that she was also tied to a chair. "What the? . . ." she started to say when the other person cut her off. "Be quiet," the voice whispered, "He's outside. He'll hear you."

"He who?" she whispered back, squinting hard to make out who had spoken to her. When he turned his head, a flicker of light from the fire revealed his face.

"D.B.? Is that you?" Imogen asked, confused.

"Yeah, it's me," he responded.

"What's going on here?" she whispered.

Before he could answer, the door of the cabin swung open flooding the entire space with light as a man in a muddy jacket and jeans entered. His face was concealed by a mass of tangled brown hair, and he was carrying a bundle of smallish logs in his arms.

"Oh, I see you're awake now," he said to Imogen as he barreled across the room and deposited the logs onto the floor next to the fireplace.

"We've been waiting for you to come around," he said as he approached her. Imogen flinched, unsure if he was reaching out to untie her or harm her. She could abandon the mission, disappear right now, but she'd come this far.

"Wait, are you Adam Curry?" she asked.

"You KNOW this guy?" D.B. piped up, incredulous. "This lunatic tossed a handful of my cash into the fire!"

"Shut up," the man shouted back at D.B. "I had to feed the fire, it was getting cold." He glanced back over at Imogen and explained in a calmer, almost apologetic tone, "I couldn't go out for kindling. I had to keep an eye on him," he said motioning at D.B.

"And besides," he said, "I'm the one asking the questions here." He glanced back and forth at both of them. "What do you want? Why are you here? Nobody comes up here this late in the year unless they're looking for something, or someone. And this guy, all that money . . . I don't want to hurt anyone. I just want to be left alone."

Imogen waited for him to stop ranting and as calmly as she could, stated, "I'm here because of Jaz."

Adam blinked and looked away. Bingo. His expression gave him away. She'd found him. She considered that she might have to come clean about who she was and where she came from. She also didn't want to have to reveal that his son had hired her. Sean was still an infant right now, in this time, but it might be the only way to diffuse the situation if she wanted to stick around.

But Adam seemed to calm down after Imogen mentioned Jaz, a name he clearly recognized. "How do you know Jaz?" he asked.

"Untie us and I'll tell you," Imogen suggested.

Adam hesitated for a moment before sighing heavily. "Okay, but let's smoke some dope," he said, pulling a baggy and pipe from the mantle. Surprised and clearly delighted at this remarkable turn of events, Imogen glanced over at D.B.

"I'm all for that!" D.B. said grinning broadly.

After he'd untied them and Adam had packed the pipe, D.B. offered him a book of matches, identical to the one he had used to light Imogen's cigarette, but this time, she noticed the Northwest Orient airline logo printed on the cover.

"Thanks man," Adam said as he took a deep pull from the pipe and held it in. "ere," he said, passing it over to D.B. who also took a large hit. Imogen was next. D.B. passed it to her and she took a turn. It was okay stuff, not quite the low-quality ragweed of the 70s, but also not the primo strains from her time, which by the way, was also legal. That bit of information would surely blow both of their minds if she told them.

Adam was the first to break the silence after they'd all smoked. "Well, I gather you know who I am, Adam Curry, but I don't know who either of you are," he said.

"I'm Imogen Oliver," Imogen said. She extended her hand and they greeted one another with a handshake. D.B. extended his, adding, "D.B. Cooper."

"Nice to meet you both," Adam said amid self-deprecating laughter. "It wasn't the friendliest welcome, I know."

D.B. smiled. "No misunderstanding that can't be settled over a friendly bowl," he said, winking. Imogen smiled and shook her head. Nothing she'd read ever about D.B. Cooper had indicated that he was a stoner, but hey, maybe he was just very good at making the best of an awkward situation.

"Please tell me about Jaz?" Adam said.

Imogen began slowly. "What I'm about to tell you is going to be difficult for you to believe, but bear with me." She hadn't planned on telling him anything but the words were out before she could take them back—she had been hired to find him, and she knew about his leaving on the day of the birth of his child because his son had told her.

Adam audibly gasped. "Wait? What? How can that be?" he asked, "it's only been six months since I left." Imogen looked over at D.B., who had leaned in to hear more of this crazy girl's far-fetched story.

"Next thing you're going to tell us you're from the future, right?" Adam said, his tone unconvinced. Imogen squirmed uncomfortably in her chair. Maybe it was the dope; maybe it was the knowledge that the mountain they were sitting on was going to blow, but for whatever reason, Imogen had blurted out everything she knew.

"Well, actually yes, that is exactly what I'm going to tell you." D.B.'s head shot up, his eyes widening. This was getting really interesting. Knowing full well how crazy it sounded, Imogen launched into her condensed backstory, about how she had established Dead Relatives, Inc. when she had discovered that she had this special gift. When she had finished, D.B. was the first to speak.

"So Imogen, how does one do this traveling through photographs, and can you take things with you, like say, money?" D.B. asked, obviously contemplating how he might learn the secret to accomplishing this trick himself. Imogen explained that one of the rules was that you could take anything with you, but you couldn't bring anything back that you didn't originally bring. While D.B. considered that bit of information, Adam was more interested in knowing about his son. "What does he look like, Sean . . . my son? How did he turn out?" he inquired.

"He's an accountant, a wealthy one even."

Adam threw back his head and laughed loudly at that. "An accountant, huh? Well, I'm sure he didn't get that from me, must have been his mother. She was always good at math."

He had more questions about Jaz: Had she remarried? Why did his son want to find him?

She felt terrible having to tell him that no, Jaz had died last year, which Adam took rather hard. Imogen waited a while for him to compose himself before resuming the conversation and explaining to him that Sean had grown up without his father, so naturally he was curious. He was going through a difficult time in his life—a divorce, and was searching for meaning that he felt he couldn't find on his own. She concluded with a warning.

"I have to tell you something else though, and you should know this too, D.B.," she said, turning to him and gesturing in the direction of the peak, "about nine years from now, this whole mountain is going to explode." She made an explosion-like noise accompanied by a blowing up motion with her hands. "Mount St. Helens is a volcano, and it's going to blow."

Their jaws both dropped a bit as Adam and Sean contemplated that impending scenario.

"One more thing, Adam," Imogen continued. "Obviously, if you were able to go back, Sean wouldn't have hired me and I wouldn't be here today, but if you choose, there is a way for you to contact your son . . . in the future." Imogen explained that Adam could write a letter to Sean and send it to a post office box that she owned. "When I return to my time, I'll pick it up and deliver it to him, and at that point, if you so desire, and he agrees, we can arrange for the two of you to meet."

Imogen noticed that Adam's demeanor had changed. His face was strained, jaws clenched, shoulders sagging like an old mattress. It seemed clear he did not want to talk about it any longer, even changing the subject by suggesting that they smoke one more bowl before hitting the sack. They could talk more in the morning.

Between the pot and the warm and toasty fire, Imogen slept comfortably inside her bedroll, and the next thing she knew, light was streaming in through the gaps in the cabin's log walls. Imogen rolled over, sat up, and looked around. D.B. was still asleep. She could hear him lightly snoring from across the room inside his own bedroll. But she didn't see Adam anywhere. Imogen got up, slipped on her boots and parka, and went outside. There was no fog this morning. She put her hand up to her face to shield her eyes from the bright sunshine and looked around, calling out, "Adam, where are you?" She walked the perimeter of the cabin and even headed up the trail a bit, but there was no sign of him anywhere. Giving up, she trudged back to the cabin and waited for D.B. to wake up. When he did, she told him that she couldn't find Adam. His pot and pipe were gone from the mantle as well as his hiking gear, and she suspected he'd packed up and gone.

They built a small fire, brewed up some coffee and ate breakfast together, and waited around to see if he might return. He didn't. Imogen couldn't help wondering if the news that his son was doing so well might have been the reason he'd left. Maybe he thought he'd screw things up and didn't want that to happen. Only time would tell.

Imogen and D.B. talked while they ate, and the conversation came back around to time travel. D.B. was more than a little curious.

"So Imogen, how does it work exactly?" he asked.

"You aren't thinking about disappearing now, are you D.B.?" she teased.

"Hmmm," he said between bites, "it may have crossed my mind, yes."

Imogen wasn't sure what would become of D.B., nobody would know for sure. Maybe Imogen happened, she figured as she expounded on the intricacies and rules and how-to of time traveling through a photograph. Essentially, she told him, "The three main rules of time travel are: you can't bring back anything from the past with you; you can't run into yourself, and you can't alter established history."

D.B. wasn't interested in bringing anything back because, of course, wherever he ended up going, he planned to stay there, in this time or some other. What he was most especially enthusiastic about was the prospect of his money being worth much more in the past than it was now, if he could figure out how to do it, that is.

"Guess, I need to get off this mountain, find me some old pictures, and put my powers of introspection to work," he said, flashing a grin, as they finished off the last bit of coffee.

"Here," Imogen said, handing D.B. the flask that she'd refilled with the remaining rum from the bottle. "For the long, cold nights ahead," she said.

"You won't need it?" he asked.

"Nope," Imogen said as she stood up and strapped her pack on her shoulders. "I need to go," she said. "It doesn't look like Adam's coming back and I have to get home and see his son."

D.B. stood up, too and they walked outside the shack together. "Perhaps we'll meet again, Imogen Oliver," he said.

Imogen winked at D.B. "I'll keep your secret if you'll keep mine."

D.B. shook her hand. "You betcha!"

Imogen turned and started down the trail. D.B. Cooper watched in stunned disbelief as the girl named Imogen began to slowly fade away, leaving behind only a puff of trail dust that, like a smoke ring, hovered above the place where she had been for an instant before dissolving all together.

2

Today, both knees sunk into the squashy soft dirt, Simon marveled at the way the sun glinted off the vibrant red Early Girls on the vine, the nubby green cucumbers, and the leafy, scarlett-streaked canopy that shielded the abundance of delicious beets hiding just below the surface. Breathing in the cool freshness of the morning and the rich, earthy scent of damp living soil he weeded around the garden's luscious bounty. Never would he have guessed that the humble act of gardening might be an appealing pastime, or that building miniature furniture from scratch might become a focused hobby. None of these things would have entered his mind at all in his past life as a school principal. But everything was different now. So different, in fact, that gardening and hobbies were the only things that made him feel grounded and sane anymore. And Imogen, of course. Imogen had been wonderful.

Since jumping through time three months ago—crazy as that sounded—naked and sick and afraid, through his struggles with adjusting to this new reality, navigating a strange landscape where people and technology had evolved and changed beyond his imaginings, through the confusion of a multitude of newfangled inventions and confusing societal norms, she had been there for him.

Of course, grabbing on to her as she was leaving to time travel home had been a purely impulse decision. He had no time to properly think things through or contemplate the potential consequences, or to even change his mind. Misguidedly, he had thought it would be easy, a cakewalk, as it were. He naively envisioned that life in the future would be an exciting adventure, like being an explorer traveling to an alien planet. Unquestionably, he'd be a stranger for a while, he thought, but eventually fit in. That's not exactly how it was turning out.

It was great, at first. Each day brought some new incredible wonder or revelation. Airplanes zipped across the globe at lightning speed, reaching faraway destinations in mere hours; cars raced down paved roads at speeds upward of 80 mph; news and entertainment could be viewed on enormous screens or on a miniature handheld device that Imogen had explained was called a "smart" phone but despite being small in size, was actually a powerful communicator capable of connecting them to information and people around the world through something called the internet. Even books could be read on these types of machines. In fact, everywhere you looked there were machines. You could procure money from a machine; a machine washed your car; one roamed about the room vacuum-cleaning your floors. There were machines for washing your dishes and your clothing, another for making coffee (Simon rather liked that one). There was even a machine that was no bigger than a croissant that you could talk to. Inside of it was Alexa, a woman's voice that could tell you a joke, play a song, look up information, remind you to turn off the lights, report on the weather, make noises of flatulence, and provide the answers to any conceivable question. As an avid reader, he'd read some science fiction, particularly Julius Verne, in which fantastical predictions of the future were made, but never could he have imagined it would be like this.

While nickelodeons that showed motion pictures in converted storefronts around town were common in his time, he had only been to the picture house once. In 1909, he paid 15 cents admission to see the silent picture *The Life of Moses.*

Imogen took him to a modern theater with the largest screen he'd ever seen in his life, and seats that reclined. The film they saw was about outer space—apparently, Imogen had said, during this century man had walked on the moon! It was filmed in a format known as 3D and was indeed a marvel to observe. While wearing the dark glasses they were provided it was as though one could reach out and grab hold of the moving objects floating in front of the eyes—it was like being magically transported into the story, rather like jumping into a good book, only better.

She took him to a country fair, but not just any fair. From the name, he was expecting a festival in some quaint, bucolic setting with wandering troubadours and foodstuffs and merchants selling wares and baskets of flowers. This country fair was quite different indeed. In fact, he'd never seen anything like it—a burst of colors on fabric called tie-dye, flamboyantly costumed people and bare-breasted women. It seemed so shocking yet so deliciously hedonistic.

It was wonderful and mesmerizing and magical all at once. He was overwhelmed by it, sure, but there were fabulous things about this century too, for instance, the music—people danced and moved their bodies with abandon, there seemed to be no social constructs governing how people could express themselves; and the fashion—again, anything goes—women with neon-colored hair and piercings; women with tattoos! It amused him now to remember how he had once been shocked by Imogen's small heart tattoo, but now understood that in her time, it was quite commonplace.

Indeed, this new time of the future held a dizzying array of options, and he was constantly amazed at the way people tackled life and the speed at which they could traverse quickly from one place to another. The food, for example, so many options it was difficult to choose—trucks and restaurants with exotic fare from around the globe. It was as if someone had flipped a switch inside him and all five senses—taste, touch, smell, sight, and sound—had turned on all at once rendering him acutely aware of everything around him—things that he had not noticed or taken for granted before suddenly coming into view as if for the first time.

He also felt immediately soothed by the comfort of Imogen's house, which had previously belonged to her grandmother Iris. Imogen's grandmother was also a time traveler and, in fact, the Iris that he had known as a youth in 1901 when he had been Andre's photography assistant. Imogen had shared with him the relics and mementos of her grandmother's time spent in the past and all of it brought back sweet memories for Simon of a carefree time in his own life, and of laying eyes on Imogen the very first time that day in the park, the first time she had traveled.

He enjoyed watching the television, although Imogen chastised him for sitting too close to the screen and turning the volume up too loud, but it was new to him and there were so many viewing options, it was hard to choose, although he was drawn in by the 24-hour news programming. No waiting around for the daily newspaper. The ability to have instantaneous knowledge of everything that was happening around the entire world at your fingertips was a constant source of amazement . . . and tremendous frustration.

Imogen had been kind and patient about answering his river of endless questions. She'd even tried to tutor him on the computer machine, the Google, but simply trying to learn how to use it to find the information felt like a crushing task. And regrettably, he had not always been so appreciative. In his frustration, he had lashed out at her when she was only desiring to help him. It was no wonder that she had wanted to get away from him. Of course, she needed to work, but at the same time, he couldn't help wondering if going back to work also meant getting a much-needed reprieve from him.

Still, although things between them had been strained, there had been good times too. Over the last three months they had gotten to know each other better. They had spent a glorious holiday together in Kauai, part of the Hawaiian archipelago, nicknamed the Garden Isle because of the tropical rain forest covering much of its surface. From the dramatic cliffs in the Na Pali Coast and the 10-mile-long Waimea Canyon to the Nounou Trails traversing the Sleeping Giant Mountain ridge, this destination was like nothing Simon had ever seen. It was paradise, a place he could only imagine himself ever visiting, yet there he was, on a tropical island in the South Pacific with his greatest love, with Imogen.

For two glorious weeks, they took early morning walks along the beach picking up rocks and sand dollars and drinking coffee on the porch of their open-air cabana. During the day they explored the island, shopping, kayaking, hiking the trails where Imogen, who had recently taken up botanical photography like her namesake Imogen Cunningham, took close-up photographs of the island's bounty of flowers—hibiscus, pink and purple bougainvillea vines, birds of paradise, sweet smelling plumeria, fragrant gardenias, densely flowered and aromatic lantana, the showy red ginger and magnificent torch ginger, and hundreds of species of orchids.

Evenings were spent drinking extraordinary cocktail concoctions with exotic names like margaritas and piña colada and daiquiri and mai tai, each adorned with a tiny, delicate paper umbrella, or dancing under the stars and feasting on roasted pig at a luau, or walking hand in hand along the beach, soft sand squishing between their bare toes. Bathed in dreamlike moonlight, they made love to the sounds of crashing waves and palm trees swishing in the tender breeze. They made a pact that on this trip neither one would speak of Teddy or Mimi Pinky nor how Simon came to be here, of Imogen's father or Simon's mother, or any of the myriad questions and concerns that had plagued them up to this point. Instead, he learned more about her life, about her childhood friend Jade and her photographer parents; that she had gone to university and majored in history, and he had shared information about his own mother.

Sadly, it had to end. They left paradise and their lovely respite from the world and reluctantly returned to reality. And after the whirlwind adventures and excitement and newness of his new life began to wear off and the truth that he was completely out of his element and unable to cope with 21st century life set in causing an insurmountable rift between he and Imogen. While she was away, however, he seized upon an idea that he thought might repair their strained relationship. Simon decided to visit a local bookstore. It looked a lot like the ones in his time. It had that same warmth and aroma of books but with updated, modern décor. Browsing the poetry section, he pulled from the shelf *Love Poems and Others* by D.H. Lawrence, the book he'd given to Imogen, which now felt like eons ago, except this copy was bound now, not in leather, but in a less appealing paper form. Opening it, he searched for one poem in particular, the one he'd chosen to read out loud to her, the one that had endeared him to her and him to her, "Kisses in the Train." His eyes were drawn down to the second to last stanza of the poem which seemed to not only encapsulate the uncertainty of their relationship of late, but also the way that he felt much of the time in this future world.

And the world all whirling
Around in joy
Like the dance of a dervish
Did destroy
My sense—and my reason
Spun like a toy.

Absorbed in reading, he was startled by a woman's voice from behind him. "May I help you?"

Simon quickly closed the book and spun around. The voice was attached to as striking a woman as he'd ever laid eyes on. She was tall and slender, not fancily dressed, wearing a simple cardigan sweater and trousers—a name badge attached to her sweater read: Abby, but what fascinated him most lay behind the tortoise shell glasses: a pair of the most unusual green eyes. Realizing that he was staring, Simon cleared his throat and a series of awkward, tortured words tumbled out, "Oh, um, excuse me, but I was just looking at poetry."

"Yes, I see that," the woman said. "D.H. Lawrence, an excellent choice." She smiled at Simon and two identical dimples framed her mouth, throwing Simon off once again. "Uh, yes," Simon said without thinking, "I purchased it when it first came out." The dimples disappeared as a look of confusion crossed the woman's face. "Are you sure," she asked, "the original book was released in 1913." Panic seized him for a moment, but Simon snorted, raising his hands as though surrendering to his error and said, "Oh, no, of course, not when it 'actually' came out; it was when the paper book came out, is what I meant." Abby smiled again and the dimples returned. "I see," she said shrugging. "Well, it's a good choice. Is there anything else I can help you find?"

Having regained some of his composure, Simon remembered what he had come to the bookstore looking for. "Ah yes, well, there is something," he said. "Poetry, but perhaps something more contemporary?"

Abby easily shifted into helpful, bookstore clerk mode. "We have a large selection," she said, fanning her fingers out to show the depth and variety of titles gracing the bookshelves. "As you can see, we have everything from feminist literature to Maya Angelou to the beat poet Allen Ginsberg."

When Simon didn't respond, the clerk glanced at the D.H. Lawrence book in Simon's hand. "Or perhaps you're interested in romance? Is it for a special someone?" Simon felt his neck growing hot and his face flushing as he shifted nervously from one foot to the other. Discussing ardor, was embarrassing, to say the least. Noticing his discomfort, Abby filled up the awkward space with a suggestion. "Here," she said, plucking a book from the shelf and handing it to him. "Might I suggest e.e. cummings?" Simon was intrigued that the author's name was lowercase. "Hmmm," he said, as he flipped through the pages. He noticed that many of the poems had sentences beginning lowercase as well, and intentional words written together, parentheses and gaps and indentation used as an artful mechanism of cadence to steer the reader toward a particular feeling. Near the back of the book he paused at the end of one poem, which read "For love are in you am in i are in we."

"If you don't like it, you can always return it," Abby suggested.

"Oh no," Simon answered, closing up the text. "This will do just fine. Thank you for all your help. After purchasing the book, he exited the bookstore leaving behind the girl with the exceptional green eyes.

After arriving home, Simon had set the book of poetry on the coffee table and was on his way to the kitchen to brew up a nice cup of tea when there was a knock at the door. Through the window Simon could see her on the front porch standing on her tiptoes, craning her flabby-skinned neck to peek in through the small window at the top of the door. Mimi Pinky. The woman Simon had only recently discovered he had the misfortune of being related to, or so it appeared. She was his grandmother, her son Teddy, his biological father. Having never been made aware of this information would have suited him just fine.

He was undecided about whether to answer, but decorum dictated that it would be rude not to. Mimi Pinky was at least mostly dressed that day. Generally, when he saw her outside, she was either immodestly attired in the skimpiest of short shorts and midriff blouses, exposing her round ball of a belly, or wearing a shabby old kimono and dirty fur slippers, her hair a rat's nest of spongy pink curlers, but always the brightest, most flaming, fiery and grossly smudged red lipstick. She never left the house without it. Even if she was in her pajamas, Mimi had those signature red lips . . . always. Today, however, her lips he noticed were a subdued shade of pink as if she was purposely trying to make a more dignified impression. She wore a plain print shirt, nondescript pants, and sandals that exposed her purple-polished toes. Her hair, though tucked beneath a teal scarf, appeared neat and combed for a change, like someone who wanted something, Simon suspected. Actually, the fact that she didn't look her usual extreme self, frightened him a little.

"Mimi, how are you?" Simon asked in the most formal, but pleasant voice he could muster. Pushing the screen door open he motioned entry. "Won't you come in?" Mimi flashed a quick half smile and stepped gingerly into the living room, looking around the room and taking it all in as though this was her first time here.

"What can I do for you?" Simon asked Mimi, who seemed

distracted by the kitchen. When she stopped turning her head around to look at everything, she answered a little embarrassed, "Oh, um, well, is Imogen here?"

Simon shook his head no. "I'm afraid she is out. May I assist you?"

Mimi fidgeted on the sofa, crossing and uncrossing her bulky legs as she struggled to find a suitable resting spot for her flabby arms. She seemed nervous and uncomfortable in Simon's presence. Come to think of it, they had never been alone together. Imogen had always been there during the few times they had been forced to interact. An uncomfortable cloud of silence drifted between them until Mimi finally spoke.

"I miss my Teddy," she blurted, clearly distraught. Although Simon was wont to believe anything Mimi said, today she seemed genuinely sincere in her sadness and Simon felt somewhat sorry for her. Of course, a mother would miss her son. It was the way he missed his own mother. That grief ran deep in a way that he could never explain to anyone.

"He was my special little Teddy Bear," she continued, blinking her eyes as genuine tears ran down her face from cheek to chin. Simon wasn't sure what to do in this awkward situation. Was this real emotion or was she trying to manipulate him? He had heard a rumor from the postman that she had been telling anyone in the neighborhood who would listen that Simon and Imogen were time travelers. Simon had downplayed it, telling him that was absurd. She was mentally unhinged. The postal worker had laughed and agreed that she did sound pretty crazy.

Simon listened to her go on, but then, as if he was no longer in the room with her, things turned weird as Mimi began to expand on her love for her son, alluding to their 'special' bond, elaborating on the gentleness of his touch as if it went beyond the natural boundaries of a mother/son relationship. Simon shifted uncomfortably in his seat, until finally she snapped out of her daydream state and shifted to praising his other traits.

"You know, my son was a brilliant businessman and a kind and good son, someone who didn't deserve the horrible treatment he received," she said sharply, squinting her eyes and shooting daggers in his direction.

Simon could feel the anger and disgust welling inside and it was all he could do to contain it, until he couldn't. "Madam are you utterly mentally unhinged?" he cried. "You know what he did to my mother. How could you adore someone like that? Only a monster would abandon a pregnant woman, especially in a place that was so foreign to her, and not merely a place, but another time, where she had no idea how to fend for herself!" Simon knew firsthand how difficult it had been to adjust to this time; he could only imagine what his mother must have gone through trying to navigate on her own, and with child!

Immediately, Simon observed a frightening and drastic change in Mimi's appearance. The tears of a few minutes ago replaced now with a scowl so horrible, so heated, it made Simon cringe. Her eyes became a pair of angry slits; her mouth turned downward at the edges as she drew herself up from the couch and lunged at Simon, thrusting her dagger-like index finger up close to his face wagging it back and forth in front of him. "Teddy was no monster!" she shrieked. "Your whore of a mother deserved what she got! She tried to trap my boy and he did the only thing he could do—get rid of her for good!"

Simon had had enough. "Get out!" he stormed, knocking her finger away from his face as he tried to keep his anger and disgust at her in check.

"You'll never get his money," Mimi blurted. "I'm the one who loved him. I'm the one who put up with his bullying and cleaned up his messes. And I'll expose you, I'll tell everyone what you people do!" she screeched as she stomped across the living room and out through the front door, her sandals making a loud clacking noise across the wooden porch as she went. Simon watched her angrily make her way across the yard, and down the street to her own house on the corner.

Simon slammed the front door shut and stood motionless for a moment, arms across his chest, fuming, on the brink of tears himself, but trying not to succumb to the emotions churning like a vortex within him. How dare she call his mother a whore! This loathsome woman, who perhaps . . . oh god . . . he could scarcely permit the words or images to fully form in his head . . . may have had intimate relations with her own son. How did he ever come from these two vile people? It was too horrifying to think about. And money? What in the world was she talking about? He noticed that his hands were shaking, his knees weak, and his breathing shallow and uneven.

After calming himself—perhaps a little too copiously—with the bottle of whiskey he'd found in the cabinet, he reflected on the encounter. Seeing Mimi brought back a mix of disconcerting and sad memories of his mother and the knowledge that she had begun her life here, in this future. It explained so much about her odd behavior, her obsession with taking photographs, the peculiar things she sometimes said. The convoluted tale had tumbled out when Imogen and Simon had come forward in time through the photograph to follow Teddy, who was also a time traveler. Simon's mother—Tiffany Rose—had been Teddy's flame. However, when Teddy had learned that she was pregnant, in a panic, he impulsively dragged her through a photograph from the late 19th century and cruelly left her there to fend for herself alone. In desperation, Tiffany began taking pictures of herself and hiding them, hoping that someone from her own time, in the future, might recognize her and find a way to rescue her.

When Imogen's father, Niles, also a time traveler, discovered some of the photos Tiffany had left behind from the past, he became suspicious and confronted Teddy about the missing girl. Afraid Niles would tell his mother Mimi what he'd done, Teddy waited for Imogen's parents to travel through their photographic portals before destroying them, trapping each in another time.

Later, cornered by Simon and Imogen, Teddy confessed what he had done to Tiffany and Imogen's parents, but then immediately vanished into another photograph—to a dangerous place that Imogen said likely he would not ever return from. Unfortunately, he got away before they could get him to reveal where exactly her parents were trapped. For Simon, the revelations of Teddy's sordid deeds also meant that this dreadful man, Teddy, was likely his biological father, and that Mimi Pinky was his grandmother.

Mimi had at first directed all of her anger at Teddy: "What did you do to that girl Teddy?" she had angrily demanded after hearing Imogen's story, but when he was gone and it seemed assured that he would not be coming back she shifted the blame onto Simon and Imogen, pressuring them to tell her what they had *done* to cause her Teddy to go off the rails. Imogen was sympathetic and far more patient with the woman than Simon would have ever been. She had explained repeatedly to Mimi that while she was sorry about what happened to Teddy, her son had done some unspeakably horrible things to Simon's mother as well as to her own parents, but in the end, all Mimi could see was that her precious son was gone for good. Since then, Simon had managed to keep an uneasy distance. Until that day.

After she'd gone Simon had retreated back to his garden to take out his anger and frustration on some innocent weeds until Imogen returned home. She had been angry and wanted to confront Mimi, but Simon was able to talk her out of it, convincing her that stirring the pot would only escalate things. Perhaps if they left it alone, Mimi would eventually let it go.

As he weeded around the tomatoes, Simon began to tug at one particularly nasty invasive perennial that had taken root in the garden. He had so far been unsuccessful at eliminating the entire root system of these pesky weeds, but he had been diligent about coming out each day and pulling out the weedy shoots. As he was pulling on it, he noticed what looked like the edge of a piece of paper poking up from the dirt, and as he gently tugged at it, he immediately recognized what it was—it was one of hundreds of photographs his mother had hidden on this very property. Brushing off the caked-on dirt, the sad, solemn face of his thin-framed mother gazed at him from the distant past, eerily frozen in time.

It felt like only yesterday that on this very same plot, he and his friend Herbert had gathered what photographs they could find and preserved them in tins for Imogen to retrieve later in the future. Still others likely were destroyed in the fire Teddy had set in Imogen's parent's photography studio, but it wasn't terribly surprising to find a loose one out here buried in the garden.

And yet, knowing the photos existed and finding one were two different things. A tidal wave of suppressed emotions over-took him as the past came roaring back and crashed into the rocky future. Simon lowered his head and breathed deeply in and out, trying hard to resist the urge to weep—for his mother, for his old life, for everything.

He wasn't sure how long he had been sitting there in the dirt clutching the photo in his fingers when he sensed movement behind him and a shadow traveled across the photograph and blocked out the sun.

3

Fletcher recognized the borderline obsessiveness of driving past Imogen's house every day, yet he felt compelled. Ever since he had come back to town, instead of driving right on past the road she lived on like a rational person, he routinely veered to the right at the last minute and drove by her house anyway. Although he never had any real plans to stop, the impulse to pull in the driveway was strong. Perhaps it was comforting to him to view the porch where they used to hang out, to remember the leisurely mornings spent drinking coffee and reading the newspaper together. Or not. Shit. It was no comfort at all. It only made him feel worse, but that didn't stop him from doing it.

Most of the time, her car was there anyway. He had heard through their mutual friend Rachel that Imogen had a new boyfriend. His name was Simon, the name she had called out one night in her sleep when Fletcher was in bed with her. But that wasn't the crazy part; she had met him while she was time traveling in the early 1900s and she brought him back with her. As ridiculous as the whole wild time travel story was, he didn't doubt it. Imogen was a horrible liar; she did not have a dishonest bone in her body. As for this Simon guy, he could only speculate what it must be like for someone to jump 100 years forward in time—the sheer profusion of history and changes compacted within that time alone would surely be overwhelming. How would someone cope with that? But more importantly, why did any of it concern him?

After the breakup with Imogen, he returned to Idaho. He tried to make a go of it with his former fiancé Molly, but he couldn't stop thinking about Imogen. He felt guilty as hell being around Molly when thoughts of someone else kept randomly popping into his head. It wasn't fair to her. Idaho wasn't the same. Moving had been a dumb idea. As for Imogen, he knew his feelings for her were silly and unrequited. If she loved this guy, more power to her. Far be it for him to insert himself into the mix. He wanted her to be happy, but damn it, what if there was a chance she wasn't? What if she realized she'd made a huge mistake? It seemed clear she'd chosen her path, yet for some reason, Fletcher couldn't squelch the possibility that maybe she had regrets too.

Today, as he glided his ghost car at a slow crawl by her house, her car wasn't there like it usually was and he spotted something else, the side gate leading to the backyard was ajar and suspiciously propped open with a garbage can full of yard debris.

This was it, he speculated, the window of opportunity he'd been waiting for. If someone was breaking into her house, well, how could he not be the hero and foil the perp's attempts? It wouldn't explain why he was there in the first place, but he'd think about that later. Parking the car out front, he walked over to the gate, moved the can out of the way, and stealthily slipped through. Across the yard, he observed a man oddly dressed in suit pants and matching vest seated in the garden surrounded by tomato plants. So engrossed in thought, Simon didn't seem to notice Fletcher crossing the yard and then hovering above him. When he finally looked up, his expression did not change—he seemed not at all alarmed that a stranger had entered his backyard uninvited. Instead, he stood up, wiped the dirt from his hand on his pant leg, and extended it to Fletcher in a welcoming gesture.

"Hello," he said in probably the most pleasant, well-mannered tone Fletcher had ever heard coming from another man. "I am Simon Elliot, how may I help you, sir?"

So this was him. Simon. Before meeting him, Fletcher was fully prepared to dislike the guy and yet, with one genteel gesture, he had completely unmoored the angry wind from his sails. Unsure how to respond, Fletcher faltered. The strong words he had envisioned himself saying at their first encounter had utterly escaped him. "Uh, well, my name is Fletcher," he managed to stammer as he awkwardly shook Simon's hand.

"It is a pleasure to finally meet you Fletcher," Simon said. "Of course, you are Imogen's friend. She has spoken highly of you."

"Really?" Fletcher said, surprised and a little irritated with himself for so easily being taken in by not only the affable charisma of the guy, but even more so, how delighted he was that Imogen had actually mentioned him to Simon.

At the same time, Simon felt strangely drawn to Fletcher, despite that he was Imogen's former suitor and, by all accounts, should be his natural enemy. There was something about him. He had one of those likable faces that made you feel instantly at ease. In another time, Simon had no use for friends, and he might well have immediately cut this man down to size with some witty aside, but he wasn't in another time, he was here. And to be honest, he was exhausted by it all, and it occurred to him that maybe a friend was exactly what he needed; not just any friend, but a male friend, someone other than Imogen to bounce thoughts and ideas off of, someone with whom he could confide in and could help him understand and perhaps learn how to better navigate this new uncharted landscape.

Simon shoved the photograph into his pocket and said, "It's getting rather warm out here. Would you care to join me inside for a beer?"

Fletcher certainly wasn't expecting this; he was unsure whether it was even a good idea. Still, it was kind of hot out and a beer sounded pretty great.

"Sure!" he agreed.

"Follow me then," Simon said smiling as he turned and led Fletcher through the back door into the cool kitchen.

Entering Imogen's kitchen again after so long felt like stepping into a happy memory. Everything was the same—the coffee mugs hanging from the pegs above the stove, the black-and-white checkered floor, the fold-down wooden table where they had shared many mornings over coffee and conversation and the

Sunday newspaper.

"Have a seat," Simon instructed as he strode over to the sink to wash the crusted dirt from his hands before reaching into the fridge for a beer.

"Thanks." Fletcher nodded when Simon handed him the cold bottle of beer. "Be right back," Simon said as he disappeared into the living room. He pulled the faded picture that had been tucked inside his vest pocket and placed it on the fireplace mantle before returning to the kitchen and grabbing a beer for himself.

An uncomfortable silence floated between them as each took sips of beer and contemplated what next to talk about, until both spoke at the same time.

"What do you do, Fletcher?" from Simon.

From Fletcher, "I hear you are not from here."

"You go," Fletcher interjected, realizing that his question was a little more probing than Simon's was."

Simon coiled his finger around a lock of hair, a nervous habit he'd acquired as a child. Clearing his throat, he asked, "I was wondering what it is you do for a living?"

"I'm an engineer," Fletcher answered.

"On a locomotive?" Simon asked inquisitively.

Fletcher snickered before realizing that Simon was probably serious. He wasn't sure, but it suddenly occurred to him that in Simon's frame of reference the term "engineer" described someone whose job was to steer a train down a railroad track.

Simon's smile faded. Had he said something wrong? Surely, he must have, and he looked away, embarrassed.

But Fletcher was quick to correct him without being the least bit condescending. "Oh, no, I'm afraid my life isn't quite that adventurous. I'm not that kind of engineer. I just work for an architectural firm. I design functional office spaces and ergonomic furniture," he said, downplaying his role.

Simon's face brightened again, but the look of confusion was plain. Once again, Fletcher realized that he'd used another term that Simon likely was unfamiliar with.

Simon was interested. He'd been building furniture on a

much smaller scale but wasn't sure what ergonomic meant. "Uh, ergonomic relates to furniture that is designed for efficiency and comfort," Fletcher said. It seemed like the right moment to also address the elephant in the room. "But I wouldn't have expected you to know that considering the time you come from," he added, glancing over at Simon earnestly, hoping that he was not offended that Fletcher knew.

Simon set his beer down on the table. "Well, yes," he stammered. "I take it Imogen has told you of my rather unusual circumstances."

Fletcher nodded. "Actually, our mutual friend Rachel told me."

"I see," Simon said. He sat still like that, not saying a word and Fletcher began to wonder if he should take his leave, but then the corners of his mouth curved into a semi-smile and Simon added, "And getting here, well, it was quite indeed a bumpy ride."

With that, the ice broke and both men began to laugh. Finding common ground—besides Imogen—in a moment of shared confidence, despite being born a century apart, each felt an immediate connection with the other.

"So, Fletcher," Simon said leaning in, "tell me more about this furniture you make."

"You betcha" Fletcher replied, "as long as you tell me everything about the 1900s!"

"Oh my, that explains a lot! Simon said. On the computer, Fletcher had shown him how to do a search in Google, not *the* Google anymore, now that he was grasping the lingo of technology a bit better. "What do you want to find first?" Fletcher had asked him.

That was easy. "Simon Le Bon, my name."

Fletcher tried to squelch a chuckle, but Simon expected that reaction. "I'm sorry to laugh," he said, but . . ."

Simon interrupted him. "It is fine. I am quite used to it now. Ever since I made first contact with Imogen and this new life, I have received the same response from everyone I meet. I'm afraid my knowledge of cultural references are lacking. And I think it's past time I learned more about this namesake of mine."

Simon was impressed. Like magic, 76,300,000 results in 59 seconds popped up on the screen. Information at your fingertips . . . in seconds . . . what a wonder, this world! This first entry was from Wikipedia, a site that he would use in the future many, many more times as his researching skills improved.

It read: "Simon John Charles Le Bon, born 27 October 1958, an English musician, singer, songwriter, and lyricist, best known as the lead singer and lyricist of the band Duran Duran and its offshoot, Arcadia." Fletcher showed him how to view images of the singer—before and after images depicting a youthful star of the 1980s and the 60-something man of today. It was striking, and Simon was hooked. It was evident why his mother as a teenager would have been taken by the handsome and charismatic vocalist.

"What about songs?" Simon asked. "My mother, as I recall, used to sing songs with unusual lyrics. I wonder if any of them could have been by this group."

Fletcher next showed Simon how to navigate YouTube where the band's entire discography could be easily browsed. He grabbed a set of headphones he found on a shelf beside the desk and handed them over to Simon. "Here," he said, "put these on."

Simon's eyes grew wide, and a satisfied smile crossed his face as the music enveloped him and whisked him away, in the same way it did for so many kids the first time they heard sound splitting in two and dancing back and forth between their ears while listening to Pink Floyd's *Dark Side of the Moon* album, for instance, through headphones for the first time.

Through the curious ear gadget, Simon was indeed transported. Never in his life had he experienced music in such intimate and crisp detail, every note, every vocal intonation seeming to echo and vibrate through his head. Although the phonograph had been invented in 1877, owning one and affording the cylinders for it was a luxury his mother, along with most other people, could not afford. In Simon's youth, music was only accessible through live performances, on the streets or via piano players in bars playing arrangements of sheet music, or orchestras in the theater.

Fletcher was enjoying himself as much as Simon—excited and pleased to be the first to introduce technology to his new friend. How often did that ever happen as an adult? All of these things he used daily and took for granted were completely brand new to Simon. What sheer joy it was to be able to share something with someone for the first time.

Simon was quickly enthralled by the accompanying music videos, which were strange, haunting. Simon made his way through Duran Duran's repertoire, internalizing the waves of sounds that seemed to be floating independently inside his head.

He recognized a couple of songs he had heard his mom humming or singing, the sad and lilting "Ordinary World" and "Do you believe in Shame?" And when the first bars of "Hungry Like the Wolf" began, Simon excitedly tore the headphones from his ears. "This one! She sang this one all the time, Fletcher!" Fletcher put the headphones on and listened for a few moments before taking them off.

Simon was confused by Fletcher's look of dismay. "This song, "Hungry Like the Wolf," it has a sort of bad connotation here in Oregon," Fletcher said.

"Why is that?" Simon asked.

Fletcher began: "In 1983, out on a country road not too far from here, a crazy woman named Diane Downs murdered her daughter and attempted to murder her other two children, but that's not all," he said, hesitating for a moment. "They say that while she was shooting them that song was playing on the car radio. It was reported that she tapped her foot along to the music as she pulled the trigger."

Simon shrunk back into the desk chair. "Oh my, that is quite a disturbing tale. Why would my mother want to sing a song associated with the murder of children?"

"I wouldn't dwell on it too much, Simon," Fletcher assured him. "It was a popular song, one of their most popular, chart-topping ones, as a matter of fact. She may not have even known about the conditions."

Fletcher was right. He had read that the band was most popular in the 1980s, but enjoyed a resurgence in popularity again in the 1990s. It would have been like his mother to have discovered them later on. She always had eclectic tastes in everything. He recalled following her to strange parts of town where out of the way, off the beaten track curiosity shops with oddities like artifacts and handmade tribal items could be acquired, not the kinds of things one might find in your typical mercantile. So, it would not have surprised him in the least that it was the same for music. She would have listened to music from many different eras.

Curious about her, Fletcher asked, "What happened to your mother, if you don't mind me asking?" Considering the immediate change in Simon's demeanor and that he abruptly got up and left the room, Fletcher instantly regretted it. But in a few minutes, Simon returned with the photograph he'd plucked from the garden earlier and handed it to him. It took a moment for Fletcher to grasp that this was a picture of Simon's mother. He wasn't sure what he was expecting—maybe a color Polaroid from the 1960s, but the old, weathered black and white photograph, he was holding depicted a woman in turn of the century clothing. Logically, he knew that, yes, of course, his mother would have been from this time, as was he, but it was still shocking, and Fletcher couldn't help noticing how heartbreakingly sad she looked. People didn't smile in photographs back then, he knew, but he'd never seen anyone this miserable before. He looked over at Simon, who seemed to be experiencing the same emotion he was.

"I apologize," he said. "I . . . I probably shouldn't have asked you . . ."

Simon gestured dismissively. "No, it is fine that you inquired," he said before adding, "she was committed to a mental institution when I was a child. I never saw her again."

"Oh," Fletcher gulped, "I am so sorry, Simon. Really, truly sorry." But then, a fleeting, brilliant idea floated into his head as they often did, his face brightened, and the thought was out of his mouth and hanging in the air between them before he could stop it.

"Why doesn't Imogen just go back and find out what happened to her for you?" he blurted. "She has the ability."

Simon pondered that for a moment. Fletcher was right, why doesn't she? he thought, but instead replied, "She has not offered, and I do not feel that it is appropriate to ask her."

"Why not? Fletcher pressed, "You would think she would want to find out about something that important to you; to help you find closure."

"Yes, it would seem," Simon said, turning his back on Fletcher. "More music?" he asked, placing the headphones back on his ears.

Several hours later, after spending the afternoon diving down the rabbit hole of YouTube, the pair retreated to the living room where the conversation turned to Simon's need for identification.

"I feel useless," Simon confessed to Fletcher. "In my time, I was a respected school principal. Here, I am nothing but a freeloader, and without identification, I cannot work. I cannot contribute." Simon sighed. "How do I prove I exist? I know that I was born in 1887 but I doubt that I had a birth certificate," he said. "The rules are perplexing, to say the least—to get identification, one must have identification!"

Fletcher nodded in agreement; his brows knitted together as he considered the *Catch 22* quandary. "Well, let's Google it!" he said, leaping from the couch and heading back to the office where the computer was. Simon was impressed all over again when Fletcher typed in, "How can I get an ID without a birth certificate?" and dozens and dozens of pages of information appeared on the screen again as if summoned by magic. The search was a bust; you really had to have a birth certificate; however, they did learn that standard certificates of live birth were not established until 1900—before that, records of birth, marriage, and death were typically recorded by the church.

Several beers later, shadows began to creep across the walls. It was getting late and Fletcher was preparing to leave. "I really need to get going, but I'll help you," he promised as Simon led him to the door. "We'll figure out some way to get you some ID."

"I appreciate all your help," Simon said, patting Fletcher's shoulder in a friendly, bro-like gesture.

His hand on the doorknob, Fletcher paused first before turning back to Simon. "But you know, there are other ways that you can make a living," he said. "With today's technology—they call it the gig economy—anyone can produce anything and sell it online through eBay or Etsy or Amazon."

"Whoa . . ." Simon said, "wait a minute. I've heard tell of the Amazon, but eBay, Etsy? What are those?"

"There are endless possibilities . . . " Fletcher said, pleased to have come up with a way to make Simon feel a little bit better about his current situation.

Simon scratched his chin. Ideas were coursing through his head at lightning speed. "hmmm, I wonder," he said out loud. "Before you go, Fletcher, come this way, I have something to show you."

Simon led Fletcher out through the kitchen door to the dark garage. "This way," he said as they navigated in the dimly lit space, before stopping abruptly where Simon flipped the switch on a large fluorescent light bar hanging low over a workstation. Awash in bright light an impressive array of small-scale furniture in various stages of production—chairs, beds, bureaus, bookcases, tables—along with neat stacks of cut and uncut wood, fabric pieces, and scraps of paper came into view. Through an enormous magnifying glass attached to the edge of the table one could see the augmented intricacies of tiny bottles and miniature plates in progress.

Fletcher was more than impressed. "Oh wow, Simon," he gushed. "When you said you made miniature furniture, I had no idea it would be this incredible!" Fletcher drew closer to examine the artful project in front of him. Picking up a chair in the arts and craft style, he gently turned it over in his hand, examining it more closely. "My goodness, I've never seen anything like this. The craftsmanship and attention to detail at such a small scale is phenomenal!" He turned around to face Simon, who stood back embarrassed, but silently basking in his friend's adoration.

"Simon, you could easily sell these online or to hobby stores . . . Geez, I would hire you this minute as a model maker in my architectural firm. These are *that* good."

"How did you learn to do this?" Fletcher asked as Simon turned off the lights and they headed back inside to the living room couch.

Simon took a breath before launching into the story. "Well . . . my mother collected scraps of many things," Simon began. "We were quite poor. I didn't have a lot of toys to speak of, but I started making furniture from the scraps she saved for a little girl that lived next door who, in comparison to me, had virtually nothing, not even a doll to play with."

In the middle of expanding on his childhood and his mother and the little girl next door, Simon stopped speaking when they both heard the sound of a key turning in the front door lock.

4

Drawing the edge of the blanket up over her ears, Imogen burrowed herself deeper into the thrift store sofa she had several years ago appropriated for her downtown office. Even though it had been several hours since returning from her journey to 1971, she wasn't quite ready to get up just yet, due in large part to the time travel "hangover" that left her feeling exhausted and head-achy for a while. Beyond that, she was a sucker for anything cozy, furry, fuzzy, warm—whether it was a blanket, a pillow, or a cat—Imogen had no qualms about lounging as long as possible, being of the firm opinion that getting enough sleep, naps, meditation, and self-care made us all better people. For that reason, she was unapologetically sloth-like.

One thing about lying awake for a while before getting up was it gave her a chance to be quiet, reflective, to think and sort out all the stuff rattling around inside her head, where and when she had just been and an opportunity to readjust to returning to now. Being one of those women who thinks too much, there were times when she wished she could turn it off, stop overthinking everything. It would be nice once in a while to let events simply play out as they will. She was getting better at it now that she'd been traveling through time for a while. Nothing she might encounter was predictable and she had learned how to be better at letting things go, relinquishing control and letting the moment happen. Simon had been instrumental in helping her shed some of those hang-ups.

Simon. On the one hand, she was unbelievably excited to see him. Knowing he was at home right now waiting for her was the best, most amazing feeling ever. The spark was still there, yet on the other, she also kind of dreaded seeing him, fearing that they would fall back into the same exhausting pattern of late, which was argue, apologize, make up, rinse, repeat. She knew it was difficult for him; how could it not be? Just because she knew her history, having majored in it in college, lived through some of it, and traveled to places all over the globe experiencing it as it unfolded right before her eyes, didn't mean that Simon shared that same cognitive context. She definitely needed to work on her patience skills.

She was also aware that some people did not adapt to change as well as she did. For as long as she could remember, change had been her middle name. She wasn't sure if it was because of losing both parents at an early age or if it was simply her character, but she had never been satisfied with staying in one spot for long—not only physically, but emotionally and mentally as well. It wasn't that she was bored necessarily—she was curious about everything, but change was exciting—whether it was dying her hair a new color—she'd experimented with a spectrum of color, from blond to strawberry blonde, and platinum blonde to super bright red, eggplant purple, jet black, pink, gray, and blue—or tossing out one wardrobe and replacing it with another. This preoccupation with change was probably why time travel had been such a natural and appealing fit for her, she figured. Every place she went, every time entered, she could reinvent herself again and again, give herself a new name, a new persona, be anybody she wanted to be. Or, maybe all along it had simply been a way of avoiding thinking about her parents.

She could only hope that Simon would understand and accept this about her, but she worried that he would not. His decision to come with her had happened so suddenly. Nothing had been planned out. He had followed his own impulses, against her wishes, by the way. And neither of them was prepared for a life together outside the shelter of the cocoon they'd built around themselves at the Benson Hotel in 1913. She smiled, remembering those blissful days spent together in room 213 as their romance blossomed, exploring each other's bodies, and discovering the patterns and rhythm of their passion. Their relationship was stumbling, for sure, but nothing they couldn't overcome. She hoped. She'd deal with it when she got home.

She had business to attend to. Top on her to-do list, visit the post office and see if Adam Curry had left any directives for her to relay to his son Sean, her client. She hoped that it was a scenario that would result in a happy ending, that Sean would be reunited with his father and that they would know one another at last.

Imogen drove to the post office, which was not far, also downtown. The town's original post office had been here as long as she could remember, and its age was apparent. Inside, long rows of postal boxes lined the wall, each metal number box festooned with ornate strands of ivy leaves. The lavish marble floor tile was original as were the high ceilings, wainscoting, chandeliers, and other turn of the century embellishments. The only part that was different was the area where you went to buy stamps and mail packages. It had been updated and modernized with shiny, stainless-steel counters, weight and bulk handling machines and whatnot that streamlined the process of mail prep and delivery.

Drawing the key to box 238 from her pocket, she inserted it into the slot and was pleased to see that there was a letter inside. The 40+ year-old letter was indeed from Adam Curry and the post date on the envelope read: December 4, 1971. It had been mailed from the general store in Spirit Lake, which provided postal service for hikers and campers and visitors. Yay, she thought. He'd come through and now she hoped beyond hope that he was still alive to set up a meeting between he and his son.

Seated in her car outside the post office, Imogen carefully removed the aged letter from the envelope. As much as she hated having to read something so personal, it was important for her to know what was in it before contacting Sean.

Dear Sean

In the time since I've been away, I have had a lot of time to think about things, things I did and didn't do, the choices I made, for better or worse.

Many times, I wondered how you and your mom were getting on. I even thought about coming home a time or two but decided against it.

I'm a coward, always have been. I got scared the day you were born. Scared about being a father and even more scared that I wouldn't be able to live up to your mom's expectations. I am sorry that I will miss seeing you grow up, but I know your mom will do a great job, probably better by herself than she ever would tangled up with a loser like me. I hope you will always find peace, son. God bless. I decided to stay on the mountain.

Adam Curry

Stunned, Imogen lowered the letter to her lap and stared out the window. It was clear that Adam had no intention of seeing his son ever again, but even more interesting was that he had written the letter without mentioning ever meeting Imogen or revealing that he knew how Sean had turned out, which surprised her a little. Perhaps knowing that he was letting his son go was enough to take in without adding a time travel tale to the mix.

Pulling out her cell phone, she dialed Sean's number. "Hello," he answered on the first ring as though waiting for her call.

"Sean?" Imogen asked.

"Speaking."

"Hi Sean, this is Imogen Oliver. Good news! I have a letter here, from your father. Can we meet somewhere this morning? I'm currently downtown, so if you want to meet up nearby, that might work."

Imogen detected the excitement in Sean's voice when he replied, "Oh yes, Ms. Oliver. Of course, I can meet you in about a half hour. Vero on Pearl?" he suggested.

"Perfect!" Imogen said. "I'll see you there."

She ended the call and headed to the coffeehouse. She would be early for their appointment, but she figured she could snag a table and then get busy on a much-required latte while she waited for Sean to arrive.

Twenty-nine minutes later, Sean walked through the door and Imogen waved him over to the table.

"Would you like to grab a coffee first?" she asked when he

sat down in the chair across from her.

"Oh no, I'm good," he said. "I'm anxious to see what you've found."

Imogen placed the letter on the table and pushed it toward him. "It's good news and bad news," she said.

Sean sighed and resting his hands palm down on the table, he gazed at the folded letter between them for a moment as though taking time to first gather up strength to read the words from a father he had never known.

After a few seconds, he gingerly unfolded the letter and Imogen watched his face intently looking for some sort of a reaction, but it never changed as he read it. When he was finished, he refolded it and tucked it away in the inside pocket of his jacket. Imogen sat quietly, waiting for Sean to speak first. He stared down at his hands on the table for another second or two before looking up. "Well, I guess that's it then."

Imogen pressed her lips together. She had hoped that she would be able to convince Adam to reunite with his son. But even so, it had been iffy, a crapshoot at best, especially considering that he had left the cabin without indicating one way or the other if he would be contacting her.

Imogen shook her head. "I'm sorry," she said, "I really thought that things might turn out differently."

Sean raised his hand, brushing her comment away dismissively. "It's all right," he said. "It was a long shot, I knew that. But there's one thing I don't understand."

Imogen leaned forward. "What's that?" she asked.

"What did he mean by 'I decided to stay on the mountain?' Did you find him on a mountain? Did you talk to him?"

How she had acquired the letter posed a problem. If she told Sean the truth about meeting Adam in 1971 it would mean divulging her unique method of finding people, something for which she'd rather not share. Only Imogen knew the true impact of Adam's statement in the letter. If he'd stayed on the mountain past 1980, he likely did not survive the volcanic explosion that blew the mountain apart. However, if he had heeded her warning and left there was the possibility that he could have survived yet still no guarantee that he was alive today. She had read that a few bodies were found after the blast that they were able to identify—one was found in a car completely submerged in ash, but she had found nothing on Adam Curry—dead or alive.

She was never good at lying, but in this case, she had no choice. She had to tell Sean something and it had to coincide with the time frame and the way in which he'd written the letter. "No, I never actually found your dad," she lied.

Sean frowned and shook his head slowly. "I don't understand," he said. "How did you get this letter?" He pulled it back out of his pocket.

"The mountain he was referring to was Mount St. Helens."

"The one in Washington that erupted back in the '80s?"

"That's the one."

"Again, I don't follow."

Some of what Imogen was about to tell him was true. "Your dad had a sister, Deborah," she began. "He mailed it to her back in 1971, hoping that she would pass it along to you. I guess he didn't have your address. She died in 2004 and the letter was part of her estate, which had been donated to a museum exhibition about the 1980 eruption.

"So you think he died on the mountain?"

"Maybe, maybe not. I don't know for sure. Beyond the letter, I couldn't dig up anything more on your dad."

They chatted a bit while finishing up their coffee. Although Sean was disappointed, he seemed to understand. It killed her inside that she couldn't tell him about meeting Adam at the cabin and sharing a cup of hot chocolate and a potent bowlful with the one and only fugitive D.B. Cooper in front of a warm fire. It made for a great story, but not something she could divulge. At the very least, she hoped the letter provided some solace to Sean. And while she hoped too that Adam Curry hadn't perished in the volcanic explosion, she felt good knowing that she had at least been able to deliver information to him about his son as well as given him an option for escape when the time came.

When it was time to go, Sean rose from the table and shook Imogen's hand. "Thank you again, Imogen," he said. He patted the place where the letter was in his pocket and said, "I feel like maybe I can finally let it go now and move on." Imogen smiled. "I hope so Sean."

Imogen was tired. These trips were physically and emotionally draining, but always interesting and sometimes rewarding, so far anyway. She started up her car intending to go home to Simon and probably more drama, but as she drove, she started thinking about change and impulsively swung the car into a strip mall and parked in front of a hair salon that accommodated walk-ins. Two hours later she emerged from the shop with a haircut in a lovely new color—chocolate cherry.

5

As she stood on the porch scrabbling with her house key Imogen heard muffled voices inside the house. Did Simon have company? Who could it be? Maybe he had the volume on the TV turned up extra high, his face plastered inches from the screen like he sometimes annoyingly did. Slipping into the foyer she tossed her keys into the Anguiano clay pot, stopped to hang her jacket on the metal peg, and then ditched her shoes before entering the living room. From where she stood, she could see several empty beer bottles on the coffee table and the backs of two people seated on the couch engaged in animated conversation. Imogen cleared her throat and they both turned around to look.

In unison, Simon and Fletcher called out, "Imogen!"

Imogen set her purse and keys down on the side table. This was certainly not the homecoming she was expecting. Reticently, she said, "Uh, hi."

Simon and Fletcher leapt from the couch as though caught in a compromising act, and Simon rushed around to greet her, surprised to see her and her new hair. "I'm so glad you're back, darling," he said reaching out and pulling her in close for a hug. "And your hair, it's . . . interesting."

It's called chocolate cherry," Imogen informed him.

Fletcher, hanging back inconspicuously, raised his hand in a half-hearted wave. "Hey Imogen," he said.

"So, what's going on here?" she asked them both.

Simon looked over at Fletcher and back again at Imogen. "Well," he explained, "Fletcher dropped by while I was gardening, so I invited him inside for a beer."

"Oh," Imogen said, glancing at the empties on the table. "A few beers, it looks like."

Imogen was most surprised to see Fletcher. After Rachel told him about Simon, as one might expect, things had been a tad awkward between them. Seeing the writing on the wall, Fletcher had decided it might be a good idea for all parties if he moved back to Idaho, but before Imogen could properly tell him goodbye, he was gone. So, this was unexpected. Why was he back now?

"How have you been Imogen?" Fletcher asked as he came toward her. He reached out and pulled her in close for an uneasy hug that lasted a little longer than it probably should have.

"Are you back for good or just visiting?" she asked when they disengaged.

"I'm back, I guess," he said shrugging. "The job in Idaho didn't pan out, so my company offered me my old job if I wanted it."

"Wow," Imogen said. "That's nice that they did that." Another uncomfortable moment followed until Simon broke the silence. "Fletcher and I have discovered that we have quite a great deal in common!"

"Oh yeah?" Imogen asked, hoping to conceal her incredulity. "How so?" This couldn't be good, she thought.

"We both like beer!" Fletcher piped up, flashing a sideways grin at Simon.

Despite how incredibly weird and socially uncomfortable this reunion was, Imogen couldn't help noticing that for the first time in three months Simon seemed excited about something. "Fletcher is an engineer and when I showed him my miniature furniture pieces, he offered to draw up some plans for building custom dollhouses," he said looking over at Fletcher, who was nodding agreement." I may have found my calling after all," he said brightly.

Part of Simon's discontent had been his inability to carry his weight. In his time, he was the headmaster of a school, quite a prestigious position back then. His decision to travel across time to the future negated all of that, making his 100-year-old degree certificate invalid. He had no credentials, no identification. He could no longer do that job or even teach as he had before. It was one of many details neither of them had thought to consider beforehand. Imogen suggested that he return to school, but he said he wasn't ready for that, he needed time. So maybe this dollhouse building thing wasn't such a bad idea after all, although the budding bromance between Simon and her ex-boyfriend made Imogen a little apprehensive. Still, this was a welcome change in him, a good sign that he might finally be making some progress adjusting to his new life.

"We're going to get together next week and discuss designs!" Simon said, enthusiasm teeming in his voice and demeanor.

"Awesome," Imogen said, and she genuinely meant it. Simon also seemed pleased that Imogen was receptive to the idea. Yet another awkward silence ensued which Fletcher took as his cue to leave.

He started moving toward the door. "Well, I guess I should be going," he said. "Nice to see you Imogen, and I'll contact you next week, Simon." Simon walked Fletcher out and when he returned to the living room Imogen was gathering up the beer bottles.

"No, no, I'll get those!" Simon said, snatching them from her hands and clearing the rest from the table to take to the kitchen.

When he came back into the room, Imogen was sitting with her back to him. "What's this?" she asked as she shifted around and showed him the book she held in her hand.

"Oh that," Simon said as he walked over to her and took the book of poems by e.e. cummings from her. "Well, I figured you'd read all of Lawrence's poems by now, so perhaps you might like some new material." When they had first met, Simon had surprised Imogen with *Love Poems and Others* by D.H. Lawrence.

"Oh you did, huh?" she said, her lips curling into a smile.

Imogen noticed a scrap of paper marking one page in particular. "Is this the one you think I should read first?" she asked. Simon winked at her. "Perhaps," he said slyly as he took the book from her. "But I'll read it to you, if that's all right?"

Imogen nodded as she settled back into the couch to listen to Simon read, as he had that first time so long ago:

. . . the great advantage of being alive
(instead of undying) is not so much
that mind no more can disprove than prove
what heart may feel and soul may touch . . .

For love are in you am in i are in we

Simon closed the book. For once, Imogen was without words. "Well?" Simon asked, "what do you think?"

She crinkled up her nose and mouth, pausing to think about it for a minute. Simon wondered if she hated it. Perhaps it was the wrong poet. Too modern for her taste? Too avant-garde?

"*For love are in you am in I are in we*," she recited. "I love that."

"It was a good choice then?" Simon seemed pleased that she liked it.

"A very good choice, Simon."

"In fact, I think it shall be our mantra from now on, our love language, if you will!" she said dramatically.

"Really?" Simon asked, a little puzzled about where Imagen was going with this.

"And we should make a pact too."

"A pact?"

"Yes," she said, "that only one of us is allowed to be crazy at a time."

Simon laughed. "All right Imogen, it's a deal," he said as he sat down next to her on the sofa. Lifting her feet up, he placed them on his lap. "You look tired," he said as he began to massage one foot.

"mmmm," Imogen said, closing her eyes, "that feels nice." Simon was a pro in the foot massage department.

Simon stopped rubbing and said, "How did it go? Your trip?"

"I'll tell you about it later. Keep rubbing," she said, closing her eyes. Snickering, he resumed the massage.

Times like this reminded her how loving and wonderful Simon truly was. She sat up next to him and wrapping her arms around his neck, planted a series of soft kisses on his lips.

"You missed me?" he asked, lifting one eyebrow.

"I did," she purred in between light kisses.

"I thought you wanted me to massage your feet," he said.

Imogen curled up closer. "Maybe I want you to massage other parts."

"That sounds like an invitation," Simon said.

As they continued to kiss, the kisses became longer and deeper and more impassioned.

Simon broke away first. "Let us go to the bedroom," he said.

"Why?" Imogen asked. "Why not right here?"

"Here?" Simon asked. So far, their lovemaking had generally been of the mission style, although Imogen had been introducing him to oral delights and a few other deliciously extraordinary activities of the flesh, that is, when they weren't arguing.

He felt ashamed now recalling the argument they'd had before she had gone on her trip. They were watching a news segment about the Me-Too Movement and Imogen had made some flippant remark about women not needing a man and it had struck a nerve with him.

"You are so smug, Imogen," Simon blurted. "You assume you are somehow superior to me because you are worldlier."

"Where did that even come from Simon?" she shot back at him, clearly surprised by his allegation, "I was only joking."

"I want to understand you Imogen, but frankly, I still have difficulty reconciling your sexual escapades with other men in the past."

"Oh my god, Simon, not this again," she groaned and rolled her eyes. "Didn't we have this very same conversation literally like 100 years ago?"

"Yes, but . . ."

Imogen cut him off before he could finish. "Yes, but you have had 'escapades' yourself! Come on Simon, times have changed. I know it's hard to wrap your brain around it, but if you're ever going to get used to living here there are things you have got to let go of, and things you must accept."

He knew now that it had been silly of him to be jealous of her former lovers. Women were magical, sensuous creatures, he was coming to realize, and anyone who had come before him was of no concern. In fact, he should thank them for helping Imogen become the goddess she was.

Imogen sat up straight and capriciously pulled her top up and over her head, much to Simon's delight. Reaching behind her back she masterfully undid her bra, exposing her lovely breasts which Simon could not resist reaching out to fondle. She unzipped his pants, pulling them down to his feet. Standing up, she removed her own pants and panties. Fully nude, she positioned herself strategically on Simon's lap. This was new and different and extraordinarily exciting. New hair, new adventures—Imogen, always so full of surprises!

When they had finished, breathless and sweaty and spent, Simon pulled his pants up and Imogen put her panties back on but left her shirt off and laid back down with her head on Simon's lap. He had begun to realize that Imogen was a master of distraction. The fact that she'd left her shirt off exposing him to her breasts meant that their lovemaking session might not be over. He gently ran his finger in circles around her belly button, and they both sat quietly as they regained their normal breathing until Imogen broke the spell. "Aren't you worried about having my ex-boyfriend around?" she asked without warning.

"Should I be?" Simon responded.

Imogen reached up and took a strand of Simon's long hair and using it like a feather teased his nose with the end of it.

"No," she said. "I'm just surprised, I guess, that you have taken an interest in someone that I used to sleep with. That has always seemed to be a hang-up of yours."

"I'm a new man," Simon declared, smiling and brushing her hand away from his nose. "That was the old Simon. The new Simon has turned over a new leaf."

"A new leaf? I see," Imogen said. "Well, I'm glad. Fletcher is a very nice person, and you could use a friend."

Imogen sat up then and put her shirt and pants back on, much to Simon's dismay.

"Are we finished?" he asked, a smidgen of disappointment creeping into his voice.

Imogen smiled. "For now," she said. "I have something I want to talk to you about.

"Uh oh," Simon said.

"It's nothing bad," Imogen assured him. "I promise. I have an idea, a way for you to be able to get some identification. You may not be able to return to your previous vocation as an educator, but it may provide you with the wherewithal to begin carving out a little independence for yourself," she said.

"That is interesting that you brought that up," Simon said, "because Fletcher mentioned that he could acquire a birth certificate that would allow me to get identification."

"Oh really, and what else did you and Fletcher talk about?" she inquired.

Simon tossed his hair aside and smiled at Imogen. "He showed me how to use Google."

"Oh, it's not *the* Google anymore?" Imogen teased.

Simon rolled his eyes. "Don't be silly, Imogen," he countered. "Actually, we looked up my name and it appears my namesake is the famous English musician and lead singer, Simon Le Bon of the band Duran Duran and its offshoot, Arcadia."

Imogen was impressed. "Wow. You have been doing your research!"

"And now I understand why so many people of this time, including you when first we met, looked at me so queerly when I introduced myself!"

"It is a rather notable name if you know your 80s culture. Well, regardless of whether Fletcher can get you a birth certificate or not, I have something for you," she said, changing the subject.

She jumped off the couch and sprinted to the bedroom returning a few minutes later with a DNA sample kit. "I know you don't want to be associated with Mimi Pinky, but if the DNA sample shows that she is in fact your paternal grandmother, there could be some benefits," she said.

Simon turned the brightly colored cardboard box over in his hand. "How does this work?" he asked Imogen.

"You give them some of your spit, send it off, and they send back data about your heritage, where you're from, all that," Imogen explained. Simon was astounded. Who would have thought that something as advanced as this could ever be possible? He opened the box and began to pore over the instructions, testing Imogen's patience.

"You can read that later," she said vying for his attention.

"I want to know how it works, what they do, the science behind it," Simon snapped, irritated. "Can't I read it?" he said, looking up at her.

"Yes, in a minute," she insisted.

Simon sighed, setting the instructions aside to turn his focus back on her.

"Okay," she said. "So do you remember when Mimi came by and upset you and you said that she mentioned something about money, right?"

"Yes, I do," Simon said recalling the day Mimi Pinky had shown up at the door. "That was a strange thing to say. I didn't understand that."

"Well, what if Teddy had money that nobody knew about?" Imogen said, her tone building with enthusiasm. "I mean, think about it. He was a time traveler. He would want to fly under the radar. He could have socked it away in various places and retrieved it later, just like I have. It's the workaround for not being able to bring stuff back with you from the past. If the DNA results show that he is your father, you may be entitled to whatever was his. Mimi can't get access to it until he's declared dead, but as his sole heir, they might put you in charge of it."

Simon squinted his eyes, and he bit the edge of his lip with concern. "Hmm, I am not confident I would feel right about that."

A flash of annoyance registered on Imogen's face. "Why the hell not Simon? After what he did to you, to me, to your mother?

Especially your mother! If anything, he owes us! It's worth a shot, and if nothing else, it will help you get a birth certificate, if that's what you want to do, of course."

"It is," Simon agreed. "But you must know Imogen, the most important thing I want is to be wherever . . . *whenever* you are." He took her hand, lifted it to his lips, and gently kissed it.

For the first time in weeks, things felt almost right between them. Imogen's anger disintegrated with his lovely words. "So tell me more about what you and Fletcher discussed," she said in between the series of small smooches she began to lavish upon his face and neck.

"Hmmm," he murmured trying to stay focused. "Well, I learned that an engineer in this time is slightly different than engineers who drove locomotives in my time."

Imogen stopped smooching for a minute to say in her best pouty voice, "It's not fair that Fletcher is the one introducing you all the cool things." Again, resuming the kissing, she asked, "And what other new words have you learned?"

"I learned that some furniture can be 'ergonomic.'"

"Hmmm, is that so?" Imogen said as she began to nibble on his ear lobe. "Well, our bed is extremely ergonomic, if you'd care to test it out with me."

Simon did not hesitate. Leaping from the couch, he raced into the bedroom ahead of Imogen and flung himself onto their ergonomic bed. "Care to join me for some efficiency and comfort m'lady?"

6

Sweaty and out of breath, Mimi Pinky Diamond stomped into the shabby house on the corner of 13th and Chesterfield, slamming the door hard enough to make the windows rattle. "What's up, babe?" a male voice drawled from a back room in the gloomy always dark house, the blackout curtains drawn tightly, because Mimi liked it that way.

Swiping the pile of empty beer cans onto the floor with her hand before flinging her hefty form onto the couch, she sat rigid and seething and too angry to answer. Moments later, an unshaven and barefoot man dressed in greasy T-shirt and baggy sweatpants, a filterless cigarette dangling from his lips, emerged from the shadowy bedroom. Snubbing out his smoke into one of several overflowing ashtrays, he approached the fuming Mimi, who had crossed her arms tightly across her round belly like some angry Buddha.

"What's eatin' you today, Ms. Pink?" the man asked. Mimi Pinky, who normally didn't like being touched or mollycoddled, yet secretly relished the attention, stuck her lower lip out in a pronounced pout, and stated, "I hate that fucking asshole!"

"What asshole?" the man asked.

"That asshole Simon, my grandson, that's who," she repeated. "You need to do something about him Carl," she said. Carl patted Mimi's arm and slid off the couch. "Well, you just tell me whatcha want me to do? I'll do it," he said, artfully raising one eyebrow and flipping up his shirt to reveal the concealed handgun he kept in a leather holster belted to his hip.

Carl Loomis wasn't a clever man, but he had a keen eye for

opportunity. His ma had always said he was cagey. "Yer gonna go far in life, Carl," she'd say. So far, she'd been right, although most of the opportunities he'd stumbled into lately had been sketchy and relatively small time—fencing stolen auto parts, selling drugs, growing pot, helping some idiot tweaker set up a meth lab in a backyard outbuilding. But when he'd been approached about stealing a rare book, he knew he'd hit the big time, well, the bigger time anyway. The money was nothing to sniff at—25 grand! Heck, he'd steal an armored truck for that much dough. Not only that, but Mimi Pinky was such an easy mark it was almost laughable.

From what Carl could gather, Mimi's blabbing to anybody who'd listen had attracted the attention of some pretty sketchy and probably dangerous characters. She was the key to getting this book, they said. All he had to do was be nice to her, listen to her wild stories about aliens and JFK and time travel and 911 being an inside job, cozy up to her a bit until she trusted him, and then get her talking about what kind of crooked business her dead son had been up to. So far, Mimi was mum on the son. She didn't want to talk about him at all. No, her focus was strictly revenge. Apparently, the grandson Simon and his lady friend were currently in her crosshair. Carl wasn't quite sure yet what the connection was, but Mimi seemed to think they were responsible for his death, although she wouldn't say how he had died.

Mimi's eyes grew wide with the sight of Carl's gun. My goodness, she didn't want him going over and shooting them. Scaring them a little, maybe, but shooting them, no. Alarmed, she asked, "Why do you have that, Carl?"

"For protection," he said snickering and flipping his shirt back down, concealing the gun from view.

Mimi marched over and snatched the gun from Carl and tossed it on the couch. "Hey!" he hollered, "you can't do that!"

"I can and I did," Mimi said defiantly. "You're not going over and shooting anybody. Do you want to wind up in jail again? You're no use to me there," she said.

Carl's face shrunk. That stung. "Why do you always have to

be so mean to me and say things like that?" he whimpered.

Realizing she'd hurt his feelings, Mimi pulled him in next to her large breasts in a bear hug.

"I'm sorry babe," she said, "but when you go off half-cocked like that it makes me think you're gonna go do something stupid and we don't want that, do we?" She let go of the embrace and looked into Carl's dejected face. "Do we?" she repeated.

Carl managed a smile, acknowledging that Mimi was mostly right. "No," he agreed.

Mimi was relieved when Carl put the pistol back inside the holster, removing it from her view. She wasn't a fan of guns. As much as she wanted revenge on those two, she didn't necessarily want them dead. No, there had to be a better way. Even if she couldn't come up with something suitable this minute, that didn't mean she wouldn't later. For now, though, getting her hands on Teddy's pawn shop was the number one priority.

On one of the numerous nights she had lain awake pondering violent retaliation, a sudden thought had popped into her head. Of course, the pawn shop was the key. If Teddy could time travel, he must have used the shop as a front. Mimi knew he had money. It hadn't escaped her that somehow, he was able to afford expensive trips and to stay at fancy hotels and such on the probably meager sales from a pawn shop located across the street from a rundown all-night laundromat in the grittiest side of town.

At best, he got guitars and musical instruments on consignment, but more likely, it was knives and guns and electronics and used bongs from druggies and thieves in need of some quick cash. No, there had to be something else he was doing; something on the side to make money. She didn't know how time travel worked, if he had some way of bringing valuable stuff back with him? All she knew was that somehow, she had to get her hands on that shop. But how? That was the big question. She would have to have him declared legally dead, but there was no body. After waving at Imogen, poof, Teddy had disappeared into thin air, the photo he had vanished into fluttering through the air to the floor.

Considering the words that were written on the back of the photograph he'd jumped through Simon and Imogen had said that he likely was dead. Not willing to take their word for it, Mimi had Googled Bikini Atoll, 1954 and sure enough, it was a nuclear bomb test site. In the unlikely event he had survived a blast, what were the odds that he got off the remote Marshall Islands? Yet, if there was even a slight chance, just to be sure, she had placed the photo on a shelf next to a bell, the idea being that should he return, the disruption of his arrival would cause the bell to ring. And if it ever did, she'd hear it. That had been months ago. She had checked it every day and laid in bed night after night listening for the sound of a bell ringing, but he had not returned.

In her own perverse way Mimi loved her son. She had hoped, and even prayed a time or two, for his safe return. He was after all, kin. Deep down she knew that the things she had done to him as a child were wrong, but she was lonely; the same way her daddy had told her he was lonely when he had crawled into her bed in the dark after her mom and brothers had fallen asleep.

And despite what he'd done to that girl Tiffany, Teddy was a good boy. He mowed her lawn, brought her donuts from time to time. It never occurred to her that perhaps her son might not feel the same way about her, that deep down he hated her, loathed her. That she made his skin crawl, yet she was his mother, and he was torn by emotion. And as fucked up as it was, sometimes, even a bad mom is better than no mom at all.

"Okay, let's think this through," Mimi said to Carl, changing the subject. "I hate those two. I really do, more than anything, but more important, I want what's rightfully mine, the pawn shop. If I can get my hands on that, I don't care a whit what happens to them. They can go to hell, for all I care, but that shop is worth millions!"

Carl perked up at the mention of money. "Millions, you say?" And maybe a rare book? he secretly thought.

"That's right, but the problem is I have no proof he's dead. Without a body or a death certificate it's something like seven years of waiting and I don't have that long to wait."

Carl nodded, the wheels turning slowly in his head. "Right," he said. He'd been waiting for Mimi to open up.

Mimi Pinky continued. "As Teddy's mother and next of kin, I'd get possession of his estate."

"But ain't ya worried about the grandson getting it?" Carl asked, "Wasn't Teddy his daddy?"

Mimi considered that for a moment before dismissing it. Even if he was related, no way would he be able to make a claim without revealing that he was born a century ago. She was sure it wouldn't happen.

"Mimi glanced over at Carl. "Don't worry about him," she stated firmly. "What I need is a death certificate."

Carl winked. "I know somebody," he said, "a friend of an acquaintance of a friend of a friend, if you get what I mean."

7

Harrison Tabor wasn't at all what Imogen pictured. He sounded much younger on the phone. The elderly gentleman seated in her office today had to be in his mid-80s, she guessed. He was also still quite attractive for his age. With a full head of neatly combed white hair, a matching bushy mustache, and a pair of very hip Ray-Ban glasses, he radiated subtle sophistication. He reminded Imogen of a gracefully aging movie star, a Cary Grant or a Sean Connery.

After shaking his hand, Imogen sat down, folded her hands together, and faced him across the desk. "What can I do for you today, Mr. Tabor?" she asked.

"Harry, please," he corrected, smiling warmly and melting her heart just a little bit. Imogen was certain the charming Mr. Tabor must have been quite the catch when he was a young man.

Yet, as warm and welcoming as his smile had been moments before, Imogen noticed that it was beginning to fade away, replaced by a look of pain. Mr. Tabor . . . Harry, sat quiet and still, seemingly gathering his thoughts before he began his story. There was always a story. It was part of the job, but so many of them were heart-wrenchingly sad; for instance, the investigation last year into the missing teenage girl who, as it turned out, had died leaving Imogen to deliver the tragic news to her sister, or the last one with her client Sean who was searching for his father. She was able to provide him with a letter, but few answers about what had happened to him. Still, there were a few happy endings and those were the ones that made the job rewarding, made her want to keep at it, to help people.

Harry finally spoke. "I'm not sure where to start."

"How about the beginning?" Imogen offered, "that's always a good place to start."

"Very well then," he said. Wetting his lips and brushing away a ball of lint from his corduroy jacket, he began his story.

"I was born in 1930 at start of the Great Depression in Garfield, Kansas, Pawnee County," he said. "Named after the 20th president of the United States, James A. Garfield it was a small, rural town. My mother said there was a bit of a baby boom the year I was born," he said. "Not sure why, but she said the population soared to nearly 500 people.

"We lived a hop, skip, and a jump out of town, out near the railroad tracks. Like everybody at that time, we were poor. My daddy was one of the lucky ones. He had a part-time job at the gravel pit. He did odd jobs too. He was a handyman, a jack of all trades. Good with a hammer. He could build anything. He didn't make much in those days, but enough to keep me and my sister Ruth in shoes.

"When I was five, the whole town nearly disappeared under a giant dust cloud. Black Sunday, April 14, 1935. I'll never forget it. We'd gotten home from church around two o'clock. Mama was fixing up Sunday supper, a chicken and potatoes, when all of a sudden . . ." Harry lifted his arms gesturing skyward. ". . . the sky went completely dark in the middle of the day. We thought it was the end of the world. I remember we had one of those single light bulbs hanging from the living room ceiling. I could barely make it out, but the dim brown glow from it was the only speck of light we had in that entire room. It buried our chicken coop and all the chickens in it. When it had finished passing over and we could see again, my parents stuffed dishtowels between the windows and doors to keep the dust at bay, but it always found its way in. Dust would be with us after that for a long, long while."

He paused and looked past Imogen as though transported in time, back to that day and the subsequent years when howling winds blew miles of piles of dust across the prairie, for days and days on end, burying homes and crops and livelihoods.

"Well, we made it through the Depression," he said, returning to his story. "But a lot of people didn't. They moved on, loading up what belongings they had and heading off for California or to other parts unknown. When the war came, things got better though, and some folks started coming back to Garfield. We stuck it out and by 1946, there was a building boom going on, and my dad was working overtime in Central City, a town about 11 miles up Highway 56. Central City was where I went to senior high school," he added. "I rode bus #17, and it was on that bus that I first laid eyes on her, Vivian Littlefield."

Harry's eyes took on a dreamy, faraway quality that Imogen noticed he got whenever he was revisiting another memory. His eyes twinkled and his mouth curved into a boyish grin as he recounted the story of their first meeting. "I remember that morning like it was yesterday," he said. "It was the first day of school, my junior year. I had just turned 16 and was quite disappointed, as I recall, that I had to get on the bus," he said. "You see, I was hoping to have a car by then. I'd been working and saving all summer long, but I just didn't have quite enough coin scraped together yet to buy one.

"The bus it would be, I figured, for a little while longer. It pulled up around 7:30 and I got on like usual and made my way to the back where I always sat, but when I looked up, what did I see?" With dramatic flair, his words hung suspended in the air for a time. Imogen leaned in close, "And what . . . what *did* you see Harry?" she asked, playing along.

"An angel!" he cried, slapping his hand down on one knee, "sitting in my seat . . . my seat!"

Imogen clapped her own hands together with supreme delight. Harry's smile was priceless. His delivery, impeccable. They both laughed and a few minutes later, he took up the story again after prompting from Imogen.

"So, tell me about this 'angel'," Imogen said.

"Oh my!" Harry stated, his face lit up with animated glee, "Vivian, she was a vision in bobby socks and saddle shoes!"

As he continued his story, Imogen was taken by the level

of detail. It was as though he was remembering something that happened just yesterday.

"She was wearing a simple dress that day, nothing fancy, but some kind of flower pattern, as I recall. She had the most beautiful auburn-colored hair, shoulder-length and held back from her face with a silver clip and when it caught the light from the back window, it looked like she was glowing, like an angel," he said, grinning again. "And she was wearing a charm bracelet with a silver heart on her wrist. I remember that, too.

Her eyes were a grayish blue—a bit like yours, Miss Oliver," Harry said, giving Imogen a friendly wink. "I know I must have stared too long because some of the kids on the bus started to snicker, but I couldn't help myself. And I also couldn't seem to get words to come out of my mouth, but finally, I managed to make a feeble pointing gesture to signal if it was okay for me to sit down next to her. And when she smiled politely and patted the seat, at that moment, everything in my world changed.

"She introduced herself and her younger sister Margaret Rose, who was seated next to her on the other side." We didn't talk much after that though," he said pausing momentarily in thought. "Funny," he said, "as much as I wanted to be nowhere else but sitting next to the loveliest creature on earth, at the same time I couldn't wait to get off that darn bus and escape after spending most of that trip to Central City sitting in embarrassed silence."

Harry would later learn from several boys and girls at school, apparently in the know, that the Littlefields had moved to Garfield from Pittsburgh during the summer. Harry was surprised he'd never met the girls, but then his nose had been to the grindstone all summer long helping his dad out of town. Getting up every day at dawn, working all day, returning home exhausted at dusk, didn't leave much time for anything, let alone socializing with girls. Evidently, they had a little brother too, William, who was eight, but he went to the grammar school in Garfield.

As the time ticked by it became abundantly clear that Harry was quite the long-form storyteller. Imogen was hoping he'd get to it a bit faster. As much as she enjoyed listening to his story, she did have other business to attend to today. Perhaps sensing Imogen's impatience, Harry picked up the pace.

"... well, even though she dressed like a typical American teenager, Vivian wasn't like one. She was different, more grown-up than her giggly girlfriends. She wasn't gaga over Frank Sinatra. She was quiet, but not shy; confident, but not boastful, beautiful, but humble. Everything about her was elegant. All the boys in school were clamoring to date her, including me. I didn't think I had a chance. Never in a million years would she go for me."

"But she did," Imogen said, filling in the blank.

Harry nodded his head. "But she did," he said, that smile creeping back at the sweet memory. He winked at Imogen once more and said, "I suppose those bus rides every day gave me an advantage over the other boys. It gave us a little extra time to get to know each other better."

"Did she become your girlfriend?" Imogen asked.

"She did," he said. "It was just like you see in the movies, young love, wild and free, kid stuff. We went to football games and bonfires together, huddled beneath a blanket to conceal the beer we were secretly drinking.

"In the spring we drove up to Pawnee Rock for a picnic. We kissed for the first time at that rock. When it started getting hot in late May and June, we jumped off the rope swing from the banks of Coon Creek to swim. Coon Creek Crossing is one of the parts of the old Santa Fe Trail and you could actually see the wagon trail ruts where they crossed on the north bank," he said, launching into some local trivia to embellish the story.

"Where is she now?" Imogen interjected, hoping to steer him back to his story.

Harry lowered his head and said, "I don't know. That's the reason I'm here, I suppose.

"Did something happen to her?" Imogen inquired.

"That I don't know," he said. "They'd built up as many houses around there as they wanted and dad needed work, so we moved away to Los Angeles. Course when we got the news, I was heartbroken and so was Viv. To this day, I can still picture the tears running down her cheeks. It was a rough goodbye."

Removing a handkerchief from his pocket, he dabbed at his eyes. "We were intimate for the first time under a tree on top of Pawnee Rock and we carved our initials HT+VL in it afterward. You never forget your first love," he said. "That must sound corny to a young person like yourself."

It didn't sound corny at all. Although Imogen knew it wasn't always the case, she felt like lovemaking back in those days really meant something. She had no such fond memories of losing her virginity. Hooking up with her stoner boyfriend Dylan sophomore year after scoring some mushrooms didn't really rate high on the nostalgia scale for her. But even if the first time hadn't been all that special, there were certainly other times later on when it had. With Fletcher, for instance. That first kiss. Wow, that was something she'd never, ever forget. And Simon, always Simon. No words could describe their first time together. But man, these kinds of love stories got her thinking too much, ruminating on things; worrying and second-guessing herself and the choices she'd made. Thankfully, the sound of Harry's voice drew her out of her head and back to the present.

"We promised to write each other," he said. "I sent letters, but she didn't write back. After a time, I figured it was over for her too, so I moved on. I went to college. I met my wife, Barbara. I became a teacher. We shared a good, happy life together, Babs and me. We had a couple of great kids, grandchildren, and then some great grandkids."

Harry paused, as if prepping himself to continue what came next. "For a long time after Barbara died, I wanted to die too," he admitted, "but I realized that she wouldn't want me to be sad. She'd want me to spend my days living, not grieving."

Imogen nodded. She knew sad, and she had an intimate, long-term relationship with grieving. She'd spent a good portion of her childhood coming to terms with the loss of her parents.

Fidgeting nervously in his chair, the story shifted focus then as he continued, "As much as I loved my life with Barbara, all these years I have wondered what became of Vivian. I didn't dwell on it a lot, mind you, but I did wonder from time to time how things might have been different if we hadn't moved away that summer. It was so long ago," he said, looking down at his hands and hesitating before adding, "I felt guilty when I thought of her, but she meant something to me, you know. She may have even been the love of my life."

Imogen leaned back in her chair and said, "You'd like me to find out what happened to her, if I can?"

Harry nodded. "Yes, if you could." He reached into an inside jacket pocket and pulled out a faded photograph and set it on the desk in front of Imogen.

"My dad bought me a used camera for my birthday, and this is a picture I took of the sisters not long before we moved away. That's Vivian on the right. She was 16, and Margaret Rose on the left there was 14."

Imogen was pleased that he'd thought to bring along a photo. Whether she ended up using it to travel through or not, it was always helpful to be able to see what the people she was tasked with meeting or finding looked like.

Typical of forties era photographs, the black and white image was small and square with a white, ribbed border around it. In it were two young girls, one slightly taller than the other, their arms wrapped around each other's waists, both wearing print dresses, ankle socks, and saddle shoes. Vivian was exactly as Harrison had described her. Fresh faces frozen in time. Forever young.

As much as Imogen dealt with old photographs, she never ceased being fascinated by them. Whenever she went to an antique shop, she looked for them—usually finding them tucked away in some corner in a file or a shoebox or a basket—and lingered over the piles of photos depicting lives lived and forgotten. It made her feel incredibly sad, but also glad that someone had cared enough to want to preserve them for all time in a photograph. This realization prompted her to write down all the names of the people in her own photo albums, the way her Grammy

Iris had. Even if one day the photos of the people she loved and cared about ended up being tossed into a bin at some antique store, they would have a name attached to them. At least future generations would know that they had lived. It was a small thing, but it seemed important.

"Whatever you find out about Vivian, I will be happy to know," Harry said as he rose with some effort from his chair. Imogen noticed that despite his youthful appearance, he didn't seem quite as nimble as when he had first arrived. Harry took Imogen's hand, thanked her, and turned and made his way toward the door.

"I'll do my best to find out everything I can, Mr. Tabor."

"Harry," he corrected, raising his hand without turning around.

"Oh Harry," Imogen said before he was all the way out the door, "One more thing; did you ever get your car?"

Harry sighed. "No, well, yes sort of, but it wasn't until after we were in California, and by that time, after Vivian, it didn't seem so important."

After Harrison Tabor had gone, Imogen lingered at her desk for a while longer gazing into the youthful faces of the two young girls in the photograph. Of course, it was quite possible that neither were still alive, in which case breaking the news to him would be tough, but perhaps not unexpected, considering his age. On the other hand, if Vivian was alive, it could potentially change his life. Whether a good news story or a bad news story, the reveal was always the toughest part of this job, and it never got any easier for Imogen.

This one might not even require time travel at all. As was often the case, especially with her elderly clients who weren't well-versed on the computer, digging up information was often only a matter of a few hours of research, made especially easy with all the genealogy sites now at her disposal, not to mention the access she had as a licensed PI to advanced databases like LexisNexis. Sometimes all it took was finding an obituary or a newspaper clipping. She never charged clients much for this service because, for one, it didn't require the time, preparation, or physical discomfort of a trip through time, but also, because it just felt good to help people who were simply seeking knowledge or closure about a family member or a lost loved one—something they may not have the expertise to access on their own, but that was easy for her to find very quickly.

Imogen tapped her fingers on the desktop, debating. Even though she had an appointment later this afternoon and could really use some lunch, curiosity about Vivian was getting the best of her. Maybe just a quick search and if she didn't find anything right away, she'd head out for a sandwich. A Google search of her name brought up several leads, a 1940 census, and then further down the page at the Find A Grave site, a photo of the tombstone. Ah, she thought, sadly Vivian had passed, but upon closer inspection, it was the date that made her pause.

"Oh, wow," she said out loud. The inscription read: Daughter Vivian Littlefield 1929–1946, Age 16. Vivian had died October 12, 1946. The page also included links to data on other family members. Imogen clicked on the sister, Margaret Rose and another image of a gravestone popped up which read: Daughter Margaret Rose 1931–1946, aged 14. Margaret Rose had died two days after Vivian on October 14. Something sudden and tragic had happened, but what? Imogen's curiosity was more than piqued now. Hunger be damned, she had to find out what happened to these girls.

Two hours later, Imogen glanced up at the wall clock in her office. 3:30. "Well, shit!" she said as she stood up and stretched. Deep into research, the hours had flown by and, regrettably, she had missed her appointment, one that had been on her To-Do list for a while, but not so important that she felt too bad blowing it off.

After finding out about the girl's deaths, Imogen was able to locate a very brief newspaper writeup about it in a local Kansas newspaper.

SECOND GIRL DIES

CENTRAL CITY, October 14 (AP) Margaret Rose Littlefield, 14, daughter of Mr. and Mrs. A.J. Littlefield, West Central City, died today of injuries received in an auto-train collision Tuesday.

A double funeral is planned for tomorrow for Margaret Rose and her sister, Vivian, 16, who also died in the accident. William Littlefield, 8, a brother, is in serious condition.

Certain there must be more details about the accident and, above all, obituaries, Imogen conducted an exhaustive search that oddly came up empty. It was curious that this was the only report to be found. Why had there not been a story? Surely, the tragic deaths of two small-town teenagers would warrant attention in the local newspaper, she thought. And even sans an obit, deaths were typically included in the vital statistics sections of newspapers.

Imogen was torn. Should she call Mr. Tabor with the news? Even without more information, it was clear that the girls had died in an accident. The newspaper clipping along with the photographs of the gravestones was sufficient evidence to pass along to him.

She knew she should just go ahead and pick up the phone straightaway and call him, but it wasn't sitting well with her, and she suspected it wouldn't with Harrison Tabor either. There really was no good reason for her to travel back there, but at the same time, questions nagged her, not only about the circumstances of the girl's death, but also many of the same ones about time travel that she had wrestled with since the very beginning.

Although she had been able to piece together on her own the basic rules that you can't bring anything back from the past with you, and you can't run into yourself; the universe won't let you, it was the last rule that hadn't been fully tested, the one about not being able to alter established history. But then, she thought, if there's an exception to *every* rule, doesn't the exception to *that* rule mean there are no exceptions?

As yet, she hadn't made any attempts at altering anything in the past. The bulk of her cases had involved only retrieving lost items or gathering information about the whereabouts of a family member.

So, if it applied to history that had been written down somewhere, did it have to be in a textbook or a scroll, carved on a cave wall? Did it only apply to historical figures, or could it be an entry in say, someone's diary, for example? Did an obituary qualify as written history? How reliable was the news? What if what was written down was a lie?

For Imogen, "what if" questions only beget more questions, which invariably sent her spiraling into an impossibly endless thought loop. Just like when she was a kid, those and other questions like: What is the speed of dark? What is infinity? Who made god? plagued her, kept her awake at night.

It also reminded her of Simon. Simon was quite possibly the only other person she'd met in her life who was as curious as her. Together, they spun fantastic, what-if scenarios—some funny, some sad, some chaotic, some impossibly mind-boggling. It was that secret something between them that set him apart from anyone else and why she knew that no matter what obstacles they faced, somehow, she'd never find anyone like him. He was a walking, talking, breathing riddle—just like her, but thrice as maddening and stubborn and irresistible.

Hmmm, so what to do? she pondered as she tapped her fingers metrically on the desktop. The question hovered at the forefront of her brain, demanding an answer. What if? What if she could change things for Vivian and her sister? What if she could save them somehow? Was it possible? She had no one to ask about how all this worked. How do you ask the universe? The answer was clear. She had to at least try.

8

As the shadows around the edges began to soften and gradually dissolve, Imogen drew a deep, purifying breath before opening her eyes and focusing on the sea of flat sunburnt land of late summer, a lonesome stretch of road—nowhere in the middle of someplace. Dusty and arid and devoid of anything resembling planet Earth, it reminded her more of a moonscape than a landscape. This must be Kansas.

With nothing to break up the flat swathe of land, not a tree or a mountain; it felt like bobbing out on the vast ocean with no land in sight in any direction—an infinite horizon of nothing but water and waves as far as the eye can see. Imogen's dad had taken her deep-sea fishing off the Oregon coast on a boat once. She was little, maybe six, and while the adventure seemed fresh and exciting and new, it was also quite frightening for a child. Imogen had questions. "What will we do if the boat sinks, Daddy? Where will we go? Will anyone save us? Will we be lost in the ocean forever?" It felt a little like that now except there was no dad around to soothe her anxieties. Except for the lone pickup truck driving past, she was alone.

She'd viewed pictures of the state beforehand, of course, but seeing it now in person was unsettling. Landing in any place you've never been before always felt a bit alien, but it was the landing in a different time that walloped Imogen every time. It was difficult to explain, how things not only looked but also smelled differently in the past. She had to laugh the other day while browsing the internet when an ad for "homesick" candles that purportedly smell like your home state popped up. Honestly, she didn't need a candle to remind her of what Oregon smelled like. It smelled like forest and the way it smelled after a first rain, that mossy fragrance that she never grew the least bit tired of. She could only imagine what the Kansas candle smelled like because here and now, there seemed to be no defining smell at all. If she was expecting sunflowers or wheat fields, a light breeze gently blowing the grassy expanse of open plains; this was the polar opposite. Everything appeared shriveled and spent and exhausted, and it was unbearably hot—icky, sticky, clammy, humidity-off-the-charts, hot. Plainly speaking, she wasn't in Oregon anymore.

Already the clothes she was wearing felt like too much, like she wanted to peel everything off and jump into a cool lake, but instead, like she always did before anything else when she first arrived, she paused to examine the clothing the universe had assembled for her this time. For some reason, she was expecting bobby socks and loafers like the teens were wearing in the picture, but her post-war attire conformed more to her level of maturity, consisting rather of a classic, yet versatile, yellow print shirtwaist dress buttoned all the way up the front and cinched with a matching belt with a hemline that extended just slightly below her knees. It had been ages since Imogen had worn pantyhose, but she immediately noticed the pinching discomfort of the 1946 version of nylon stockings, which came only up to the thigh and fastened with garters to an itchy, too tight, hot girdle.

In her research, Imogen had discovered an interesting bit of trivia about nylon stockings. Stockings had been rationed during the war. Women made do, coming up with innovative ideas like using a pen to draw a black line up the back of both legs to simulate the line in the hosiery of the day. But after the war ended and rationing was lifted, real, actual *nylon riots*—women clawing and clamoring for stockings—broke out in front of department stores in cities around the country. In fact, at one store in San Francisco she had read, they had to stop selling stockings after it was mobbed by 10,000 manic nylon stocking-deprived women. Crazy!

Still, in spite of the scorching heat and the itchy stockings, she had to admit, she was rather keen on the super cute pair of calfskin peep-toe wedge heeled shoes she had on. Although she couldn't properly check it out at the moment, when she touched her shoulder-length hair, she could feel that the sides were rolled up and pinned away from her face and held in place with two fancy jewel-encrusted clasps. Even with no mirror handy to take in the full effect, she was more than confident that she not only suitably blended in, but at the same time, looked quite stylish.

The canvas tote bag she'd brought was now a chic soft leather satchel. Inside was a coin purse with money, a few toiletries, and the digital camera she'd packed, which was now a slightly later version of the Brownie No. 2 she'd had when she was back in 1913. This one, the Brownie Flash Six-20 had a metal box body and an odd trapezoidal shape that she remembered had been introduced in July 1946, making it nearly brand-new here. She'd also packed a couple of rolls of 35 mm film, which were now a size 620 to fit the Brownie. These cameras were quite popular for their indestructibility. But the main purpose, of course, was to experiment with the rules, which was to shoot some photos, develop some here to see if they could be brought back intact and to stash the second roll for later retrieval to test whether it was possible to time travel through them even though she'd been the one taking the pictures in that time. She was pretty sure it wouldn't work, but there was a learning curve for navigating time, and it was important to test the rules whenever she could. More rules would be tested later, but for now, she needed to get her bearings and find her way downtown.

Because it was always best practice to be as inconspicuous as possible, Imogen avoided using photographs that her clients had supplied. It put her too close to the subjects. Fortuitously, she was able to obtain a photo near Central City taken within the correct time frame, roughly three weeks before Mr. Tabor said he'd moved away but before the train accident. Landing in town early would give Imogen time to scope things out.

If the label on the back of the photo was accurate, she had

landed roughly two tenths of a mile outside the town proper, not far from Main Street and within walking distance of a hotel that she knew would be there in 1946 for her to check into. Straightening her dress, Imogen started walking. Flat farmland, a smattering of farmhouses, and dusty roads soon gave way to a paved street as she turned the corner into town. In the heat, a mirage of shimmering waves danced above the hot road like jitterbug fairies.

Like any municipality, the usual businesses hugged Main Street—a barbershop with its spinning red and white pole, a beauty salon, a market, a dress shop. Along the route, planters filled with summer flowers and elm trees shaded the walkway and Imogen soon forgot that she was far from home, not only in distance but in time by about 80 years, as she breathed in the pleasant aroma of lavender and lilac and honeysuckle. Lilacs were her favorite. She wondered why people in cities pooh-poohed small towns like Central City, Kansas, thinking that anyone who lived there must be backward and out of touch, and the land so hard and dusty and unforgiving and ugly, but Kansas was growing on Imogen. It didn't matter where you lived, she figured, as long as you were with your people.

Lost in thought, Imogen continued strolling along the picturesque sidewalk, taking in the sights and smells, marveling at the bounty of fresh fruit and vegetables on display in a multiplicity of crates at an outdoor farmer's market. She stopped to pluck a fuzzy peach from one of the crates and held it up to her nostrils. A sentient feeling washed over her as she breathed in the fresh aroma and pondered whether she should purchase some fruit to take with her to the hotel when suddenly without warning grinding gears and the roar of a car's unmuffled engine shattered the tranquility of the near perfect scene. A late model convertible bursting with what looked like an impossible number of teenage boys careened around the corner, barely missing the curb and coming dangerously close to the spot where Imogen stood. As they sped away, fragments of the boy's hooting and shouting, whistles, and wolf calls clearly aimed directly at her—*Hey Blondie! Get a load of them gams*!—hung uneasily in the stifling air. And then, everyone on the sidewalk stopped what they were doing to look in her direction as though somehow it was her fault. This was clearly not what she wanted to happen. "Oh my," Imogen said, mortified. The looks of displeasure on the faces of a group of prim, hat and glove wearing ladies made Imogen feel even more embarrassed. Setting the peach back inside the crate, she made a hasty retreat. "Excuse me," she said, lowering her head and brushing quickly past the disapproving women as she crossed over to the other side of the street.

Imogen walked briskly without turning to look back, hoping that she hadn't drawn too much attention to herself and that they would soon forget about the unfamiliar woman in town who had caused such a stir at the vegetable market. Suitably fitting in with the right attire was one thing when traveling to another era; drawing attention to yourself was unwanted. In her experience, it was vital for her to be as inconspicuous as possible. The universe had always served up drab, nondescript clothing, so she would blend in unnoticed, so it was puzzling why this time she had been given such a stunning, look-at-me kind of getup. But then, it occurred to her that perhaps she actually *was* blending in, because she'd read that after the war and rationing, women were tired of drab. They wanted to feel pretty again, to wear bright fabric and to be noticed. Maybe those prim and proper women weren't as shocked as they let on. Maybe that kind of thing was happening in towns all over the country after the war.

She remembered studying in her history classes that a sort of giddy relief settled in after 1945. After five long years of rationing and sacrifice and fighting Nazis and wars around the world, people just wanted to return to some sense of normal. There was a building boom, as Harrison Tabor had mentioned, along with a baby boom. Returning servicemen were looking to settle down and needed places to live. It was a time of hope and great prosperity and it certainly seemed evident in Central City, Kansas as Imogen strolled through town. Businesses were booming as women pushing strollers with young ones in tow shopped and mingled with their neighbors. Imogen knew it wasn't perfect.

The so-called good old days weren't so good for a lot of people, for Black people and LGBTQ folk, for instance, or women who were driven from the labor force when the men returned from war, relegated to office jobs or the kitchen. Still, the shared collective experience and the social contract made people pull together as a society, something Imogen wasn't seeing too much of lately in her own time. Technology was great but sometimes she wondered if it caused people to be more isolated, divided, separated into like-minded bubbles. Visiting simpler times provided her with a unique inside perspective, but if one thing time travel had taught her, simpler times weren't necessarily better, and history definitely repeated itself.

"Hey lady, watch where you're going," a voice barked from out of nowhere.

Struggling to maintain an unassuming posture after the catcalling incident, Imogen had been keeping her head down as she walked along. When she looked up, the owner of the voice, a pimply boy, filter less cigarette protruding from his lips, rolled up at the cuff blue jeans, scuffed loafers, and a white cotton shirt doing his best at being tough guy cool, sneered at her. Beside him, a girl, presumably his girlfriend, also smoking a cigarette and blowing smoke rings from her pouty cherry blossom red lips. The last thing Imogen needed was to invite trouble but honestly, she wasn't the least bit intimidated by these two. "Pardon me," she said, confidently stepping around the couple and moving along. Sensing that she wasn't a pushover, the boy shrugged then took a dramatic bow, gesturing for her to pass on by. As it turned out, the encounter was serendipitous because if Imogen had not looked up at that precise moment, she might have missed the Help Wanted sign posted in the window of the diner. A few more kids loitered around outside, but quickly dispersed, jumping into their cars and driving away, likely escaping the stifling heat that kept them from hanging around outdoors too long.

Imogen pushed open the glass door with the name "Mary's on Main" stenciled in bright red. A bell attached to the top announced her entrance. At 10:30 a.m. it looked like the breakfast crowd had mostly cleared out, all but a few stragglers lingering over coffee and a couple of elderly men sitting on barstools, probably regulars, chatting with the waitress.

It wasn't much cooler inside, but a slow-moving fan and the air from a swamp cooler, its droning sound emanating from somewhere in the back, almost made it feel like a cool oasis compared to outside. Almost. It was your typical local diner. Nothing fancy, vinyl booth seating, metal and vinyl barstools at the wraparound bar facing the waitress station, a couple of cooks behind the window and the spinning carousel for order tickets, a milkshake/malt-making machine, a pie rack. And, each table featured an early model tabletop jukebox, the kind where from the comfort of your table you could turn the red knob and browse through 40 songs, deposit five cents for one song or 10 cents for two, then push the red button and wait for your tune to queue up.

All in all, the vibe was convivial and casual. Diners like these were one of those things that never seemed to change. Even with technology and fast-food chains—whether it was 1957 or 2019 or 1946—in nearly every town dotting the interstates across the US you could still find a diner or cafe, similar in style to this one. A comforting constant, not so much a throwback to a bygone era but a reminder that we crave the familiar, that even if change is happening so fast around us it makes our heads spin, at least we can still count on finding a place like this somewhere.

While Imogen took in the surroundings, a waitress, dressed in a crisp white uniform with short, cuffed sleeves with green piping and a sort of fanned out headpiece bobby-pinned to her head, a notepad visible in her apron pocket, burst from the kitchen through swinging doors. Without really looking at Imogen, she called out in her general direction, "Sit anywhere you'd like, hon," as she grabbed the coffee pot and bustled over to a table to offer up refills.

Imogen raised her hand in the air in an effort to get her attention, but the waitress briskly moved on to the next table without glancing her way.

"Um, excuse me," she said. Her voice was scratchy from not talking to anyone, but the woman, still not looking at her, held up one index finger indicating she'd be with her in a moment as she refilled the cups at a couple more tables before finally making her way over to where Imogen stood waiting.

"You can seat yourself," she repeated, this time with an irritated tone. Up close, she read the name Darla on her badge.

"Thank you," Imogen said politely as she turned slightly and gestured toward the window, "but I saw your sign in the window out there . . . that you're hiring?"

Darla brought the horned rimmed grasses, which hung at her chest suspended by a silver chain, up to her eyes to get a better look at Imogen. "Oh, you're here for the waitress job?" she said.

The unpleasant tone of Darla's voice didn't deter Imogen from answering cheerfully, "Yes, yes, I was hoping I might be able to speak to someone."

The waitress eyed Imogen suspiciously. "Have you had any experience as a waitress before?" she asked.

Imogen nodded. "Um, yes, sure I have." Her mind scrambled for the correct response. She had picked up some mad skills as a barista in college at the Beanie Barn, but had to remind herself not to mention barista, knowing that Darla would have no clue what that was. Imogen often struggled with not blowing it and giving herself away as a time traveler. She blurted out the first things she could think of. "I know how to take orders. I can juggle dishware and make change."

Awaiting Darla's response seemed an eternity. She couldn't tell whether her blank expression meant she was impressed or inclined to dismiss her. "Well," Darla finally said, placing her hands on her hips, "I'll have to speak to Mary. She owns the place. She'll have the last word, course, but I'll tell her you'll do." With that, Darla bustled back through the swinging doors, returning a few minutes later with a wrinkled uniform. Shoving it into Imogen's hands, she said, "Come back tomorrow morning, 6:30 sharp, for the breakfast rush. We'll see how you do." Turning on her heels, she abruptly turned and walked away, but stopped mid-stride and pivoted, adding, "And make sure that uniform is ironed crisp as a cracker!" She marched away with intent then, leaving Imogen holding the crumpled uniform and wondering whether she'd ever even used an iron before.

After checking into the Merchants Hotel downtown, Imogen grabbed a quick bite before settling into her room. It had been quite the productive day. She had rented a room and landed a job, not that she needed one necessarily, but working at the diner held the potential for gaining access to conversations that could help her learn more about the townspeople in a relatively short period of time. At the Beanie Barn, people loved to linger for hours over their espresso and Danish, either that or they brought their laptops in to work, soaking up the funky atmosphere and using the background sounds of clattering cups and plates and the buzz of people chatting around them as white noise. Imogen was pretty sure that the same held true, even in Central City, Kansas 1946, only here they probably came in and gossiped over iced tea and key lime pie. It was perfect really. And those tabletop jukeboxes were a clue that teenagers probably frequented the diner as well, something Imogen was hoping for. Teenagers did nothing but chatter and socialize, and Imogen was prepared to take full advantage of it, to eavesdrop a bit, and maybe even run into Harrison Tabor and the Littlefield girls, if she was lucky.

Not only that, but the job was also perfect in another way. Because waitstaff had a tendency to come and go with some regularity, she could easily work for a few weeks and when it was time to leave, she'd quit. Things were falling into place. Now all she had to do was locate an iron to smooth out the wrinkles in her new uniform.

9

Simon relished subdued moments of reflection, those times when he could spend solo time with his thoughts, sort things out a bit, but his insides today felt as empty and still as the house. Uninspired by anything, he didn't feel much like working in the garden or on his miniature furniture. Even listening to music through the headgear or watching television didn't appeal.

Not sure how to shake the feeling, Simon paced about the quiet living room looking for something to distract him. From across the room, he spotted it on the mantel, the faded photograph of his mother he'd found while digging in the garden. Scraping off some lingering dirt from it he sat down on the sofa and held it gingerly between his fingers, staring at the woman in it. She was not what one might call a classic beauty. Her eyes were shallow, her lips thin. Her hair was by far her finest feature. She pinned it up atop her head in a loose bun as was the fashion of the time, but he remembered that small wisps of it were forever falling across her face, which she constantly blew away or brushed aside or nervously twisted between her fingers. When she released the clips holding it up and let it down in the evenings though, it was a lovely curly dark brown lion's mane that she was forever trying to manage.

Perhaps someone had told his mother to smile because the camera had captured one of those rare moments when she had. Possibly he had taken this picture. He liked to think that he had been the one who caused her to smile, but he could not remember. There had been so many occasions. Although he now understood the depth of her obsession, her desperate attempts at rescue, it saddened him to think that she had been unable to move on from what Teddy had done to her, to carve out a happier life for herself in that time. After all, she did have one good thing, didn't she? Her boy, him, Simon? Why couldn't that have been enough?

Still, despite her melancholy and during those times when he and his mother were barely scraping by, there were small joys to be found, always a small glimmer of hope that something good could potentially be waiting just around the corner. She had a way of turning whatever they were doing into a game or distracting him with some fantastical story she'd made up.

"Who needs books," she would say, pointing her finger to her temple, "when you have access to a whole world of imagination inside of your own head?"

Thinking of his mother today did not bring him joy. No, what he felt was a dull ache in his gut that he could not suppress. He had avoided letting anyone know how much he missed her, especially Imogen. How could he burden her with yet another of his copious challenges? Adjusting to this new life, bombarding her with a million questions, expecting her to prop him up? It was too much.

And yet, he couldn't shake something that Fletcher had said the other day about finding his mother. He had asked Simon why, if it was that important to him, had Imogen not herself offered to find out what happened to her. She had the capability to do so. Finding people in the past is what she did for a living, after all.

Certainly, mother was long dead now, probably 70 years or so. That much he could wrap his head around. He guessed it was not knowing how her story ended that bothered him most. He had been separated from her at an early age, shipped off to the orphanage, for his own good, Herbert Doran, the man who had done the separating had said at the time. She was mentally unstable, couldn't take care of him. Had she languished in some dirty, draconian mental hospital? He had a name. Crestview Sanitarium. More than once he'd debated asking Imogen to go back for him, to find out, but again, it seemed too much to ask. He had resigned himself to the fact that he might never know.

As he scrutinized the photo, Simon tried hard to concentrate, to will himself to enter into it, the way Imogen did. If only he could master time travel himself, he could learn what happened to his mother on his own. Imogen had described it as a deep meditative state, but no matter how long or how hard he looked at this one or any other photograph for that matter—he'd tried it before, many times—nothing happened. Dozens of times since he'd arrived here, he had flipped through Imogen's grandmother's old photo album, looking at the picture of his dear friend Iris Graham and his old boss Andre, reminiscing on that time and realizing that he actually knew these people and that the blurry person riding the bicycle through the image was him. It all seemed so terribly long ago and far away, another life, the memories fading away with time.

Setting the photo aside, he picked up a book he had been reading from the table and brought it to his lap. A gift from Imogen, the encyclopedia set had provided Simon with a straightforward linear view of history, a way to catch up with all that had happened between the time he left his own point in time and the present. It had not been easy reading about events that had occurred shortly after he departed in 1913, especially the chapter on World War I, a conflict for which he was certain he would have been called upon to enlist in; followed by the devastating flu epidemic of 1918 that snuffed out so many lives. He shuddered to think how many of his friends and colleagues must have died during those two events alone.

He was surprised and enamored though by the "roaring 20s." Although, like any time, there is good and there is bad—crime, opium dens, he might have enjoyed experiencing the jazz music, learning to dance the Charleston and the Foxtrot, discovering the literature of F. Scott Fitzgerald and Virginia Woolf for the first time, viewing the nonconformist art of Pablo Picasso or Salvador Dali, the clandestine experience of entering an underground speakeasy during prohibition and the carefree abandon of the flappers he'd read about. He was not disappointed to have skipped the misery of the collapse of the stock market in 1929 and the Great Depression of the 1930s that followed, or the dust storms in the Midwest. Imogen had filled him in a bit on what that was like for Iris, her grandmother, and it did not sound like a pleasant experience.

After reading the chapters covering World War II Simon had become so distraught, he had set the book aside for several days to process all of the shocking and grisly images and passages. It was a lot to digest in one sitting. He had not thought anything could possibly top the horrors of the first World War, but he had been wrong. Nazis, the holocaust—six million Jews, Gypsies, gay people, the disabled, and others, slaughtered. It seemed more like something from a work of fiction than actual, true history. And the equally horrific end to the war that culminated with atomic bombs dropped on Hiroshima and Nagasaki, two Japanese cities, killing and maiming and scarring millions of innocent citizens.

After the war, he read that the US had continued testing of a nuclear bomb on an island called Bikini Atoll—he remembered that name because it was scribbled on the back of the photograph that Teddy, his father had vanished into when Imogen had confronted him about trapping her parents as well as Simon's mother in the past. After reading more about it, it appeared wholly unlikely that Teddy could have survived the 15-megaton explosion.

He was certainly ready to leave that bit of history behind and move on, but as he flipped ahead through the next section, it was evident from these photographs that the 50s and 60s had also been turbulent times in the United States: Two more wars in Asia, the assassination of a popular president and his brother and several civil rights leaders; the disturbing images of a Black female student trying to attend school, an angry mob of snarling white people shouting behind her, their faces contorted by unbridled hate; Black boys sitting at a lunch counter surrounded by a hoard of enraged white men; white people milling about at a lynching as though it was an ordinary Sunday-after-church picnic, the burned beyond recognition body of a Black man suspended from the limb of a tree. Simon felt ashamed now thinking back about how in his own school there had not been a single Black child in attendance.

As the school's principal, he had overseen the curriculum and was mortified now to think about what was being taught in terms of history, or perhaps what wasn't being taught. Back then, in his time, the Civil War was barely 50 years past, yet Black folk, though no longer enslaved, were nonetheless considered inferior members of society. From what Simon could make of the current news, the topic of racism remained front and center and since his time teaching, much of what had been taught in history classes was a glossed-over version intended to depict America as a beacon of fairness and freedom, leaving out the uglier, much different experiences and history of its Black, Asian, and Indigenous citizenry.

Coming from an entirely different century, Simon possessed a rare perspective on change, and it seemed abundantly clear that change in society never came quickly. It was a slow, nuanced process, and trying to absorb all of the changes that had occurred over the last century at one sitting was more overwhelming than he had anticipated. It also made him realize just how much he didn't know. Making the choice to follow Imogen into the future meant that he'd bypassed everything leading up to now, and as a result, he had no context, no history, no basis for comparison . . . about anything.

Still, he read on. Flipping forward were more frenzied images of protesting women carrying signs that read "Equality Now!" ringed by dozens of sneering men, their furious fists raised in the air. He recalled a memory from his own childhood, of seeing the women, the suffragettes on the street, dressed all in white and carrying signs. He had asked his mother at the time why the ladies seemed so cross. "They want to be free and equal to men," she had answered. She had also said that she wished she could join them but could not because she was afraid of losing her job. Her first obligation was to taking care of Simon.

He flipped back to the 1900s section to look at the photographs of women suffragists like the ones he'd seen marching down Pennsylvania Avenue in Washington DC in 1913. He had read of this in the newspapers, of course, but it had seemed so far away and removed from his own daily life, at the time he hadn't given it much thought or attention. One passage from the text caught his eye: "One especially notorious event, the 'Night of Terror,' when 33 suffragists from the National Women's Party, who had been arrested for protesting outside of the White House, were brutally beaten and tortured at the Occoquan Workhouse, a prison in northern Virginia." It took place a little over 100 years ago on November 14, 1917." Stunned, Simon laid the open volume across his lap. Of course, he had left before this event occurred, but how could he have missed all of this when he was right there?

But again, like racism, in which people naively believed had been resolved, had only been pushed underground, waiting for the next time to resurface and rear its ugly head again. The same seemed to be true for women. And women! Oh my! How the world had changed for them. It appeared to be improved in some regard, but from what he could gather, they still struggled with equality and issues of pay and recently, a vile US president who had so angered the women they had evidently knitted pink hats and taken to the streets in protest.

On bold display in graphic detail, were stories of discontent and sexual abuse, a movement called "Me too." In Simon's time, a man who verbally attacked a woman was no gentleman. Even worse, they were viewed as cowardly. And a man who made unwanted advances toward a woman often found himself skewered by said lady, sometimes fatally at the end of a sharp hatpin. Simon did not have a desire to harm women. He loved women! And they adored him. He had fancied himself a thoroughly modern man, in part because he was raised by a strong-willed woman, which made sense now that he knew that she had come from a future where women seemed to have made great advances. But he had also been aware that many men of his time were not nearly as enlightened as he. Women of his time, it was assumed, should be content to live their lives in service to their husbands and children. It caused him to fear for his mother. If women were treated in this manner as routine, who could say what might have befallen her in the asylum?

Another chapter detailed how women, who had worked in factories building airplanes during WWII, were pushed aside when it was over, and sent home to make room for the returning men. There was a sense of pause during this era. After a world war that had scarred a nation so deeply, there was a desire for a return to normalcy—to take a break from conflict and unrest. Women were encouraged to stay in the home and nurture their families, to put them first and foremost, to put her own wants and desires aside for the greater societal good, for healing.

Women found themselves desperately striving to define themselves based upon their ability to be the "perfect" wife and mother, to have the most gadget-lined kitchen, or to bake the best-tasting brownies. Likewise, men often found themselves adrift in meaningless jobs and endless routines in an effort to support their emergent families while maintaining a middle-class, suburban lifestyle. This, of course, was not a sustainable model.

Turning back to the place he'd left off, a black and white image of a woman stood behind a dais above a caption that read: "Feminist, activist, and author, Betty Friedan helped launch the women's movement of the 1960s with her groundbreaking book, *The Feminine Mystique*."

And below the photo, the text described Friedan's views on what she had identified as the "problem that has no name."

"The problem lay buried, unspoken, for many years in the minds of American women. It was a strange stirring, a sense of dissatisfaction, a yearning [that is, a longing] that women suffered in the middle of the 20th century in the United States. Each suburban [house] wife struggled with it alone. As she made the beds, shopped for groceries . . . she was afraid to ask even of herself the silent question—'Is this all?'"

Simon looked up from the book. That was it. He wasn't a woman, of course, but the concept seemed to encapsulate precisely what he was feeling. How could you name something if you didn't know what it was? But the simple question, "Is this all?" resonated with him. What sort of life did he even have now? What was his purpose? He felt useless and adrift. Conceived in one time, born in another, he wasn't quite certain where, or *when* he belonged. But he was beginning to understand now how his mother must have felt being torn away from everything she knew and forced to try to adapt to another time. As horrible as that was, had she been a man, might it not have been easier? At least in Simon's case, he had been given the choice.

As he continued reading, he was fascinated and surprised that despite their earlier efforts, even as late as the 1970s, women were still struggling with equality. A woman could not get a divorce. She had no control over her body because abortion was illegal. She could not get a credit card in her own name. And what of Black women? Information was sorely lacking about them in this book. He might have to summon more information from the Google after all. Likewise, the more Simon read, his understanding of Imogen began to grow as it explained much of why she was the way she was. Flipping through the pages, looking into the earnest faces of the protesting women united by a common cause, and the angry mobs of menacing men that surrounded them, faces contorted, mouths opened wide in howling shrieks, he could envision Imogen—had she been alive then—being right there, defiant and right in the thick of it.

And then, strangely, Simon thought he heard the faint sound of distant voices: "What do we want? Equality! When do we want it? Now!" Had he left the television on? He wasn't sure where it was coming from exactly, maybe from inside his own head, but was that chanting?

The room shifted. It was a subtle shift, something he might not have even noticed had the corners of the room not begun to turn noticeably darker along the edges, creeping phantom shadows that turned up before folding back into themselves. But it was the way he felt more than what he saw that grabbed his attention—his arms and legs began to prickle with sticky-hot heat.

What is happening? his mind screamed. In the moment, a rising panic seized him. Was he having a heart attack? A stroke? He felt uncertain of where, or *when*, he was. Had he dozed off while reading? Was this a dream? Would he wake up again?

Too terrified to open his eyes, Simon felt a disconcerting sensation of falling as his body seemed to tumble this way and that, end over end into a bottomless abyss, until being interrupted by a disorienting jolt and then a sense that he had miraculously landed somewhere, unhurt and on his feet. Even without opening his eyes, scorching heat and bright light assaulted him and the loud chanting and jarring cacophony of overlapping voices were disorienting. Nauseous and unsteady he opened his eyes and reached out for the nearest object next to him, quickly realizing that he was clutching another man's sweaty arm. The man gave him a dirty look and Simon quickly withdrew his hand. As crazy as that seemed it appeared he was at the epicenter of the crowd of men from the picture in the encyclopedia. In the growing chaos closing in all around him, the oppressive heat of many bodies, an overpowering stench of perspiration, and the swirl of wildly waving arms and fists and angry voices shouting and screaming, was suffocating.

Not far from where he stood, the soaring chants of the women coalesced with the foul invectives the men spewed as they passed in front of the barriers they were being forced to stand behind. "You look pretty good for being oppressed!" "Fuckin' bitch, who do you think you are?" "Cunt! I'll give you something," one shouted as he jumped about, clutching his crotch salaciously for lurid effect. Simon felt an elbow slam into his upper back and turned around to see the person responsible, a short, portly man in a striped polo shirt, jostling his way to the front. "Sorry dude," he apologized politely to Simon before turning back around and launching into another abusive tirade. Witnessing this raw, seething anger on public display made Simon ill. He was disgusted by it and the overwhelming desire to extricate himself immediately from the scene took hold somehow and—silence. Miraculously, he was back in Imogen's house again, lying on his back on the living room floor staring upward at the plaster swirls on the ceiling. The encyclopedia must have toppled to the floor because he could feel it poking into his backside.

He felt dizzy and confused and sick, and it took him a minute to process what he guessed might have just happened. When his stomach stopped doing flip-flops Simon sat up and looked around, relieved to be home. "Holy Toledo!" he shouted. "What the Sam Hill just happened?" He took a quick assessment of his person. He seemed all to the mustard; all in one piece, at least.

When he stood up, he at once felt woozy and had to grab the edge of the coffee table to steady himself, but by golly, a bit of dizziness couldn't deter his excitement. "I did it!" he shouted to the empty room, shaking his head, amazed. "I can't believe I did it!" His mind raced. He wanted to do it again; he *must* do it again, but could he do it again? Excited, he flipped through the pages of the book, looking for a test photograph, someplace safe, somewhere other than a war zone or in the middle of a violent protest. The problem: the encyclopedia was, of course, filled with photographs of major events, some that he'd rather not be a part of.

Not to be deterred Simon raced to the bookshelf where Imogen kept Iris' old photo album. When he plucked it from the shelf a loose photograph tumbled out from between the pages and fluttered to the floor. He picked it up and turned it over. He had never seen this one before. It appeared to be of a group of teenagers sitting at a table in a diner, one of them looked a lot like Iris, although it was difficult to tell because the photograph was cloudy and a smattering of what looked like small dust particles coated the surface. Simon shrugged and was about to tuck it back into the album when without warning—*baloomp*—the room rolled over in another giant somersault, sending Simon twisting and bending into a spiral of swirling miasma of dark and light. When the world finally stopped spinning, Simon found himself seated in a booth at, presumably, the same diner in the picture he had just been viewing. Several teenagers seated in another booth over glanced up briefly from their cokes before turning their focus back on each other and resuming their conversation. It was peculiar, like they had noticed him, but . . . didn't.

The diner was standard fare making it difficult to judge what era he might have landed in.

A waitress, Darla, it read on her badge, approached him carrying a pot of coffee. "What can I get for you, hon?" she asked with a hint of a Midwestern accent.

"Um, coffee," Simon spluttered. Darla flipped the turned upside down cup over and poured the coffee, filling it to the brim. "Anything else?" she asked. Simon shook his head no and Darla walked away.

Simon stared at the coffee and wondering if it was real, took a sip. It was hot and very real. Whomever had last been sitting in the booth before he got there had left behind a folded newspaper. Simon unfolded it and noted the name at the top: *Central City Gazette* and the date: October 2, 1946. A bold headline splashed across the front page read: "12 Nazi war criminals sentenced to death in Nuremberg" accompanied by a grainy photograph of a courtroom full of men. Simon barely had time to take a second sip of his coffee before it happened again. The edges around the room began to wobble and transmute into murky smoke-like clouds. He could feel his body stiffening and his mouth turning "O" shaped, sort of like the subject in Edvard Munch's painting *The Scream*, as the diner slid away, the walls and ceiling folding and dissolving. Tumbling this way and that and back again felt like being inside of the oscillating cylinder of a washing machine amid a churning eddy of darkness and light and chaos and confusion.

The next thing Simon felt was a hard wooden bench against his legs and the sensation of other people's arms touching his on either side. Considering that he had been looking at the picture of the diner right before he arrived there, he grasped that he must have now been transported to the last picture he had viewed, which was the one on the front page of the newspaper. He realized he was sitting in the packed visitor's gallery overlooking the iconic paneled walls of Courtroom 600 at the Palace of Justice in Nuremberg where the leaders of the Nazi regime were being tried for their crimes before an international military tribunal.

Simon glanced at the large clock on the wood-paneled wall. It was just past 3:00 p.m. and Judge Geoffrey Lawrence, who was presiding over the court this day, began to speak.

"In accordance with Article 27 of the Charter, the International Military Tribunal will now pronounce the sentences on the defendants convicted on this Indictment.

"Defendant Hermann Wilhelm Goering, on the counts of the Indictment on which you have been convicted, the International Military Tribunal sentences you to death by hanging."

Not only was it strange to be witnessing the event that he had only just learned about a day ago from a book, but equally sobering to watch Goering, Adolph Hitler's second-in-command and head of the Gestapo, knowing that before his sentence to be hanged would be carried out he would commit suicide in his cell via a cyanide capsule.

Judge Lawrence continued.

"Defendant Rudolf Hess, on the counts of the Indictment on which you have been convicted, the Tribunal sentences you to imprisonment for life.

"Defendant Joachim von Ribbentrop, on the counts of the Indictment on which you have been convicted, the Tribunal sentences you to death by hanging.

"Defendant Wilhelm Keitel, on the counts of the Indictment on which you have been convicted, the Tribunal sentences you to death by hanging . . ."

Kaltenbrunner, Rosenberg, Frank, Frick, Streicher, Funk, Doenitz, Raeder, Baldur von Schirach, Sauckel, Jodl, Seyss-Inquart, Speer, von Neurath, and Bormann. Simon listened as each Nazi war criminal was sentenced. On the one hand, it was remarkable to be bearing witness to history in real time; on the other he struggled to grasp what was happening to him personally. Why was he jumping from one time point to the next? Hadn't Imogen said that you could only go to one place at a time, that you had to return to your anchor photo first before entering a different one?

These thoughts had scarcely entered his mind when like before, the courtroom began to dissipate and the universe began to toss him this way and that like a rag doll.

When everything had stopped spinning, more or less, and he could safely open his eyes, Simon couldn't believe what he was seeing. It seemed like eons ago he'd entered these four walls. Everything about it appeared the same, yet it felt different . . . old. He turned around and surveyed the room, spotting a calendar on the wall. December 1913. Herbert's apartment, one of the last places he'd been before grabbing hold of Imogen and traveling to the future. Imogen! Oh my god, he thought, what had he done? Had he trapped himself here? Would he never see her again? Just then, Herbert entered the room, and the last thing Simon saw was the look of surprise on his face and the distant sound of his voice shouting "Simon" as he came toward him. It couldn't have been more than a split second, a lightning flash, and then the universe abruptly dropped him back into his own living room!

How had that happened? Was it because he had been thinking about home and Imogen that he was brought back? Which place was home? Was the universe confused about which home was home? The turn of the century home he was born into or the home he was conceived in and currently resided? Simon was both exhausted and exhilarated and a little bit sick. But he had traveled through time and made it back in one piece!

His first impulse was to take a look at the photograph of the diner he'd been to in Iris' album and to check if it was the same one, but he was also afraid to look at it. What if he was swept away again against his will? Who knew where, or when he might end up or whether he would be lucky enough to return, or even arrive back in one piece? This was madness. Clearly, he had no control over this.

With no one to answer his questions and his body screaming with fatigue Simon was content in the moment, just lying on the floor getting lost in the swirly patterns on the ceiling. Yes, he could see them now, the cat and the skull, right there. Imogen had called the patterns of light and shadow that caused you to find familiar objects in random places like plaster and clouds, pareidolia . . . and as everything went black and he lost consciousness, he thought he heard pounding somewhere in the distance.

Fletcher pulled into Imogen's driveway and parked. He couldn't help thinking how now that he and Simon were friends, he no longer needed an excuse to drop by. The funny thing about it though was that he didn't need an excuse, he truly liked the guy, enjoyed being around him. He hadn't seen him since last week though and he knew Simon was struggling a bit with his new life. It wouldn't hurt to check up on how his bud was doing whether Imogen was at home or not.

He rang the doorbell a couple of times and waited. No one came. He knocked on the door, but no answer. It was possible that nobody was home. He could come back later, but for some reason Fletcher decided to take a quick peek through the front window. And what he saw was disturbing. Sprawled out in the middle of the living room floor, lay Simon, his arms and legs splayed unnaturally as though he had been dropped from the sky. This didn't seem right at all.

Fletcher rushed back to the front door and began to pound hard, over and over, hoping that Simon would hear and wake up. No luck. He rushed back to the window and peered in. No response. Simon hadn't moved a muscle. Really worried now, Simon dashed to the side gate and sprinted through the yard to the back door. Feeling around in the bushes he located the special rock that he knew Imogen always hid an extra key under. Letting himself in through the kitchen, Fletcher bolted into the living room where Simon lay motionless. Was he dead? Passed out? Had he been drinking? Fletcher grabbed his shoulders and called out his name. "Simon . . . Simon, are you okay?"

Grasping Simon's wrist between his fingers he felt for a pulse. Yes! Thank god, there was one, so at least he wasn't dead.

But what was wrong with him? He tried lightly cuffing Simon's cheeks to arouse him. Still no response. Rushing into the kitchen Fletcher filled a glass up with water, rushed back and poured the cold tap water on Simon's face and smacked his cheeks a couple times more. This seemed to work because he moved and slowly began to come around.

"Wha . . . what? Who . . .?" Simon muttered.

"Simon, it's Fletcher, are you okay? What happened here?"

Confused and still in a stupor, Simon clutched Fletcher's arm and attempted to open his eyes. "Where am I? Fletcher?"

"You're here at home, in your living room, Simon." He made a weak attempt at lifting his head but gave up and fell back exhausted. "Don't try to sit up yet," Fletcher said, "just lie back and tell me what happened.

Groggily, Simon said, "I fell asleep. I think." His words were slurred like he had been drinking.

Fletcher stood up and threading his arms through Simon's, dragged him across the floor to the couch where he lifted him up and propped a pillow behind his back. "There," he said. He took the glass into the kitchen, refilled it with water, and handed it to Simon to take a sip.

"Okay, now tell me why you were passed out on your living room floor, Simon."

It took a few seconds for Simon to feel like he could speak properly, but at least he was able to string together more than a few words.

"I . . . I don't know," he stammered. "One minute I was lying on the floor and the next thing I remember is you slapping me and throwing cold water in my face."

"Dude, I thought you were dead!" Fletcher replied. "You scared the shit out of me."

Simon managed a weak smile. "Sorry, I must have fallen asleep."

"But on the floor? What the hell were you doing before that?"

It all came flooding back, the women's protest, the diner, the Nuremberg trials, Herbert Doran's apartment, dark and light, falling and tumbling and out of control. Was it a dream? It couldn't have been, but Simon was confused. He wasn't sure that he wanted to share that part with Fletcher, but who better? Well, Imogen, but he didn't feel like he wanted to tell her just yet either. And why didn't he? He wasn't sure about anything right now.

Simon looked at Fletcher, whose face, filled with nothing but sincere concern for a friend, was comforting. It was the face of someone he strangely felt he could trust with his life.

"I time-traveled," Simon blurted.

"What?" Fletcher wasn't expecting that explanation. "What do you mean, you time-traveled?"

Simon felt much better now. His mind was sound and clear. It was real. He was certain of it. He had been to each one of those times and places. And he needed to tell somebody.

"I didn't think I could," he began. "I tried many times before and it never worked, but I'm telling you Fletcher, this time, it did, it really did!" Simon could barely contain the excitement he felt.

Fletcher knew that Imogen had the skill. She had finally spilled the tea to him a few years back. It was a day he'd probably never forget; the day he'd foolishly asked her to marry him, and she had turned him down flat. But they had grown closer when she had come clean to him about her peculiar superpower and the weird job she'd turned it into because, she said, she wanted someone to worry about her if she didn't come back and Fletcher was more than happy to be that person. He would do anything . . . anything for her. Not an understatement.

But then, three months ago, she brought Simon back with her from one of her time traveling trips. And Fletcher had tried so hard not to like the guy, but he was so darn likable it was near impossible. He was intelligent and talented and unbelievably humble, and Fletcher sensed that they were both in need of a friend.

"So . . . so what happened? Simon's excitement was infectious, and Fletcher wanted to know more. "Tell me everything!" he said.

Simon filled Fletcher in, how he had been reading the encyclopedia, catching up on his history and unexpectedly found himself situated in the middle of an angry crowd of men at a women's march in the seventies, back here, then to a Midwestern diner and then the Nuremberg trials in 1946, and then finally, in the apartment of a friend from his own time in 1913. He told Fletcher how he had returned the first time, but the next time was propelled willy-nilly from one time to the next, and that it had happened so fast, he wasn't entirely sure that it wasn't a dream.

A look of concern flashed across Fletcher's face. "So, what you're saying is you involuntarily jumped from one time period to the next?" Simon nodded.

"That's strange, because according to Imogen you have to return to the original picture you came through, that it's your portal or anchor or whatever, and that making sure it's secure is important for getting back to your own time. So, how was what you did even possible?"

Simon felt as perplexed as Fletcher. "I don't know," he said as he fiddled with a strand of his hair.

"I don't know," he repeated. "It happened so fast, I mean, I was here and then I was there and when I did come back, I was so exhausted I must have fallen into a deep sleep on the floor and that is how you found me."

"But without a portal how did you manage to get back home, to here, to now?" Fletcher asked, clearly confused.

Simon scratched his head. "Well, when I was in Nuremberg, I do remember thinking about home and that's when I jumped back to 1913. I was barely there for split second when I thought of Imogen, and then somehow I ended up back here."

"Do you think that when you initially thought of home, the universe sent you back to your own time, but then thinking of Imogen caused you to be sent back here, to your current home?

"Possibly," Simon answered. "Honestly, I don't know how it works or why it was so different for me than it was for Imogen."

"You should talk to Imogen," he suggested. "I'm sure she'll have answers that I don't have."

Simon's reaction was swift. "No, I don't want to tell Imogen anything yet."

Fletcher was surprised by his response. "Why not?" He hated himself for even thinking it, but were there cracks in their relationship? Were they not as tight as they let on?

Simon felt a pang of guilt about withholding information from Imogen, but the truth of it was, he wanted to experiment on his own first, see what he could do before telling her. He also hated drawing Fletcher into his deception, but it was too late for that now. Lying seemed like the best option.

"I think Imogen has a lot on her mind right now. I don't want to trouble her," he explained. "And to be honest, I'd like to experiment a bit before telling her, see what I can do first. Do you understand?"

"Of course," Fletcher said. He didn't want to make Imogen angry, but at the same time, it felt good being included, privy to a secret that only he and Simon shared. And besides that, he had always wanted to time travel, maybe Simon would teach him.

"I agree, it might be too much for her, but . . ." A key turning in the lock and the sound of the front door being pushed open caused Fletcher to stop what he was saying mid-sentence.

Like a naughty boy caught in the act, Simon reacted by throwing up both of his hands and shooshing his partner in crime, Fletcher. "shhh," he whispered, "act natural."

"Imogen dropped the keys in the bowl in the hallway, removed her sunglasses, and entered the living room where Simon and Fletcher were fidgeting, looked guilty.

"Hi guys," she said, a little surprised to see Fletcher again so soon. "What's going on?"

10

Imogen arrived outside Mary's early at 6:45 a.m. sharp, dressed and ready to go in her "crisp as a cracker" uniform, as Darla instructed. Last night when she had gone downstairs to inquire about an iron, Loretta, the hotel desk clerk had brought out an ironing board and set it up for her. Imogen could feel the women's eyes on her, and finally after about 10 minutes of watching Imogen struggle with the hot iron and starch, she took over, showing Imogen how to use long, straight strokes and to iron creases.

"Voilá," she said as she pulled it from the board and hung the now perfectly wrinkleless uniform on a hanger, ready for Imogen to slip into. When Imogen came down the next morning dressed in her uniform, she was surprised to find that Loretta had gotten up early and prepared coffee and a light breakfast.

"Good luck," she said.

"I think I'll need it," Imogen said.

"First days are always stressful, but you'll do fine," Loretta reassured her.

Imogen looked at her watch. "I'd better get going," she said pushing her chair away from the table. "Oh, would you mind taking a photo first?" Imogen asked, remembering the experiment with the camera as she rushed to her room to retrieve it. Imogen posed and offered up a cheesy, selfie type grin for the shot before grabbing her sweater and rushing out the door for her first day.

Stretch, the morning cook, opened the door and let Imogen in. Greeting her with a broad smile, he winked and said, "Are you ready?" Imogen returned the smile. "I think I am," she said nervously, uncertainty beginning to sink in now that she was really here. From the kitchen, Darla bustled into the room and handed Imogen a fresh order pad and pencil. "Here you go honey." She gave Imogen the once over and nodded approval of her freshly pressed uniform. "You'll do fine," she said with only a hint of cynicism creeping into her voice as she walked away.

It was 11:00 a.m. Imogen had been here only four hours, and already she was exhausted. Except for the short 10-minute break, she'd been on her feet all morning long, rushing from one table to the next, taking orders, juggling platefuls of pancakes, eggs, bacon and sausage and hash browns, and biscuits and gravy—so much biscuits and gravy—pouring coffee and carrying juice and milk and glass bottles of sticky syrup. She hated being sticky. Oh my god, being sticky was the worst and here she was now, literally drowning in the sticky! Her apron looked like breakfast had vomited on her.

It had been nonstop from the minute the doors opened. If she'd had a moment to ponder it, Imogen would have been amazed. Was this the only eatery in town? Surely it couldn't be, but it sure seemed like it. Christ, the Beanery had never been this busy, even during the big windstorm when the lights went out and all the college kids got stuck inside to ride it out. A few stragglers lingered over cups of coffee, but the breakfast storm had finally passed. Imogen wiped off the table that Stretch had just bussed.

She pushed a stray hair off her face. "Is it always like this?" she asked him. "Eh, sometimes it's not. It's the Sunday church crowd." He gave Imogen a crooked smile and hurried back to the kitchen carrying the bin full of dirty dishes.

"You did pretty well." Darla had come up behind her, startling Imogen and almost causing her to drop the tacky syrup bottles she was holding. "Now it it's time to prep for the lunch crowd," she said, handing Imogen a basket of condiments to fill the sugar and salt and pepper shakers.

When her shift mercifully ended at 2:30 p.m., Imogen

dragged her weary body back to the hotel. Exhausted, she flung herself face down onto the bed, closed her eyes, didn't move. She was nearly asleep when a few minutes later there was a soft tapping at the door and Loretta pushed her way in carrying a large pan of hot water.

"I brought you up some water to soak your feet in," she said sweetly. Imogen groaned as she lazily turned over onto her back. Loretta gave her a hand so that she was sitting upright on the edge of the bed. She gently pulled each sock and pump from Imogen's tired feet and Imogen couldn't help feeling bowled over by the kind gesture and the water that was like manna from the gods. "Oh, dear lord, Loretta," she said as she accepted the healing warmth of the water on her sore heals and arches and toes. "This is fucking amazing," she said, almost immediately realizing she'd screwed up again. Caught up in the moment, the curse word had just automatically rolled off her tongue, but when she looked over at Loretta to gauge her reaction, there was none. She simply smiled. "I'm glad it's helping," Loretta said.

"Honestly, Loretta, I don't know if I can do this again tomorrow," Imogen moaned.

"Oh, don't be silly, of course, you can," Loretta answered, adding "Women can do anything that they set their minds to."

If it had seemed odd to Imogen a few minutes ago that Loretta had no reaction to her dropping the F-bomb, red flags were up now. Could Loretta be a time traveler too? Her statement about women certainly sounded suspiciously progressive coming out of the mouth of a woman living in 1946 Kansas.

At the same time, it was nice to make a new friend. Imogen didn't have many. And she was surprised how quickly she and Loretta had clicked. That wasn't something that happened easily or often.

For once, she chalked it up to misguided perceptions about people and times, lumping generations into stereotypes, making assumptions about people's morals and motives, forgetting that everyone is different, no matter where you go . . . or *when* you go.

Bouncing effortlessly on her heels, notepad and pencil at the ready, Imogen made the rounds, feverishly refilling coffee cups and asking customers if they needed anything. After Loretta's warm water therapy Imogen's feet had made a full recovery. In the three days she'd been working at Mary's, Imogen knew the ropes, mostly, and she'd picked up on a few other things too, one that just a block over within walking distance was the high school, and two, that at seven minutes past noon, a raucous throng of teenagers would burst through those doors, pushing and shoving and angling for available tables. Imogen was overwhelmed at first—so many of them! But she was ready for them now. In fact, the countdown had become a bit of a game between she and Stretch as they watched the clock over knowing looks while the second hand ticked off the minutes. And then, just as it clicked to exactly seven after, boom! a rush of girls and boys surged through the doors, breaking the sound barrier as they poured in, and the lunch crew sprang into action.

Working alongside the other waitress—Imogen knew nothing about her, other than her name, which was Nan—they quickly bounced from station to station taking orders, mostly for hamburgers, fries, malteds, Coca-Cola, the occasional hot dog. A discordance of youthful voices shouted their orders, barely paying attention to Imogen, distracted by each other and which songs to play on the tabletop jukeboxes.

It was a race to get the tickets over to the spinning carousel, where Imogen caught a glance through the window of Stretch, who gave her a quick thumbs up as he artfully flipped burgers on the greasy, sizzling grill. Once orders started showing up, it was another mad dash to get the food to the tables. Imogen toggled between balancing several plates of food and then rushing back to grab the drinks that went with them. If anything, she was getting some great cardio in! But aside from the excellent workout, she rather enjoyed the physical labor, of doing something repetitive and rigorous, something that took her out of her own head for a while, distracted her from overthinking. It was nice to only have to think of her own needs for a while. She loved Simon, loved spending time with him, but often it seemed as though his needs trumped hers. As the first wave of kids left, their tables were quickly snatched up by other waiting teenagers—it seemed that the high school staggered their lunch breaks, so the actual lunch rush extended to 2:30.

Kids lingered at a couple of the tables, slow-sipping Coca-Cola through straws in frosted glasses, but for the most part, things had settled down. Imogen refilled their drinks and then picked up stray napkins and straws off the floor. At around 1:30, the bell over the door chimed, and two small groups of kids came in. One headed straight for a table that had been bussed but not wiped down. Grabbing a wet rag, Imogen scurried over to wipe up the salt and ketchup from the table's surface before they sat down. Setting the cloth down on the next table over, she dried her wet hands on her soiled apron and snatched her order pad from her pocket.

"Sorry about the dirty table," she said, "what can I get you guys?" During the chaos, the faces of the kids had become one big blur, but now in the calm, she had time to make out individual features and there was no doubting who these kids were. Imogen immediately recognized Vivian Littlefield from the photograph, and the boy seated next to her, had to be 16-year-old Harrison Tabor himself. She had been right about him. He was a looker. Even when the 85-year-old version of him had walked into her office, she knew. In this iteration, Harry's head of hair was still thick but instead of being white, it was a dark ebony, with almost a bluish tint to it. Like the others, Harry and Vivian were too preoccupied with choosing a song, and with each other, to notice their waitress, Imogen.

Vivian leaned in close to Harry, whispered something, and giggled. Harry smiled and said without really bothering to look up at Imogen, "Uh, she'll have a chocolate malted and some fries, and give me a burger, fries, and a Coke," before turning his full attention back on Vivian. Imogen hadn't noticed the third person with them, a girl, until she turned toward her to take her order.

"What can I get . . ." the words, as if falling off a cliff one by one in slow motion, ended abruptly with a gasp. Noticeably shaken, but trying not to show it, Imogen pitched backward; the order pad and pencil slipped from her hand and a fuzzy gray cloud coalesced around her eyes. Her legs turned rubbery beneath her frame as she fell.

The first thing Imogen saw when she opened her eyes was the slow-turning fan on the ceiling and she realized she was lying in a prone position on the floor. What happened? She tried to push herself up with one arm but felt faint and wobbly. A hand gently pushed her back down and the soothing voice of a girl said, "Lie back. Don't try to get up too quickly." The voice sounded oddly familiar, like she'd heard it before, but a long time ago.

And then, a youthful male voice said, "Iris, help me lift her up and get her over to one of the tables." Arms pulled her up and guided her to a nearby booth. Still discombobulated it took a moment for her eyes to fully focus, and when they did, she was looking into the face of Grammy Iris. How this could be happening, she wasn't sure, but she knew it was her because, well, in about a year or so from now, or 118 years ago, depending on which direction in time you were moving, she'd be spending an afternoon in the park with 18-year-old Iris Graham, a young Simon, and Grammy's beau André posing for photographs. She felt a little too scrambled right now from the shock of seeing her dead grandmother to process what the heck Grammy was doing here now, on this day in 1946 in Central City, Kansas, but that was the least of it. Part of her wanted to reach out and throw her arms around her and hug her tight. How she'd missed her sweet grandma. She had so much to tell her. But she knew she could not do that. She was pretty sure that this young version of Grammy had not yet discovered time travel or had any inkling that the crazy waitress that had fainted when she saw her was her future granddaughter.

"Are you okay?" the girl . . . Grammy . . . asked with the same look of worry that Imogen remembered. Imogen smiled. It wasn't every day that you were rescued by your own grandmother. A bit of a shock, yes, but not altogether unpleasant either.

"Thank you, I'm fine now, really," she said as she attempted to stand up. Instantly, both Iris and Harrison stopped her, pushing her back against the vinyl seat. "Why don't you sit here with us for a few minutes longer," Harrison suggested. "It's not very busy. Hardly anyone is in here now." Imogen glanced up at the clock on the wall. It was a little after 2:00. Her shift was almost over. It was probably okay if she took it easy for a few minutes. Just then, Stretch came toward them carrying a tall glass of ice water. "You okay?" he asked, genuinely concerned. He handed the glass to her, and she took a sip. "I'm okay, thanks," she answered. "Don't worry about a thing, I got you covered," he said, winking and heading back to the kitchen.

"Imogen, that's an interesting name," Iris said, tapping Imogen's name tag with her finger. "I don't think I've ever heard it before." You will, Imogen thought surreptitiously. For some reason, she'd neglected to pick out an alias on this trip, but once here, figured Imogen sounded old timey enough for someone in 1946.

Imogen looked down at the tag pinned to her chest. "Oh, thank you. My dad named me after Imogen Cunningham. She was . . . or I mean she *is* a photographer, like my father was."

Harry perked up with the mention of photography. "Holy mackerel, that's killer-diller! My dad bought a camera for me this summer for my birthday, and I've been taking pictures like crazy!" "He has," Vivian teased, "mostly of me."

Harry blushed. "She's quite photogenic," he said, which obviously pleased Vivian, who giggled and gave him a quick peck on the cheek. Young love on full display. It was sweet, but in the back of her mind, Imogen couldn't sweep away the gruesome knowledge that in a couple of weeks Vivian would be dead. It made her realize how vital it was for her to stay on task and not get distracted by the fact that she had just run into her dead grandmother.

Her thoughts were interrupted by Stretch who appeared at the table with plates of food for the group. "I'll get out of your way," Imogen said, starting to stand up again. Iris reached over and gently touched her wrist, "Are you sure? It's fine with us if you want to stay here and rest a bit longer." In between chewing their food, Harry and Vivian both nodded in agreement.

Her grandmother's touch sent a wave of emotion surging through Imogen, memories of her hands; holding her soft, wrinkled hand at the store, tucking her in at night, showing her how to can peaches, waving goodbye. There was a strange connection again, like the time she'd accidentally traveled into the photograph in college. Grammy hadn't known her yet, but somehow, she did know. There was something between them, electricity, a spark, a memory that wasn't quite yet a memory, but still, something there, a connection she couldn't explain. Imogen withdrew her hand from Iris even though it felt painful to let go.

"Oh, thanks," Imogen said. "That's sweet, but I'm fine, really. My shift is over, so I'll go straight home and rest."

"We'll come in at lunch tomorrow and check on you," Iris said brightly.

"That will be great. And thank you for your help today," she said as she rose from the table and started to leave the teenagers to finish their lunch.

"Oh wait," she heard Harry say as she was walking away. She turned and saw that he'd pulled a camera from his pocket. "Since we saved your life and all, do you think we can we take a photo together?"

"Sure, Imogen said, a little surprised, but also pleased. Harry asked one of the kids at a neighboring table if they'd take the picture. "Let's get all of us in it," he said as he grabbed Vivian's hand and pulled her out from the booth. "Iris, you stand next to Imogen," he directed. The girl who was taking the picture, counted: "one, two three . . ." and they smiled for the camera as she pushed the button and then handed it back to Harry. Imogen wondered how much of a wreck she must look after just recently being passed out on the floor, but she was also excited to have met them. Now she could begin the work she'd come to do.

"Cute dress," Iris said appreciatively when she opened the front door. "Thanks!" Imogen said, "I took your advice and did a little shopping on my day off." Iris ushered Imogen inside the modest house where she lived with her aunt. Pushing a couple of pillows out of the way she invited Imogen to sit down on the sofa. "It's nothing fancy," she said, "but Aunt Phillis keeps it nice."

"It's lovely," Imogen said and meant it. Everything in the small living room was as neat as a pin, something that wouldn't exactly rub off on her grandma—Imogen often described Grammy's home as controlled chaos, yet she always knew where something was if she ever needed to find it.

After her fainting spell in the diner, as promised Iris had come back the next day to check on her, and from there they had hit it off, chatting during Imogen's breaks and meeting up after her shift a couple of times to talk. It appeared that Iris was desperately in need of someone to talk to, and she'd found it in Imogen, which made sense considering they were related. But Iris didn't know that.

During their getting to know one another stage, Iris heard some old stories and discovered a few new things about her grandmother's past. She imparted the many times repeated "Dust Bowl to deliverance" story of Grammy's family fleeing Missouri in 1932 to escape the choking dust, and how when Iris was seven, after the death of her sister, her folks had sent her to Central City to live with her Aunt Phyllis. Aunt Phyllis, she learned, was a pleasant woman, if not a bit stodgy and strict. She'd never married and had insisted that Iris make no messes ever in her tidy house. Dust was her singular nemesis. She was also quite religious, which provided Imogen a clearer understanding of why Grammy had been so quick to embrace the church after her parents had disappeared. The missing part of that story had been revealed the day of Grammy's stroke when Imogen was in college and had literally stumbled upon this "gift" while researching one of Grammy's photographs from the turn of the 19th century. She'd found herself inside the photo where she met face to face with the 18-year-old version of her Grammy (Iris).

Afterward, Grammy had no choice but to tell Imogen the truth, all of it, not just the time travel part. Since she was nine, Imogen had believed her parents had died in an automobile accident, only to find out Grammy had lied to her. While they were time traveling, someone had destroyed their anchor photos, trapping each in a different time period, lost and unable to return.

It was difficult recalling the lies Grammy had told, especially now sitting in the same room with her, but apparently it had been too much for her too because she'd suffered a stroke and died several days later, something that Imogen would always blame herself for. Lost in her own thoughts, the sound of Grammy, er Iris' voice brought her back to the here and now.

"Um, would you like to look at some of my grandfather's photographs?" Iris asked. "He was quite an accomplished photographer."

"Of course," Imogen answered. "I'd love to see them."

Iris jumped up and pulled the album from one of the built-in shelves that lined one wall of the living room. It was a beautiful album, ornate with hand-carved bas relief wood over a plush purple velvet backing, very similar to Grammy's, which Imogen had thumbed through as a child. Iris seemed excited to show someone the album. In typical schoolgirl fashion, she plopped down on the sofa next to Imogen and carefully opened it up to the first page, which was a visual feast.

"Oh my," Imogen gasped. "These are stunning." Her grandfather certainly did have an eye. Page after page of black and white images captured every imaginable facet of turn of the century city life. Women strolling through parks in enormous hats and parasols, men in their dandy suits and bowler hats, spring flowers and cherry blossoms, a Ferris wheel, horse-drawn carriages snaking down cobblestone streets. A rush of memories of her time spent with Simon around the same time flooded Imogen's mind. It was no wonder that Grammy had also become so enamored with this period. From the photographs it seemed a simpler time, which was an illusion, of course, but you wouldn't know about any of the bad components looking at any of these photographs. As she slowly turned each page, taking in each image, she imagined the effect it would have had on a young, impressionable Iris. And then it dawned on her, in just a few short months from now Iris would discover her gift for time travel and disappear into one of the photographs in this very album.

About a third of the way through, one photograph, in particular, took Imogen's breath away making it quite difficult for her to keep her expression of surprise from giving her away. The picture was of two gentlemen who were setting up camera equipment and Imogen immediately recognized who they were. In fact, she'd met them before—Andre, Grammy's future beau and his young apprentice Simon Le Bon Elliot—Imogen's Simon.

Imogen quickly turned the page pretending like nothing was out of the ordinary.

Iris reached out and flipped back to the previous page. "I think I went somewhere once," Iris said dreamily. "I was looking at a photograph and fell asleep. I thought it was a dream, but I wasn't so sure. What do you think Imogen? Do you think it could have been real?"

Imogen only had memories of her own experience, but she needed to frame it in a way that wouldn't give anything away. She paused to assess the current situation she found herself in. How weird was it to be the older adult, the granddaughter giving advice to the adolescent, her grandmother, in this strange upside-down universe? So weird though that it made her smile despite everything. Imogen closed the album and looked over at her grandmother at 17, an innocent, fresh-faced high school senior—her whole life in front of her, only able to imagine what lie ahead.

"Well," Imogen said. "If you concentrate very hard, you never know what might happen."

Iris frowned and looked away, obviously disappointed in Imogen's vague response.

"May I be forthright with you, Imogen?" she asked.

"Of course, you can," Imogen said, gently patting her grandmother's hand.

"I'll be graduating from high school soon and I don't have any idea about what I want to do," she said. Her words came spilling out like water through a crack in a dam. "I know the war is over and I should be happy and hopeful, but I can't just put all the horrors behind me like some people can. My Aunt Phyllis will want me to move out, or get married . . . or . . . or something."

"Have you thought at all about college?" Imogen asked.

"A little, but I don't know that I'm ready for that. I feel sad and adrift, and I don't know why. And the future seems so scary and uncertain."

Imogen couldn't help chuckling, remembering how she had felt at that age. "It's supposed to feel that way, but it is possible to be both scared and excited about it," she said. "No, you don't know what's ahead, but even if you did, you might not choose that path anyway," she said, adding, "and even if you knew that one day in the future you would meet prince charming and live happily ever after, it's not to say that a bad boy named Snake in a leather jacket might show up tomorrow on his motorbike, scoop you up, and ride away with you into the sunset first."

Iris laughed out loud at that. It was wonderful seeing her grandmother like this, smiling, laughing, youthful.

"Well," Iris said, rolling her eyes, "I don't know anyone who rides a motorbike around here, or any boy named Snake, for that matter!"

"You never mentioned how your sister died," Imogen asked Iris casually from across the table. After looking at the photo albums, they had moved to the kitchen where Iris had prepared a lunch of cucumber sandwiches and iced tea for them. Iris had mentioned earlier on her own that she had an older sister who had died and although Imogen knew it was a deeply probing question, it was the opening she needed to get Iris on the topic of suicide and specifically if she suspected that Vivian might be unstable—unstable enough to stop her car on the tracks in front of an oncoming train. Iris shifted in her seat, her body language revealing that she was uncomfortable talking about her sister, but Imogen also sensed a hint of relief as well.

"I was a little girl when Lillian died," she said. "She was 13, eight years older than me and I didn't understand it, why she was there one day and just gone the next." Tears were beginning to form in the corners of her eyes as she spoke.

Imogen suddenly felt remorseful for bringing it up at all. "I'm sorry Iris, you don't have to talk about it if you don't want to. Forgive me for asking."

Iris wiped away the tear from her cheek. "No, I want to," she said. "My family sent me away so I would forget about it, but I haven't forgotten. It's good to be able to talk to someone about it finally."

Sighing again, she clasped her fingers together and scooted up closer to the table. Iris launched into the story, but this time, coming from the younger Iris, the memories were recent and raw and Imogen could tell that this was terribly difficult for her.

Imogen was certain that Aunt Phyllis had never discussed the matter with her nor encouraged her to talk to anyone else about her feelings. The remedy in those days for getting over trauma seemed to be fresh air and being sent away to a new place where one could forget. At least until it came up later in life after being neatly tucked away under the rug only to resurface because it had never really gone away.

"We left Kansas because of the dust storms and daddy needed a job. I was young, but I remember that the trip was long and hard, and it seemed like it took months rather than weeks. Days and days of driving on dusty roads, camping in a tent outdoors at night, sleeping sometimes in the back of the pickup under the stars. I had my rag dolly. Her name was Elsie. I played with her when we stopped for picnic lunches in parks along the way."

Imogen could see Iris' reliving the memories of that journey like it was yesterday as she went on to describe the good and bad parts of the trip—from the kindness of strangers who offered them water to drink from their hose and fresh fruit to eat to the filthy bathrooms, days of dirt and grime, and the hobos who one day stole their tent when they were inside a mom-and-pop store getting sodas.

Iris shifted gears. "My sister Lil was a lot like my mother," she said. "Mother was, I'm not sure how to say it, hard, unforgiving. She never hugged us or asked how we were doing. It was as if she had no feelings. Lil shielded me and stuck up for me. But she was sad, not just sometimes, all the time. And she talked to people that no one could see but her. She called them the shadow people. We shared a room and at night I could hear her saying 'No, no, I won't do that.' I asked her if she was talking to the shadow people and she said, 'they are talking to me.'"

Imogen recalled the photograph in Grammy's photo album of Lillian gazing blankly across the prairie. She wondered now if the shadow people were speaking to her when it was taken.

"She rarely spoke to anyone, but me and . . . well, the shadow people, and when we got to Oregon it got worse. The day before she jumped off the bridge, she told me that she loved me, but she couldn't control the pain or tell them no anymore. I didn't know what she meant. I think I probably asked her if she was hurt or something and she had smiled. I remember that. Lil hardly ever smiled. I will always remember that she smiled for me.

"I asked mother where Lillian was, and she said she died. I wasn't sure what dying meant. All I knew was that my sister was gone. There was no funeral, no goodbyes. No one explained to me what had happened. But not long after that when my cousin Harlan was visiting, he blurted out that Lillian had committed suicide, jumped off the bridge, he said. I didn't know what suicide meant so I asked my mother and she said it meant Lillian was a selfish girl, who didn't care about anyone but herself and it was best for everyone if we forgot about her. But I couldn't forget, and then I couldn't eat or sleep. I was so sick and sad that my folks decided to send me back to Kansas. I have to admit that it did help to be away from mother. Aunt Phyllis was never the affectionate sort either, but she has always been kind to me, and I appreciate that she took me in.

"Once, when I was about 12, I looked up suicide in the library and I asked Aunt Phyllis why Lil had done it. She told me that it was because she was schizophrenic, another word I didn't know and had to look up. She said they didn't know what to do with her. They talked about sending her to a hospital, but they were afraid people at church would shun them if word got out that my sister was crazy."

Iris paused, looked away and finished with, "I guess they found out anyway when she jumped off that bridge."

This was the first time Imogen had heard the full story and it was as gut-wrenching hearing it as she was certain it was for Grammy Iris to tell it. At a complete loss for words, Imogen instinctively reached over and pulled Iris in for a hug. Hugging her grandmother and having her hug back was the best Imogen had felt since coming here and she felt terrible for it. It was a horrible thing to use her grandmother to gather information about a client, but at the same time, was it so wrong to take pleasure in the touch again of her beloved, long passed grandmother?

Imogen sensed that her impulsive and intense show of affection may have seemed embarrassing for Iris as she patted Imogen's arm and gently extricated herself from her embrace. Totally worth it though, Imogen thought.

The awkward moment passed, and Iris was the first to speak. "It's why I worry about my friend Vivian sometimes," she said.

"Vivian? Why?" Imogen asked, surprised that Grammy was freely offering up this information.

She doesn't hear voices like Lil did, but she's impetuous. She doesn't think before she does things. I have a bad feeling about her, and I don't know why.

The days passed quickly, and Imogen found herself falling into a pleasant routine between work at the diner where a friendship with Stretch and even the gruff Darla, who she'd managed to actually draw out a smile from a few rare times, had taken root; long discussions about everything in the universe with her lovely new friend Loretta at the hotel at night, and spending time with her carefree young friends Iris, Harry, Vivian, and Vivian's younger sister Margaret Rose.

Out for a spontaneous outing with a hastily thrown together picnic and a blanket that she and Loretta were sharing as they watched the teenagers frolicking in the lake, Imogen was beginning to understand now why her Grammy Iris had been drawn to another time and, how once she got there, had so effortlessly fallen into friendships and routines that would make her want to stay. She had told Imogen that in 1901 where she had gone, that it was a simpler, less complicated time, and there was André, the dashing photographer with whom Iris had fallen deeply in love—not unlike she and Simon's story—yet she had decided to return to her own time because despite everything, she missed her parents. They were the only family she had, and she unselfishly wanted to have grandchildren that they could know and love. It was not lost on Imogen either that had her grandmother not returned and met her grandfather, she would never have given birth to her father Niles which, of course, meant there would have been no Imogen.

"Come in girls. The water's swell!" Harry called out to them as he turned to splash a giggling Vivian.

Imogen snapped off the remaining pictures left on the Brownie's roll of film of the teenagers frolicking in the water. She would stash and retrieve this roll later to develop because it was full of the moments and people she had come to care for; she wanted to remember their sweet faces. The second roll she had snapped random shots of street scenes, buildings, landscapes, plants, and the like. It would be the experimental film that she would leave in the camera as she traveled back to her time to see if, one it would even make it through, and if it did, what might the pictures reveal.

These thoughts reminded her that the clock was ticking. In just a few short days from now, the dreaded event loomed. The train accident. The reason Imogen was here.

"So what are your long-term plans, Imogen?" Loretta casually inquired. "I don't mean to be a nosy Nellie, but you aren't planning to stay in the hotel indefinitely, are you?" Do you plan on renting a place?

Imogen dreaded this conversation. People always wanted to know what your plans were, part of what made interacting with people problematic when she was traveling. But before she could answer, they were interrupted by Harry, Vivian, and Margaret.

The three wet teenagers grabbed towels from the trunk and began vigorously drying themselves off. "We have to go," Harry said. "I've got to have the car back by four."

A few days later while she was briskly wiping down tables and refilling the sugar dispensers after the first lunch rush, Imogen didn't notice Harry, Vivian, and Iris come in and slip into their usual booth. It wasn't like them to be so stealth; they usually entered the café in a mad flurry of chatter and bounce. But today, they sat quietly, morose, Harry and Vivian on one side facing Iris on the other, only looking up when Imogen strolled over with her pad and pen.

"Why the sad faces," she asked, although she was sure she knew why already.

Harry spoke first. "My dad told us last night that we're moving . . . to California. He was offered a job and we have to leave right away . . . day after tomorrow." Imogen could see that Vivian was trying very hard to hold it together, but her façade was about to crack open like a delicate egg.

"How could they do that? Just take him away from school and his friends . . . and me. It's not fair!" she blurted. Iris reached over and gently touched her friend's arm.

This is it, Imogen thought. Go time. She had already worked out a few scenarios in her head to stop the tragedy she knew was inevitably coming, but even the best laid plans could be derailed. All of it depended on how things played out. She could only try. She knew the date, October 12. She knew the time, 8:42 a.m. Her goal was to figure out a way to keep Vivian, her sister, and their little brother far away from the train tracks.

Last night in her hotel room, for the umpteenth time Imogen pored over the map of Pawnee County spread out across the bed. She had been studying it for weeks now, pondering which route Vivian might take, which one she should take. Route 56 connected Garfield to Central City and the train tracks paralleled the route all the way down from Central City to the other side of Garfield where the tracks ended abruptly.

According to the police report Imogen had obtained from a record search, the accident occurred at a railroad crossing at G Road. That much she knew. What she didn't know was why Vivian was traveling that route at that particular time with her brother and sister in tow, but today's conversation with the kids had provided the answer; the railroad crossing paralleled an unmarked, unpaved road that led to Harry's house. Obviously, Vivian must have been on her way to or from Harry's house when the train collided with the pickup.

In theory, it seemed straightforward: divert Vivian or delay the train somehow. There were a variety of ways to delay a train: an anonymous call up the rail line, reporting that the tracks were out, placing an obstacle on the tracks, forcing it to stop, starting a fire, yet none of these schemes felt like a failsafe plan. Something else gnawed at her. This was serious business. Two lives were at stake here. Why not simply tell Vivian not to drive that morning? What could be the harm in Imogen telling her she was from the future? Imogen rationalized. Vivian was a teenager after all. Teenagers forget most of what you tell them. And even if it seemed strange to her at the time, the memory would fade over time. And Vivian and Margaret Rose would live; young William, who was only eight, would be spared a year of rehabilitation from his injuries and the guilt and trauma of surviving while his sisters did not. Wasn't it worth the risk?

Imogen decided it was. When the kids got up to leave, Imogen pulled Vivian aside. "Vivian, may I speak to you alone for a moment?

"Sure," Vivian said.

"We'll meet you outside," Harry said as he and Iris headed for the door.

"What is it?" Vivian asked.

All of sudden, Imogen felt very nervous and unsure about her words, not something she was normally prone to, but she had to phrase this correctly.

"Um," Imogen hedged. "Look, I know you are really upset about Harry leaving. Losing someone you love is never easy, but . . ."

Vivian frowned. "What are you trying to say?" she asked.

"Okay, I don't know how to put this, but on Tuesday you need to get on the bus and go to school. Don't borrow the car. Don't drive, and don't cross any train tracks."

"I don't understand," Vivian said, her face registering a look of utter confusion. "How? Why do you know this?"

Imogen sighed as she tried to explain, hoping she wouldn't have to blurt the crazy part about being from the future, that maybe Vivian would think that Imogen was some sort of freaky but harmless psychic, tea/palm/tarot reading lady.

"It's a feeling I have, okay. I get flashes of . . . things . . . future things . . . sometimes," she stammered. "Please, Vivian," she pleaded. "Just promise me that you'll do this, on that day." During her speech, Imogen had taken Vivian's hand and was probably squeezing it too tightly. Visibly uncomfortable Vivian mumbled something that sounded like, "I promise," as she withdrew her hand from Imogen's vice-like clutch.

Imogen peered out through the window blinds watching

Vivian as she joined her friends. As she talked and gestured in the direction of the café, Harry and Iris looked over. She knew that Vivian was telling them what she said, but it didn't matter really. She felt better for telling her; for at least trying. Imogen would have a backup plan, of course.

The next couple of days had been tough. The kids hadn't come back in again, which made Imogen think that what she'd told Vivian had scared them away from her. It saddened her that she would not be able to give them a proper goodbye, but most of all, that she would not see her Grammy Iris again.

At the end of her shift on Monday, Imogen regretfully turned in her resignation at the café, making up an excuse that she'd been invited to stay with relatives back east. The hardest part had been saying goodbye to Stretch. He teared up a bit, and even Darla seemed a teensy bit sad, although she tried not to show it. Loretta had reluctantly agreed to let Imogen borrow her car. The plan was to get up early in the morning and set her plan in motion. Before she went to bed, Imogen fiddled with the ancient-looking alarm clock, with it's weird little bells on top. Figuring out how to set it to go off at 6:00 a.m. seemed an impossible task compared to setting the alarm on her smart phone. This particular analog model had a knob on the top and separate key winders for time and alarm with individual setting stems for each. After several test attempts, Imogen felt relatively confident that she had done it correctly, she hoped.

The high-pitched shrill of what sounded like a thousand clanging bells pitched Imogen awake from a night of restless sleep and anxious dreams of darkness and shadows, screeching and screams. Groggy, she reached over to the nightstand to turn it off, but missed the mark, sending the confounded noisy thing banging to the floor where it continued to ring and ring and ring. "Stop, damn it!" she yelled at it. Pushing off the covers she plucked it from the floor and after several attempts at pushing levers and buttons, was finally able to silence it.

Something was wrong. It should be dark, but light was seeping through a gap in the curtains. Snatching up the clock, Imogen was immediately horrified. It was 8:14. She had 38 minutes to stop a train.

Without bothering to comb her hair, Imogen dressed quickly and threw on a pair of shoes before rushing out to the lobby to use the payphone. "Operator, how may I help you?" the voice on the line answered. Imogen knew that all payphone calls were operator-assisted, an obstacle she didn't need at all right now.

"Operator, connect me to the Littlefield's residence please," Imogen said, trying hard to temper the rising panic welling up inside of her. After depositing a nickel in the slot for the call, Imogen fidgeted while the operator dialed Vivian's number. "I'm sorry, that number is busy," the operator informed her. "Shit!" Imogen blurted.

"Excuse me?" the voice on the line said.

"Sorry, can you keep trying and call me back if the line becomes available?" The operator didn't sound nearly as pleasant after hearing Imogen curse, but politely agreed to keep trying anyway.

Within five minutes, which felt more like eternity, the phone rang loudly, jangling Imogen's already frayed nerves. "Yes, hello, hello?" she said into the receiver, hoping not to sound overly anxious.

"Your call is going through now, please deposit five cents," the operator said.

Imogen dropped the nickel into the slot again. A woman's voice, presumably Vivian's mother, picked up at the other end, "Hello?"

"Uh, yes, um," she stumbled, "is Vivian available?"

"Vivian left for school a few minutes ago," the woman said. "May I ask who's calling?"

Ignoring her, Imogen blurted, "Did she ride the bus?"

There was a pause on the other end of the line. "No, she

drove her brother and sister to school today. Who is this?"

Imogen hung the phone up and paced, pushing her hair back from her forehead. "Shit, fuck."

"Who are you shit/fucking now?" a voice asked from behind her. It was Loretta.

"Oh geez, Loretta, I'm late, I'm so fucking late. Can I please borrow your car?"

"Of course, Imogen. I told you that you could last night. Just let me grab the keys."

The plan, had she gotten up earlier to execute it properly, was to drive out Route 56 under the cover of darkness and plant an obstruction on the tracks ahead of the crossing to Harry's house, just as a precautionary measure in case Vivian had ignored her warning and taken the pickup to school anyway.

Growing increasingly more impatient as she waited for Loretta, Imogen paced harder. "Loretta? The keys!" she called out.

"I'm looking," Loretta called back from the kitchen. "I swear they were right here last night." Imogen rushed to the kitchen and began frantically pacing around the room, her eyes flitting from the counter to the table, to the sink to the floor, anywhere that Loretta might have set them. After a minute of searching, Loretta spotted them on the floor under the table. "Here they are. They must have slid off the counter."

Imogen snatched them from her hand and rushed outside and jumped into the 1941 Nash 600 parked out front. She put the key in the ignition and turned it. Nothing. She tried again. The engine turned over, but did not engage. Imogen slammed her hands against the big steering wheel. "Oh my god," she wailed. "Why is this happening?" A third time yielded the same result. Imogen vaulted out of the car and ran inside calling out to Loretta, "Where are you? The car won't start!"

Emerging from the kitchen with a look of irritation, Loretta asked, "What now Imogen?"

"The car, it won't start. What do I do? I don't know what to do," Imogen said frantically, close to tears.

"Come on," Loretta said, pulling Imogen out to the car by

her arm. "Get in," she ordered. Imogen obeyed. Put it in neutral, push the clutch in and when I tell you, pop the clutch and hit the gas. Can you do that?"

Imogen nodded and Loretta scurried around the back and started to push. Luckily, the road had a slight incline, and the Nash began to slowly move. In the rearview mirror, Imogen saw a neighbor rushing over to help Loretta push. Between the two of them, the car began to pick up speed. "Now!" Loretta shouted. Imogen popped the clutch, hit the gas pedal and the engine turned over, lurched forward, and then rolled to a dead stop. Loretta caught up to the car and appeared at the window. Imogen had lain her head on the steering wheel in defeat. "It's no use," she wailed.

"Don't be silly, you can do this. This time when you let the clutch out, be sure to hit the gas," Loretta instructed. Imogen sat up and pushed the clutch to the floor. Through Loretta and the neighbor's efforts the car began to move again and when it had picked up some speed, Loretta hollered, "Now!"

Imogen popped the clutch again and stomped on the gas pedal hard. The engine revved and as Imogen began to drive away, she could see Loretta running alongside the car.

"Get back, Loretta!" she called out as she sped away.

With only 15 or so minutes left, it was too late now to stop the train but perhaps she could still stop Vivian. Damn it, she'd run her off the road if she had to!

She rolled onto Main Street. There was a bit of traffic, but not enough to delay her too much. As soon as she got out of town and hit Route 56, she'd have plenty of time. These calculated thoughts were racing through Imogen's mind when, up ahead, suddenly a gray cat darted into traffic. Like watching a disaster in slow motion, the pickup truck ahead of her swerved to miss it and crossed the center line hitting an oncoming car and dumping its payload of dirt onto the street, snarling traffic and leaving Imogen completely boxed in. Exasperated, Imogen slapped her palm to her forehead.

So, this was how it was going to go. She was ready to give

in to it, but damn it, how could she not try? It was an epic battle now. Imogen vs. the universe. Time was ticking. Imogen began to repeatedly honk the horn, which was exceptionally deafening and really annoying, by the way, not like modern horns which conveyed a sort of kinder and gentler "excuse you for cutting me off back there, asshole" sound. This horn literally shrieked "OUT OF MY WAY!" Amazingly, the people in the cars who were stuck behind her began to slowly back up, peeling away like the parting of the sea. Inch by inch, there was just enough of a gap between Imogen's car and the one in front of and behind her for her to maneuver her way out of the tight space until finally she was able to navigate out of the tangled traffic turn onto a side street. "Yass! That was crazy fucking amazing!" Imogen shouted out loud as she gunned the motor on the 600 and raced out of town toward Route 56 and the train crossing at G Road.

With her sister Margaret Rose and little brother Willie in tow, Vivian had headed out that morning to Harry's house for one last goodbye before he moved away from her. She wasn't thrilled about having to bring her siblings along with her, but the only way mother would allow her to borrow the pickup was if she promised to give them a ride to school. It was still too early to drop them off, so she figured she'd have enough time to see Harry off and get back in time. And yet, there was this niggling thought in the back of her mind that wouldn't go away. Imogen's words. Don't drive today and specifically, steer clear of railroad tracks, but to get to Harry's house she'd have to cross the tracks twice. She promised herself she'd be extra, extra careful.

The goodbye was harder than she could have ever imagined. Seeing the empty house and Harry and his family with their belongings loaded into a trailer was more than she could bear. When she returned to the pickup, her eyes red and stinging, she wiped away the tears streaming down her cheeks and with a heavy heart, drove away, realizing this was probably the last time she'd ever see Harry Tabor again. She looked both ways at the railroad crossing. All clear. Turning onto Route 56 as they headed back toward Central City, neither Vivian nor her siblings noticed the black Nash 600 roar past them in the opposite direction.

Even as fast as she was going, Imogen, however, did notice the brown pickup truck with three kids pass her going the other way—and heading back to Central City, thank god! Slowing down she glided the Nash to a stop on the shoulder of the road. Putting it in park, Imogen laid her head upon her arms on the steering wheel and heaved an enormous sigh of relief. She'd been hyperventilating ever since she'd left town. There would be no more tracks for Vivian to cross. She'd beaten the universe.

In the pickup, Vivian began to weep. She had failed to tell Harry something—something important, something she suspected, but wasn't sure about, even though she'd been so tired lately and sick every morning. She had to tell him. Slowing down, Vivian impulsively pulled a U-turn and headed back in the direction of Harry's house.

All at once, a cyclone of emotions erupted within the cramped cab of the pickup. "What are you doing Vivian?" Margaret Rose shrieked at her sister. "Where are you going? We're going to be late for school!"

William joined the chorus of outrage. "Vivian," he wailed. "I'm gonna miss band practice!"

Margaret Rose reached over and clapped her hand over her little brother's mouth. "Shut up Willie," she barked.

At that moment, Imogen glanced up to see the pickup passing her again, but in the other direction—back toward Harry's house—at a fast clip. "Oh my god, no you can't go back! Why are you going back?" she screamed. "Like I said, Vivian, I'll run you off the road if I have to!" Imogen reached out and grasped the clutch jamming the Nash in gear. And then—just like that—the engine stalled.

"No, no, no, no, noooooo," Imogen wailed in panic and desperation as she pumped the gas pedal again and again and again, to no avail.

"Stop! I'm telling," Willie hollered back at his sister as he attempted to pry her hand from his mouth. The wrestling match happening in the front seat was more than Vivian, who was sobbing now, could take.

Behind the waterfall of tears flowing from her eyes and streaming down her cheeks, nose, and throat, the world at that moment in time was a massive, incalculable blur as Vivian navigated the pickup onto G Road, her voice rising briefly above the cacophony of squabbling siblings as she cried out, "Quiet you two!" her words drowned out by the thunderous screeching of metal wheels braking on tracks and the deafening impact of the freight train slamming into the pickup, sending bits and pieces of metal and shards of glass spiraling into the air in all directions.

It was 8:42. Universe 1; Imogen 0. In defeat, Imogen banged her hands against the steering wheel and wept.

As they headed west, away from Central City along Route 56, Harry felt a strange urge to look back. Turning around in his seat he glanced out the back window at the wide, flat expanse of Kansas, the only home he'd ever known, and pondered sadly if he'd ever again see the sunflowers or the angel he'd left behind.

11

On January 7, 1839, members of the French Académie des Sciences were shown an invention that would forever change the nature of visual representation: photography. The astonishingly precise pictures they saw were the work of Louis-Jacques-Mandé Daguerre (1787–1851), a Romantic painter and printmaker most famous until then as the proprietor of the Diorama, a popular Parisian spectacle featuring theatrical painting and lighting effects. Each daguerreotype (as Daguerre dubbed his invention) was a one-of-a-kind image on a highly polished, silver-plated sheet of copper.

The process revealed on that day seemed magical . . .

Kevin McCord was bored. It was a slow day as most workdays at Daguerreian Society headquarters were. As a data monitoring technician in the Department of Temporal Anomalies (DTA), Kevin's primary job was to observe time travel activity, not every minor incident, mind you, but the anomalies—those that fell outside the norm that might constitute unusual activity or arouse suspicion in the real world. Jackson, Kevin's partner, who lovingly referred to him as Kevie, compared the agencies function to that of the Ministry of Magic in the Harry Potter realm or Shield in the Marvel movies—but *real*—its mission: to both monitor and be the guardians of the universe.

On days like this when it was slower than slow, Kevin liked to retrieve a few of the first-person testimonials from the vault to read. The society held a vast library of resources and access to a database of documents, newspapers, and wire services, to which the other part of his job was to serve as a librarian of sorts tasked with overseeing the agencies extensive collection of ephemera. Most of the books, documents, pamphlets, photographs, and newspaper clippings had been digitally archived and easily accessible on the computer, the originals were stored in a dark, temperature-controlled acid free environment.

Today, Kevin had pulled one of the oldest files, dated 1858, Nadir, Paris. Even with the protective white gloves they were required to wear he enjoyed the tactile feel of the aged paper, and experiencing with his own eyes, the beautiful cursive script in its original form.

He began to read the narrative account of Odette Lumiere as reported by her longtime caretaker, Madame Geneviève Renaud:

Odette Lumiere was quite fond of the photographic image her uncle, Gaspard-Félix Tournachon, had recently presented her. Gazing back at her was a girl of 16, powdered and primped and anxious to be noticed. In her later years, she would speak of an enigmatic stranger who had appeared as if by magic transport in her room one day. He seemed confused, but upon his discovery of the lovely, albeit stunned Odette, he was taken by her rare beauty. He was gentlemanly, polite and when he bowed and kissed her hand, she invited him to sit. For several hours they conversed. Mostly, she listened as he spun a fantastic tale of machines and events that Odette could only imagine to be the musings of that of a gifted storyteller or of a madman. When she asked him to stay, he said that he could not and as strangely as he had arrived, he vanished like a phantom, leaving her curious as to whether the incident happened at all.

Kevin had been a traveler once too, but for reasons that no one could explain, he started getting very sick after each time trip. And it was not the normal time travel "hangover" that most people experienced. And when after what would become his final trip, he became so violently ill he was rushed to the hospital and nearly died, he knew that was it, he would never travel through time again. Fortunately, working for the society, though not as satisfying as being a traveler, was the next best thing. He enjoyed reading the firsthand accounts and tracking the journeys of those who could.

According to its public description, the Daguerreian Society, founded in 1988, was an organization of hundreds of individuals and institutions sharing a common interest in the art, history, and practice of the daguerreotype, along with its descendants and variations. Privately, however, the society, which began in the 1830s during photography's infancy, started with only a handful of photographers (chemists) who had control of the medium. A few of them discovered they could naturally time travel; they found each other and formed the group to study the phenomenon.

Over time, as their knowledge base increased, they became the keepers of the universe, essentially, although their mission was to examine the risk and limit their involvement, only stepping in when absolutely necessary. And as technology advanced, they employed sensitive instruments able to detect subtle changes that occurred in the historical timeline and monitor the temporal journeys of time travelers and the time streams they entered. Although they could not possibly observe the routine comings and goings of every single traveler on the planet, their central purpose was threefold: maintain secrecy, educate, and provide traveler assistance whenever possible.

Time travel, like alien abductions was a nebulous premise, so far unproven, and the fodder of which powered internet conspiracy platforms and the grocery store tabloids. The society's challenge was to keep the concept of time travel within the realm of disbelief, hearsay, and conspiracy theories.

Educating time travelers was a lofty but essential goal, and not always achievable. Time travel was interesting and fun but with great power comes great responsibility—something not all time travelers understood or possessed. Although the universe naturally self-corrected, subtle alterations perpetrated by travelers could change the course of people's lives in hidden ways. The society had a name for it: the Misery Index. Something as seemingly innocuous as retrieving a piece of jewelry from the past had the potential to send a ripple effect through the smooth fabric of the cosmos that could cause people to lose wealth or opportunities that might have been used, for example, to educate someone who would say, one day find the cure for cancer.

To explain the Misery Index, the society's employee manual applied the example of a watch: A man works his entire life and is rewarded upon his retirement with an expensive gold watch as a gift from the company. When the man dies his son receives the watch and sells it to purchase a home for his family. That stability is the foundation that establishes their wealth going forward, allowing them to send their daughter to college, perhaps the first in the family to graduate. If that watch, however, were to be stashed away by a time traveler, not only might this family never achieve financial stability, but the world would suffer the small but potentially significant loss of wealth as well.

This ripple effect that changed the dynamic of that family, could change the outcome of everyone connected to the watch. For instance, the man who would have purchased the watch for his store no longer has a very expensive watch to sell to someone else. As a result, his business fails, he starts drinking, his wife divorces him. One can imagine if everyone was making these slight modifications, the Misery Index would be more than noticeable as items disappeared from circulation and the world became poorer. When and if the watch does eventually resurface, wealth would return to the world but never as much as its absence cost.

The third prong in the society's mission—providing traveler assistance, was another challenging goal. A clear known was that an anchor photograph was necessary for a traveler to safely navigate between the target destination in the past and their home base in the present. If an anchor photo should be destroyed, a traveler with no portal to return through could become stranded or stuck within that time. Finding these unlucky travelers was unfortunately not an exact science. Certain recurring loop notifications might be detected, and a field agent could be dispatched to help, but only a handful of cases had been resolved. The Society did not have nearly enough field agents to investigate every single anomaly.

Again, the universe was self-correcting, but there were instances where things could go awry, unusual events could alter history or people's lives in such a way that might be noticeable. It was looking out for the huge blips, but it was also monitoring a known time-traveler's activities over time.

Kevin glanced up at his monitor. While he had been reading, a curious anomaly had popped up on the screen. From the co-ordinates, it was coming from a Kansas 1946 time stream. Kevin zoomed in for more detailed information:

```
    Suspected attempt to interfere with recorded
historical train accident incident. Traveler Name:
#082858 Imogen Oliver.
```

"Hmmm, interesting," he said as he typed the name into the search bar and a record popped up. Although they kept electronic records, Kevin found that using paper files suited him better, probably in the same way he liked the tactile feel of the original documents. After returning Ms. Odette Lumiere's file to the secured vault, Kevin went to the row of file cabinets to retrieve Traveler #082858's file.

Kevin carried the file over to his desk to spread out and properly peruse. In due course, he discovered that hers was an interesting case with connections to other travelers. The agency had launched a separate file on her in the late 2010s when she had started up a private investigator business, Dead Relatives, Inc. A paper-clipped note indicated that there were separate related files on her parents: Niles Oliver (#032522) and Francis (#101027) Oliver, both professional photographers, who were known travelers, but nothing more on them after 1997, as well as a mention of her grandmother, Iris Graham Oliver, who had a connection to famous early 20th century French photographer André Mimieux. It was not clear whether she may have been a traveler too. And before the 2000s, the society's tracking technology was not as advanced as it is today. Imogen Oliver didn't show up again in records until 2005 when she had traveled once, and then not again after that incident until she started her business, presumably around the time she had discovered that she had time travel capabilities.

However, she did have an interesting connection to Theodore (Teddy) Diamond (Traveler #051395) and his mother Mimi

Pinky Diamond. Kevin snorted. What kind of a name was Mimi Pinky anyway?

Kevin got up and retrieved his file from the cabinet and brought it over to his desk. Teddy Diamond, with whom the society had been keeping close tabs on, was a known traveler who kept a low profile, using aliases and primarily traveling to stock his pawn shop with unopened, never-before owned collectibles, and never using information for personal gain or passing information along to others who might do so. Three months ago, however, Teddy had disappeared under mysterious circumstances. And interestingly, in the notes it appeared the Society had been preparing to recruit Teddy before he vanished. It was standard practice to invite seasoned travelers into the fold to be able to better monitor their activity, for their "safety," but to also ensure they weren't doing anything unethical.

In Diamond's case, it looked like there were some unanswered questions. First was a handwritten notation briefly describing an ongoing investigation into a notebook that may or may not be in Teddy's possession, possibly of great value, and a last name of Eastman underlined three times. Next, a copy of an attached news clipping.

October 9, 1997--Tiffany Rose Van Elder, an 17-year-old high school senior was reported missing Thursday evening by her parents. The Albany High School senior left her western Oregon home around 7 a.m. and was expected at school. She did not arrive for class, or return home that day setting off an intense search for the missing teenager, which is currently underway. Lane County Police are urging anyone who may have knowledge about her disappearance to contact them immediately.

Van Elder was not a traveler, but it had been noted in the file that she had been dating Diamond at the time of her disappearance, which coincided with his first known jumps. Kevin wondered if there was a connection between the Oliver's and Tiffany Van Elder—they had all gone missing the same year, 1997. He pulled a highlighter from his desk drawer and underscored the dates.

A final item noted that since Mr. Diamond's disappearance, his mother, Mimi Pinky Diamond, had become quite vocal about the existence of time travel. Field agents who had been monitoring her actions, observed that she had been contacting news reporters and anyone else who would listen to her story about time travelers living among us. For the most part, though, she had been mostly unsuccessful in her efforts as news outlets had not been at all interested in promoting her wild allegations. She had been dismissed as a non-threat.

Ms. Oliver, however, was a bit of a problem. She made mistakes. According to the record, although it was inconclusive, agents suspected she may have revealed to subjects she had come in contact within the past that she was from the future causing larger than usual ripples and disturbances on the time continuum.

Kevin shifted in his office chair. His stomach growled, loudly. He looked at his watch. 12:30. Jackson packed his lunch every day, usually a deli meat sandwich, chips, fruit, and a surprise snack treat like a candy bar or a piece of carrot cake. Normally, he went down to the break room to eat and chat with his coworkers Norman Bolger and Kristi Chase, also technicians, but decided he better take lunch at his desk today, in case any additional info came in. He checked his email and played a couple rounds of Solitaire while he ate.

When he logged back into the work screen at 1:07 p.m. more details had indeed come in about her latest incident. For whatever reason, perhaps to test the universe, traveler #082858 Oliver may have tried to interfere with the outcome of a teenage girl. Historical records showed that the girl in question—Vivian Littlefield, age 16, died Oct. 12, 1946, in an auto-train collision. Her sister Margaret Rose, age 14 died two days later. The data indicated that she had made attempts to alter the events, albeit unsuccessfully, but her efforts had once again shown up as an anomaly.

Kevin hit the PRINT key to add a paper version to the file and was on his way to the printer room to retrieve it when he heard loud beeping coming from his monitor. Grabbing the printout, he hurried back to his desk. On-screen, was an anomaly, but unlike any he'd ever seen before. This was a bright crimson, vigorously flashing dot that danced erratically across the screen. Unlike your typical anomaly alert which stayed in a static position, this one was jumping crazily from one place to another in rapid succession.

"What's this? This is new," Kevin said aloud, baffled by the anomaly's jarring combo of sound, appearance, and unpredictable behavior. He tried to scroll over it with his cursor, but it moved too quickly making it virtually impossible to get a reading on it. Even more surprising, was the sudden unexpected entry into the room of his boss Caleb Willis. Willis was a society muckety-muck, a corporate higher up who would never, ever in a million years venture down here to Kevin's floor unless it was something really important.

"What's happening here McCord?" he barked at Kevin who was frantically still trying to pinpoint the moving dot's location.

"I'm not sure Mr. Willis!" he answered, hoping that he could gain some control here to impress one of the bosses.

"Out of the way," Willis asserted, physically pushing Kevin out of his seat. Kevin slinked off to the corner as two more higher ups—Kevin could not recall their names—burst into the office and stood behind Willis in front of the squawking, blinking monitor.

"What is it?" one shouted at Willis as the other one clapped his hands over his ears to quell the noise.

"Don't know, the universe has gone mad" he shouted back at him, "but it's big, that much I can tell!"

Willis finally gave up trying to track the dot and chaos that reigned for several more minutes before the blinking dot simply stopped moving. It continued to flash but the angry alarm ceased at last, and silence filled up the room.

"Oh, thank god that stopped," said the one who had covered his ears.

Willis moved the cursor where the now static dot had finally settled. The three men and Kevin, who had moved in closer for a better look, leaned in to read the single message that appeared on the screen:

```
   Multiple jumps recorded between temporal time
streams - east coast August 26, 1970; Midwest Oc-
tober 2, 1946; Germany October 1, 1946; west coast
December 17, 1913. Traveler Name: case# unknown
Simon Le Bon Elliot
```

Willis looked at the others, who were looking back at him, bewilderment etched across each face before shouting excitedly, "Multiple jumps guys! We got ourselves a goddamn Manifold Outlier!"

The normally unassertive, Kevin blurted, "What the fuck is a Manifold Outlier?"

12

After the crunching, sickening, ear-exploding sound of impact between train and pickup stopped, an eerie silence consumed the void. Imogen knew that William was badly hurt. Instinctively, she reached for the key in the ignition hoping the engine would roar to life, sensing it would not. Devastated, defeated, stalled, and too far away to get to the scene on foot, Imogen sat numb and motionless in the car, awaiting the emergency vehicles that would surely be coming at any moment. Within 15 minutes, police cars, an ambulance, and a firetruck, lights whirling and sirens blaring, thundered past her. She tried the key again, anticipating a different result. She was right.

Without the cosmos pushing back to stop her, the engine turned over easily. The universe had won. It had no need to delay Imogen Oliver any further. Putting the Nash in gear, Imogen turned the car around and headed back in the direction of Central City. She did not need to see the wreckage. She already knew the outcome. Nothing left to do now but go home.

Back at the hotel, Imogen placed Loretta's car keys on the kitchen table along with a note tucked underneath thanking her for all she'd done to make Imogen feel welcome. Slipping upstairs to her room, she packed her camera in her handbag. These were the only two items she had arrived with, and they were all she would be taking back. Yesterday, she had mailed the experimental roll of film to a rented postal box located near her home office for retrieval when she returned. Taking a last look around the room, she looked over at the freshly starched and ironed uniform with the green piping, the bleached clean apron, and hat hanging on a hanger in the closet. She had promised Darla she would return it to the café after it had been laundered but evidently Loretta had taken it upon herself to iron it and hang it up. Imogen hoped she would remember to return it as well.

Seated on the edge of the bed, feet planted firmly on the floor, she closed her eyes and concentrated on the photograph of Kansas back in her rented office space. Her stomach lurched and even with her eyes closed she could sense the creeping shadows as the gaping vortex of time opened and swallowed her up.

She arrived unceremoniously in the office on her hands and knees, retching. At once, she crawled to the toilet to finish. This was weird. She had not had such a violent reentry like this in a long time. Exhausted and sick, Imogen collapsed on the couch. Tossing a blanket across her legs, she closed her eyes, and an unexpected thought streaked bright across her brain like a comet: *I don't want to go home.* What? Imogen thought. Where did that come from? Out of the blue, something else, another random word. *Andaman Sea.* Andaman Sea? What the hell? Where was that? Had she been there? Why was she thinking of it now? Puzzled, she dismissed it as she waited for her stomach to settle down. But then, it hit her. Of course! Several months earlier while going through her dad's office desk, she'd found a stack of photographs labeled "Andaman Sea."

Still feeling woozy and out of sorts, Imogen was careful to get up slowly from the couch where she made her way over to the metal file cabinet next to the desk. Rifling through various work-related papers, she came across what she was looking for at the back of a drawer, a stack of bundled photos held together with a single rubber band. Before tossing them in the file cabinet, she recalled thinking she'd go through them later, but had never gotten around to it. Looking at the stack, another memory slid into her brain, of her mom and dad talking about an island they had visited. She couldn't recall whether they'd both visited it or individually or even when, but the name had been tossed around.

It was abundantly clear as she sorted through the photos it was a stunningly gorgeous place—an ideal spot really to hide if that's what one needed to do. At this point, she wanted nothing more than to hide away and give herself time and space to deal with what had just happened in Kansas. She certainly wasn't ready to go home and face Simon or to resume her normal life as if nothing had happened. And most of all, she wasn't prepared to deliver the sad news about Vivian and her sister to Harrison Tabor. It might have been easier had she not become involved with each of them on such a personal level. Her mistake, but she had done it and there was no changing that now.

Perhaps decompressing after trips was the purpose of her parent's trips too. Traveling into the past was not only hard on you physically but it screwed with your head sometimes too. Whatever, she thought. All she needed was a soft bed and a nice tiki bar where she could order Manhattan's and chill for a few days.

Powering up the laptop on the desk Imogen did a quick search for Andaman Sea. Wikipedia described it as a sea bordering Myanmar and Thailand with several islands that were part of an archipelago in the northeastern Indian Ocean. Perfect. Clutching the assortment of photographs Imogen slumped back in the desk chair. She was drained and still feeling a little bit queasy but the idea of resting on the sand under a warm, tropical sun, a gentle wind blowing; the Zen-like ebb and flow of the waves—similar to what she and Simon had experienced a few short months ago on their trip to Kauai—tugged hard at her. No, she debated with herself; she should go home. She had things to do, responsibilities; she shouldn't worry Simon, although the way time travel worked, a much-needed week away would only cost about an hour of Simon's worry time.

"Screw it," she said aloud, as she pulled one of the photos from the stack. On the back in Niles' handwriting, "Bakunawa."

A layer of soft, squishy sand embraced her body, cradling her in warmth. The calming sound of ocean waves breaking in the surf and palm leaves rustling in the tropical breeze soothed her yearning soul, and yet, something about it didn't feel right. From above she heard a sort of low humming sound like a plane engine—perhaps carrying whoever had taken this picture, but it was what she heard coming from all around that concerned her most—many loud and angry overlapping voices speaking in a language she did not understand. Afraid to open her eyes but knowing she had to, above her a group of scantily dressed, bow-wielding natives came into focus. Imogen was confused. What was this? Had she dropped in on a movie set? Who were these people?

She had taken an anthropology course in college and learned that a few remote untouched tribes of people still existed. Could this be one of those? She wanted to sit up but was afraid that any sudden movement might set them off. They looked fierce and plenty hostile. Gradually drawing herself up, she raised her arms slowly indicating surrender. One of the men came extremely close to her face and began to interrogate her in a language she did not understand.

"Fte uko chea? ftch uko chea toko? ftoko xe chea yequo wkequ? ftoko ij cheak zeuh?" *(Who are you? Why are you here? Where do you come from? Where is your boat?)*

A second man lunged at her shouting in her face, "Poh'j ripp bado!" *(Let's kill her!)*

Several others picked up the mantra, "Poh'j ripp bado! Poh'j ripp bado! Poh'j ripp bado!" and their voices rose to a fevered pitch in a menacing synchronic chant.

Although she did not understand the words, it was apparent that the natives were quite agitated and probably instigating violence against her. The best course of action at this point would be to concentrate hard, as hard as she ever had in her life, on the photo back home, ignore whatever ugly words they were shouting at her, and get the hell out of there . . . fast, but before she could begin, an elderly Native, arms raised above his head, stepped forward. Gesturing at the others, he said, "ne! fuih! i tugo joon tok bado zoweko. Ih ij hto bado ew nipoj Niles. *(No! Wait! I have seen this face before. It is the face of Niles.)*

"What??!" Imogen heard herself crying out, "What did you say? Did you say Niles? Niles, he is my father, my *father*!"

The older man, D'ar, made an attempt to imitate the sound Imogen was making. "Fa-tur, Niles?" he asked.

"Yes, yes! Imogen said, clasping her hands and arms together in a cradling a baby gesture and then pointing to herself. "I am Imogen, Niles' daughter."

The elder sounded out: "Im-oo-gen" and then turned to the others and said, "Jto ij hto xuavthok ew nipoj." (*She is daughter of Niles*). With that, they all began to nod, a couple of them even displayed toothy smiles. A good sign. Imogen nervously sighed with relief. Maybe at least they weren't going to toss her on the spit and barbecue her for supper, not right now anyway.

The elder extended his hand, which Imogen took. Helping her up, he said, "Ome, ome Im-oo-gen, xuavthok ew nipoj Niles." (*Come Imogen, daughter of Niles*)

Gesturing to her, he summoned her to follow him into the rain forest, navigating a course through tall grasses, palms, deciduous trees, and wild orchids, and candlewoods. A short walk from the beach they come to a small clearing and an overgrown shelter which looked as though it had not been inhabited by anyone for some years. Built with mangrove wood it was nearly buried in flora. Stepping forward, the elder pulled palm fronds from the structure and gestured for Imogen to enter. Still quite nervous, Imogen was hesitant to go in. Was this a prison? Were they planning to hold her captive? Sensing her reluctance, the elder entered the shelter first, waving for her to follow.

"Ome yequo fihtin" (*Come within*). Imogen had to stoop to enter the small enclosure. Once inside, it was quite cozy and in the far corner was a small bed, constructed of sturdy bamboo. But the thing that made her gasp was the pair of black canvas Converse All Stars sitting on the floor next to the bed. Dad's shoes. Imogen turned to the elder and asked, "Niles?" He nodded.

As she moved in for a closer look, on a wooden chair were a pair of reading glasses, a yellowing notebook, and a writing instrument, a thinly shaved piece of charcoal. Imogen was astonished that everything was still here as though awaiting his return, that her dad, Niles had been here, stayed here, lived among these people. Seeing his personal possessions like this brought back memories of him along with a wave of emotions that caught her off guard. How she missed him. Tears began to involuntarily spill down her cheeks. Seeing her reaction, the tribe's elder touched her hand. "Jhuch toko, kojh" (*Stay here, rest*).

Imogen did not understand the words, but the kindness and concern written in his face was universal. Considering that Niles' things had been preserved and untouched here, it seemed clear that he had been fond of her father and, in turn, was eager to welcome his daughter in the same way. Smiling, he turned and left the hut, leaving Imogen alone with her father's notebook.

How long had it been since he had been here? Imogen wondered. It could be 20 years ago or yesterday, depending on what photograph he came through, but considering the condition of the faded and yellowing pages of the notebook, it had to have been many years. Imogen sat down in the bamboo chair, opened Niles' notebook, and began to read.

At first, the Native peoples I encountered on the island were hostile. I feared for my life, but something dissuaded them from killing me, why? I'm not certain, but I believe now they were either curious about me or afraid of me. I did not understand their language but through a rudimentary method of pointing at objects I was able to discern a few words. One word, zeuh *I quickly learned meant boat, which they used quite often when speaking to me, which was in tandem with another word,* quuviy*. It occurred to me then that what they kept asking me was "Where is your boat?" The only means of getting to this island is by boat and because I didn't have one, I took the word quuviy to mean magic or sorcery. I believe they viewed me as some sort of god or magical traveler, which very likely saved my life.*

Reading her father's words, made Imogen ache for him. She could hear him speaking in his calm, measured voice. Niles was a scholar. His desire to learn, his quest for adventure, and his curiosity and sense of wonder about the world around him knew no bounds; he had instilled that same sense of inquisitiveness about everything in his only daughter, and she loved him for that. She also suddenly appreciated that unlike Simon, who grew up without a father, she at least had hers for nine years and was so grateful for the time they had together. Reading his notebook made her feel close to him again, a feeling she had pushed away before to avoid the pain, but it also contained something that would prove quite useful in Imogen's efforts to communicate with the tribe—a glossary of common words Niles had compiled.

Despite the scary first encounter, the Native people of the island could not have been warmer and more welcoming. Each day they invited her to dine with them on a bounty of fruits, from papaya and mango to plantain and figs. They roasted wild boar and entertained her with an array of impressive dance and drumming performances. A couple of the young girls showed Imogen how to weave using palm fronds and to make beaded bracelets from seeds they had collected. The best part, in Imogen's opinion was a concoction they made called "quuntuhhun." It wasn't quite as cosmopolitan as a Manhattan and it didn't come with a fancy paper umbrella, but it was exceptionally delicious, not to mention quite potent. They were curious and friendly but also seemed to step back to give Imogen her space, seeming to understand that the reason she was here was for rest and reflection.

For the first time in months, Imogen allowed herself the time and space to do that; to breathe, to reflect, without distraction. Along with spending time with the islanders, she took long walks on the beach, watched sunrises and sunsets and added her own thoughts to her father's notebook. The simplicity of handwriting her feelings on paper was therapeutic. It forced her to slow down, dig deep, let go.

Niles had evidently used his time there for the same purpose. Some of his entries centered on her mother. It appeared that they were facing some challenges in their marriage. Niles wrote that aside from their common interest in their daughter, they had stopped talking to one another, that Francis had grown distant and how he missed their conversations, how it used to be. He pondered whether there was any hope of salvaging their marriage. It made Imogen sad, not only that it was happening, but that she hadn't been aware of it, as children rarely are.

The time also forced her to see how much she had avoided ever properly mourning her parents, and now, with the knowledge that they weren't dead at all and might still be alive and living in another time somewhere out there, gnawed at her insides. At least believing they were dead had given her some measure of closure; not knowing their fates was far worse. She vowed to search harder for them. There could be a news clipping or a census record or something about them out there that might offer a clue to their whereabouts, perhaps lead her to the time they were trapped in.

Avoidance was much on her mind too when it came to Simon. She had to concede that for the past few months, she had been using her job as a way to sidestep discussing their relationship. He seemed to be enjoying his hobbies and ever since Fletcher befriended him, he'd seemed happier. Yet Imogen worried that it wasn't enough, that *she* wasn't enough. Could he truly be happy living in her present?

And finally, Imogen pondered whether this whole time-travel business was even right for her. After the catastrophe in Kansas, she wasn't so sure anymore. She had been vaguely aware that recorded history couldn't be changed, but the temptation to test it was strong and look how it had ended up. Despite all her efforts to change things, to create a happy ending, Vivian and Margaret Rose died anyway. And getting to know them on a personal level had been her biggest mistake of all. It is one thing to be in the present and know that the people in the past are dead and gone, but to go back and meet those people in their time, witnessing them vibrant and living, they become real; not a statistic, not a memory, not just another name etched onto a gravestone—but real people with feelings and emotions and opinions.

Thinking about the past few weeks she'd spent in Central City, getting to know Harry and Vivian, Margaret Rose and Darla and Stretch and Loretta brought her to tears. They were more than characters in some time travel scenario. They were friends. She knew them and cared for them and missed them now. Imogen vowed to never again get involved in the lives of the people that she interacted with in the past, no matter how much she thought she wanted to help them. She simply could not allow herself to become emotionally entangled. It was too hard. It was too sad.

Time travel had been fun and exciting, an amazing adventure at first, but the more she learned, the more it seemed she doubted herself and her own intentions. Was she doing more harm than good? Was she truly making a difference in her client's lives? Why not look for a real job? She could teach history, but would that really make her happier?

And yet, much to her chagrin, Imogen couldn't seem to quell the lingering, unanswered questions that continued to float around in her mind—things she still wanted to test out but knew she shouldn't for fear the answers might turn out to be as devastating as seeing firsthand how the universe would not allow recorded history to be changed. No matter what, that freight train, on that date, was going to collide with Vivian's pickup, but what about history that had been recorded but was ambiguous or lacking details? For instance, a murder where there was no eyewitness or a fire where no bodies were found? Could history be changed in those cases? She didn't have to make a decision now, but it was something to consider moving forward.

That night, Imogen dreamed that Vivian and her sister didn't die. The train wreck never happened because Imogen had successfully stopped it. In it, an unwed Vivian gives birth to Harry's baby but is shunned by the community. Skipping ahead in time, her boy is now a teenager. He is a menace and a bully and ends up murdering several people.

The dream sequence shifted again. Imogen was sitting on the beach with her own mother, who turned to her and said, "The universe does what it must, Imogen, and the worst isn't always the very worst."

Imogen wasn't sure what the dream meant, but she was certain it was time for her to go home now. Time to face Simon and Harrison Tabor; time to begin searching for her parents in earnest; time to make some hard decisions about her future.

13

After her restful reprieve on Andaman, Imogen's return trip to the present was much improved, less bumpy, no vomiting on arrival. It made her wonder if there was a correlation between how rough or smooth a return trip was depending on the trauma one may or may not have experienced while engaged in the past. Geez, there was so much to learn about time travel, so much she still didn't know, notwithstanding her little failed experiment with trying to change the outcome of a tragedy. She quickly shoved that unpleasant memory from her mind. She was curious to see how the photography experiment turned out though. Would both rolls—the one she'd left in the camera and the one she'd mailed—come out?

One thing was certain, time moved slower when you were in another time. After all that had happened in Kansas and then on the island it seemed like she had been gone for weeks and weeks, when in fact, it had been only hours. Even more so than the physical trip itself, that's what made returning to the present so jarring. Weeks, months, years of memories and events condensed into real time took time to process. She wasn't sure she'd ever get used to that part, but the recovery time following a trip had its advantages in that it provided guilt-free time to wrap up a few things before returning home to real life, and Simon.

Knowing that she could not use that specific picture again Imogen filed the Andaman photo away in the USED PHOTOGRAPHS file. She wasn't quite ready to call Harrison Tabor with the news about Vivian, but she did want to see if there was anything new in the newspapers about the accident. She turned her desk computer on and navigated to the newspaper site where she'd found the original brief. It was still there, and it read the same. This confirmed it. She had changed nothing. But a second headline also caught her eye:

CAT SNARLS DOWNTOWN TRAFFIC

CENTRAL CITY, October 13-- Traffic was snarled for several hours on Thursday when Mrs. Harriet Gilbert's cat ran into traffic on Main Street.

Swerving to miss the cat, Grover Vineman crossed the center line, hit an oncoming car driven by Gladys Mooney, and dumped his entire payload of dirt onto the street, causing traffic to back up until the vehicles could be towed and the dirt removed from the street.

Neither Vineman nor Mooney sustained any injuries in the collision. Mrs. Gilbert reported she later found "Whiskers" safe and sound and hiding under her porch.

Imogen snickered. Despite witnessing this craziness firsthand and remembering her own panic in the moment when all this occurred, reading it now was nothing short of comical. A comedy of errors! How many small-town stories had she read just like this one where it seemed that everything that could go wrong, went wrong—Murphy's Law! It seemed too outlandish to be true, or was it the universe on autocorrect? One could only speculate. She was happy that Whiskers was unscathed anyway.

Turning off her computer and locking up the office, Imogen's next stop, the post office to see if the film she'd mailed was still waiting for her after 70-some years.

Imogen loved going to the post office downtown. With its marble flooring and high ceilings, and rows upon rows of postal boxes lining the wall, it was a comforting marvel. Because the universe wouldn't let you use the same place for retrieval, she had to rent a new box under an alias every time she needed to send something forward from the past, but it was fairly easy to keep track of it and postal workers didn't care if your name was Imogen Oliver or Rumpelstiltskin, they'd rent a post office box to anyone. As long as she knew that the post office was still standing in her own time she could essentially pay for a box in perpetuity.

Inserting the key into this new box 113, she was happy to see that the package she'd sent in 1946 had arrived intact. When she gently pulled it out, something else tumbled out from the box and fell to the floor; a letter, addressed to Imogen Oliver. "What's this?" Imogen whispered aloud. This wasn't supposed to happen. There should *not* be anything in here but the package she had mailed containing the roll of film. Imogen felt the anxiety rising. Who could have known to send something to her at this PO box?

Reaching down she plucked the plain white envelope from the floor and turned it over in her hands. It was old like the package but curiously, the mail date stamp read 1973 and there was no return address. Imogen quickly locked the postal box and hurried out to her car. She carefully opened the envelope and removed the letter from inside. She unfolded it and read the brief handwritten note:

Dear Imogen,
I hope you don't mind, but when you were here, I copied down the PO box number from the package you were mailing so that I could contact you. I could be wrong about you, but I thought I'd take a chance anyway.

If you're ever in 1973, look me up.

Your friend,
Loretta Ross

"Oh," Imogen gasped. Loretta was a time traveler. It was a surprise, but also explained a lot about Loretta's rather forward-thinking behavior. She'd never met another traveler, well, aside from Teddy although she didn't know it at the time. I wonder what she was doing in 1946, Imogen thought. Hmmm, so she'd traveled to 1946 from her current time of 1973. It seemed so weird to think that in 1946, they were roughly the same age, yet Loretta was probably about 45 years older than Imogen. "Wrap your head around that one," Imogen said to herself before grabbing her phone and typing "Loretta Ross" into the search bar.

A fairly common name, many Loretta Rosses came up, but

which one? As she scrolled through, one entry leapt out at her: Loretta Ross, 1947–2013, author of *Love on the Kansas Prairie*. She clicked on what appeared to be an obituary.

Loretta Ross, celebrated author of 37 historical romance novels, died of cancer at the age of 66. Known for her highly detailed and descriptive novels set in small towns across the US, Ross' first novel "Love on the Kansas Prairie" published in 1976, about teenage love in 1946 Kansas, was critically received. Other novels followed, including "New Mexico Enchantment," "Green Mountain Romance," "My Sweet Magnolia," Winter of the Midnight Sun, et.al.

"Ross' writing is remarkably researched and descriptive, almost as if she herself experienced the times and settings and lived the lives of the characters she created.
– Margorie Brown, *New York Times* Book reviewer

Imogen looked up from her phone and stared out the window. "Wow." If that was the Loretta Ross she had encountered in Central City, it was quite possibly she was there researching her first novel set in Kansas. Could she have modeled her characters for the book after Harry and Vivian and Margaret Rose and Iris, Imogen's grandmother! Excited to read it, Imogen searched for the book online and ordered a copy. But when she finished, excitement turned to sorrow with the depressing realization that her friend was no longer alive. How nice might it have been to meet her now and find out all about her life and perhaps even learn from another fellow traveler. It always hurt thinking that the people she met in the past were often long dead in her present. She tried not to think about that too much. But still, she could always travel back to 1973 and look her up. Loretta had invited her, and maybe one of these days she would!

Setting the letter aside, Imogen started up the car and headed to her next stop, Jet's Photography to drop off the rolls of film—from her camera and the one in the package that she'd mailed to herself from Kansas.

After waiting an hour for the film to be being developed, Imogen came away disappointed with the results. "Shoot!" she said as she opened the first envelope containing the pictures developed from the roll she'd left in the camera. All of them were a bust. She had taken random pictures of sunflowers and buildings, landscapes, cars, people on the street—none of which came out. You could see shadows and vague outlines, but for the most part nothing in them was distinguishable, and they were all cloudy with a smattering of what looked like small dust particles. She wasn't terribly surprised that the film might not make it through time. She wasn't sure about the science of it, but she suspected that there was a lot of transformation going on inside the Brownie camera of 1946 as it shifted to the modern point-and-shoot camera she'd taken with her and the Kodak film inside returning to 35 millimeter. Maybe next time she would try finding a vintage camera to take back with her, see if that would make a difference.

Setting those aside, she opened the second envelope containing the pictures from the roll she'd mailed from Kansas to herself. Gazing back at her, frozen in time, wearing bobby socks and saddles shoes were three young girls: Vivian, Margaret Rose, and Iris Graham . . . Grammy. Imogen couldn't help it, it brought her to tears seeing them here together in the photograph, so vibrant and alive; knowing that all three were gone. Imogen grabbed a tissue from the glove box and wiped her eyes as she looked at the next photos—pictures of a young Harry Tabor, laughing and joking with the girls at the river; the four of them, posing with their heads together at the diner; photos of Darla and Stretch. Imogen paused at the next picture. Loretta, sitting on the blanket they'd laid out on the banks of the river for a picnic. She was smiling, being silly, her hand raised in a cheesy slow-motion parade float wave.

Imogen stared blankly out the window. At this moment she would never think of pictures in the same way again. Of course, she knew that all those baskets of discarded photographs and postcards in the antique shops were real people with real lives, people who had existed once, who had lived and breathed and danced and cried and fell in love and had children and grandchildren. But suddenly, it felt all too real and so, so overwhelming.

Imogen prided herself in being brave, an expert at keeping her feelings locked safely inside. Even after promising herself on the island to open up, let it out, move on, why was she still torturing herself? Would she ever find the courage to let someone in or would her irrational fear of one day losing the people she loved prevent her from ever getting too close? she wondered as she tucked the pictures back into the envelope, started up the car, and headed out of the parking lot for home.

14

Pulling into her driveway, Imogen felt a surge of relief. It was good to be home at last. On the drive over she was still trying to process it all—Kansas, Andaman, the photographs, the letter from Loretta. She didn't have a good poker face, at all. It would not be easy to keep from telling Simon about all of it. And why didn't she want to tell him? she wondered. The time on the island had been therapeutic, for sure, but for some reason, she didn't feel ready yet. So much had happened, so many details and unresolved emotions. She was exhausted from thinking about it herself, let alone retelling the story to someone else, even if it was Simon. All she really wanted at this point was a warm shower and to sleep in her own bed.

After unlocking the front door and dropping the keys in the bowl by the door, she entered the living room. "Hi guys," she said, a little irritated to see Fletcher again so soon. "What's going on?"

Their heads tucked together like a couple of schoolgirls discussing something, they both turned to look at the same time. Fletcher managed a wave and a weak "Hi."

Simon arose from the couch. "Hello darling," he said cheerfully. Something seemed off, suspect.

"You two are becoming as thick as thieves," Imogen noted as she glanced past them around the room. She had meant for it to come off in a jokey kind of way, but instead, it came out sounding sarcastic.

The thing she noticed first was the mess. It looked like a cyclone hit the living room. Pillows were strewn here and there and everywhere. The rug was skewing sideways and flipped up in one corner. Open encyclopedia books were spread out all over the floor. Imogen was annoyed.

"What's been going on here?" she asked Simon, who had backed away, deciding that maybe it wasn't the best time to approach her.

Before he could answer, Fletcher stood up. "I should probably get going," he said to Simon.

"Thank you for dropping by," Simon said nervously.

"um, yeah, I'll see you soon, Simon. You too Imogen," he said. Imogen gave Fletcher a look as he filed past her to the front door.

At first, after Fletcher had gone, Imogen didn't say anything, instead sending Simon a questioning glance as she surveyed the room with raised eyebrows and hands. "Well?"

Simon seemed nervous as though searching for an explanation. "I'm sorry about this. Uh, Fletcher and I had a wrestle."

Imogen was taken aback. "A wrestle? You two had a wrestle? What does that even mean?"

Simon struggled for a good answer. "A wrestle, you know, we were wrestling one another . . . for sport."

"For sport?"

He nodded. "Yyyyess, that's correct."

Imogen wasn't sure how to respond to that. "Um, okay then," she said as she began plucking the pillows up off the floor one by one and tossing them back onto the couch.

"What's this?" she said, as she stooped to pick up a photograph that was lying face down on the floor. Turning it over, she let out a tiny gasp. It was one she had never seen in the album before—a picture of Harry and Vivian sitting together in a booth at the diner, probably one that Grammy had taken. She had a camera too, as Imogen recalled.

"It dropped out of your grandmother's album," Simon said. "I must have forgotten to put it back." Imogen pressed it back between the album pages and then noticed on the fireplace mantle leaning upright against a book, a second photograph that she had never seen before either.

"Is that you and your mother?" she asked.

"Oh, yes, I-I found it when I was digging in the garden," Simon stumbled. Knowing how he still grieved the loss of his mother, Imogen imagined how hard that must have been on Simon to come across yet another photograph she'd hidden. She honestly didn't want to be angry with him about the mess, but damn, she'd only been away for a couple of days. Simon took a step toward her.

"I apologize for the condition of the room," he offered. "I'm such a bonehead. Fletcher and I, well he wanted to demonstrate karate movements and we began to get nutty and soon we were romping about and the next thing I knew I was on the floor, and we had made quite the mess, I'm afraid." He stared down at his feet, feeling terrible about the room, but even worse about the egregious lie he had just fed Imogen. "We had only moved to the couch when you came in," he lied.

Imogen couldn't help but giggle. "So what you're telling me is Fletcher was showing you karate moves and you got into a wrestle together?"

Simon nodded. It was close to the truth. He had been traveling from one place in time to another, and Fletcher had gotten down on the floor and wrestled with him trying to help him, which didn't fully explain the water spilled on the floor that he'd tossed in his face to revive him, but Imogen hadn't noticed that yet. He quickly scooted the rug back into place with his foot to hide it, hoping to mop it up as soon as she left the room. The karate part he made up, but that was a minor detail, he figured.

"Alright," Imogen said smiling. "I forgive you, but no more wrestling in the living room when I'm gone!" It was hard to stay mad at Simon. He was so darn charming. Yet, at the same time, it gave her an excuse not to have to deal with explaining the whole Kansas fiasco to him right now. Planting a kiss on his forehead, she headed off to the bathroom for a shower.

Simon had fallen asleep reading on the couch, snoring, a book lying face down on his chest. Imogen needed to check her email, but she was curious about that photograph that had been on the floor. Tiptoeing by the sleeping Simon, she pulled the album from the shelf and took it back with her to the bedroom. Tucked into one of the pages, she pulled it out to take a closer look. As with the ones she'd developed, this one too had a hazy, grainy look and those strange particles on the surface. If this new picture had shown up what other items might have Grammy saved from 1946? She couldn't recall seeing anything before, but it was worth checking.

After Grammy died, Imogen had painstakingly gone through all of her lovely possessions, keeping a few sentimental items for herself, giving away some of it, and lovingly storing other mementos away in labeled bins in the garage. Dragging the ladder out from the corner, she climbed up to the eaves to get the bins. There were four in all, some were laden with books and dishes and pictures in fancy frames, others were filled up with textiles and pressed flowers and letters and the like. After retrieving each one, she pulled up a stool and began to carefully rummage through them. She didn't know what she was looking for exactly, but so far, everything seemed to be unchanged from when she'd packed it all up years ago, that is until she got to the third bin—the one that contained Grammy's diaries. Grammy had kept a total of three, but now there was a fourth that Imogen didn't recognize. Bright red and frayed around its edges as if it had been heavily used, it appeared to also have come from a different era than the others.

Imogen gently unhooked the tattered clasp and opened it. At the front it read: "Property of" and in a youthful scrawl the name: Vivian Littlefield. Also, inside was a note. Imogen recognized the handwriting.

According to the date, it had been penned by Grammy on

November 17, 1946, and it read:

This is the diary of my friend Vivian Littlefield, who with her sister Margaret Rose, was killed in a terrible train accident. The day of the funeral, I took it from her room because she told me that if anything ever happened to her, she didn't want anybody to read it. I promised I would I keep it safe.
Iris Graham

Imogen refolded the note and began to scroll through the diary. Most of the entries chronicled the usual mundane events—gossip, school, subjects she was doing well in and not doing so well in, teachers, friends, football games, and expressions of love for a boy named Harry Tabor.

"I met Harrison Tabor on the bus this morning. I think I like him."
"Iris and me went to lunch today and Harry was there with another boy. I wanted to tell him I liked him, but he left before I could."

And a few months later:

"Harry and I kissed at the rock today and he asked me to go steady with him. I am the happiest girl alive!"

As she flipped through the pages, she discovered one entry near the end in which Vivian had mentioned Imogen by name.

"There is a waitress at Mary's named Imogen who is very nice. She isn't much older than us and I can talk to her about things."

The sad part about reading this was that Imogen knew the date it would end and why it did, but she couldn't stop reading.

"July 12, 1946: Today was so much fun, Iris, me, Margaret Rose and Harry went swimming at the river. Imogen and her friend Loretta came too and packed a picnic lunch."

And later in the entry:

"Harry had to take his dad's car back home but mom let me use the truck

so Harry and I went back out to the river. It was so romantic sitting under the stars. Pretty soon we started necking but it turned into more. I was scared at first but Harry said he would be gentle. I guess tonight I am no longer a virgin. I'm not sure how I feel about that."

Imogen skipped to the last entry in the book, dated October 10.

"Harry is moving in two days! I don't want him to go. It's not fair. I have to tell him but I don't know for sure yet if I'm P.G. If I tell him and I'm not that will be terrible, but what if I am and he leaves? I will never see him again. If I tell him his life could be ruined and my family will hate me. They already think something is wrong with me in the head. They might send me away to a home and I won't be able to stand that. I don't know what to do."

Some of the ink had smeared in places suggesting to Imogen that Vivian had likely been crying when she wrote it. This was even more heartbreaking than Imogen imagined. Pregnant! No wonder Vivian had turned the pickup around and gone back to see Harry the second time. She was struggling over whether to tell him that she might be pregnant. Had she been prepared to raise the child alone without a father to spare him the shame and embarrassment, but changed her mind? If only she had told him sooner before that fateful day. How might things have been different if she had? Might Harry have stayed behind? Imogen could only imagine how crushed Mr. Tabor would be now knowing that he not only lost his true love, but their child as well.

So immersed in what-ifs, Imogen hadn't noticed Simon, awake from his nap, standing in the doorway holding up a package. "This arrived for you in the post," he said.

"Oh Simon, you startled me," Imogen said.

"Sorry," he said as he entered the garage and handed the package to her. Simon looked down at the bins on the floor. "What are you up to in here?" he asked.

"Oh, just going through some of Grammy's old things," she answered as she closed Vivian's diary and laid it aside. "I was missing her a lot, so I thought I'd reread some of her diaries, that's all." That wasn't the whole truth, of course, but not telling everything wasn't really lying, she reasoned.

Imogen opened the package and pulled out the book she had ordered, *Love on the Kansas Prairie*, by Loretta Ross. Ironically, the cover art featured a freight train barreling down the tracks against the flat, dusty landscape of the Kansas prairie. The tagline read: "Can Hudson and Violet, two passionate star-crossed teenagers, find lasting love on the windswept Kansas prairie? Or will tragedy and heartbreak derail their love forever?"

The fact that the characters Hudson and Violet shared the same first letters as Harry and Vivian was not lost on her. Imogen held it up for Simon to see. "I was not aware that you enjoyed romance novels," Simon noted.

"Normally, no, I don't," Imogen answered, but I ran into this author recently and was curious about her books."

Besides delivering the mail to her, Simon had been feeling guilty about the lie he'd told Imogen earlier, about wrestling with Fletcher. "Fletcher and I weren't really wrestling," he blurted.

"You weren't?" she asked. "What were you doing then?"

While she'd been in the shower, he had decided to tell her what really happened, well almost what really happened. Leaving out the time travel part of the story, he rationalized, wasn't technically lying.

"As I mentioned before," he stated, "I'm a bonehead. When I came in from the garden, I was reading but when I got up, I experienced a bit of a dizzy spell and I fell and hit my head."

Concerned, Imogen closed up the bins and went to him, placing her hand on his cheek. "Simon," she said, "Are you okay? Are you hurt?"

"No, yes, no, I'm fine," he reassured her. "But Fletcher, who happened to be at the door at that time saw me through the window lying on the floor, apparently out cold. He came 'round the back and revived me."

"That sounds like more than a dizzy spell, Simon," Imogen said. "Thank goodness Fletcher was there when it happened!" She wrapped her arms around his neck for a second before pulling away suddenly. "You should have told me!" she said in a stern tone as relief turned into concern. "You could have suffered a concussion and you went to sleep! Are you okay? Maybe we should take you to the ER."

Simon jumped in to calm her. "Imogen!" he said firmly. "I am fine, truly I am. No need for you to worry."

Somewhat reassured, she asked, "You're sure?"

"I'm sure," he said. Simon, feeling less guilty now and Imogen, having successfully avoided a discussion she did not wish to have yet, embraced, which swiftly turned into kisses.

"I missed you," Simon murmured in between smooches.

"I wasn't gone that long," she said.

"Any time away from you feels like a long time," he said, burrowing his face in her neck. "Mmmm, you smell good," he whispered in her ear, sending goosebumps running up and down her arms. With her arms still locked around his neck; Simon began to walk her back out of the garage.

"Where are you taking me," she asked, as they frog-walked together in the direction of the bedroom.

"I hear tell that you love romance," he teased.

"Meh, it's okay," she said, amused.

Simon gently pushed her onto the bed and began softly kissing first her thighs and then pulling her shirt up, he planted a series of little smooches across her belly. Lifting her arms, she allowed him to remove her shirt and unhook her bra and many more kisses ensued. Imogen moaned as he fondled one of her breasts and began to lightly nibble on the nipple of the other.

"How are you liking romance now?" Simon asked.

"Mmm, liking it more and more," Imogen purred.

As even more clothes were removed, passions soared, doubts disappeared, and both let go of themselves in the moment.

Imogen awoke the next morning to Simon curled up big spoon behind her, one arm flung across her shoulders. She managed to wrangle her phone from the bed table. Shit, it was 8:30. After last night's lovemaking, they had both fallen fast asleep in each other's arms and stayed that way all night, apparently. It felt wonderful to be back in her own bed again and clearly, the tensions of yesterday had melted away. However, she'd almost forgotten that she had an appointment this morning with Harrison Tabor. The bed was a twisted mess and with Simon tightly wrapped around her it took a moment to extricate herself from beneath his arm. Leaving him snoring, she got out of bed and ready for her meeting with Harry.

Promptly at 10:00, Harrison Tabor pushed open the door to Imogen's office. "Hellooo," he called out as he entered. It was such a corny old guy thing to do, but Imogen loved it and was barely able to suppress an amused chuckle.

"Hellooo yourself," she answered him back. Even though he was decades older, the delightful character of the 16-year-old Harry she had recently gotten to know in Kansas shown through.

"And how are you this fine morning, Miss Oliver?" he said, grinning.

"Very well, Mr. Tabor." Imogen wished she could keep this sunny conversation going indefinitely but knew all too well that it couldn't last long considering the news from Kansas she was about to deliver. She hated being the bearer of bad news, making people sad, and she felt especially sorry today about having to tell a gentle soul like Harry Tabor what she knew.

"Harry," he corrected her.

"Harry, yes, have a seat," Imogen said.

Harry sat down and smiled at Imogen. This was much weirder than she anticipated. It was the first time she had ever interacted with a client that she had met both in the present and in the past. Mere days ago, she had been spending time with the youthful teenage Harry and now seated in front of her, 70 years later, was elderly senior Harry. Much different versions of each other, but with the same affable smile and gentle eyes. Imogen sighed.

"Bad news?" Harry asked, his smile turning to a frown.

Imogen bit her lip. "I'm afraid so." Opening the file folder with his name on it, she removed the printouts of the newspaper clipping and the images of Vivian's and Margaret Rose's gravestones and placed them on the desk separating them. Harry removed his glasses from his shirt pocket, put them on, looked at the pictures of the gravestones, set them aside and then read the brief news piece.

When he had finished reading, he glanced up at Imogen over his reading glasses. "Both of them, yes?" he asked.

Imogen nodded. Harry removed his glasses and stared at the desk for a moment before speaking. It was a lot to take in, and Imogen could see that he was struggling to keep his composure. He took a handkerchief from his pocket and dabbed at the corners of his eyes.

"I didn't tell you this before, but that day, the day I left, the day of the accident, we quarreled," he said looking down at his hands. "It was silly. She accused me of liking Iris more than her. In hindsight, she might have started a fight with me on purpose to make it easier to say goodbye, I'll never know for certain."

Imogen knew that was only part of the reason she had turned the truck around and gone back. She brought the red diary out from a desk drawer and handed it to him. "There's something else," Imogen said. Opening it, he immediately saw that it was Vivian's.

Imogen had attached sticky notes to the pages where Vivian had talked about Harry and she watched Harry's face light up as he read, in Vivian's own hand, about their first meeting, the dates they'd had, the fun times they had shared. It was obvious that a thousand memories were flooding back. It made Imogen feel only slightly better that he was smiling and nodding, at times chuckling at the passages. That changed, however, when he finished reading the final entry, the one where Vivian had spoken about Harry moving away and expressing her concern that she might be pregnant.

Harry seemed stunned. "Pregnant," he said, shaking his head back and forth. His hands began to shake, and Imogen was concerned for him. "Harry?" she asked, "are you okay?"

He motioned with his hand that he was, but Imogen could

see that he was choking up trying to hold back the tears that were now streaming down his cheeks. She got up and walked around the desk and rested her hand on his heaving shoulder as he openly wept into his frail hands. She wished she could do something to ease his pain but decided the best thing to do was remain steady and quiet and just let him get it all out. After a moment, he patted her hand and straightened up in the chair.

"I'm fine now," he said, clearing his throat and wiping his eyes again with his handkerchief. "The train accident was a shock, but I wasn't expecting . . . well, that . . . that she was . . . you know." Imogen squeezed his shoulder again before returning to her desk.

"I am so, so sorry Harry. I know this is difficult," she said, knowing her words offered little comfort.

Harry closed the diary. "How did you get this, if you don't mind me asking?" She felt uncomfortable having to stretch the truth a bit, but obviously, she didn't want to reveal that his friend Iris was Imogen's grandmother.

"I found a relative of hers that had possession of some of her things and she said I could take it," she lied.

Harry turned the book over in his hands before looking back at Imogen. "Would you mind if I kept it?" he asked.

"Certainly. Of course," Imogen replied. "Oh, I have something for you," she said. "I think you might enjoy it." She handed Harry *Love on the Kansas Prairie,* Loretta's book.

"Hmmm," he said. "Loretta Ross, the name sounds familiar."

Imogen offered a weak smile, knowing that there was nothing she could possibly say to make Harry Tabor feel better. He had come to her seeking answers about what happened to Vivian Littlefield and Imogen had delivered. She hoped it would bring closure for him, as much as for herself. It was a sad ending for him, but a hard lesson for her in getting involved and trying to interfere in things that weren't meant to be meddled with.

"Well, I must go," Harry said, as he slowly pulled himself up from the chair, both knees creaking as he did so. Extending his hand to shake hers, he said, "Thank you for everything Miss Oliver."

"Call me Imogen," she said, smiling.

"Oh, that reminds me," he said. "After our first meeting I got to feeling nostalgic and while I was rummaging around in my keepsakes, I came across the old Brownie camera my dad had bought me for my birthday." He drew a faded photograph from his pocket and continued, "I'd forgotten about this day back in '46. A group of us had gone down to the river for a picnic." He handed the picture over to Imogen.

"It's curious," he said, "one of the girls in this photograph—her name escapes me now—she looked quite a lot like you."

In the photo, mugging for the camera on the picnic blanket, were all five girls—Vivian, Margaret Rose, Iris, Loretta, and Imogen. Imogen tried not to react as she brushed off what she was certain he was implying. She responded with a nervous laugh and glibly replied, "Oh well, I have some relatives from that area. Who knows? Could be one of my identical cousins . . . you know, like Patty Duke!"

Harry flashed a knowing smile and Imogen understood she probably wasn't pulling a fast one over on the very astute Harrison Tabor.

Imogen lingered in the office for a while after Harry had gone. It had been hard breaking the news about Vivian, as she knew it would be, but at the same time, he seemed relieved. It was always like that. People needed closure, an opportunity to end one chapter and start another, kind of how she was feeling about Simon now. The past few months had been difficult. Admittedly, she didn't know what Simon was going through, she'd been so preoccupied with work and keeping her own secrets that honestly, she'd not taken the time to ask him.

But something had changed. He seemed different, calmer,

more confident, less confused about things—like the old Simon that she'd fallen head over heels in love with at the Benson Hotel.

Yesterday had been a good day for them, the first in a long while. The sex was great—more than great. What had changed? She wondered if Fletcher might be somehow responsible. Could having a male friend have restored what had been missing in his life?

The questions reminded her of how she had been thinking a lot about fathers the last few days—her own dad, after reading his notebook on the island, about Harrison Tabor's grief over the loss of the child he would never know, and about the impact dads made in general on a child's life. At least she had hers around in the formative years. Simon, however, was raised by his single mother and had no such male figure to guide or influence him. Almost certainly, his biological father Teddy Diamond would have been a dreadful father, but Simon never spoke of it.

Imogen thought she was a master at avoidance, but how much was Simon holding in? Maybe it was time for them both to confront their feelings head-on instead of dodging them. First thing when she got home, she decided, she would sit him down for a chat.

Simon rolled over expecting to feel Imogen's sleeping form beside him in bed only to find an empty impression on the mattress where she had been. "Imogen," he called out. No answer. He tried again. "Are you out there?" he called. He rolled over and got out of bed and walked through the house calling her name, looked out the window, didn't see her car in the driveway. Where did she go?

The phone rang. It was Fletcher. "Hey, do you mind if I drop by?" I want to talk to you about an engineering project I'm working on, get your opinion, if that's okay."

"Sure, come on over," Simon said. After witnessing Imogen's

less than enthusiastic reaction yesterday to his presence he was mindful that he might be spending too much time with Fletcher, but she wasn't here. Surely, she wouldn't be cross that he came by when she was away, right?

When Fletcher arrived, Simon had coffee ready. "How are you doing," Fletcher asked, accepting the cup from Simon and making himself at home at the kitchen table.

"Doing okay," Simon answered a little contemplative.

"Did you tell Imogen about what happened, about the time traveling?"

Simon hesitated. "No, I thought about telling her," he said. "I probably should have, but I don't know, I feel that I want to explore this on my own a bit first; find out what I can do before I involve her."

He paused and Fletcher could tell that he was struggling with something. "Is there something else?"

"Yes," he admitted, "to be completely honest, I still can't say I am not disappointed that she never once offered to go and find out what happened to my mother for me."

Fletcher frowned. He knew he'd planted that particular seed and now he felt bad for it. "I apologize. I didn't mean to bring that up the other day."

Simon brushed his comment aside. "Don't be silly. It is not as though I hadn't entertained the thought myself before you spoke of it."

Both sat quietly drinking their coffee for a minute before Fletcher spoke. "Hey, maybe now that you can, you know, time travel, you won't need an ID, or you can pick one up somehow or some time."

Simon nodded. It wasn't a terrible idea. "Perhaps I will," he answered. After finishing their coffee, they resettled at the computer for Fletcher to show Simon some of his furniture designs.

"I sent you an email earlier, can you check to see if it came?" Fletcher asked.

Simon was embarrassed. Fletcher had set up an email account for him but so far, he hadn't gone back to check it because he couldn't remember how to get to it.

"Um," he hedged before admitting, "I'm not sure how to check it."

Fletcher was quick to reassure him that it was perfectly fine. That was what Simon liked about Fletcher. He was ever patient. Unlike Imogen, who always seemed to be in a rush to the next thing, Fletcher seemed to welcome Simon's endless inquiries about how things worked.

Fletcher navigated to Simon's mailbox and Simon was surprised to see it was filled up with nearly a page of unread email messages.

"Wow! Who are all these from?" he asked excited. Getting messages was almost as thrilling as receiving a letter in the post.

Fletcher snickered. "You won't be so enthusiastic when you start getting tons of spam. See," he pointed at the screen. "They've already found you!"

Fletcher was right, the majority of the messages were either invitations to sign up for newsletters, travel promotions, or product come-ons. "Penis enhancement?" Simon turned an incredulous eye at Fletcher. "Does that work?" he asked.

"Of course!" Fletcher said with a straight face before busting up. "Nah . . . joking," he admitted.

One message, though, caught his eye: "Your DNA Report is ready to view." Simon's curiosity was piqued. He'd completely forgotten about that. He knew so little of his mother's family or background. It might be interesting to learn about his roots.

After they had finished reviewing the files Fletcher sent, Fletcher showed him how to download the DNA report to the computer. It didn't disappoint. Simon was fascinated that so much information could be obtained from the one small vile of saliva he'd sent off a month ago. A map of his ancestry composition indicated that he was primarily Northwestern European comprising Scandinavian, British and Irish, French, and German. Good to know. Other reports exploring his neanderthal ancestry were equally illuminating, but it was the tree showing DNA relatives that confirmed his worst fear. He and Theodore Diamond were a match. In the back of his mind, he had hoped it wasn't true, but the report confirmed it, Teddy was indeed his biological father. Teddy's mother was also on the family tree, but the name listed was Grace Alexandria Diamond.

Grace Alexandria? Who was that? Simon was confused. Was not Mimi Pinky "The Horrid," Teddy's mother? Could it be a nickname she used?

Imogen pulled in next to Fletcher's car in the driveway and took a deep breath. The old Imogen would be upset and angry that Fletcher was here . . . again, but not the new Imogen. Nope. She'd turned over a new leaf.

When she entered the room, Simon was staring intently at the monitor. "Hey hon," she said, placing her hand lightly on the back of his neck. "What's up?" Simon jumped, startled.

"Oh hi," he said, patting her hand. "What do you make of this?" he said, pointing to the screen.

"You got the DNA results back I see."

"Yes, and as we suspected, regrettably, Teddy is my biological father." Imogen frowned at that.

"But who is Grace Alexandria?" He pointed to the name on the tree. "Do you think that's Mimi Pinky?"

Imogen leaned in for a closer look. The tree branched out from Grace, or Mimi's side through her mother with other ancestors, including a George Eastman, which Imogen thought was interesting. Could it be *the* George Eastman, of Eastman Kodak? She wondered. "Hmmm, I don't know," she said, "but I can find out." She wasn't thrilled about getting sucked into this. She had hoped to come home and have a serious conversation with Simon . . . alone. It was always something, she thought.

"Scoot," she said, shooing Simon from the desk chair so she could sit down. Simon watched in amazement as Imogen navigated the computer with lightning speed. She was a pro. She quickly pulled up one of her private investigators search sites, typed in the name "Grace Alexandria Diamond," and waited for the results.

The result was interesting. Grace Alexandria Diamond; *aka*

Grace Fitzpatrick, Grace A. Fitzpatrick, Mimi Pinky Paulson, Mimi Pinky Diamond.

Now it was Imogen who was becoming easily distracted. This looked intriguing enough to send her down a rabbit hole. "Well, Grace is Mimi," Imogen said, "but right now I'd really rather talk to you about . . ." She was interrupted mid-sentence by Fletcher who entered the room stopping abruptly when he saw Imogen.

"Oh, hi Imogen, I didn't know you were here," he said. By the look on his face, she could tell he was surprised and maybe a little embarrassed to see her.

"Hi Fletcher," Imogen said brightly. Her cheerful greeting was not at all what Fletcher was expecting, but he was certainly happy about it. "Have you guys had breakfast yet?" Imogen asked them, "I'm starving."

With the air cleared, and Imogen, having turned over her new leaf, the three of them headed for the kitchen for coffee, breakfast, and a bit of long overdue amity among friends.

After clearing away the dishes, Imogen walked out to the mailbox to retrieve the mail. Simon had a bad habit of forgetting to go to the mailbox and check the mail and it tended to pile up. A few bills, tags for their car, ads, and an official-looking envelope from a law firm: Yates, Turnbull, Davis, and Hall LLC.

Imogen was reading the letter as she walked back into the kitchen. "What is that?" Simon asked.

"It's a letter from a lawyer firm," she said, without looking up. "We've been summoned, day after tomorrow, 10:00 a.m. in their office . . . for the reading of Theodore Diamond's will."

15

Without discussing the summons or having the private conversation she had hoped to have, Fletcher and Simon retreated to the garage and Imogen to the computer to check her email. The only valid message was from a client about her next case—retrieving a lost opera cape that had been left behind in a 1920s New York City hotel cloakroom. The rest of the messages, she methodically deleted—the usual spam come-ons from credit card companies and advertisements for discounted cruises and penis-enhancing products, and poorly written, misspelled, and sketchy requests to transfer money into bank accounts of foreign entities. Delete, delete, delete as she scrolled through, almost deleting a message with a curious subject line that instantly caused her to pause: Childhood friend reaching out . . . *What's this?* she thought as she opened it and began to read.

Hi Imogen

It may seem strange to be receiving an email from me after all these years. I'm not sure if you even remember me, but I remember you, and our friendship. I have never felt so welcomed as when we moved in across the street from you. And our connection, well, since you, I have never experienced that kind of instant bond with a friend again.

You are probably wondering why we moved away suddenly without telling anyone. There is more to the story, and it has bothered me all these years so much that I feel you deserve an explanation. I am in town on business this week until Friday and I would love to meet up with you and catch up. If you are at all interested in seeing an old friend, please respond to this email or

```
call me at the number listed below. I hope to see you
soon.

    Best,
    Jade Delaney
```

Imogen shrank into the desk chair. "Oh my god," she whispered as she attempted to digest this shocker. It was a message from Jade—her childhood companion, the little girl with the freckles and braids—the only genuine friend Imogen had ever had, the one who had moved away mysteriously in the middle of the night the summer she was nine. Over the years, she had thought often of trying to locate Jade, but because she had never thought to ask her what her last name was, finding her was virtually impossible, even for a PI like herself. Delaney, well, now she knew.

It seemed so long ago, yet it was a childhood memory that had never faded. Imogen had tucked away the hurt but whenever she thought of Jade, it triggered a nagging ache right below the surface, probably because her leaving coincided with the disappearance of her parents shortly afterward. She had tried to be brave like Grammy told her to be but with practically everyone in the world that she loved gone, Imogen had bound her feelings up tight crying only when she was alone in her room. Friends had come and gone, weaving a trail of good and not so good memories, but after Jade, she didn't have the emotional bandwidth to reciprocate a friendship with another person. It was too hard, too painful—she always had all the excuses at the ready.

So yes, here it was, that whole emotion thing again. Was the universe trying to tell her something because she'd certainly had plenty of feelings lately—first Kansas, then finding and reading her dad's notebook on the island, having to tell Harrison Tabor the bad news about Vivian, and now, out of the blue, a message from her long-lost friend, Jade?

Of course, there was no question she would meet with her. But at the same time, she felt oddly unsettled. What would she be like? Would they have that same connection they had as children? Would it be awkward? Imogen hated the way she overthought every situation, but she couldn't stop herself from doing it, no matter how hard she tried. But . . . what if Jade wanted something from her? She knew nothing about her beyond their short time together as kids. She had mentioned in the email that she was in town on business, so she must be someone who has a job, and a job that requires travel. Well, enough with the speculation, just do it. Imogen hit reply and began to type: Dear Jade, I was quite surprised to hear from you. Of course, let's get together while you're in town . . .

Imogen entered the former Beany Barn, renamed the Coffee Grind, the coffee shop where she had worked during college, which seemed like a million years ago. The place had changed ownership several times since she'd worked there although nothing much had changed décor-wise, the same rustic wood plank booths and tables and chairs, plants growing willy-nilly everywhere, and funky-weird guerilla artwork on the walls, although she noticed they had expanded their menu beyond coffee, smoothies, muffin tops, and scones to include specialty soups and deli sandwiches.

The second thing she noticed was the only person of color seated near the back of the restaurant. There was no mistaking it was Jade. A taller, but equally stunning version of her mother, Jade rose from the table to greet Imogen and Imogen was instantaneously enamored with the natural beauty, grace, and confidence her old friend exuded.

Stylishly dressed in a pair of black slacks and low-heeled pumps, a freshly pressed white shirt accentuated by a classic houndstooth patterned blazer, Jade was even lovelier than Imogen had remembered. Immediately, Imogen began to question both her cherry chocolate hair color and the fashion choices she'd made today—yoga pants, a sweatshirt, red converse tennis shoes? What was she thinking?

Topping it off, Jade's hair, which was styled in hip interwoven box braids piled atop her head in an elegant bun, had replaced the tiny braids and barrettes that Imogen remembered, but she still had that same patch of freckles marching across her lovely cheeks.

Imogen at once felt intimidated by this so stunningly put together creature, but when Jade without hesitation reached out and embraced her in a warm hug as if no time had passed between them, her fears that her friend had changed were unfounded and Imogen eagerly hugged right back.

"Look at you!" Jade gushed, sounding like an elderly aunt cooing over a niece she hadn't seen in many years. "How gorgeous and grown up you are!"

For some reason Imogen didn't mind the attention her friend was conferring on her one bit. Everyone in the room was staring at the gorgeous, impeccably groomed woman, who must certainly be a model, fawning over that other average-looking female human.

After the hugging and gushing was done, they sat down across the booth from each other and for a minute, simply stared at one another across the table, smiling, saying nothing, until the silence became uncomfortable, and each attempted to break the silence at once.

"I'm so glad to see . . ." Imogen began.

"It's been so long . . . " Jade started to say. They both laughed. "You go first," Jade offered politely.

"I can't believe you're sitting here," Imogen said. "It's been like, what? eighteen years since we last saw each other?"

"Something like that," Jade agreed.

"How is your mother? And your baby sister? Sasha, wasn't it?" Imogen asked, happy that she was able to retrieve the name of Jade's sister from her memory.

"Mother is well," Jade answered. "She's a professor in the English department at the University of Baltimore."

"Oh my, and Sasha?"

"Also doing well. She's in college now," Jade said, "studying law."

"That is so fantastic!" Imogen said, although she inwardly

wondered how the family had managed it. Circumstances change, of course, but at the time she knew the family, they had been living in the shabby little house across the street with rented furniture, not to mention that Jade had told her that her father was serving time in jail for abusing them, but she pushed those recollections aside for now.

"And you?" Imogen continued inquisitively, leaning forward.

"I'm a junior executive at an architectural firm in Detroit," Jade said. Imogen detected a sense of pride in Jade's voice, but in a genuinely unpretentious way. "I oversee urban renewal projects all over the city to help preserve the buildings but also make them better and more people-centric," she said, unable to quell the excitement she had for her job in her tone. "I'm out west for a sustainability conference in Portland."

Imogen was more than impressed. "Wow, that's awesome. I am so proud of you Jade," she said.

Jade paused and folded her arms together. "But enough about me Imogen, what have you been up to? I have wondered about you, forever," she said, her lips forming into a perfect smile. Suddenly, after hearing how successful Jade and her family were, Imogen felt a bit deflated about her own career choice. Her response was an offhand gesture meant to show her reticence about talking about herself.

"Pffff, me," she scoffed. "I'm just a lowly private investigator."

Jade tilted her head to one side and said, "I don't believe you're a lowly anything, Imogen. If I remember correctly, you were the most bold and curious and fun and entertaining person I have ever encountered in my whole life, and I imagine that if you are a private investigator, you are likely the best one money can buy! Am I right?" she inquired with a sly nod of her head.

Imogen blushed, bringing her hands up to her face while blowing away a wisp of hair that had fallen in front of one eye.

"Okay, well, I am pretty good at what I do," she conceded.

"Of course, you are!" Jade said, reaching out impulsively and grasping Imogen's hand.

"Oh Imogen, how I wish we could have known each other longer, what fun, what adventures we could have had but missed out on all because I had to move away." Imogen's smile faded at the memory, and she pulled her hand slightly away from Jade's grasp. "I'm sorry I left you Imogen, but I swear, there really was a good reason."

Imogen sensed that Jade thought Imogen was overwrought about her leaving, when in fact, it was so much more than that. She didn't know that Imogen's parents had disappeared shortly after too.

Detecting a shift in Imogen's demeanor, Jade attempted to lighten the mood. Leaning back and folding her hands together on the table, she asked, "So, how are your parents doing Imogen?"

There it was. There was no way to avoid talking about it. As much as Imogen wanted to keep their reunion light and breezy and focus exclusively on the excitement of seeing one another again, she knew that, of course, Jade would get around to asking about her family, too. May as well just throw it out there, she thought. Imogen leaned forward, sighed, and spoke. "Not long after you left, my mother and father disappeared."

Jade's smile faded into alarmed concern. "Disappeared? What do you mean they disappeared? Where did they go?"

Imogen was ambivalent about revealing the true circumstances of how they had vanished. First, because it was a very long story, and second, she wasn't sure she was ready, nor that she even wanted to or should share the intricacies of time travel with someone she barely knew anymore. Still, she had to say something to satisfy Jade's curiosity. She hated to do it, but the lie spilled from her lips before she could stop it.

"They were killed in a car accident."

Jade's appearance transformed again from concerned to confused. "I thought you said they disappeared?"

Having gotten pretty good over the years at backpedaling on errors she sometimes too often made while traveling in other times, Imogen did a quick edit of her words. "Well, I mean they did disappear, initially," she said." "While they were missing, they were in the car accident."

Jade gasped in astonishment. "Oh my god," Imogen, "I'm so sorry. That's horrible. "I . . . I don't know what to say."

Ever since learning from Teddy the true circumstances of her parent's departure, Imogen hadn't thought about how devastated she'd been at age nine when Grammy had delivered the stunningly big lie about her parent's deaths in a fiery crash, but in a rush, it all came flooding back—the shock, the denial, the years of praying to a god that didn't listen to please bring them back—and though she tried very hard, Imogen could not hold back the tsunami of emotions those memories invoked. Her bottom lip began to quiver uncontrollably, and she felt the tears pooling around the corners of her eyes threatening to spill over the edges. Immediately, Jade flew from her seat, coming around to Imogen's side of the table where she scooted in next to her and engulfed Imogen in a close embrace. "I'm so sorry this happened to you Imogen," she whispered. "And I'm so sorry for bringing it up."

Surprised by Jade's open and sincere display of concern, Imogen allowed her friend to cradle her head as she sobbed quietly into her sleeve. After a minute, Jade grabbed a napkin off the table and handed it to Imogen to dab her eyes. Embarrassed, Imogen started to wriggle away from Jade's taut grasp, but Jade held on tight. "I'll let you go when I know for sure you're okay," Jade whispered softly in her friend's ear. That made Imogen laugh a little. "I'm sorry for being such a big baby," she said sniffling.

"Don't be silly," Jade said. "As I recall, you and I shared quite a few ugly crying sessions together when we were little girls. Do you remember?"

Imogen smiled feebly up at Jade, "Yes," Imogen admitted, "I do remember that."

They both noticed then the waitress guardedly hovering nearby patiently waiting with pad and pen in hand to take their order, but clearly not sure if now was a good time or not. Jade unwrapped her arms from around Imogen and they both gestured for her to come on over. They shared a Reuben sandwich but engaged in little talk, other than chitchat as they ate. But when Jade had finished eating and was sipping her coffee, she decided to wade again into deeper waters.

"Imogen," she said. Imogen, mid-chew, gazed up from her plate. "I know you're still eating, but I just want you to listen."

Imogen took a drink from her water glass and swallowed the bite still left in her mouth. "Sure Jade, I'm listening. Go ahead."

"My biological father's name was Darrell Schmidt," Jade began. Imogen wiped the corners of her mouth with her napkin and settled in deeper against the booth's cushion to listen to Jade's story. "Before we moved in across the street from you," Jade continued, "my mother found out that he had been sexually abusing me and had recently started messing around with Sasha too. When she confronted him, he beat her up, really bad this time though, worse than any other time before when he had only punched her and given her a black eye or two. She was lying on the floor crying. He had gone and she told me to call the police. So I did."

Imogen could tell that this was a difficult story for Jade to tell too but she listened quietly as Jade pressed on. "Well, they arrested him, and he went to jail. My mother got a restraining order and we moved to your town to try to get away and start a new life there. We thought we were safe, but a friend tipped my mom off that Darrell had been released early, he knew where we lived, and he was coming for us," she said, pausing a moment before continuing her story, "and that's why we had to leave in the middle of the night.

"We tried to start over again, in another town that was farther away in another county and things were pretty good for a while, maybe about six months or so, but as it turned out, we weren't safe there either. One Sunday, Mom, Sasha, and I came home from church and as we were walking up to the front door of the house, Darrell showed up. He grabbed me from behind and held a knife to my throat. He told my mother that he'd leave us alone for good if she'd give him money. We found out later, that before he came to our house, he had tried to rob a gas station, but the clerk had fought back, and Darrell ran off empty-handed. He was desperate and, on the run, and he needed cash to get away."

Jade paused and drew in a deep breath as though she was resisting an urge to cry. And Imogen, who had leaned forward in her seat resting her elbows on the table, chin in her hands, enthralled by her story, blurted out, "Were you okay? What happened? Did he hurt you?"

"No," Jade said, "because out of nowhere, this man came up from behind and hit Darrell in the head with a rock! When he stumbled backward, he let go of me. I ran inside the house with my mom and Sasha, we locked the door, and mom called the police. When the police got there, Darrell was lying bloody in the grass in our front yard, his hands bound behind his back with a garden hose. At first, the police wondered why these two white guys were fighting in our yard," Jade said, "but then the message came over the radio about Darrell robbing the gas station. So they arrested him on the spot and this time he was sentenced to prison for a long, long time.

"And the man who saved you? What happened to him?" Imogen asked.

"Well, he became friends with my mother. I was a child, so time was immaterial, but it seemed like he was with us for a short time, a few months maybe, and he helped us with handyman type chores, mowing the lawn, fixing the sink, painting, stuff like that."

"Where did he go?" Imogen asked.

"I don't know," Jade mused. "We left. He didn't think we were safe there and he bought us plane tickets to Baltimore. He said he knew people there who could help us. And he gave my mother money, and it must have been a lot of money, come to think of it—enough for her to enroll in school."

Imogen wasn't quite sure why, but Jade's story sounded really implausible. "So let me get this straight, this mystery man, he just shows up out of nowhere, saves you guys, and then gives you enough money to fly across the country to start a new life? Didn't that seem kind of strange to you?" Imogen asked, incredulous.

Jade nodded agreement and shrugged. "I don't know what

his motives were Imogen. Like I said, he helped us. He was there for like two months and then we were gone, to Baltimore."

But then she stopped as though she'd suddenly remembered something else. "He gave me this," she said, pulling out a necklace with a dark green stone that had been hidden beneath her blouse. "I thought I'd lost it, but somehow, he had it," Jade said.

Imogen gasped. "Jade! Oh my god, that's the necklace I found in your front yard. It was hanging on my bureau mirror and after my dad disappeared, I noticed it was gone."

Jade brought her hand up to her mouth and gasped, "You don't think . . .?"

"What was the man's name?" Imogen cried out.

Jade faltered as she tried to retrieve the man's name from her recollection. "Poole," she said. "Yes, he said his name was Frank Poole, that's it."

That name, Frank Poole, it sounded vaguely familiar. But who was it? Could it have been one of Niles photographer friends? He had belonged to a dark room photography club. But Imogen could barely contain the rising excitement in the pit in her stomach.

"What did he look like, Jade?"

"Do you think it was your dad?" Jade asked.

"You met my dad, Niles, wouldn't you know if it was him or not?" Imogen asked.

"Honestly, I don't know, Imogen, he had a beard, and he may have resembled your dad in a way, but . . ."

"Jade, please," Imogen pleaded. "It's important. Just try to remember whether it was him or not. I need to know!"

Jade was visibly shaken as she tried to provide Imogen with the answers she knew she so desperately wanted. "This guy had longer hair than I remembered your dad having, and a beard," she added. "I was a little girl for heaven's sake. I can't say for sure."

Imogen was frustrated, too. It had seemed like her dad had grown a mustache at some point, but never a beard, but she couldn't be certain either. "Is there anything else that you remember about him Jade? Anything at all?"

Jade hesitated for a moment, nervously tugging at her hair and causing one of her braids to fall carelessly onto her neck as she struggled to remember more. Imogen sighed, ready to let it go, when suddenly Jade straightened up. "I do remember something now," she said.

Imogen straightened up too, excited. "What? What do you remember?" she asked.

"This man, Frank, I remember that he kept a journal, well, it was actually smaller than a journal, more like, what do you call it? A reporter's notebook. He kept it with him in his pocket and he was always writing stuff down in it, and the night before we were to leave for Baltimore, I saw him bury something in the backyard. I wondered what it was, and I had planned to sneak out later and find out, but my mom sent me to bed. I fell asleep, and that was that. Early the next morning we flew out to the East Coast, and I have not been back since that day, 18 or so years ago."

Ever since Teddy had divulged that he was responsible for their disappearance, Imogen had entertained the thought that her parents could still be alive somewhere, but with no clues where they could be, for self-preservation, she tempered her feelings. But now, now that there was even a slight possibility of locating her dad, Imogen felt a wave of unexpected hope. So many memories. All at once. Niles, dad, had always been the one who was there for her, playing catch, tucking her in at night; being the nurturing parent that she relied on.

"Can you take me there, Jade?" Imogen asked. "Can we go to that house now?"

"I wish we could," she said, "but I don't remember where it is or even what town it was in. It was so long ago, Imogen, I'm sorry."

"Does your mother remember?" Imogen asked.

"I asked and she says she doesn't remember either," said Jade. "I think she wanted to forget all about that time in her life."

So close. Her shoulders slumped as Imogen sunk down into the booth, crestfallen, defeated.

"There might be a clue though," Jade said.

"What?" Imogen answered gloomily.

"A letter," Jade said. "I sent you a letter after we'd moved. Do you remember? If you still have it, there might be an address or a postmark from where it was sent, at the very least."

Imogen perked up. "Yes! And you sent a photo too, I remember, of you standing in front of your house!"

"That's right," Jade said.

"I bet that was the photo that Teddy destroyed!" Imogen was getting excited again.

"Teddy?" Jade said, a frown creasing her face. "You mean creepy Teddy, that guy in the neighborhood with the weird mom that we used to spy on all the time when we were kids? What does he have to do with this?"

"Never mind, it's a long story. I'll tell you later," Imogen said as she pulled a twenty-dollar bill from her wallet and plunked it down on the table for their meal. She stood up and grabbed hold of Jade's hand. "Are you busy, right now? Can you come back to my house for a bit?"

"No, I mean yes. I guess so, sure, why?" Jade asked.

"We have to find that letter!"

16

Imogen was not the least bit surprised to see Fletcher's car parked in the driveway again—he was becoming a regular fixture at their house. But ever since they had reconciled their differences and restored harmony during their coffee klatch session the other morning things had been much better between them.

"Here we are," Imogen said without noticing that her friend was preoccupied, gazing intently across the street at the house where her family had once lived.

"It hasn't changed much, smaller than I remember," Jade said softly as she pushed the passenger door open and stepped out of the car.

The house, still a rental, was empty and in between occupants. "A lot of different neighbors have come and gone over the years," Imogen remarked.

"Would you mind if we went over and took a peek through the window?" Jade asked.

"Of course not," Imogen said. "Let's go." Linking arms with Jade, the old friends strolled side by side across the street they had once lithely capered barefooted across so many years earlier. With the exception of a few fleeting memories here and there over the years, Imogen hadn't devoted much thought to the pleasant remembrances of life in the neighborhood, pre-parents disappearing. Those happy times, with them and with Jade, had been clouded over by the sad years that had followed. But today, with Jade beside her, the sweet childhood reflections of that summer inched slowly back into focus—making chalk drawings on the sidewalk together, playing in the sprinkler, or reading chapter books in the afternoon when the temps climbed into three digits; spying on Teddy at her dad's studio; evenings lying on their backs on the cool grass in the back yard, staring up at a sky filled with a gazillion twinkling stars; and cooler nights spent at Jade's house making shadow puppets with the flashlight and giggling beneath their makeshift blanket fort.

Jade crossed the yard and approached the ranch style home. It was painted a pale green now. When she had lived there it had been freshly painted a perky yellow, but the paint, which was chipping here and there, revealed the rainbow of shades it had undergone over the years. Jade walked up to the big front window and peered in. "It's so small," she remarked with surprise. Having never moved away in her life, Imogen knew about, but wasn't all that familiar with, the phenomenon of returning to one's childhood home and feeling like it seemed much smaller than you remembered. Of course, like Alice through the looking glass, when you are small everything seems bigger and when you grow up, it seems smaller, but because she had grown up along with her house, she supposed, it didn't seem like it had changed at all.

Jade smiled and turning to Imogen, said, "Remember that night we laughed so hard you blew milk out your nose?"

"Oh my gosh, yes!" Imogen said, chuckling. "I can't even remember what was so funny though."

"Me either, something," Jade said, amused by the memory. "What about mom holding Sasha and dancing around with us to her jazz records? She sure loved her smooth jazz!" They stared into the empty living room for a few moments, each revisiting their shared memories in silence. After a minute, Imogen reached out, and encircled Jade's waist with her arm. "Good times, eh?"

"Good times," Jade repeated, returning the smile.

"Let's go see if we can find that letter, shall we?" Jade said. Imogen nodded and the two headed back across the street to Imogen's house.

As they climbed the steps to the porch, Jade called out from behind, "Lots of memories here too."

"Yep," Imogen, said opening the front door and ushering

Jade into the foyer. A muffled sound of male voices echoed from somewhere in the house, and Imogen called out, "Simon, where are you?"

"We're in here, in the kitchen," his voice returned.

As Jade paused in the living room to take a glance around at the other house that had also been a center of their childhood activity that summer, Imogen headed to the kitchen where she found Simon and Fletcher poring over a set of blueprints spread out across the kitchen table.

Resisting the urge to appear too excited to see her, Fletcher glanced up nonchalantly when she walked in. "Hi Imogen," he said raising his hand in a welcoming wave.

"Imogen!" Simon said, bouncing over and planting his lips upon her cheek. "How did the lunch date with your friend go?" he asked. Imogen had filled him in earlier about the message from Jade. She was excited now to tell him that not only had she reconnected with her old friend, but they had news about Imogen's dad, but before she could answer his question, peeking her head around her, Jade appeared in the doorway behind Imogen, "Oh, and this is Jade," Imogen said, pulling her friend around her through the door.

Simon and Fletcher stopped everything they were doing, neither bothering to hide their besotted expressions as they gawked at the stunning creature that had just entered the space.

"Um, hello," Imogen ventured, attempting to break the spell Jade had apparently cast on them. As though snapping out of his transitory trance, on reflex, Simon remembered a gentleman's decorum and grasping Jade's hand said in his patently polite turn of the century vernacular, "Oh my, please pardon my staring, I am so happy to finally meet you Ms. Jade!" he said, graciously kissing her hand lightly. Jade flashed a self-conscious grin but was thoroughly enjoying the attention of this charming man. "Why, thank you," she said, "It's a pleasure to meet you as well."

"And this is Fletcher," Imogen said.

"Pleased to meet you," Fletcher said, offering his hand to Jade. A rush of confusing sensations flooded his brain. Not since meeting Imogen back in college had he experienced that level of attraction, but there was no mistaking the electric current that seemed to be flowing between his hand and Jade's.

"Likewise," said Jade. Imogen took note of the prolonged handshake. Not sure how she felt about this, Imogen decided to quickly usher Jade from the room, claiming they had girl things to attend to. She'd tell Simon the news about her dad later once Fletcher had gone.

In the bedroom, Imogen placed a footstool in front of the closet, climbed up, and began rummaging through a number of shoeboxes and bins stacked on an upper shelf. "I'm pretty sure it's here somewhere," she said to Jade who had seated herself on the bed.

"How do you know Fletcher?" Jade asked.

Imogen continued to search for the right box, but answered, "Well, actually, he's my ex-boyfriend. We met in college," she said. "Here it is," Imogen said triumphantly, as she pulled a plastic bin from the shelf. She stepped down from the footstool and placed the bin on the bed between them.

"Your ex, huh? And Simon?"

Imogen shot Jade a questioning look. "Are you sure you really want to hear this now? It's a very long story."

Jade nodded. "Yes, I'd love to hear about it," she said. "I told you my story . . . well, part of it. I want to hear yours."

"Tell you what," Imogen said, "Let's find the letter first and then I'll tell you all of it, about Teddy and my parent's disappearing and everything that happened after that summer, okay?"

"Okay," Jade agreed.

Imogen removed the lid from the container to reveal a pile of old postcards, letters, photographs, and various mementos from her childhood. She dumped it all on the bed and the friends spent the next half hour reminiscing and laughing over the random array of 90s stuff Imogen had stashed away—from the oh-so-trendy Tamagotchi slap bracelet and colorful butterfly hair clips to scented highlighter pens and a movie stub for *The Lost World: Jurassic Park.*

Imogen removed an envelope from the pile. It was the letter. From Jade. Imogen carefully opened it and pulled out the neatly creased letter written in pencil on lined paper. She unfolded it and began to read the words written in Jade's uneven nine-year-old's hand.

Dear Imogen, I'm sorry I didn't get to say goodbye to you. We had to move. I started at my new school and I like my teacher. Her name is Miss Norton. She is nice. Our house is smaller than our old house but I like my room and the back yard. I miss you alot and I hope we will always be best friends.
Love, Jade

Imogen looked over at Jade, who gently took the letter from Imogen's hands. She could see that Jade was trying extra hard not to tear up, and she was having trouble herself.

"Wow," Jade said. "I can't believe you kept it all this time."

"I keep everything, as you can plainly see," Imogen said, waving her hand over the pile of assorted memorabilia on the bed. "You also sent a picture of you standing in front of your house. I think it must have been the one my dad used," she said.

Jade looked up from the letter, confused by what Imogen had just said. "How did your dad *use* it, Imogen?" she asked.

Imogen gulped. She shouldn't tell, she knew this, but what choice did she have if it meant there was a chance of finding her dad still alive?

"I was four the first time it happened," Imogen began, "the first time I went into a picture."

Although D.B. Cooper and Adam had gotten only the condensed account of the story, for the second time in so many weeks Imogen launched into the full version this time around. She told Jade about meeting her mother on a beach for an instant when she had been looking at pictures in Grammy's album when she was four, how when she was nine, she had come home from school to learn that her parents had been killed in an automobile accident.

She described what happened in college when she was writing an essay about the turn of the century, how she had entered a picture from 1901 and encountered her grandmother there, which forced Grammy to tell her the truth about her parents—that they were time travelers too, and the truth about their disappearance, that they hadn't died in a crash as she had been told, but had each become trapped inside different photographs somewhere in the past.

Of course, Jade had a million questions about time travel. How did it work? What was it like? Was this how she found out things for people who hired her? Are there rules? What are they?

Imogen spent another good 45 minutes discussing the intricacies of time travel and still didn't cover everything. Jade listened intently, never questioning the validity of Imogen's story, never doubting her. Her only question next was, "And Teddy, what did he have to do with all this?"

They spoke briefly of Teddy and his disturbing proclivity for exposing himself to little girls. Reacting to the nauseating memory, Jade's features knotted into an "ew" face. "He was a vile, horrible boy," she stated.

"Yes, he was," Imogen said, frowning, "but he was even worse than that."

Before she could continue, they heard a soft rapping at the bedroom door and Simon slowly pushed it open as he entered. "Quite sorry to interrupt," he said as he guardedly entered the room, "but I thought you two might enjoy a cup of coffee."

"Awww, how sweet," Imogen and Jade vocalized at the same time. "We love coffee!" Imogen said. "Did you remember to put my favorite special hazelnut syrup in mine?" she asked, tilting her head sideways teasingly and winking at Jade.

"Of course," Simon said earnestly, thoughtful male companion that he was.

"This was so considerate, thank you Simon," Jade said when he handed her the mug of hot brew. She leaned in close to Imogen and whispered, "He's a keeper."

"I know," Imogen whispered back.

Simon planted a soft kiss on Imogen's cheek. "I'll leave you two alone now darling," he said as he headed for the door.

"We won't be too much longer Simon," Imogen said. "And thanks for the coffee!" she called out as he was shutting the door behind him.

"He is quite well-mannered," Jade ventured. "I don't think I've ever met anyone so polite."

"Probably not in this century, for sure," Imogen said. "In a minute, you'll understand that better too, I promise."

"Okay," Jade said suspiciously as she brought the mug to her lips and took a sip.

"So where were we? Oh yes, Teddy." Jade's smile faded to a frown with the mention of his name.

"You remember that Teddy worked in my parent's studio, right?" Imogen asked.

Jade nodded, "Oh yes, I will never forget what he did to us there." Imogen knew exactly what she meant. Teddy had exposed himself to them. They had run away, but neither one of them told on him. "I was afraid to tell anyone," Jade said.

"I know," Imogen said, "Me too."

"We should have told on him!" Jade exclaimed. Imogen could see the justifiable anger in Jade's eyes. Imogen didn't know the extent of the abuse Jade had endured by her own father as a child, but she could only imagine how horrible it must have been. Imogen was angry too. It made her blood boil thinking about how girls then and now were still afraid to speak up about harassment, or touching, or abuse.

"I'm glad we had each other though," Imogen said. "I can't imagine going through that alone."

Jade nodded and grasped Imogen's hand. She knew that besides the incident with Teddy, Imogen was also referring to what had happened to her as a child. While she appreciated her friend's concern, she didn't want to detract from Imogen's story. "So what happened next?" she asked, encouraging Imogen to go on.

"Well, my parents knew how to travel," Imogen continued. "My grandma told me that they tried to help people, in the way I do as a PI, but for them it was more of a side gig. Anyway, I think Teddy saw something, maybe saw them enter a photo, and he must have figured out how to time travel himself."

Jade shuddered. "I do remember how he was always lurking around all creepy-like, watching us and those girls who came in for photos."

"Yeah, well that's not even the half of it. One of those girls—I don't know if you remember her—Tiffany Rose—she started dating Teddy."

"Ew, I can't imagine anyone wanting to date Teddy!" Jade said, disgusted by the thought.

"Well, evidently she did, and that summer, she went missing."

Jade's jaw dropped. "No!"

"Yep, and I don't know all the details, but my dad, Niles, he called Teddy out because he found a photo of her in the studio." Imogen reached around behind her and brought out a couple of the many photos that Tiffany had left around the studio for someone in the future to find.

Jade looked down at the pictures and gasped, "This is her?" she asked. "But these are old pictures. How could . . .?" She shook her head back and forth bewildered. "I don't understand, Imogen."

"This will sound so crazy, but she found out she was pregnant and when she told Teddy he took her through a photograph from the late 1800s and left her there," Imogen blurted, the anger coming back now as raw as the first time she'd learned of this a few months ago.

"No way!" Jade said.

"He trapped her there with no way to get back!" Imogen said, shaking her head. "So she started taking pictures of herself and leaving them all over the place hoping that one day someone in the future might find them and come save her."

"And your dad could have saved her," Jade said, understanding dawning on her. "Oh my god, Imogen do you think he was responsible for your parent's disappearance too?"

"I *know* he was!" Imogen exclaimed, "because he destroyed

the two anchor photos they had each traveled into making it so that they couldn't come back either."

Jade stared at Imogen in shock. Neither said anything for a minute or two while she processed the story Imogen had just told her. "How did you find all this out?"

Imogen sighed. "It's complicated, but I'll give you the short version."

Jade leaned back against the headboard and made herself comfortable as Imogen began her story. She smiled and laughed when Imogen told her how she and Simon had met, about their roller-coaster courtship and romance. She gasped in dismay at the parts about Teddy admitting to trapping Imogen's parents and the stunning disclosure that Simon's *mother* was Tiffany Rose and that his father, shockingly, was Teddy; and how Teddy had set fire to Imogen's dad's studio killing her beloved cat and had then disappeared into a photograph forever.

Jade's emotions were all over the place—happy that Imogen had found Simon, elated that Teddy was probably dead, sad about her parents and Tiffany Rose and Luxe. On top of learning that people could actually travel though time, it was a lot to absorb in one sitting.

"We need to find what your dad buried in that backyard!" she said.

Imogen looked at the envelope the letter was in. It was date stamped September 1, 1997. "Look, a return address!" she said excited, although also noting that Jade had not included her name, which was the reason she was never able to find her. "Let's go look it up online."

Using a real estate app, it was a snap finding the house, which was located in Stambourg, a town about 20 miles away. And luckily, the house had been sold recently so there were loads of pictures of the exterior and the interior, satellite, and street views. They should have no trouble finding it. The only problem was that if people were living there, it might be problematic getting into the yard.

"I'm thinking the owners probably wouldn't appreciate us

knocking on their door with shovels asking if we can go on a buried treasure hunt in their back yard," Imogen said.

Jade looked at Imogen who also looked defeated. "Right, so what do we do?"

"Well, hmmm," Imogen said, tapping her fingers anxiously against her chin. "I guess we'll just have to sneak in there at night."

Jade's reaction was predictable. "What!? Are you joking? That's so crazy . . . not to mention dangerous," she said. "What if the owner has a vicious guard dog, or . . . or, a gun? We could get arrested!"

"Do you have a better plan?" Imogen asked.

"No, not really," Jade admitted.

Imogen turned back to the computer and went through the images again, checking to see if there was any way to easily get access to the yard.

"Look!" she cried, pausing on one shot of the back yard. "There's a gate, do you see it?"

"Where?" asked Jade.

"Right there, behind that rosebush." Imogen zoomed into the picture for a closer view. "I bet there's an alleyway behind the house. We could come in from that way and they wouldn't even know we were there . . . probably . . . maybe."

She opened a maps program and zoomed around in the street view to the end of the street and there it was, just as she suspected, an alleyway. They didn't do it much anymore, but in the older neighborhoods, people used to be able to put their trash cans in the alley for the garbage truck to drive down and pick up.

Jade was optimistic, but also skeptical. "Maybe we should do some reconnaissance first before we actually do anything, you know, reckless."

"Okay," Imogen said, closing the programs on the computer. "Good plan! What are you doing tomorrow afternoon? I have a thing at 10:00 o'clock but we could drive over to Stambourg later, scout around, scope it out."

Jade pulled out her planner. "I have meetings, but I'm free

after noon."

Imogen flashed a conspiratorial smile. "Perfect! All right then, backyard spy mission, ON!"

After bidding farewell to Simon and Fletcher, who were huddled deep in a project in the garage, she drove Jade back to her hotel downtown. "So pick you up tomorrow then?" she said as she grabbed Jade's briefcase from the trunk of the car.

"Tomorrow," Jade replied.

Expecting a hug, Jade was surprised when instead Imogen spontaneously reached over and touched her friend's braids. "May I?" she asked. Jade smiled. "Of course, you may, silly girl."

"You are so beautiful Jade, just the way I always remembered you."

Touched, Jade pulled Imogen in for a hug. "I'm so glad I found *you*," she said. They lingered like that for a moment before Imogen pulled away. "Do you remember that time you braided my hair all over like yours?" Jade smiled at the memory.

"I looked awful," Imogen said, laughing. "I know now that it's wrong for white people to appropriate Black culture, but when I was little, I saw your braids as a superpower that I didn't have. You were exceptional and I felt . . . ordinary. Through my little girl eyes, I thought it was cool to be Black without understanding what it meant for you to actually *be* Black."

Jade returned an understanding nod and started to go but turned around and said, "I envy you, you know."

Imogen was genuinely perplexed. "My goodness, Jade, why?"

"Because the adventures you have are out of my reach," she said. "Can you imagine me, a Black woman, showing up out of nowhere in say, the 1950s South, or *anywhere* during the 1860s? As a person of color, it would be far too dangerous for me to travel back to most of the times and places that you are freely able to visit and blend into."

Imogen had not considered this and immediately felt horrible. "I'm sorry Jade, I never seem to have the right words."

Jade patted her friend's arm reassuringly. "We've all had a lot to learn and work through, Gen. We still do."

17

Imogen shivered as she and Simon climbed the stairs outside the law offices of Yates, Turnbull, Davis, and Hall. She wished now she'd grabbed her sweater off the chair. It was late September, that seasonal limbo time, between summer and fall, when you never know what to wear—sandals or shoes, a sun dress or sweater; when you fiddle with the thermostat because the house is too hot one minute, too cold the next. Today was like that, deceptively warm in the bright sunlight, but noticeably chilly in the shade.

Autumn was on its way, and with it, for Imogen, stark reminders of dad. It was their favorite season. So many memories of hiking the butte with him, the sound of their boots crunching through the dry leaves that had fallen on the trail, the earthy smell of the forest mixed with a distinctive fall-ish scent, and then reaching the summit to shoot aerial photographs of the glorious red and orange and golden leaves on the trees that blanketed the city between two mountains below. Who knew what in the world Teddy might have left her in his will, or why? But her mind wasn't on that today, it was on him. Dad. They were so close to maybe finding out what happened to him. Would she see him again, truly be able to save him tomorrow or the next day? And if so, what would he be like? Would he be the same? Different? Would he remember her? So many questions that only time would answer.

When they reached the landing at the top of the stairs, Simon paused before opening the door to the lawyer's office. "Are you ready?" he asked.

Imogen smiled. "Yep. Let's do this."

The receptionist at the front desk directed them to the waiting area, the attorney would call them shortly. When they entered the room, Imogen was not surprised to see Mimi Pinky, but Mimi Pinky was shocked to see Imogen and Simon and immediately stood up and waddled toward them.

"What the hell are you two doing here?" she demanded, wagging her finger in their faces. The sketchy man that was with her, stood up, like backup and joined her.

Imogen pulled from her purse the letter the lawyers had sent and held it up for Mimi to see. "I was invited," she said.

Angrily snatching the paper from Imogen's hands, Mimi held it between her pudgy fingers as she scanned the content. "This can't be right," her voice rising to a shrill decibel as she tossed the paper dramatically into the air where it floated to the floor. "Teddy would NOT have left anything to YOU in his will," she hissed. "You should go . . . right now. I don't want you here!"

Carl, projecting a menacing presence at Mimi's side, glared tough at Imogen and Simon and made a lame attempt at bullying them. "You heard the lady," he growled. "You ain't wanted here."

Imogen could feel the rage building. "Who are YOU?" she demanded, leaning in close to the beefy six-foot-tall Carl, brave and unafraid. Carl puffed his chest up in a retaliatory stance and started inching toward her when Simon interjected, wedging himself between the two.

"Please take it outside!" the startled receptionist called out.

Simon took Imogen's hand and guided her to a seat across the room. Carl grabbed Mimi Pinky's arm and dragged her back over to where they were seated. "I'm not afraid of Carl," Imogen whispered angrily. But they waited quietly despite Mimi lobbing a barrage of deadly daggers in Imogen's direction from across the room.

A few more minutes of glaring at each other passed before the receptionist's phone finally buzzed. "You may all go in to see the attorney now," she said.

Imogen started to get up, but Simon pulled her back. "Wait, let them to go in first," he said. Still scowling in their direction, the receptionist led Mimi and Carl down the hall and into the office of Jason Turnbull. Imogen and Simon got up and followed. Fortunately, the office was large enough that the chairs were arranged a considerable distance apart.

"Hello folks," Jason Turnbull welcomed them cheerily, clearly misreading the room. "How are we all doing this morning?" His pleasant smile faded though when Carl and Mimi Pinky walked past him and sat down without speaking.

Imogen, at least, returned the professional courtesy, extending her hand to shake his. "I'm Imogen Oliver," she said.

Simon followed suit. "Simon Elliot," he said as Turnbull gestured for them to also take a seat.

Acutely aware now of the heightened tension in the room, Turnbull wasted no time getting to the point of the meeting. "I won't take up too much of your time. I've summoned you all here today because I am the executor of one Theodore Diamond's will, for which some of you are beneficiaries."

With that, Mimi Pinky leapt from her chair, turned, and pointed one ruby red, nail-polished finger at Imogen and Simon and emphatically stated, "Then why are they here? They . . . they, are NOT beneficiaries of my son's will!"

"Please, sit down Ms. Diamond," Turnbull said calmly but forcefully. This was nothing new. He'd dealt with angry relatives before and knew how to defuse this type of situation, although the women's companion seemed rather large and menacing, perhaps even prone to violence by the looks of him, but hopefully, it wouldn't come to that. "As I said, I am the executor of the will. Mr. Diamond entrusted me with this responsibility several years prior to his untimely death. It is my duty now to simply relay his wishes as he requested without comment or outburst until it has been read in its entirety. He looked directly at Mimi and Carl. "Are we clear?" he asked. Mimi frowned but nodded yes.

"How about you Mister . . . ?"

"Loomis," Carl replied.

Mister Loomis?" Carl begrudgingly rolled his eyes, but nodded agreement as well. The attorney stepped around behind his desk and sat down. "All right then," he said as he pulled an official looking document from a manila folder and began to read.

"I, Theodore Diamond, residing at 1134 S. Main St., Stambourg, Oregon, declare this to be my Will, and I revoke any and all wills and codicils I previously made.

"I direct my Executor, Jason R. Turnbull, Attorney at Law at Yates, Turnbull, Davis, and Hall to pay my enforceable unsecured debts . . ." As the lawyer covered the legalese mumbo jumbo before finally getting to the parts that concerned them Imogen and Simon listened attentively. Mimi and Carl slumped in their chairs, looking bored.

"ARTICLE III: Real Estate," Turnbull began, causing Mimi to perk up in her chair, fully stealing herself for that glorious moment when she would smugly give Imogen and Simon a richly satisfying smirk as they realized exactly who Teddy would be leaving his estate to. After all, she was the one who had done all the hard work raising him and putting up with his peccadilloes. And she was the one who had gone through all the trouble of getting a fake death certificate and submitting the paperwork. Maybe he'd felt sorry for Imogen and left her a trinket or something, but no way was she going to get anything substantial.

Turnbull continued. "I give all my tangible personal property and all policies and proceeds of insurance covering such property to Imogen Oliver. I further give all my residences, subject to any mortgages or encumbrances thereon, and all policies and proceeds of insurance covering such property, to Imogen Oliver."

Imogen audibly gasped and Turnbull raised his hand gesturing that he was not finished. "I give all the rest, residue, and remainder of my estate to Mimi Pinky Diamond, which includes . . . one brown 1987 Buick Grand National."

Like a gaping sinkhole Mimi's mouth transformed into the shape of a giant "O" and then, all holy chaos ensued. "Noooooo!!!!" Mimi shrieked. Like some crazed banshee, she flew out of her chair, catching her heel in it and knocking it over, intent on one goal and one goal only: inflicting pain and bloody hell on Imogen. Carl tried his best to grab her and pull her back, but she kicked him away and pounced on Imogen, clawing at her with her long fingernails. "You won't get my son's estate," Mimi screeched. Simon tried to intervene but quickly realized his help was not needed—Imogen was no slouch. She was perfectly capable of fending off Mimi's assault. Imogen didn't want to hurt her, so instead, spun Mimi around twisting her arm behind her, locking her up and preventing her from attacking her any further. By that time, Carl, who had come over to help Mimi, lunged menacingly at Imogen.

"Let go of her, you bitch!" he bellowed at Imogen just as Jason Turnbull stepped between them holding a baseball bat in which he kept handy for such occasions as this when clients behaved badly.

"Back off Lurch!" Turnbull pronounced as he held the bat aloft and trained it on Carl's head. Carl raised his hands in the air and complied, backing up a few steps.

"All right now people," he said without lowering the bat, "You," he said gesturing with the bat at Carl, "are going to walk out of my office and wait in the other room. My receptionist Marlene will be watching you and if you don't sit there quietly, she will call the police. Understood?"

A subdued Carl nodded and retreated from the office. Turnbull stood in front of Mimi Pinky. Her lipstick was smeared, and her hair was disheveled. She looked like she'd gone a couple of turns in the dryer.

"As for you, after Ms. Oliver lets you go," he said, "you are going to park yourself in that chair over there and not move or say a word. Got it?" Mimi nodded and Imogen let go of her arm and quickly stepped away from her.

"Sit," Turnbull instructed, to which Mimi obeyed. Once she was seated, he continued, "Okay, now here's how it's going to go." He lowered the bat to his side but did not put it away. "We're going to finish this up and there will be no more shouting, no more fighting. Do we all agree on that?"

"Yes," Simon and Imogen said in unison. Mimi pouted.

From his desk, Turnbull produced two sets of keys, to which he placed at either ends of his desk. "These are the keys to the

1987 Buick Grand National." He placed a piece of paper next to them. "This is the address where the vehicle is being stored. You must pick it up within 10 days, or you will be responsible for all storage fees. Is that clear?"

Mimi nodded. It was more than clear. This was about more than a stupid Grand National, this was Teddy's grand parting shot from the grave. It wasn't enough that he'd left everything to someone he barely knew, someone who had been partially responsible for his death. It went beyond that. The goddamned car was a message, punishment for what she'd done to him when he was 16, how she had made him perform certain favors, sexual ones with her in order for him to borrow the car to go out. And for a fleeting moment in her miserable life, Mimi Pinky felt a small stab of remorse. He must have hated me so much, she thought. A tear slipped down her cheek and Imogen, who glanced over, felt sorry for her.

"These are the keys to Teddy's building, the pawn shop downstairs, and the upstairs apartment," Turnbull continued. "In this folder is assorted paperwork regarding the transference of the deed and ownership of the property and its contents therein."

With that, he stood up and handed Mimi's paper and car keys to her. "You may leave now."

Mimi Pinky stood up slowly, pressed the wrinkles out of her gaudy dress, and snatched the items from him, but not before lobbing a hateful look at Imogen and Simon as she exited the office.

"That was rather unpleasant," Simon said to Turnbull. "Thank you, sir, for handling it so well."

"Oh, you mean the bat," Jason said snickering. "You would not believe how often this sort of thing happens." He handed the ring of door keys and folder to Imogen. "Good luck with your new business venture," he said.

"Thanks," Imogen mumbled as she and Simon exited the law office. Outside, Imogen glanced around checking to see if Mimi Pinky or Carl Loomis were lurking anywhere nearby, waiting to ambush them when they came out.

"What are you doing?" Simon asked.

"Checking to see if Mimi and her friend are still around. I don't see them anywhere," she said. "How about we grab a cup of coffee?" They ducked into a coffee place a block down, ordered their coffees and sat down. Imogen sighed. "Well . . . that was certainly eventful, wouldn't you say?"

Simon returned a weak smile. "Yes, you could say that."

"What do you think the significance of the car was? Why leave that to Mimi?" Simon was pretty sure he knew the answer.

"Do you remember when Mimi came over to the house that day?" Imogen nodded. "And do you remember me telling you what she said? About her unhealthy bond with Teddy?"

Imogen drew her hands to her forehead. "Yes," she said. "Yikes, now I remember. So awful."

Simon continued. "I suspect that the car had something to do with that. She may have used it as an inducement to continue their 'relationship' as it were. Perhaps letting him use it in exchange for . . ." he hesitated, "you know, sexual favors."

"Ugh, that is so nasty," Imogen said shaking her head in disgust. "What kind of mother does something like that to her own son? I have no love for Teddy, but geez, no wonder he was so messed up."

"It doesn't justify what he did to my mother though," Simon added.

"Oh, no, of course not," Imogen agreed, "but maybe, this is a good thing."

"How so?"

Imogen leaned forward. "Well, there's the satisfaction of denying Mimi what she wanted most."

"True," Simon acknowledged.

"But honestly, what am I going to do with a pawn shop?" she asked.

Simon shrugged. "Sell things, I don't know." That made Imogen smile. Simon could be so funny at times.

"Well, yeah, but I already have a job, a job that I'm good at, one that pays really well. But you don't." Simon looked away, ashamed. "Oh no, I didn't mean it like that," she quickly added, clutching his arm. "What I mean is, you could run it." Simon rolled his eyes.

"Think about it," Imogen continued. "It's the perfect operation for selling the miniature furniture you design. You'd sell other stuff too, but you could even branch out and build dollhouses to sell in the shop. You'd have the time, not to mention more space to work. Anything has to be better than the garage, right?"

Admittedly, the more she talked about it, the more Simon was warming up to the idea, although it still felt monumentally wrong to accept anything from Teddy. He had done the unthinkable, trapped his mother, nothing would ever change that. On the other hand, Imogen was correct about one thing—it would certainly be a devastating blow to Mimi Pinky. One couldn't put all the blame on Teddy's abhorrent behavior without also looking at the horrific damage his mother had inflicted upon him.

Imogen wasn't always so pragmatic, but in this instance, Simon had to concede that she was right. Accepting the shop would give him legitimacy in this time, and now that he could time travel, there was the potential for using the shop as a façade in much the same way Teddy had. It appeared to be the best option at the moment, despite his misgivings.

Imogen looked up at the clock on the wall: 11:30. "I have to go," she abruptly announced.

"Go? Where?" Simon asked, confused. She hadn't mentioned anything about having to be somewhere.

"I have to meet Jade," she said. "Remember, I told you. We're driving out to scope out her old house today."

"Oh yes, of course," he said. "I forgot."

"I have an idea," Imogen said. "Why don't you come with us. We're both going to Stambourg anyway. I can drop you off at the pawn shop." She pulled the keys out of her purse and held them up to him. "You can check it out. See what's there. What do you think?"

Simon pondered the idea. "Okay, but how will I get home?"

"I can pick you up. I'll text you if we're going to be late, but maybe you could call an Uber?" she suggested, cocking her head to the side sheepishly.

He was still getting used to using the smart phone, but he knew about Ubers and taxis and things, sort of. "Sure, I'll find a way back. Don't worry about me," he said.

Imogen gave him a quick peck on the cheek. "Okay! Let's go!"

18

See you later?" Imogen said to Simon after he had exited the car. He knew later meant late as it always was with Imogen. He'd likely need to get a ride, but that was okay. He was quite curious to see what was inside Teddy's shop.

"I'll see you at home," he said, waving goodbye as Imogen and Jade drove away. A gust of wind whipped up around his legs, and Simon watched as it picked up dry leaves sending them swirling end over end down the street. Stambourg, at least this part of town, was markedly rundown. Here at the south end of Main Street, most of the businesses catered to a different crowd than the more upscale Northern portion of the city. A coin-operated laundry across the street, liquor stores, a few seedy pubs, a couple of bawdy houses, a few restaurants—a chop suey joint, a diner, and a taqueria and, of course, Teddy Diamond's pawn shop, which traded in guns, jewelry, musical instruments—things people were willing to part with, Simon assumed, if they were down on their luck and needed a little cash or drink.

Simon breathed in, hesitating before placing the key in the front door's lock and turning it. What am I getting myself into? he contemplated. Everything still seemed strange, he always felt out of place no matter how hard he tried to pretend it wasn't so. It was a constant struggle, but what did he have to go back to, honestly? His job as a school principal, alone, no family.

As he pushed the door open, the wind followed him inside with a whoosh, sending not leaves skittering this time, but hundreds of papers wafted through the air like the ticker tape parades he'd read about. Books and papers littered the floor everywhere.

A few chairs were tipped over. It looked as though the books had been yanked from a bookcase along the back wall. From what he could surmise the glass display cases appeared undamaged, the items housed within them still there, but it appeared that the place had been ransacked by someone searching for something specific.

Concerned that the person or persons that had done this might still be lurking about, Simon quickly closed the front door behind him and dead bolted it. He carefully waded into the mess, picking up things here and there as he cleared a path. In the back office behind the main shop, all the drawers of a filing cabinet had been flung open and invoices and business papers tossed about the room. In the hallway, he felt cold air coming in from the bathroom and upon inspection found that the window was wide open. That must have been how they got in.

Closing up the window, locking it, and searching through every room, Simon felt satisfied that he was alone before returning to the shop space to begin the laborious job of cleaning up. Not sure where to begin, he first created a haphazard pile of the papers to sort through later. That took a good while, but the books were heavy and there were many of them. Some of them were old and tattered. Thinking they might be rare; Simon took special care in handling them. Back and forth he went, picking them up and replacing them on the bookshelf. Realizing he'd filled up most of the bottom shelves that he could comfortably reach, he searched around for a footstool to get to the higher shelves.

As he was placing books on one of the upper shelves, his hand brushed against something in the back corner. At first, he thought it might just be a flaw in the wood, but upon closer inspection, he realized it was a button. Curious, Simon pushed it. A panel slid open, revealing a hollowed-out space in the wall behind the bookshelf. Reticent about sticking his hand into a dark, unidentifiable place where spiders or rats might be in residence, Simon climbed back down and went searching for a flashlight. He located one and shining the light inside didn't reveal any vermin, thank goodness; however, there were several journal-like books inside, which he reached in and carefully pulled out. They seemed nothing special, the kind of inexpensive essay writing books you might pick up at a college bookstore, but they must be important, Simon speculated, otherwise why would someone have bothered to hide them inside a wall? After returning the rest of the books to the bookcase, righting the overturned chairs, and mostly straightening things up, Simon returned to the journals he'd left on the end table. Sitting down in an old, but surprisingly comfy chair upholstered in a floral fabric from some bygone era, he opened up the first one and began to read:

My therapist said I should write stuff down. So here goes. She started it when I was about seven. She called me her little man and her Teddy bear. At first, I liked the attention. It was nice to snuggle up in the big bed with her. She was warm and squishy, and it felt good to be loved. But when her boyfriends were there, mother wouldn't let me come into the bed with her.

One time, after Dale moved out, she asked me to get in bed with her, but when I got in under the covers, she wasn't wearing anything. The first time she touched me I knew it wasn't right, but I just wanted her to love me and hug me like she used to. I hated Mimi but I loved her too and she ruined me.

Simon stopped reading. Obviously, this was Teddy's journal. Written on the behest of his therapist, he had laid out every painfully gross detail of the unholy alliance he shared with his mother, Mimi Pinky. Reading it was like watching a train wreck; you wanted to look away, but you couldn't. At times, Simon had to set it aside and take a breather before continuing—it was that disturbing. Mimi Pinky was a monster. Imogen was right, it was no wonder Teddy turned out the way he did.

When I was 16 I got my driver's license. I was really happy about that, except like everything else, using Mimi's car came at a price. I had to have sex with her to borrow it. I know how twisted and sick that sounds, and it was. I hated myself and I hated everything about that car. I really did. It was this ugly piece of shit brown 1987 Buick Grand National. I hated driving it, but it was worth it to get out of the house and away from her.

"Ah," Simon said aloud. Just as he had suspected. The car was the only thing Teddy had left to Mimi in his will. It was a slap in the face and the shocked look on Mimi's face at the lawyer's office today confirmed that she too understood the significance of it.

To pay for gas I got a job working part time in Niles Oliver's photography studio and that's where I met Tiffany Rose Elliot.

Simon gulped reading his mother's name written in the journal. Here we go, he thought, preparing himself for what would come next.

I liked Tiffany a lot. She didn't mind that I smoked pot. She liked riding in the car with me, but she was annoying too. I hated the way she was always fiddling with her hair. Sometimes I wanted to smack her, but she let me touch her boobs, so I put up with it. One night when we were parked out in the country we were making out and I guess I was frustrated because she wouldn't let me do what I wanted. I got really mad at her, and I know it was wrong now, but I forced her to have sex with me. We stopped seeing each other after that but a few months later she told me she was pregnant. She wanted to get married. When I told her I didn't want to she said that I had to because I was 18 and she wasn't. She said she'd tell everyone I raped her, and they would send me to jail. I was scared and mad. I shouldn't have done it, but I didn't know what else to do. I had figured out how to time travel from watching Mr. Oliver, so one day, I took Tiffany to the park by the high school. I had an old picture of our town, and I took her with me through it. I can still hear her screaming when I left her there.

Before noticing it, Simon's hands were gripping the book so hard his knuckles were turning white. He could barely contain the rage surging through him as he finished reading Teddy's passage. Any empathy he had previously felt for the guy was gone. Nothing, . . . nothing, could ever make up for what he had done to Tiffany—his mother.

Simon slammed the notebook closed and chucked it across the room. On an intellectual level, he knew the story, he knew what Teddy did, but reading it now written down in Teddy's own words, in his own handwriting, made it even more devastatingly real and raw. He raped her, goddamn it! Simon felt sick, like he might vomit. The thought of what he had done to her was bad enough, but the knowledge that this deplorable human being was his father made a million times worse. Simon stood up and began to pace, his fists clenched. He wanted to hit something, a wall or someone, anything to calm the fuck down. He needed a drink. Yes, that's what he needed.

There was a liquor store nearby, he knew, but maybe there was something stashed here in the store somewhere. Simon marched back to the room behind the main shop. He hadn't paid much attention before when he'd been in here to how big it was. Imogen was right, it would make a great workshop—much better than the garage. This was good, he thought. Thinking other thoughts helped soothe his seething anger a bit, but he still wanted that drink.

In a far corner of the room, was a small kitchen area with cupboards, a sink, and a counter with a microwave and coffee maker on top, and beside it a small refrigerator. This must have been used as a break room, he thought. Simon began rifling through the cupboards. The first contained a few mismatched plates and coffee mugs. A second cupboard held more promise. As he rummaged around behind the instant coffee, assorted boxes of tea, and packages of ramen noodles, he found a bottle of pretty good scotch, about a third full, stowed in the back. "Eureka!" he bellowed, pulling it out and then grabbing a coffee mug from the cupboard to pour the liquid into. The bastard at least had moderately good taste. "To dad" he said sarcastically, lifting his glass and killing it in one gulp.

Three shots later, Simon felt reasonably ready to return to Teddy's journal, although it didn't get any better.

. . . I respected Mr. Oliver, Niles. He was always straight up with me, and it seemed like he wanted to help me get somewhere. Nobody had ever done that for me before, but when he started asking questions about Tiffany, I knew I had to do something. He found an old picture of her. I guess she thought that if she took pictures of herself in the place and time I'd dumped her she could leave them for someone in the future to find and rescue her. It might have worked if I hadn't done what I did. I knew it was wrong too, but I didn't have a choice, so when I saw the photo that Niles had gone into I tore it up and burned it. There was another picture there too, one that Mrs. Oliver, Francis had went to probably. It looked like San

Francisco. I knew she went there sometimes. I burned it up too. I didn't think about Imogen or how she would be an orphan. I just wanted to keep them from finding out what I did to Tiffany.

Simon couldn't take much more, flipping forward, he turned to the last few pages of the journal.

I loved them. They were the family I wished I had. I was always jealous of Imogen. I never hated her though. I kind of loved her, even though she was just a kid. That's why if anything happens to me I want her to have the pawn shop. She'll know what to do with it, how to use it.

My mother, Mimi Pinky, she will never, ever get her hands on it. I will see to that. She deserves nothing. I HATE her.

Simon shut the book and poured another shot. He sat quietly nursing his scotch for a while, absorbing Teddy's words, wishing he hadn't read them, but also glad he did. When he finally leaned over and picked up the second journal a photograph fell out. It was a sepia photo of a Colonial Revival mansion. Simon recognized the design. It had been popular among the wealthy when he was growing up around the turn of the 20th century. Much like the dollhouses that he designed and built his miniature furniture for, the homes were typically large, stately, and distinguished, two stories with a symmetrical façade, hipped roofs and dormers, columns in the front, and side porches or sunrooms.

This one was quite large. Obviously an estate, it featured a massive, landscaped lawn and garden with many trees and an array of ornamental shrubs and flowers in front. Simon set the photo aside and opened the notebook.

Different than the first, which had been Teddy's personal confessional, this one contained detailed notes—names, dates, times, events, places, contacts, directions, aliases he had used. Clearly, it was information Teddy had gleaned from his travels through time. Many of the contacts in the book appeared to be businesses you didn't hear of anymore, names like Shiels Jewelers, Pickwick Records, Littleton Coin Company, Vroman's Bookstore, Goldblatts, Ax Billy Department Store—Simon remembered that one, he had visited the Ax Billy as a child. It was long gone now.

Simon hadn't made his way upstairs yet to Teddy's living quarters, but from the looks of it, he suspected that he had used the pawn shop as a front for his true business—gambling, betting on ball games and boxing matches, and other events, which he knew the results of beforehand, and through the later retrieval of items from the past that he knew would be valuable in the future.

As he scanned the pages of the notebook, a name on one page jumped out at him—Eastman. Where had he heard that name before? Simon wondered and then he remembered. Oh yes, just the other day, from the DNA results. Someone with that name was listed on his family tree. About him Teddy wrote:

Doing some genealogy I found out that my great grandfather was George Eastman of Eastman Kodak company. When I had some downtime, I decided to go back and poke around . . .

Teddy stood in front of George Eastman's 8.5-acre urban estate in Rochester, New York. It was always a bit of a shock entering a black and white photograph and seeing the vivid colors pop into view on the other side. He'd looked it up online. The estate was equipped with working farmland, formal gardens, greenhouses, stables, barns, pastures, and the 35,000-square-foot, 50-room mansion was made of reinforced concrete.

"This must be da place," he said, amused by what he perceived as a clever New York accent. He couldn't wait to get inside. He'd read that the house, which was built in 1905, had a slew of modern conveniences, unusual for the time, an electrical generator, an internal telephone system with 21 stations, a built-in vacuum cleaning system, a central clock network, an elevator, and a pipe organ. Reading all of this had especially piqued Teddy's interest. That stuff would be worth a mint now. And if this truly was his great grandfather, might he be inclined to leave some of his riches to a future grandson?

It was the Eastman Museum in Teddy's time, but other than a few additions and modifications, the place looked the same . . . big, formidable;

he wondered how he might get in, but there didn't appear to be anyone around at the moment, so Teddy strolled up the pathway unimpeded, marveling at the grandeur of the gardens and the four huge pillars that greeted visitors at the elegant front door. He thought to knock, but on a lark, pressed the handle to which, surprisingly, the door opened. Pushing it open slowly, he tipped his head inside and looked both ways, making sure no one was around before ducking inside. The entryway was huge, and the grand staircase cascaded down like a waterfall from the upper floor. Fine tile flooring covered with dozens of fine oriental rugs and sitting chairs filled up the room. Most impressive was the sheer number of very large potted plants that seemed to be situated in every conceivable nook and cranny, creating a jungle-like vibe.

Teddy wandered in and out of spaces, each more impressive than the next—a living room with high carved ceilings and walls and a massive fireplace, a library filled with shelves upon shelves of books, even a billiard room! Now that was something Teddy would love to have. But the conservatory was even more over the top. Mahogany and glass French doors opened onto a view of a spectacular terrace garden. High ceilings covered in windows drew light into the space filled with even more giant plants, a collection of strange and exotic taxidermy animals, and mounted on the wall, an elephant's head!

Teddy stealthily ascended the stairs to the second floor, which featured many bedrooms, sitting rooms, an office. On the third floor, he found what he assumed was Eastman's screening room, workshop, and dark room where he began poking around, opening and peering into cabinets and looking in drawers, which mostly held miscellaneous photography tools, glassware, drying trays, and chemicals. He wasn't looking for anything in particular, just curious mainly. One drawer he opened contained an ordinary notebook, which he may have ignored had the title not caught his attention: A Guide to Photographic Time Travel.

"What's this?" Teddy mumbled under his breath, lifting it from the drawer and opening it up to the first page.

"Everyone can travel forward in time. We do it at a steady rate of one second per second. Einstein's theory of relativity suggests that we live in a four-dimensional continuum in which space and time are interchangeable. The faster we move through space, the slower we move through time. However, while Einstein's theory attempts to explain time travel to the future, it stops short of how one might move backward in time, to the past.

Now, that question has been answered. Through experimentation with photography, the capability of time travel to the past has been revealed, but there are rules and consequences, which will be outlined in more detail later in the text."

"Excuse me," a weak voice said, "who are you?"

Startled, Teddy jumped, closing the book and attempting to hide it behind his back. A frail man with a cane, wearing a fancy dressing gown and slippers stood in the doorway.

"Uh, um, I was just looking around," Teddy stammered, certain that he'd been caught.

"Have you an interest in photography?" the man asked.

Teddy was relieved. Seemed he wasn't in trouble after all. "Why yes," he answered, "I do."

The elderly man took a wobbly step forward, his face wincing as though he was in severe pain. Teddy set the book down and walked over to the man. "Can I help you," he asked, reaching for the man's arm. Teddy could be quite charming when he needed to.

"Yes, yes," the gentleman said as Teddy guided him to a nearby chair to sit.

After he was seated, Teddy was taken aback when the man bluntly asked, "Are you a traveler?"

"Well, yes," he said. "I'm from the Northwest."

"Not that kind of travel dummy," he said. "What year? What year are you from?" How did he know? Teddy wondered.

"Are you George Eastman?" Teddy asked.

"I am," the man answered, his voice shaky, yet growing impatient. "What year?" he repeated, sighing.

Teddy hesitated before answering. Okay, the jig was up. No use pulling out an alias to use. This guy obviously knew he was out of time. He was probably the one who wrote that book. He was George Eastman after all, inventor of Kodak cameras and roll film.

"My name is Teddy Diamond," he said, "I'm from the year 2019."

Eastman barely batted an eye, his facial expression remained unchanged.

"I saw you looking at the book. I assumed that's what you came here looking for."

Teddy was honestly confused. "Uh, no, I just found it in a drawer, saw the title, and was curious, that's all."

Eastman raised his eyebrow suspiciously. "Are you sure this is the first time you saw it?"

Teddy nodded his head. "Yes, sir.

Eastman seemed relieved. "Have a seat Teddy Diamond. We'll have a little chat. Bring me the book, and can you close that door first?" Teddy went back and retrieved the book from the drawer, closed the door to the workshop, and pulled up a chair across from George Eastman, who took the book and holding it tightly on his lap, began to slowly speak.

"In 1906, I stumbled upon a formula for time travel. It involved one entering a deep meditative state. He paused and looked at Teddy. "On account of you being here, evidently it works," he added.

"I shared my discovery with several of my colleagues, fellow scientists, and we agreed that the finding and the existence of the book should remain a secret," he continued.

"The Spiritualist movement, which has an interest in ghosts, levitation, contacting the dead through seances, and the like, had been gaining popularity since the late 19th century. This included spirit photography, which attracted the attention of many intellectual figures, including scientists Alfred Russell Wallace and Charles Richet, and author Sir Arthur Conan Doyle, among others," he explained. "But charlatans preying on the emotions of grieving individuals, took to manipulating photographs by adding in preexposed images of their dead relatives."

"Like photoshopping them," Teddy interjected.

"If that means using trickery, then yes," Eastman answered, shooting Teddy a salty look for interrupting him.

"At any rate," he continued, "people were leery of photography, many even believing that taking someone's picture could steal their soul.

"If photography itself was suspect, we believed that the public was not ready for something as groundbreaking as time travel. We did not know how having this knowledge might change the world. If everyone could time travel, would it rip the universe apart? Could items that might be removed from circulation in the past, what we named the "misery index," cause a ripple effect with catastrophic results in the future? We agreed that the phenomenon required more study."

"So, why are you telling me all this?" Teddy asked as he shifted uncomfortably in his chair.

"I am dying," Eastman said sighing.

"Are you sick?" Teddy asked.

"My spirit is sick. It is broken," Eastman said, "and when the spirit dies, the body follows." Eastman leaned forward and said, "I'll ask you again, son. Are you here for the book?"

Teddy was intrigued by Eastman's story, sure, but what did he care about a bunch of scientists fussing over photoshopped pictures and misery indexes, whatever the hell that was? "Look, mister," he said, "the only reason I came here was because I was curious. I don't give a rat's ass about your stupid book or any of that. I was just looking up genealogy stuff and it said you were my great grandpa. I never met anyone famous that I was related to, that's all."

Eastman didn't react or respond at first, but after a moment, reached out and grabbed Teddy's hand with some urgency and said, "You must take the book, Teddy, and hide it. Keep it safe. People are looking for it. Bad people. People who want to kill me!"

Suddenly, the door flew open and a woman in a starched white nurse's uniform and cap entered the room. "Mr. Eastman!" she cried out, stepping forward. "What in the world are you doing out of bed, and who is this visitor?" she demanded to know as she glared at Teddy.

Eastman shoved the book into Teddy's hand and whispered, "Take it. Put it somewhere safe." Teddy did not understand any of it, but it seemed important to his grandfather. He took the book from him and slipped it inside his jacket just as the bossy nurse approached.

"It's all right Ruth," Eastman reassured his agitated caretaker. "Teddy is a friend," he said as the woman helped him get up from his chair. Ruth shot Teddy a stern look. "Teddy, is it?" she asked. Teddy nodded. "Please show yourself out now. Mr. Eastman needs his rest."

Eastman nodded knowingly at Teddy as Ruth steered the shuffling elderly man toward the doorway. Before exiting though Eastman briefly turned back to glance at Teddy and smiled weakly before giving his future grandson a parting wink.

. . . When I got back, I put Eastman's notebook in a safe in my apartment. I always keep the key with me at all times because I hope to one day find the right buyer for the right price.

A key? Simon hadn't noticed any keys lying around, and then it dawned on him—the keys to the shop, of course. The key to the safe must be on the keyring, he hoped it was anyway. Pulling the keys from his pocket, he noticed several other keys on the ring. Well, he'd only know by trying. Simon hadn't made it upstairs to Teddy's apartment yet. Who knew what he'd find there? Would it be picked over and vandalized too? He laid Teddy's notebook aside and stood up. Time to find out.

But where might the entrance be? He assessed the bottom level, opening closet doors, looking for stairs, but found none. The only thing he could think was that the entrance must be on the outside. When he left the shop to go outside to look, he made sure to lock up and headed toward the back of the brick building.

Tucked around the back he discovered a separate entrance with a steel door double locked with a deadbolt. Simon pulled the keys from his pocket and tried one of the larger keys. It worked. After several tries, a secondary key opened the deadbolt. A staircase led to the top level where Simon was met with yet another substantial-looking door. Simon had to wonder why Teddy's living quarters were secured like a fortress, but the pawn shop was not. Perhaps he kept the most valuable items there?

He had wondered why there were so many keys on the keychain, now he understood why. He unlocked the door to Teddy's apartment and entered it. In stark contrast to the bland, no frills pawn shop downstairs Teddy's domicile was a virtual palace, not for its creature comforts nor its orderliness—the place was a mess—but for its treasures. Every conceivable corner was cluttered with items. Stacked from floor to ceiling were rarities and antiquities from around the world, alongside piles of collectibles still in their original packaging, statues, books, jewelry, and paintings. Simon stared in awe of the sheer volume of accumulated stuff stowed in this one room.

No wonder he kept it under lock and key. This was where

the real money and deals were made. As he suspected, the pawn shop was a front. And no wonder Mimi Pinky wanted it so bad, it was likely worth a fortune. Imogen would never have to work again ever if she chose.

Temporarily distracted by the room's contents, Simon nearly forgot what he had come up here looking for—Eastman's notebook. Teddy had written that there was a safe somewhere but locating it in this chaotic mess would be a challenge. Where to even begin? He started by canvassing each room, checking the obvious places—behind books in the bookcase, around the television stand, in closets, behind pictures on the wall. He figured it wouldn't be so obvious as to be under a floorboard, but he scooted rugs aside and checked just the same. Teddy's bedroom, the only room free of clutter—was meticulously clean, the bed perfectly made, everything tidy, a sort of stylish man cave removed from the chaos of the other rooms. It was complete with a massive wall-mounted television, stereo sound, a mini-bar—so it appeared that, at least in here, Teddy did enjoy a bit of the good life.

Moving on, he entered the kitchen. It was nice, modern, clean. He searched through cupboards and drawers, and found other things stashed, for instance, an envelope full of cash taped to the outer side of a silverware drawer. He opened the pantry where Teddy's food supply consisted mainly of an abundance of what Imogen despised, processed foods—packaged mashed potatoes, mac and cheese, ramen noodles, soup, cereal. Moving from shelf to shelf he meticulously pushed items aside but found nothing. He was ready to give up when on the second to the bottom shelf, he pushed some boxes of dressing aside and bingo! Another button like the one he'd found downstairs behind the bookcase. When he pressed it, a door in the wall opened revealing a hidden safe in the wall. Fishing in his pocket for the keys, Simon tried several until one of the smaller ones worked. Inside he found some jewelry and papers, which appeared to be an assortment of fake birth certificates, and an envelope stuffed with several loose photographs. The ones on top were old and showed Tiffany and Simon as a child. These Teddy had probably removed from the studio to keep Niles from finding them, he figured. The last few surprised him—pictures of Imogen in various stages of life—as a child, in a silly pose in the front yard, the sun reflecting off her golden hair—innocent, happy; as a teenager dressed all in black—jet black hair, black dress, black boots, pale skin, lots of black eyeliner around her eyes, looking angry and quite morose.

The last few were more recent, and it looked as though he had taken these from afar, perhaps using a powerful camera lens to zoom in close. The final shots in the pile were startling, to say the least. The subject of these was quite unexpected—Imogen's mother Francis. They were candid shots of her as she posed playfully uninhibited, seductively for whomever was behind the camera taking the pictures. The obvious assumption was that Niles must have taken them seeing as how he was a professional photographer, but how and why would Teddy be in possession of them? He may have stolen them from Niles, but a darker option crossed Simon's mind, could Teddy have been the one taking the photographs? It raised a lot of puzzling questions, for certain.

Placing the photos back in the envelope, he reached back into the safe and retrieved what he was looking for—a notebook, with words written on the front in fancy script: *A Guide to Photographic Time Travel.*

Simon flipped through the pages. A quick scan showed that it was filled with diagrams and a lot of text. Inserted inside of it was a newspaper article on George Eastman's death by suicide in 1932, along with a photocopied image of Eastman's suicide letter, dated March 14, 1932.

The inventor of film on rolls and the Kodak camera—the father of popular photography—had been quite ill and shot himself in the heart with a luger pistol at the age of 77, or had he? Simon wondered aloud. Teddy had written in his notebook that Eastman said that he feared for his life. If someone was trying so hard to find his notebook now, might someone in 1932 have harmed, even murdered Eastman to get to get their hands on it?

Seated at the kitchen table in Teddy's apartment, Simon focused hard on the photograph lying in front of him. He had been sitting like this for the past 25 minutes, but so far, nothing was happening. Could he have imagined that he time traveled? Perhaps the first time had been a fluke after all. He pushed those thoughts away and pressed on, surrendering his mind, allowing his thoughts to drift away on a tranquil sea of nothingness until the darkness began to surround the edge of his peripheral vision. Teddy's apartment began to lose shape and become opaque until it completely disappeared altogether and time pulling him backward, deposited him to a sidewalk outside a mansion in 1932.

19

Daddy?"

"What Imogen?"

"Is there a god?"

"That's an awfully big question for a little girl?"

"Well, is there one, a god?"

"I'm not sure. Why are you asking?"

"I learned a new word," she said brightly. "Infinity. I looked it up and it means something that has no beginning or end. Andy, my friend at school told me that at his church they said that god has always been there, forever and ever, and so I started to think about infinity and I tried to imagine a god just always being there, but who made god? I thought about it so much it made my head hurt." Niles chuckled and patted Imogen's hand.

"Try not to dwell on it too much Imogen. I know it's hard but thinking about infinity will drive you crazy."

"Did you think about stuff like that when you were a kid too?"

"Oh yes," he said, nodding, remembering. "Here's the thing, Imogen. We all want the answers to the universe and it's frustrating when we can't get them." He really didn't want to get into a lengthy explanation tonight about religion, but he forged ahead hoping she'd be satisfied with his explanation. "People have their own beliefs and that's fine. It helps them cope with things they don't understand. But the one thing I do believe in is science. You can always count on the validity of something if there is scientific evidence to prove it. If there is none, then it is only someone's opinion and that doesn't make it true."

Satisfied with his answer, Imogen yawned and rubbed her eyes wearily with her knuckles. "Okay Daddy, I think I'll go to sleep now."

Niles tucked the blanket in around her. "Good girl. No more thinking about infinity tonight, right?"

She turned over on her side. "Right."

"But daddy?"

"Yes Imogen."

Is time travel real?"

"Goodnight, Imogen."

"Goodnight, Niles."

"Imogen . . . Imogen!"

Imogen heard her name, but was so lost in the memory, it barely registered. "Gen!" the voice repeated, this time louder. Jade was shaking her arm. "My goodness, where were you?" Jade asked. "I was afraid you were going into some time travel trance and were ready to disappear on me. I wondered if I needed to be ready to take the wheel!"

Imogen laughed. "Oh, I'm sorry Jade. I was just lost in thought. Driving does that to me," she reassured her friend. "And besides, I need to focus on a photograph to travel somewhere."

"I wasn't sure how it worked," Jade said, twisting toward Imogen in the passenger seat. "So, what were you thinking so hard about?"

Imogen looked over at Jade. "I was thinking about my dad." Jade nodded, unsurprised considering they were headed off to find him, who knows where.

"Do you think we'll find him?" Jade asked.

Imogen sighed. "I don't know," she said. "I want to find him, but I also *don't* want to. Does that make sense?"

"It makes perfect sense," Jade said. Imogen's face became a wrinkle of worry. "The last time we saw each other, I was nine," she told her friend. I'm afraid he won't remember me."

Jade rubbed Imogen's shoulder. "Don't worry. How could he not remember you? You were so 'Daddy's Girl.'"

"All my life, I wanted a dad, just not my dad—*your* dad," Jade continued. "He was everything I thought a dad should be. You don't know how lucky you were, Imogen."

"He was good, wasn't he? I do feel lucky to have had him

for a little while. I didn't have much interaction with my mother. He made up for it though," she said. "I loved your mother, Jade. She was so awesome. Do you remember when she used to sing?" Imogen asked.

"I sure do, and she still does!" Jade answered conjuring up a memory of Monique and breaking into a song by Sade, one of her mother's favorite smooth jazz artists. *No need to ask, he's a smooth operator*, Jade sang in a silky voice as she began to bob and weave her head and move her shoulders to and fro in perfect rhythm. Imogen laughed and joined in.

Smooth operator,
Smooth operator,
Smooth operator . . .

They were still singing when they turned the corner into Jade's old neighborhood. Imogen followed the GPS directions, rolling up to a small and simple white stick house on Juniper Lane. "Is this it?" Imogen asked Jade.

"I believe it is," Jade answered. It looked much the same as she remembered it, although it appeared the neighborhood had undergone a makeover since she lived there in the 90s. Back then, the houses were a bit rundown and neglected, but now all the houses and yards along the block were neat and tidy.

"Should we drive around back to the alley?" Jade asked.

"That might look suspicious," Imogen said. "Maybe we park the car around the block and walk down the alley?" Jade agreed and after parking a short distance from the house the two women got out and headed for the narrow stretch separating two blocks of houses. Once a gravel road that served as the garbage pickup route, it was now a paved shortcut. Imogen counted houses as they walked until they reached the fourth one down on the left.

"This is it," she said, walking over to survey the fence. There was an outline of a gate and hinges. "Well, there's a gate here," she said, turning back to Jade. "What do you think, should we go for it? Doesn't look like anyone is home."

Jade felt uneasy. "I don't know Imogen; it's still light out," she said as she glanced around. Why don't we wait and come back after dark?"

Imogen looked at the time on her phone. It was 3:30—still a few hours until dusk. "Let's go get dinner. I'll call Simon and see if he needs to be picked up." Imogen tried his cell phone, but it went to voicemail. "Simon, it's me. Jade and I are going to grab dinner. Call or text me if you need a ride home. Love you, bye."

Jade and Imogen finished their dinner and at around 7:30 drove back to Juniper Lane. They first drove past the house. No lights were on inside; it didn't appear that anyone was at home. Parking in the same place as last time, Imogen grabbed a small shovel from the back, and they walked down the alleyway until they were again standing outside the gate.

Jade was still not convinced this was a good idea. "How do we know that they won't come home and catch us?" she asked.

"We don't," Imogen whispered as she leaned the shovel against the fence and began pushing against the area of the fence where the gate was outlined. She managed to get it to budge about an inch, but something on the other side was blocking it. "Help me," Imogen instructed Jade and they both pressed their weight against it. Finally, it opened wide enough that Imogen could push her arm through. On the other side, she felt metal and the shape of a bicycle and a few other bin-type things. Pushing as hard as they could, they managed to move the contents in front of it enough for them to squeeze through.

Imogen went first, pushing her body through the opening and into the backyard. It was dark, but she could tell that the yard was fairly large and there were a number of trees and bushes, which would be good for concealment.

"Come on Jade," she whispered through the gate. Jade followed her through the gap. "I can't believe we're doing this Imogen," Jade said, "This is so illegal. Is this what you do? As a PI?"

"Sort of," Imogen answered. Once they were both on the other side, Imogen turned to Jade, "Okay, can you remember approximately where Niles dug the hole?" She remembered playing in this yard, but a lot of the bushes had grown up since she was here last. Glancing toward the house, she did recognize her old bedroom window.

"There," she pointed, "right there on the right, that was my bedroom, and I recall looking out the window and it seemed like I saw him digging by the fence straight across from me."

They crept along the fence until they were in a direct line of the window Jade had pointed out.

"So here, you think?" Imogen said, placing the shovel in the spot.

"I guess," Jade said, shrugging. "I'll go first." Imogen handed Jade the shovel and she stuck it into the ground and stood on top of it with both feet to get it started. Luckily, there was no grass, only dirt, so at least it wouldn't be too noticeable that someone had been digging. She pulled up a large chunk, tossed it aside and continued digging. She had dug down about six inches when she abruptly stopped and looked around.

"Did you hear that?" she whispered.

Imogen scanned the yard. "No, keep digging."

"I thought I heard something," Jade said.

"I didn't, but let's hurry up," Imogen said, taking the shovel from Jade's hands and starting to dig faster. Just as the shovel struck something, they heard a dog barking, and the back porch light switched on.

Jade began shifting nervously from one foot to the other. "Ooooh, shit, hurry up Imogen!"

They heard the back door open, and a male voice shout, "Who's out there?"

The dog was still barking frantically from inside the house. Imogen dropped the shovel and reaching into the hole with both hands she began to tug on something wrapped up in plastic. They were off by a few inches, but she pulled as Jade frantically dug the dirt out from around it.

The dog's barking was getting louder and closer. Evidently the owner had released it from inside the house. "Got it!" Imogen said, triumphantly holding it up.

Jade grabbed Imogen's arm. "Run!"

They sprinted along the fence to the gate and Jade squeezed through it with Imogen close behind her. Imogen managed to get through just as the barking, growling dog reached them. Imogen pulled the gate closed behind them and without looking back they hightailed it down the alley and around the block to the car where they both jumped in and closed the doors, out of breath and breathing hard.

"Go!" Jade cried as Imogen fumbled with the keys before inserting the correct one and starting up the car.

"Shit! We forgot the shovel," Imogen said as they drove away.

"Oh my god, that was close," Jade said once they were safely out of the neighborhood.

"Did you see that dog?" Imogen said. "All big and snarly—I thought for sure it was going to bite me!"

Imogen drove to a convenience store and parked under a streetlight to inspect what they'd dug up. Picking it up off the seat, she carefully opened the dirt-encrusted baggie. Inside was a faded yellow notebook.

Her memory jogged by the yellow color; Jade gasped. "That's it. I remember it—it's the one he used to carry around with him all the time," she said.

Imogen tried calling Simon again without success. "Let's swing by the pawn shop and see if he's there." She placed the book back inside of the plastic, and said, "We'll look at this at home later, okay?"

When Imogen and Jade pulled up outside the pawn shop it was dark and deserted. Imogen tried the front door, but it was locked up tight. She knocked a few times, no answer. Figuring Simon must have called an Uber and was probably on his way home, they headed for home too.

Imogen's house was dark when they arrived and there was no sign of Simon. Imogen was slightly worried, but also eager to open a notebook written by her dad that had not seen the light of day since the late 90s.

Delicately removing the notebook from the plastic again, Imogen opened it up. Tucked inside the front of it was a folded letter containing a Polaroid photo. Imogen turned the picture around for Jade to see. In it, Jade and her mother, who was holding her baby sister Sasha, stood in front of the very house from which Imogen and Jade had fled from earlier tonight. Jade took the photo from Imogen and examined it more closely. "I don't remember this being taken," she said "but I do remember the dress. It was my Sunday school dress, so this was probably before or after church."

Imogen opened the letter and began to read:

Dear Imogen,

I know this will sound crazy to you but bear with me. If you are reading this, it means that you have found my journal and somehow, some time, Jade must have led you back to this place. I hope sooner than later. Your mother and I are time travelers. We are able to enter the time of any photograph.

Two months ago, in my timeline, I tried to return home, but discovered I could not. I think something may have happened to my portal, a photo Jade had sent to you, the one of her standing in front of her new home that was pasted on the mirror in your bedroom. Your mother was traveling at the same time. I fear that whoever tampered with my portal may have done something to hers as well. I don't dare leave this at our house if someone did this to us.

Enclosed is a different photo. Please ask your grandmother for help. She is also a traveler and will know what to do.

My journal recounts the last two months. I do not know what will happen tomorrow when I reach my original launch date, October 10, 1997, the day that I entered the photo. I don't know whether time will reset or something worse.

I hope that you will be able to find a way to help me.

With Love, your dad, Niles Oliver

Imogen laid the letter aside on the coffee table and looked away.

"Are you okay?" Jade asked. Imogen drew a deep breath. "I think I know where he's been, or where he is, if he's still there, that is."

"Where?" Jade asked.

"I may have gone there once back in high school," Imogen said.

"I had been looking at a picture. It was of you and me and dad and all of a sudden, I wasn't in the bathroom anymore. I was outside lying on a lawn, but there was nothing else around me, no house, nothing—just grass and darkness, but I could hear voices and sounds and smell the barbecue. Granted, I had eaten some mushrooms," she added, "but still, this was real, and terrifying. I didn't know anything about time travel then.

"Later on, when I remembered back on it, I assumed that the universe must send you to some limbo place to prevent you from running into another version of yourself. I was able to think about where I was before it happened and go back, but I wonder if my dad, because there was no photo to go back to, got stuck in that same limbo spot and maybe he's still there, all this time, in some sort of strange halfway house purgatory."

Memories of that dark place came rushing back at once and Imogen teared up. Being there for only a few minutes was terrible for her; picturing her dad trapped in a place like that for years was too horrible to contemplate.

"Oh Imogen, don't cry sweetie," Jade said, trying to comfort her friend. She put her arm around her and pulled her close.
"I can't imagine being trapped in that awful place," Imogen sobbed. "All this time—who knows what's become of him. He could be a raving lunatic."

"Don't think like that," Jade consoled. "Your dad's a strong person. I'm sure he's okay."

"Really?" Imogen cried, pushing Jade away. "You're sure?"

Jade struggled for a response, "Well no, I'm . . . I'm not sure, but . . ."

"But you don't know." Imogen started crying more. "What if

he's crazy, or worse, dead? Honestly, I don't think I could bear it again Jade. For most of my childhood I believed he had died, and it took me a long time to accept that. But then, when my grandma told me that it wasn't true, that he was alive, but lost out there somewhere, I didn't know how to feel. And now that I know where he is, I'm so afraid of what I'll find."

Unsure what to say or do, Jade took Imogen by her shoulders and said, "Look, your dad saved me. He saved my family," she said. "He knew the risk he was taking when he came back to find us. But you told me yourself, he did it for you—because he loved you and he couldn't stand seeing you, his little girl, unhappy. He's given you a way to help him. You owe it to him, and to yourself, to do what he asks, no matter what you might find when you get there."

Imogen squeezed her eyes tight in an effort to squelch the outpouring of tears that didn't seem to want to stop and impulsively reached out and wrapped her arms around Jade. "I'm sorry," she said, spilling wet tears onto her friend's neck. "You're right. I do need to know." Imogen pulled away and Jade grabbed a tissue for Imogen to dry her red, swollen, damp eyes.

"You don't know how scary that place was," Imogen said, "but I'll go. I will. I only wish Simon was here."

"Are you sure you're ready," Jade asked.

Seated at the table, the picture Niles had left for her in front of her, Imogen nodded yes, closed her eyes, and began to focus. In no time, the edges began to creep up around her and Imogen knew the dark was coming. She hoped this dark wouldn't lead her to an even murkier, scarier, darker place.

But it wasn't dark at all. It was light. She opened her eyes on a bright sunny day, facing the same house she'd visited last night, only this was the 1997 version. It was clear, and a relief; Niles had not been trapped in the dark limbo place as she had feared.

As he said in the letter, this must be the day before he caught up with his launch date, and likely the same day he had snapped the photo of Jade and her family. Maybe he was caught in a loop—sort of like Bill Murray was in that movie *Groundhog Day* where he kept reliving the same day, only Niles relieved the same two months over and over again. Either scenario—dark limbo place or looping for 25 years—couldn't be good. She was about to find out.

The man standing beside her looked familiar, but he had a beard. When he noticed her standing there, he dropped the camera he was holding in his hand. If this person was her dad, surely, he'd be overjoyed to see her, but that wasn't what happened next.

He started backing away from her, a look of fear registering on his face. "Who are you?" he demanded. Everything about him seemed wrong, off.

Imogen slowly approached him. "It's me, dad, Imogen."

"No! You're not Imogen. Imogen is a little girl." Of course, he wouldn't recognize her. The last time they had seen each other she was nine.

"I know I look different, but it is really me, dad, I swear," she repeated calmly as she moved closer. He continued to back away, but Imogen inched close enough to touch his hand, and for a split second, it seemed like there was a small spark of recognition in his eyes, but in an instant, it was gone.

"You're not Imogen," he said, shaking his head.

All I need do is grab hold of him and go, Imogen thought as she moved closer. She was almost ready to grab him when he turned and ran off. "Noooo," he yelled as he sprinted away from her down the street. Good thing I wore my running shoes, Imogen thought as she pounced into action and took chase after Niles. He was fast—weirdly, they were close to the same age now—but she was faster. She caught up to him and pitching herself forward, tackled him to the ground. Imogen tried to hold on, but he was strong. They wrestled like that on the street for a moment until Niles abruptly stopped struggling. Imogen turned to see why. Jade was standing over them.

"What are you doing to Mr. Poole?" she asked Imogen.

Jade—nine-year-old Jade—the way Imogen had always remembered her. More than anything, she wanted to speak to her; to reach out and hug her, tell her who she was, but realized she could not. Seeing the crazy woman tackling her family's truest friend and then vanishing with him without a trace would be enough trauma for a little girl. Instead, she forced herself to look away, wrapped her arms tightly around Niles' chest locking her fingers together in a vice grip, and focused, harder than she ever thought possible, on the portal at home. As Jade, the house, and 1997 slipped away, together again, father and daughter began their journey home at last.

Jade watched in terrified wonder as they appeared seemingly out of nowhere. Imogen's arms were still wrapped tightly around Niles' chest, but his knees buckled beneath him. He dropped to the floor and was immediately violently ill.

"Quick, get a pan!" Imogen screamed. Jade jumped up and raced to the kitchen cupboard and back and placed it under Imogen's dad's face. When he was finished, he rolled over on his side and laid in a fetal position, breathing hard, not saying anything, vomit clinging to his beard and hair. Imogen and Jade stood back unsure of what to do. Imogen quickly grabbed a throw blanket off the couch and draped it across his frame in case he was cold. She knew what it felt like to travel through time, the chills, the nausea—like a hangover, times a million. It had been this way for her the first time, and she suspected her dad was experiencing this reaction because it had been so many years since he'd last traveled.

Imogen and Jade looked at each other, then back at Niles who had appeared to have fallen asleep almost instantly. "What happened?" Jade asked. "What did you see? Was he in that place?" Imogen shook her head. "No, thank goodness. He was at your house . . . with you." Jade's eyes widened as an old/new memory suddenly drifted into her mind, of a strange woman chasing Frank Poole down the street and wrestling him to the ground, and then . . . the two of them vanishing into thin air. And she remembered screaming, running back to her yard, to her mother and sister—horrified by what she had witnessed. Not understanding what had happened.

"Oh," Jade said, realizing that although Imogen had been gone only minutes, what she had done in 1997 in that short amount of time, had altered the rest of her childhood, haunted her dreams, made her from that moment forward question what was real and what wasn't.

"What . . . did . . . you . . . do, Imogen?"

Imogen tossed her head downward, her arms drooped at her sides, defeated. "I think I fucked up," she said.

While she should have been ecstatic about saving her dad, here was yet another odious revelation about the consequences of time travel, something she had not foreseen—that nine-year-old Jade might be severely traumatized seeing two people evaporate into thin air. It was so far outside the realm of normal, even for a child. Her actions today had, in an instant, forever changed her beloved friend's childhood.

Imogen plunked down on the sofa and covered her face with her hands. "I'm so, so sorry Jade. I didn't realize . . ." Jade came over and sat down beside Imogen and placed her arm around her. Still reeling in a state of shock herself, the memories rushing over her like a tsunami, she still could not blame Imogen. "It's okay," she said. "It's not your fault. What happened, happened. It can't be changed now." Imogen appreciated Jade putting up a supportive front, but yes, it was her fault. She did it. Nobody else. For the second time in so many weeks she again found herself questioning time travel. Was meddling in people's lives worth it? Was she doing more harm then good?

She began to weep and when she looked up, saw that Jade was sobbing too. "We'll ugly cry together, okay?" Jade said. Imogen grabbed her friend close in a tight embrace.

"It was amazing though," Imogen said after they'd both

blown their noses and dried their eyes. "I got to see little Jade again, the you that I had remembered all these years."

"Was I acting goofy?" Jade asked, making Imogen laugh.

"No, but I was so tempted to reach out and give you a hug," she admitted. "I know I couldn't have been anywhere near as traumatized as you were seeing dad and I vanish, but a long time ago you vanished too, from my life, in the middle of the night, and I never stopped missing you all this time."

Jade smiled at Imogen. "We were both traumatized," she said, "but we found our way back to each other, didn't we?"

Imogen smiled back at her friend. "Yes, we did."

Just then, Niles stirred under his blanket. "He's awake!" Imogen said, leaping from the couch and rushing over to where he lay on the floor. Niles opened his eyes and began to shriek, "Who are you? Where am I? Why are you here?"

Imogen tried to calm him. "Niles . . . dad, don't you know me? It's Imogen." That had the opposite effect that Imogen was hoping for. Niles became ever more distraught. Throwing the blanket off of himself, he stood up and wavered as though he would topple over. "Let me help you," Imogen cried.

"No!" Niles said. "You, stay away from me." He looked at Jade and ran to her side, taking her hand. Jade led him over to the couch. For some reason she was able to calm him down. "It's all right, Mr. Oliver," she said.

"Who is that?" he asked her clearly confused. Jade continued to soothe him. Imogen approached him again. "Dad?" she said, touching his arm. Niles recoiled in fear, turning his head and refusing to look at Imogen. Why did he recognize Jade as an adult, but not her?

Frustrated, Imogen gave up and walked away. Reaching for her phone, she dialed Simon's cell phone. No answer. "Shit!" she said, "Where the hell is he? Why isn't he here?"

After poking around the grand estate for a time, Simon made his way unnoticed upstairs to the second floor. Hearing someone approaching, he quickly ducked into the nearest room and hid behind the door. As he waited for the coast to clear a shaky voice in the room startled him.

"Are you another traveler?" the person inquired.

Simon turned in the direction of the voice. An elderly gentleman in a dressing gown was seated in a beveled chair beside a huge four-poster bed, smoking a cigarette through a fine black and gold holder.

"Excuse me?" Simon asked.

"I said, are you another traveler, from a different time?"

Surprised by the man's directness, Simon responded by asking, "Are you George Eastman?"

The man calmly took a puff from the cigarette holder and expelled a whiff of smoke. "I am," he answered, "and who sir might you be?"

Simon wasn't sure how to respond but decided to go with sincerity. "My name is Simon Elliot," he said. "And truth be told, yes, I am here from another time."

"Perhaps you know Theodore?" Eastman inquired.

Simon was confused. "Theodore?"

"My grandson of the future, Theodore Diamond, he was here not more than 15 minutes ago," he said. "Do you know him?"

"I do," Simon answered, realizing that Theodore was Teddy and that this man might be his great, great grandfather. "He is my father," he said.

Eastman seemed pleased. "Well then, Mister Simon Elliot, you must know that I asked him for a favor. Did he follow through?"

Unnerved that he had missed running into Teddy by mere minutes, Simon understood the meaning of Eastman's question. "Teddy . . . er, Theodore did as you asked," Simon said. "Your book is safe in the future."

"Very good," the man answered, "my work is done."

On the kitchen table, Simon's cell phone began to vibrate. The opening couplet of Beethoven's *Für Elise* played several times over before switching to voicemail. Into the empty air of Teddy's apartment, Imogen's voice pleaded, "Where *are* you, Simon? Please . . . answer your damn phone!"

20

A knock at the front door sent Imogen scurrying to answer it. Maybe Simon had forgotten his key. But when she flung open the door, it wasn't Simon standing on the porch. It was Fletcher. Surprised to see him at this late hour, she shouted, "Fletcher! What are you doing here?"

"Looking for Simon," Fletcher said. A look of confusion crossed his face as he entered the room. "What's going on here? Who is that?" he asked, pointing at the sobbing man seated on the sofa next to Jade.

"This," she said, "is my father, Niles."

"What? Oh my god, you found him? Is he okay?" Fletcher asked as he ventured closer to the trembling man. Tilting his head and crinkling up his brow, he observed him, "He doesn't look okay."

"You're right. He's not okay! Okay?" Imogen responded, annoyed. "Where is Simon?" she demanded. Still distracted by Imogen's dad, who was not the older man he had expected to see, without thinking Fletcher blurted, "I don't know where he is, Imogen, probably time traveling somewhere."

"What!?" Imogen shrieked, startling Niles who, cringing at the noise, burrowed himself further into the sofa. "What do you *mean*, he's time traveling? Simon can't time travel!"

Realizing his blunder, Simon gulped nervously, unsure what to say knowing that he'd spilled the beans. "You know something, don't you Fletcher," she said. "Spill it," she said, "right now!" Fletcher knew better than to cross Imogen when she was angry. Although she was normally pretty chill, she was stubborn, and you knew when you'd crossed the line.

"Uh . . . um . . ." he stammered, searching for a suitable answer, knowing there wasn't one. Just then, the door opened and both Imogen and Fletcher turned to look. This time it was Simon.

Imogen pounced. "Where have you been?" she shouted.

Simon scanned the room, puzzled. What had he walked in to? Fletcher looked like he wanted to run away, Jade was sad, and a man, likely Niles, Imogen's dad, although he looked much younger than he should, was openly weeping into a pillow on the sofa.

"I was at the pawn shop, in Stambourg," he said. "You dropped me off, as you recall."

"And where . . . or should I say *when* did you go to from there? After I dropped you off."

Simon glanced at Fletcher who looked mighty guilty. "I'm sorry, it just slipped out," he shrugged. "She asked me where you were and . . ."

". . . and he said you were time traveling!" Imogen finished.

"I meant he was *trying* to time travel . . ." Fletcher interjected, attempting to fix things.

Imogen immediately cut him off. "Shut up, Fletcher, yes you did," she said.

Turning back to Simon, she said, "How could you keep something as important as that from me?" she asked, a hint of hurt seeping into her voice.

Simon hated confrontation, but even more than that, he hated confrontation in the presence of others. It was disconcerting but also something proper people did not engage in. Quarrels were meant to be kept private, as he saw it, and he sought to draw Imogen away.

"Let us go to another room and discuss this?" he suggested to her.

Hands on both hips, Imogen stood firm. "No!" she said. "I needed you tonight and you were gone, who knows where, gallivanting through time, doing who knows what, and you didn't even have the common courtesy to call me or even to tell me that you could do this. How can I ever trust you?"

Simon took Imogen's verbal onslaught until he could no longer suppress his own feelings. Staring angrily back at her, he divulged something he had held inside for months. "Why did you never offer to find my mother?" he demanded to know. "You have the nerve to stand there, self-righteously and accuse me of doing something behind your back that you yourself could have accomplished, quite easily, had you offered. I thought you cared about me, but not once . . . not once did you say, 'Simon, let's find out what happened to your mother.' Did you ever stop to think about how I felt, Imogen? No, you did not," he said, answering his own question.

Imogen had never heard Simon raise his voice in anger, to her or to anyone, and it was upsetting and unfamiliar. She did not like it one bit, but he was right, and she could not think of a single thing to say in her defense.

"Simon, I'm sorry . . . I didn't mean. . ." she said taking a step toward him.

Simon threw his arms up in a defensive stance. "Too late, Imogen. You're on your own," he said abruptly turning away from her and heading for the front door.

"Simon, wait!" she called out to him from the porch, but to no avail as she watched him disappear on foot into the dark night.

Fletcher came to the door and tried to press past her to follow Simon. "Where do you think you're going?" she questioned him.

"To find Simon," he said.

Imogen grabbed his arm. "Oh no you're not. I need you here to help me with dad."

Fletcher balked as he tried to extricate Imogen's hand. "Let it go, Imogen," he said. He was fed up with her too. Simon was right. She hadn't been paying attention to anyone but herself lately, him included.

"Fletcher," she said, reluctantly letting go of him. "Please, stay. I need your help," she pleaded. "Jade is leaving tomorrow, and dad won't talk to me. I can't handle this by myself."

It had always been hard telling Imogen no, and tonight was no exception. Standing there, looking at her with those sad, pleading eyes, it was too much, and grudgingly he agreed to stay the night.

Frustrated, Imogen plopped into a nearby chair. Head down, her elbows resting on her knees with her hands cradling her head, she shook her head back and forth. "Why is he afraid of me?"

"I don't know," said Jade, who was again seated on the sofa beside Niles. He had stopped crying finally. Last night she and Fletcher had managed to get him cleaned up, calmed down, and to sleep with the help of a sleeping pill, but this morning he was silent and still refusing to acknowledge Imogen.

"Maybe he's afraid to look at you because deep down he knows it's you, but his mind can't accept that you're no longer a little girl," Jade suggested.

"But surely he knows how time travel works," Imogen said. "Time in the past moves slower than it does here, so he should have recognized that while he wasn't aging much in his timeline, I was growing up here in my own time."

Niles laid down on his side on the sofa and curled himself into a fetal position, eyes open, staring blankly past her. Jade leaned forward. "You know I'm flying back to Chicago today," she said, pulling a blanket down and tucking it in around Niles' legs.

Imogen rubbed her eyes with her fists. "I know," she said. "I wish you didn't have to go. And not just because I need help with Niles," she quickly added, "but because I'll miss you. I could get used to you being around all the time, you know."

"I could too, but some people say I have to work," Jade said.

That made Imogen laugh. "Speaking of work," she said, "I have an appointment with a client later and I'm not sure what to do about dad. I wouldn't feel right leaving him here alone, especially this soon. It's hard to tell if he even knows where he is, at this point."

"Maybe Fletcher can stay with him," Jade proposed.

"Yeah, maybe," Imogen said.

Jade's taxi driver pulled up to the curb in front of the house and tooted the horn, and the moment Imogen was dreading had arrived. She was never particularly good at goodbyes anyway, but this one felt especially difficult. After finally finding the one friend she had ever truly known and loved she was leaving again.

"Everything will work out with your dad, Imogen. He'll come around, you'll see." Imogen wasn't so sure, but she tried not to reveal how worried she was to Jade. Tears were starting to pool in Imogen's eyes and Jade reached out for her. "Come here, you," she said, pulling Imogen close to her and squeezing. They stood like that, touching noses, tears mixing, for a minute before Jade said, "I'll keep in touch Gen. We won't lose each other again."

Imogen sniffled. "Promise?"

"I promise," Jade said.

Fletcher came out of the bedroom. "Bye Jade," he said.

"Bye Fletcher," Jade said, as she grasped the handle of her suitcase and pulled it to the front door. Turning back, she blew Imogen a kiss. "I'll call you when I get home."

Imogen watched Jade get into the cab and drive away. Why did it feel like people were always weaving in and out of her life, and never staying? Nothing seemed permanent or long lasting, fleeting moments of happiness that she could never quite keep ahold of.

On his way into the kitchen to pour himself a cup of coffee Fletcher walked past Niles asleep on the couch. "How's he doing this morning?"

Imogen sighed. "Well, he's calmed down at least. He seems super tired, and he still won't look at me. That pretty much sums it up."

Fletcher returned from the kitchen with his mug and sat down. "I'm glad he's better, but he doesn't look too good."

Imogen agreed. "I can't even imagine what it was like for him to be stuck in a continuous loop for so many years."

"Do you think that's what happened to him?" Fletcher asked.

"I can't be sure, but it's the only thing that makes sense." She described to Fletcher how 22 years ago Niles had entered a photograph that had been taken two months earlier. When Teddy destroyed it, that meant that Niles couldn't return so when he caught up to the date that he had left in his present time, he'd loop back to two months prior. Essentially, from what I can gather, he must have relived the same two months more than 100 times. The closest she could come to imagining it was to compare it to the movie *Groundhog Day.*

Fletcher took a sip of coffee and said, "That was a good movie, but every time Bill Murray woke up to the alarm playing *I Got You, Babe* it made me feel sort of anxious thinking about what it would be like having to relive the same day over again and again."

"Yes, I would think it would be horrible," Imogen agreed before changing the subject. "But . . . you and I have other things to discuss this morning."

Setting his cup aside, Fletcher knew what was coming next and tried to get in front of the anger he was sure Imogen had been holding in since yesterday when he blurted out that Simon might be time traveling.

"Imogen . . . I am so sorry for not telling you, but Simon didn't want me to." That was mostly true, although Fletcher had also done his share to encourage Simon to keep it to himself. He waited for her response, but surprisingly, the anger he was expecting from Imogen didn't come. She seemed more sad than mad, almost contrite.

"I don't care that you told me, or even that he can do it," she said. She looked down at her hands and replied, "I'm upset that he didn't feel like he could share something as important as that with me."

Everything inside him screamed it was wrong, but at this moment Fletcher's desire to comfort Imogen was far stronger than his friendship with Simon. He approached Imogen and boldly took her into his arms. All the old feelings that he took such care to suppress were right there again as strong as ever. Why did he adore her so much? Why couldn't he let her go? And when she embraced him back, it was all he could do to keep from telling her how he felt. When she began to sob into his shoulder all he wanted to do was hold her like this forever.

"I feel so stupid," Imogen finally said, pulling away from him and wiping the tears from her eyes with her sleeve. "It seems like all I do anymore lately is cry." Fletcher was reluctant to disengage, but she untangled herself from him and sat down in the chair again. "When . . . where did Simon go? Do you know?" she asked.

Fletcher sat down across from her and paused before speaking. "Do you remember that day you came home and the house was a mess?"

Imogen had to think for a minute—the house was always a bit of a mess. She couldn't recall. "I think Simon may have told you that the two of us were wrestling?" he ventured, to jog her memory.

"Ah, yes," Imogen said, remembering what an odd conversation that was. "He said you were demonstrating karate moves."

Fletcher looked away unable to suppress a snicker. "Uh, yeah, well, that's not quite what happened."

"I figured as much," Imogen replied, "But he revised that story later. He said that he had a dizzy spell and fell and hit his head and you found him passed out on the floor."

"Yes! That part *is* true!" Fletcher said, pleased that Simon had come up with a better explanation later.

"Okay, so I take it he was like that when you found him because he had been time traveling, is that correct?" Imogen asked. Fletcher nodded. "All right, do you know where he traveled to?"

"That part is hazy," Fletcher said. "I remember him telling me that he went to a bunch of places, a protest march, a diner, some trial somewhere in Europe, I can't remember all the details."

Imogen jumped in. "You're saying he went to all those different times and places, all at once?"

"Yeah, he said he kept jumping from one place to the next."

Imogen bit her lip, baffled by what Fletcher was telling her. "All at once, you say, not in separate trips?" Fletcher felt like he was ratting Simon out, but he couldn't backtrack; the cat was all the way out of the bag now.

"Simon said he went through the first picture but then kept jumping to the next and the next. He didn't know what was happening but then finally he said he remembered thinking about you and home and that's how he got back."

Imogen couldn't believe what she was hearing. "That's crazy," she managed to say.

"It was," Fletcher said. "Neither one of us understood it."

Imogen sat silently pondering this new information before asking Fletcher a final question, "Did he tell you why he didn't want me to know?"

Fletcher shrugged, "I guess partly he wanted time to make sense of it on his own, and well . . . you heard what he said last night."

"That I never offered to help him find his mother," Imogen finished.

"Yeah," Fletcher said, "that too."

Imogen stood up then and glanced at Niles, who was still sleeping. "Listen," she said. "I need a favor."

"Anything," Fletcher said. "I want to help, if I can."

"I have an appointment today with a client," she said. "Can you stay here with dad? I won't be gone long."

"Sure, of course," Fletcher said, eager to get back into Imogen's good graces.

Imogen plucked the car keys from the bowl in the foyer on her way out. "I'll be back in a couple of hours," she said, closing the door behind her.

Fletcher returned to the living room. Niles had apparently woke up when Imogen shut the front door and was now sitting upright on the sofa. "How you doing, Niles?" Fletcher asked. No response from Niles, who sat quietly, hands folded in his lap, distantly staring elsewhere at something locked within his own head.

Fletcher's cell phone rang. It was Simon. "Hi Fletcher," Simon said, "What are you doing right now? I could use some company here."

"Where are you?" Fletcher asked.

"I'm at the pawn shop, in Stambourg. Listen, I found this book . . . it's about time travel."

Before Simon could say more, Fletcher interrupted him, "I'll be there in just a bit." Why had he told Simon he'd go? he thought after hanging up. Because damn it, he wanted to go. But he should stay here with Niles. Imogen would be really mad if he left. He was torn as the debate raged in his head.

Seizing the remote from the coffee table, he turned the TV on, which was tuned to a house hunting show. Niles seemed to perk up, interested. He knew he shouldn't, but Niles seemed fine. He'd lock all the doors, he rationalized.

"Niles," he said, "I'm going to go, but Imogen will be back soon."

"Imogen?" Niles asked. "Where's Imogen?"

"She left, but she'll be back soon," Fletcher repeated.

"We were going out for a photo shoot today. Is she with her mom?"

"Uh, I don't know, maybe," Fletcher played along. "But anyway, she'll be back, so watch TV and don't go anywhere, okay?" he said.

"Okay," Niles replied.

This is wrong, this is very wrong, Fletcher repeated in his head, stressing himself out. He should stay, but if Simon was going to time travel, he wanted to go too. He moved around the house checking that everything was turned off, except the TV, the windows and doors locked.

"Okay Niles, I'm going now. If you get tired, just lie down there and take a nap." He picked up the throw blanket that had slipped from the sofa onto the floor. "Here's a blanket," he said, handing it to him. Niles laid back down on his side and pulled the blanket up over his legs. He seemed content for now watching the home show.

"See you later buddy," Fletcher said as he exited the house, locking the behind him.

21

Despite it being the first New Year's celebration without legal liquor, New York City's Plaza Hotel on December 31, 1920, was packed with jolly merrymakers. Imogen could barely squeeze through the swollen crowd. It was the onset of the jazz age, the era of speakeasies and bootleg gin. The excitement was palpable. Mostly, she loved how the loose-swinging chiffon flapper dress swished-swished against her legs. With hundreds of hand-sewn beads, it was a shiny thing-lover's dream. Two long strands of white and black beads to accentuate it bounced at her neck. She had caught a glimpse of herself in the mirror on the way in. With her hair, styled in a short, perky bob embellished with a decorative beaded clip in a leaf motive that sported two elegant white feathers, she was the embodiment of cute.

Maybe this was where she needed to be, Imogen thought, inside this shimmering hotel with its opulent décor and chandeliers. Considering all the bad and sad that had happened recently—Vivian and Margaret Rose, the train wreck, her father's inability to recognize her, the blowout with Simon. Who wouldn't want to stay here and party forever?

This morning, she had planned on only meeting with the client Marguerite Sims today and working the case later on so she could get back home quickly to dad, but as it turned out this would be a quick trip. Get in, get out. Mrs. Sims had found a receipt in her grandmother's possessions for an opera cape that had been left behind at a coat check at a hotel party. She had come up empty trying to track it down on her own through family and exhaustive online searches. Apparently, it had meant a lot to her grandmother who had written that the cape had been a special gift from her mother and how upset she was to have lost it. The receipt named the hotel—the Plaza in New York City, and the date—December 31, 1920—New Year's Eve. With all the essential info wrapped up neatly in a bow, this should be a cinch. All Imogen had to do was present the coat check, retrieve the cape, and go. What could go wrong? She might even get home sooner than she had originally planned.

Catching a glimpse of a sign that read COAT CHECK Imogen broke away from the throng of people heading for the hotel's ballroom and made her way toward it. Inside her fancy bejeweled purse was Marguerite Sims' grandmother's receipt. Imogen waited patiently in line until it was her turn. Although most people were checking *in* hats and garments, Imogen was singularly focused on checking *out* and hoping that her timing was right—that Marguerite's grandmother had already dropped the cape off for her to slide in and pick it up. Removing the ticket from her clutch, she handed it to the clerk, who gave it a once over, nodded, and departed into the depths of the cloakroom to retrieve the item. A few minutes later, she returned with the cape—a stunning black velvet wrap with exquisite corded passementerie design work interspersed with a black chain beading design woven in and out of the cording, fur trim, and a brilliant fuchsia lining. No wonder Marguerite Sims was searching for it. It was one of a kind.

Imogen took the cape and thanked the clerk. Thrilled at how smoothly everything was going she couldn't resist a modest smile as she turned to go, cape tucked neatly over her arm. But her pleasure was short-lived because at that very moment, someone unexpectedly knocked into her, spilling a drink down the front of her dress, although mercifully, missing the cape. The woman responsible gasped and with a distinctly Southern accent drawled, "Oh my, I'm so sorry." And before Imogen could react, the woman had clutched her hand and began to pull. "Come! Let's get that cleaned up before it stains," she declared as she began to weave in and out through the dense crowd with some urgency, tugging Imogen along behind her.

They entered the ladies' powder room, which was as stunningly opulent as every other part of the elegant hotel, to a row of freestanding sinks. Pulling a fresh cloth towel from a rack, she dampened it with soap and water and began to dab at the large, spreading spot on Imogen's dress. It gave Imogen time to get a better look at her. She was young and fresh-faced, her skin as smooth as porcelain, her lips accentuated with a bright vermilion lipstick. Her blonde hair was curly and clipped in a sassy poodle bob and wrapped up in a colorful boho scarf. The light from the overhead chandelier made the thousands of beads sewn into her dress sparkle like tiny twinkling stars. She'd seen this girl before, in pictures.

You're Zelda Fitzgerald, aren't you," Imogen said.

The girl looked up and snorted, inquiring playfully, "Who wants to know?"

Imogen couldn't believe it. Zelda Fitzgerald, Zelda with a capital Z. The original wild child. Legendary tabletop dancing, naked fountain diving, pearl twirling flapper and party girl. Writer, muse, and wife of F. Scott Fitzgerald, right here, in the flesh.

"There," Zelda said, as she added the finishing touches to the spot. "You can scarcely see it at all now." Carelessly dropping the towel on the floor for someone else to retrieve, she flew off the chair, whisking Imogen into a separate room, the ladies' lounge, furnished with an assortment of plush velvet sofas, and along one wall, a row of tasseled posh stools positioned in front of a long line of vanity mirrors.

The beads on her dress made a pleasing rustling noise as Zelda sat down on one of the vanity chairs facing a mirror. She fluffed her curly bangs with her fingers and then snapped up the glass atomizer sitting atop the ledge, squeezed the bulb, and liberally spritzed her neck and wrists with a fine mist of the free Chanel perfume.

"I love your dress," Imogen ventured, unsure about what to say to Zelda Fitzgerald.

"These glad rags?" she drawled. "You look spiffy too, what's your name baby?" She patted the adjacent stool and gestured for

Imogen to come sit down next to her.

"Imogen, Imogen Oliver."

"Imogen, why I do like that. It's the cat's pajamas," she said winking and expelling a big sigh.

"Well, I'm truly bored and tired of being everyone's muse," she announced, flinging her hand to her forehead for dramatic effect. "Let's go have some fun, Miss Imogen. Let me buy you a drink to make amends for spilling my drink on you."

"Oh, no I don't think so," Imogen hedged. "I really need to be going actually." She stood up, but Zelda pulled her back down.

"Oh please, please, pretty please, just one itsy-bitsy drink?" she begged.

Imogen wasn't sure that everything she had read about Zelda Fitzgerald was true, but she was certainly charming and persuasive. Imogen shook her head, resolute, trying hard to stick to her guns. "I really have stuff to do."

Zelda tilted her head to one side. "Stuff?" she said, as though the word was foreign to her patois. "You slay me! I dig the crazy way you talk. It is like you come from another planet or time!" Imogen laughed out loud. If only she knew, she thought. "Come on," said Zelda, tugging at Imogen's arm.

"All right," Imogen acquiesced, holding up one finger. "One drink."

Zelda clapped her hands together excitedly. "You're a peach! Let's go downstairs to the Grill Room. That's where the real party is!"

After leaving the powder room they wended their way back through the throng of people mingling about on the main floor. Imogen followed Zelda down a flight of stairs then zigzagged through several very long, lonesome, diffusely lit basement hallways deep in the bowels of the Plaza Hotel that seemed to go on forever, past a sequence of wooden doors, finally stopping abruptly in front of another nondescript door that to Imogen's eyes looked pretty much the same as all the others they had passed. Zelda winked and slowly turned the glass knob. "Ready?" she asked Imogen as she pushed open the door.

Wisps of disembodied voices and laughter, the frenetic sounds of a jazz band playing, and the pungent smell of cigarette smoke wafted out into the hallway like ghosts inviting them to join the secret soiree within. Through the haze and dim lights flappers glided across the parquet floor, martini glasses clinked in clandestine corners, patrons sipped gin martinis and Bombay Sapphire from coffee mugs. In contrast to the party upstairs, it was far from dry and certainly much livelier. Imogen felt goosebumps forming on her arms, and she shivered with anticipation. Although this experience seemed similar to the way she often felt when arriving in another time period, this felt strangely different—fun, vibrant, electrifying, and slightly more dangerous. Evidently secrecy and lawbreaking made this New Year's Eve revelry even wilder.

Standing beside her, Imogen noticed that Zelda seemed as nervous as a cat. It was like she was buzzing from the inside out.

"Why are you looking at me that way?" Zelda asked.

Imogen smiled. "Sometimes you just need to dance it out."

"Yes! That's exactly right!" Zelda liked this girl!

Like being pushed from behind by invisible hands, the room devoured them both, whisking them away into the swirling vortex of whirling, twirling, spinning, writhing bodies, all moving in frenzied abandon, arms flapping, slapping, clapping on thighs, legs bouncing and flailing, to the cacophonous chorus of wailing horns and woodwinds, suffused with the feverish pulsating thump thump thumping beat of the drums.

At last, the music faded and then stopped and Imogen and Zelda, spent and bathed in sweat, tossed their arms about each other's waists, and headed toward two empty seats at the bar.

Zelda ordered two shots from the bartender. "Best bootleg gin in town!" he said and together they toasted tonight and tossed them back.

"Tomorrow we may die, so let's get drunk and make love!" Zelda roared, catching the passing eye of an expensively clad gentleman seated at a table to the right of the bar.

"Oh my god, is that . . .?" Imogen managed to get out of her mouth before Zelda finished her thought. "F. Scott, yes, that is indeed my dear, clever husband," Zelda said with a touch of disdain. She raised her glass up to him in mock cheer and he nodded back to her in return before turning his attention back to his adoring audience of young literary wannabes and hangers on.

It was astounding to be hanging out with Zelda—famous and fascinating in her own right—but Imogen hadn't expected to also run into the great F. Scott Fitzgerald, author of *The Great Gatsby*, one of Imogen's favorite novels, friend to Lost Generation luminaries Gertrude Stein, Picasso, Cole Porter, and Ernest Hemingway, sitting in a smoky speakeasy on the eve of 1921 tossing out bon mots to his captivated fan club.

Imogen watched as Fitzgerald extricated himself from the group and approached Zelda. "Hello, my darling," he said. She turned her cheek to allow him a small kiss. "Are you enjoying yourself? he inquired.

"I am," Zelda replied turning away and ordering two more shots from the bartender. Imogen felt compelled to interject. "Oh no," she implored, "no more for me, remember? One drink?"

"That's applesauce, Imogen," she said. "We are just getting started!" Imogen had a feeling Zelda's response was intended more for her husband than her. She'd read they had quite a contentious relationship, especially when they were drinking. Fitzgerald gave her a sly smile and when he turned, noticed Imogen. "Who is your lovely friend here?" he asked.

Zelda flung her arm around Imogen's neck. "This is Imogen. My new friend. She's the bee's knees, this one!"

He gallantly took Imogen's hand in his and kissed it, lingering a little bit too long. "It is very nice to meet you Imogen," he said gazing intently into her eyes. Imogen thought she would burst. *Oh wow, oh wow*, she thought. It wasn't like meeting Bowie or Elvis Costello or Lady Gaga, but in the literary world, Fitzgerald was a rock star.

Zelda turned away and after downing another shot, tossed out a bon mot of her own, "Excuse me for being so intellectual," she quipped. "I know you would prefer something nice and feminine and affectionate."

No matter how thrilling it was to have captured the attention of the famous author, Imogen felt embarrassed at his very overt public display of affection, especially because it was so blatantly on display in front of his wife. Imogen smiled though and politely removed her hand from his, dropping it to her side and stepping back and away from the volatile couple.

"I should go," Imogen said.

"Drink your shot," Zelda said brightly. Fitzgerald smiled at Zelda; Zelda smiled back. The awkward moment between them seemed to have passed, and Fitzgerald was already turning and taking his leave. Zelda turned back to Imogen and grinned, admitting, "I'm hopelessly stuck on him, you know."

In her wildest dreams, Imogen could not have envisioned that she'd be hanging out in a speakeasy partying with Zelda Fitzgerald, but here she was. And surprisingly, she was enjoying herself . . . immensely, in fact. She sensed that despite her wild ways, heavy drinking, and penchant for riding on the roofs of taxis, Zelda was lonely and in desperate need of a friend, a girl friend in exactly the way Simon needed Fletcher, Imogen suddenly realized, a male friend that he could confide in.

And that is what Zelda did. For the next few hours, she entrusted Imogen with the most intimate details of her life, divulging her overwhelming desire to write, of living in the shadow of her famous husband, how she felt held back and often put upon to live up to the unrealistic assumptions and expectations people had of her.

And then, a jazz beat she couldn't resist came up and Zelda rushed off to the dance floor leaving Imogen alone for a time with her thoughts. Maybe it was the alcohol, but she couldn't help thinking that if Kansas hadn't been enough of a wakeup call, speaking so openly with Zelda tonight confirmed it. These were real people with real dreams and passions and lives. Clearly, she had compartmentalized them to save herself from having to recognize them as people rather than mere players in her own private universe—to be dealt with only as an effort to further her own personal goals. It had been a way to block out her own sorrow about being an orphan. But now that dad was back, perhaps she could let it go, break down the walls and start carving out a life with him and with Simon, a life that might actually be more satisfying. Carried away in her own thoughts and enthralled by the music and the tipsy patrons, she hadn't noticed the man that had slipped silently into the seat next to her, but she could smell him before she saw him. His breath, reeking of alcohol, preceded him.

Knocking up against her shoulder, he growled into her ear, "Hey sweetheart. Couldn't help noticing ya got some nice gams there. You are *it*, baby." Imogen grimaced and scooted away from him. Where was Zelda? she wondered, searching the room hoping to spot her. "Don't be a wet blanket, doll," the man persisted, moving in closer again.

Thankfully, the music stopped, and Zelda breezed back over squeezing in between her and the creeper, creating a welcomed wedge between them.

"Hey, beat it chippy!" the man scowled at Zelda. "I'm talkin' to this dame here."

Plainly, that was the wrong thing to say to Zelda. Rearing back, her eyes narrowing into the tiniest of angry slits as she slung fierce invisible daggers at him, she demanded, "Who are you calling a chippy?" Defiantly, she crossed her arms together forming a barrier, daring him to cross it. "Breeze off Hank, she's not interested."

"Hank" threw his hands in the air in a gesture of surrender and slinked away but not before leaving a parting shot. "ahh," he said, "you're nothing but a Dumb Dora anyway."

"Was he bothering you?" Zelda asked concerned.

Imogen took a nip from her drink and brushed it off as no big deal. "It's okay, not for very long."

"That goon," Zelda added, shaking her head. "He gives me the heebie-jeebies. He's a wrong number if I ever saw one."

One hand—smelling of stale cigars and sweat and gin—was clamped hard against her mouth and nose. Another fumbled to pull her dress up and her panties down . . . and then, things went black.

Imogen woke up in Zelda's hotel room, hungover and sick. After throwing up in the ice bucket, Zelda handed her a cup of what smelled like tea with lemon—the same concoction a friendly Uber driver had once suggested she try the last time she drank too much. But after one sip, it was obvious this one came with a kick. Imogen's stomach lurched, "What's in this?" she gasped, crinkling her nose.

"Oh, a little hair of the proverbial dog," Zelda said gleefully. "It works wonders, and I should know!"

Suddenly realizing that the very thing she had come here for might be lost, Imogen sat up and cried out, "Where is the cape?"

Zelda gently pushed Imogen back into the folds of the silk pillow. "Relax baby, it's right here," she said pointing to the bed, where Imogen could make out its lovely fur trim and magnificent fuchsia lining.

Imogen sighed with relief, but after glancing down at herself was confused by the condition of her dress. Big chunks of beads were missing in places as if they had been torn off. She touched her hair. It felt like a cat had sharpened its claws in it and, clearly, the decorative beaded clip she had been wearing and the two elegant white feathers were long gone.

She looked to Zelda for answers. "What happened last night?"

"That sloppy sap at the bar slipped you a Mickey, doll!" Zelda answered breathlessly as she launched into the exciting retelling of the events of the previous night. " . . . And if Georgie hadn't noticed the jam you were in and punched him straight in the beezer, you might be pushing up daisies today, or worse!"

Imogen was at a loss. "Wait, a Mickey? What's that?" She

thought she was up on 1920s slang, but this particular euphemism she was unfamiliar with.

Zelda giggled. "Oh Imogen, you slay me!" she said. "A Mickie is a drug slipped in a drink. That Hank is no good, I tell you. I've seen him before. I don't know why they let him in. But he won't be coming back for a long time. They hauled him off to the cooler."

As Imogen listened to Zelda riff, she tried not to let on, but she was severely rattled, especially now after hearing what had happened. She remembered parts of it now, that vile man's nasty breath in her face and his disgusting hands groping her all over. Drugged! My god, she thought, the what-ifs dancing in her head. This could have been so much worse than a hangover. What if someone hadn't intervened in time? She could have been raped or killed. Why, oh why had she been so fucking careless . . . again? What happened to 'get in, get out?' And the looming question, notwithstanding, 'What is *wrong* with me?' She pulled the pillow up around her face and began to cry softly into it. Zelda heard her sobs and rushed over, wrapping her arms around her.

"There, there, don't cry, honey," she said as she cradled Imogen's head in her hands.

Trying to lighten the mood, she picked up a leftover party horn lying on the table next to the bed and blew into it, creating a flat ta-doo-dah sound. "Happy New Year," she exclaimed brightly. Imogen proffered a weak smile.

"We're friends now. I won't let anything happen to you," Zelda whispered, causing Imogen to cry more.

"I have to go, now," she said, suddenly pulling herself up even though doing so made her feel like she was going to be sick again.

"No! Why?" Zelda protested, trying to make Imogen lie back down.

"I can't," Imogen stammered. "I have to be somewhere . . . right now!" Determined, she stood up and the room teetered. "Whoa," she said, grabbing hold of the chair rest for support.

"You need to rest a while, Imogen. Please," Zelda persisted.

"Have more tea and then you can go." Zelda did her best to try and talk her out of it, but Imogen was adamant. She needed to be gone from this place, far away from this time, now. Scooping up the cape, she gave Zelda a quick but sincere hug. "Thank you," she said. "I am so glad I got to meet you—you have no idea."

"But we will see each other again soon, won't we?" Zelda said, decidedly sad, as Imogen was leaving.

Imogen opened the door and stepped out of the hotel room but not before turning back and blowing her friend a kiss. "You are the cat's meow, Zelda Fitzgerald, and don't let anyone tell you otherwise!"

Closing the door behind her, Imogen sprinted down the hallway, down the stairs, and out onto the sidewalk in front of the Plaza Hotel, this morning littered with thousands of paper hats and confetti and party blowers and various discarded paraphernalia from last night's revelry. After a night of speakeasy smoke filling up her lungs, she paused for a moment to breathe in the fresh air before stepping onto Fifth Avenue and hailing a cab to west 52nd Street, where she entered the third-floor law office of Dagmar Coleman, esq. Making sure the cape was securely wrapped and labeled, she entrusted it to his safekeeping with explicit instructions for the date and manner wherein it would be retrieved in the future.

She knew she looked a hot mess. Didn't care. Today, the air was cold and crisp and everything that Imogen required in this minute to feel marginally better. She turned and slowly began to stroll along the avenue, savoring the sights and sounds of New Year's Day 1921 in NYC, before anyone noticed that the flapper with the torn dress and missing beads and disheveled hair had ever been there at all.

Three hours had passed since she first entered the photograph of the Plaza Hotel 1920 but although time moved slower in the past it couldn't allay the booze and drug hangover or heal the physical parts of being brutally assaulted in the form of the very real and painful bruises and gashes on her body. And not even close to the mental trauma she felt when she landed back in her office.

She had tried to keep it together with Zelda, pretend that she was strong and unaffected, that it hadn't bothered her—just another crazy night out on the town, right? but as she willed her aching body to wobble painstakingly to the sofa and curled herself up into a wee ball, the façade began to crumble, the pain burbled to the surface overflowing like lava that turned into great wracking sobs. Never in her life, had she needed someone so bad as she did right now. "Simon," she sobbed into the pillow. "Where the hell are you?"

22

The sun was shining when Fletcher pulled onto route 34 heading west toward Stambourg, but looming in his rearview mirror a gathering bank of dark clouds on the horizon ominously stalked him. The wind had been steadily picking up during the drive too, strong gusts sent loose leaves twirling and twisting across the freeway in front of him.

When the first big drops of rain began pelting the windshield, the steady thwump-thwump—thwump-thwump of the wipers lulled him into a contemplative mood and pangs of guilt slipped into his mind for leaving Imogen's dad alone. He shouldn't have left him, he knew, Imogen would be furious, but the temptation of having a time travel adventure with Simon was hard to resist. Plus, he felt awful about divulging Simon's secret to Imogen. It wasn't his place to do so, and it was his fault they were fighting. Yet, while a part of him hated that, there was also the nagging thought in the back of his head that hoped they might break up so he could have another chance with her. But he cared for Simon as well. He bandied these thoughts back and forth as he drove. Clearly, he was torn between his love for Imogen and loyalty to Simon. Was it possible to love them both? That seemed wrong, and yet, if he was to be honest with himself, it was true.

Even with the wipers turned up high they could not keep up with the steady onslaught of water now falling out of the sky. And by the time he rolled up to the curb in front of the pawn shop in Stambourg, the storm was a gully washer. To exit the car, Fletcher had to first leap across a fast-moving tributary of water before darting to the front of the building. Either there were never awnings attached to the exterior of the building to shield people from the elements or they had blown off and he was now getting drenched as he stood in front of the shop pounding on the door. He could see lights on inside. Simon must be in there. After a moment, the door flung open.

"Fletcher! Get in here before you drown," Simon commanded, pulling him through the open door by his collar.

"I'm already soaked," Fletcher acknowledged, as he removed his jacket and observed the puddle of water pooling around his shoes on the wood floor. "It's crazy weather out there!" he said, taking off his drenched coat. Simon closed the door behind him and locked it before taking Fletcher's coat and hanging it up on the coat tree by the door where it continued to drip.

Sensing an urgent need to get things off his chest right away, Fletcher began to profusely apologize. "Hey, man I'm really sorry about what happened between you and Imogen."

"Oh, no," Simon said, "it's not your fault."

"It is," Fletcher interjected. "I didn't mean to say anything. It just slipped out. I wasn't thinking."

"It's okay, Fletcher," Simon reassured him. "She would have found out sooner or later anyway."

Fletcher wasn't convinced. "Yeah, well, it shouldn't have been me telling her. It should have been you."

Simon squeezed his friend's shoulder. "Don't beat yourself up over it," he said as he walked over to the table and picked up the bottle. "Care for a drink?" he asked, holding up the whiskey.

Fletcher's eyes lit up. "You betcha!" he said, sauntering over to examine the label. "That looks like it could do some damage."

"Indeed," Simon agreed.

They sat down and Simon poured them each a drink. "How is she? . . . Imogen, and her dad?"

Fletcher wasn't prepared to lie to Simon, although he hedged a bit. "She's okay. She had to go meet a client."

"Oh?" Simon seemed surprised. "I would have thought, considering her dad's precarious mental state, that she might not want to leave him alone."

Fletcher nodded. "Well, she asked me to stay with him, but he seemed perfectly fine when I left."

"Are you sure?" Simon asked, skeptical. "He seemed rather agitated when I was there."

"He calmed down a lot after you left," Fletcher replied. Technically, this was true, if you counted barely speaking at all now as calm.

Simon nodded, satisfied with Fletcher's assurance that things were under control. "I should call her later though."

Before Fletcher arrived, Simon had been perusing the Eastman notebook and he pulled it out now to share with him. "Is that the time travel book?" Fletcher asked.

"It is," Simon replied, handing it over to him. "I met him, you know."

"Met who?"

"George Eastman."

"The guy who wrote this . . . the Kodak guy?"

"That's where I was when Imogen was trying to reach me. Turns out he is my great, great grandfather."

"Wow. Really?" Fletcher was impressed.

"But I must say, I'm somewhat disappointed, really."

Fletcher set his drink down and opened *A Guide to Photographic Time Travel.* "How so?" he asked.

"I suppose I imagined it would be more scientific," Simon explained. It appears to be a lesson in meditation—methods and strategies to enhance deep concentration gathered from around the globe—India, the Middle East, Japan, China, Egypt, Africa—lists of potent and powerful medicinal herbs and fragrances that one can use, as well as a recipe of sorts—a drug concoction that can ostensibly help one reach a focused state in which to achieve time travel."

As Fletcher flipped through the pages, skimming the contents, he suggested, "Perhaps the importance of the book is not in its instructions *per se* but in the proof that time travel is in fact achievable."

"Hmm . . . an interesting hypothesis," Simon said. "That

could be a possibility, I suppose.

"It wasn't clear to me," Fletcher said, "but did you say someone was looking for this book? You mentioned it was in a safe?"

"Yes, Teddy wrote about it in his diary. Eastman gave it to him for safekeeping, said he feared for his life. And when I arrived here yesterday, the place had been ransacked. Things were thrown about everywhere. I discovered the book in a hidden safe in the wall, but whomever was here was looking for something specific."

Simon unfolded the newspaper article that had been inside the book detailing George Eastman's death by suicide in 1932 and handed it to Fletcher to read. Fletcher was familiar with the famous inventor of rolled film and the Kodak camera, but this was new information.

"It says he shot himself in the heart with a luger pistol at the age of 77," Fletcher said, his eyes widening with suspicion. "Do you think he could have been murdered for this book?"

"Perhaps," Simon said. "I wondered the same thing, but frankly, I can't see why anyone would want or need this. Again, in its essence, it is a how-to book for meditation."

"But," Fletcher said excited now, "returning to my original hypothesis about the existence of time travel, what if, in the wrong hands, the knowledge that time travel is possible could potentially put the people who can travel at risk of perhaps being manipulated or used for criminal purposes?"

"I don't know Fletcher," he said. "It is a mystery."

Fletcher handed the notebook back to Simon and he slipped the newspaper article back inside.

"He does offer up an interesting concept he called the "misery index, however."

"What is that?" Fletcher asked.

"As I understand it, when people travel to another time, they can make subtle changes that cause ripples in time—taking items out of circulation, for instance, or sharing information that could alter the course of someone's life path."

Fletcher nodded. "It sounds fascinating. I'd be interested in reading about how that works."

"I would as well," Simon replied, "because it is possible it may have effected two friends of mine—Herbert Doran and Georgia Bitgood. Before Imogen and I left 1913 together she told them that she was from the future."

"I don't follow," Fletcher said. "What's that have to do with Eastman?"

"Nothing," Simon replied. "The thing is, I want to find my mother and to do that I must go back and find Herbert. He promised to continue the search. The question is, did we set the Misery Index into motion by telling them? And if their lives were somehow altered, if things may have changed, will I be able to find them again?"

"I knew the story about your mother and how Teddy dumped her in the past, but I don't know anything about this man, Herbert, how is he involved?" Fletcher asked.

Simon explained how Herbert had befriended his mother and had helped her take and leave photographs in the vicinity of where she had been abandoned in the hopes that someone in the future might find them and come back to rescue her.

"He sounds like he was a decent man," Fletcher said.

"He was," Simon said, adding "but he was also a minister and very much a product of his time."

Simon told Fletcher that even though Herbert had helped his mother, he had a reputation as a man of the cloth to uphold and when it was reported to authorities that Tiffany had been making wild claims about being from the future, he was duty bound to have her committed for observation at a mental hospital to protect Simon, who was a child at the time.

Fletcher was shocked hearing this new information. "Wow," he said, "so this 'decent' guy had your mother committed to an insane asylum? I take back what I said before about him being a nice guy. That certainly doesn't sound very Christian-like."

The pain registering on Simon's face was evident and Fletcher immediately regretted being so flippant about it. "I'm sorry, Simon," he apologized. "And what happened to you . . . when they took her away?"

"I went to live in an orphanage."

Fletcher felt compelled to give his friend a hug whether he wanted one or not. "I'm really sorry," he said, stepping forward and grasping Simon by the shoulders.

Simon wasn't used to displays of affection, especially among men, nor was he at ease divulging his feelings, but admittedly, the hug wasn't awful. Still, he brushed it off, quickly disengaging from Fletcher and steering the conversation back around to Herbert.

"I know it probably sounds strange, but despite what he did, Herbert helped me gather up the pictures my mother had left for someone to find. He wasn't exactly a father figure, but other than my mother, he was the only person that genuinely seemed to care about me."

Growing up on the farm in Idaho, the third youngest of four rough and tumble boys, Fletcher knew he was lucky to have had a dad that took him on fishing trips, taught him how to ride a horse, a bike, and a tractor; shoot a gun, buck hay, and play football. He led a charmed life compared to what his friends Simon and Imogen had experienced. He couldn't imagine what it might have been like growing up without his dad, or his mom, and he was grateful not to have to know what that was like.

"Herbert also had a secret to keep," Simon said. "He was a homosexual, and he was terrified of anyone finding out. In those days, it was considered an abomination. When he saw Fletcher cringe at the word, Simon quickly realized his gaffe. "Um, what I meant to say was, he was gay," he corrected himself. Fletcher nodded acknowledging that Simon sometimes still struggled with the changing use of language. "At any rate," Simon continued. "It is difficult to fault the man knowing that he felt he had no choice. And, he believed that it would only be temporary, that they would evaluate my mother, and then she would be released."

Fletcher knew the answer to his question before he asked it. "But she wasn't released, was she?"

"No, she was not. Herbert and I visited the place . . . Crestview Sanitarium. So many years had gone by, and she was no longer there, of course. They said they had no record of her, that she had likely been transferred elsewhere."

"And you never found out what happened to her?"

"Right," Simon said sadly.

"Well then," Fletcher said, "we have to find out, don't we!"

Simon gave him a sardonic look and snickered. "We?" he said, as he poured them each another drink, took a sip, and paused before adding, "I do wish to find my mother, and remarkably, after reading Teddy's diaries he confirmed that even if you don't have the ability to travel to time on your own, it is possible for me to take you with me."

"Are you kidding me?" Fletcher bellowed.

"I must warn you," Simon said, "it could be a bumpy ride!"

"I don't care!" Fletcher remarked gleefully. "Take me with you!"

For the next hour, the two discussed strategy, how and when and where they might have the best luck locating Herbert. Simon explained that when he and Imogen had left at the end of 1913, the country was on the brink of war and most certainly Simon would have been called up to fight. And then when World War I was coming to an end, the deadly Spanish flu swept the globe, killing millions of people. Simon estimated that around 1917 might be the optimum time to go. Although the war was still going on, they wouldn't be sticking around long enough to be drafted, and the pandemic wouldn't occur until 1918. It would also have allowed Herbert enough time to unearth any news about his mother if he was able to.

All they needed now was a photograph. That part was relatively easy. It didn't take more than a few minutes of searching to locate Teddy's stash of photographs. Because his business model was based on traveling to the past and making contacts with buyers and sellers, his vast photo archive, located in several filing cabinets, was carefully organized, color-coded, and cross-cataloged by dates, subjects, and usage. One folder contained numerous photographs of varying dates devoted solely to the Benson Hotel—likely from the time he was trailing Imogen. Finding one taken in 1917 should be easy.

"Eureka!" Simon said, pulling the photo from the file. "We're in business."

"Are you sure that's going to get us there at the correct time?" Fletcher asked. Time travel seemed like a great adventure in theory, but now that he was coming close to actually doing it, his confidence was beginning to waver.

"It should be fine," Simon assured him. "The hotel is within walking distance of Herbert's apartment and if he is there, we should be able to find him. If he is not, well, we'll have to come back and try again with a different photo."

Fletcher followed Simon around the downstairs shop and through the apartment making sure that every door and window was locked up securely. Simon didn't anticipate anyone breaking in again what with the storm still raging outside, but he wasn't taking any chances this time.

When they were ready, Simon stashed some extra cash in his pocket in case they might need it and placed the photograph upright on Teddy's table. Stepping in front of Fletcher, he locked forearms with him and instructed him, "Keep your eyes closed. Hold on tight. Do not let go, no matter what happens." For a moment, Simon's thoughts returned to the time he impulsively grabbed hold of Imogen at the last moment, unable to bear the thought of losing her again. He never dreamed of ever seeing his own time again but it was about to happen. Fletcher tried not to let on how anxious he felt, but the telltale clamminess of his hands gave him away.

"Ready?" Simon asked, gripping Fletcher's arms tighter.

Fletcher nodded uneasily. "Ready."

Simon trained his gaze on the photograph and began to concentrate. This time, the room immediately began to shift, sooner than it had the last time. Perhaps with practice he was getting better at this. In his peripheral vision he could see the dark sneaking up in the corners. "Close your eyes," he instructed Fletcher, who gladly obeyed.

His skin prickled with electric energy, hairs standing on end as they were plunged into darkness and an explosion of air pulled them spinning together into the maelstrom. Simon felt Fletcher's fingers digging deeper into his skin as they plummeted into the nebulous void. He thought he heard a faint scream escaping Fletcher's lips as they clung tightly to one another. This was Simon's least favorite part of time travel. It was terrifying, yet also strangely peaceful—the act of letting oneself go, of being carried away by the unknown, was exhilarating. And as abruptly as the time journey began, it stopped. Before Simon opened his eyes, he knew he was home. He could smell it and feel it. And when he did, the Benson Hotel, with its magnificent red brick and glazed terra-cotta exterior and forest green awnings, loomed large in front of them as they stood outside on a sidewalk covered completely with delicate white blossoms.

Simon released Fletcher and they looked at one another. "Are you all right?" Simon asked. "I think so," he responded, glancing down at his feet. He seemed to be in one piece.

"How do you feel?" Simon inquired.

Fletcher noticed the early turn of the century duds the universe had provided—a fancy vest with a chain and jacket that had replaced his 21st century sweatshirt, gray cotton trousers for jeans, and a brown felt derby, which he removed from his head for closer inspection, Fletcher did a thumbs up and said, "Great!"

Simon was relieved that Fletcher wasn't sick. He wondered if that might only be a side effect of returning to the future. He supposed they'd find out when they made the return trip. With wide-eyed wonder Fletcher could not stop marveling at the sights and sounds unfolding in front of him in a time 100 years or so before he was alive. "Oh, my goodness, look, Simon did you see that?" he said as a succession of Ford Model Ts and Model As tooted their horns, *meep meep*, as they passed by them. People were everywhere, walking, riding bicycles and motorcycles, some with sidecars attached, and not a cell phone in sight.

For Simon, the experience was slightly different, like waking up from a long sleep. How many times had he entered those glass revolving hotel doors with Imogen on his arm during their glorious courtship? He missed her madly, but how things had changed for them since that time. He longed to go inside to room 213 where they had spent so many hours together entangled in each other's arms.

He wondered if the desk clerk, Marvin or Otis the lift operator were inside. He was tempted to find out but decided against it. Best to keep a low profile. They were here for a reason and one reason only—to find Herbert.

Simon tugged at Fletcher's sleeve to get his attention. "Let's go," he instructed as he started to walk in the direction of Herbert's apartment. After about 20 minutes, Simon abruptly stopped and began turning around in a circle as though struggling to get his bearings. "Are we lost?" Fletcher asked. "What are we looking for?"

"I could be wrong, but this seems to be where the mercantile used to be, he said, pointing at the rundown building in front of them with a sign above the door that read WEST END BOARDING. Dangling precariously from a single nail attached to the front door was a lopsided APARTMENT FOR RENT sign. Simon glanced at Fletcher, shrugged, and they went in.

Seated in a ragged lounge chair in the back was a wiry fellow with hollow eyes and sunken cheeks. A scribble of greasy black hair drooped across his sullen face. The mercantile was gone, obviously replaced by this scruffy boarding house. Clearly, a lot had changed in the four years since Simon had last been here. Fletcher hung back as Simon approached the man.

"Excuse me," he said, "I'm looking for a gentleman by the name of Herbert Doran."

"Upstairs, second door on the right," the man grunted, barely looking up from the newspaper he was reading.

Fletcher and Simon climbed the steep stairway to the second floor and Simon rapped on the door of the second apartment down the hallway. No answer. He knocked again. He waited a moment before turning to Fletcher. "Perhaps he isn't home or doesn't live here anymore."

They started to leave, but stopped when they heard the

sound of several locks clicking inside and then the door opening up a crack. "Who is it?" a tired-sounding voice responded from within.

"Herbert?" Simon asked, turning back to face the door. "Is that you?"

"Who is it?" the voice repeated.

"It's me, Herbert . . . Simon . . . Simon Elliot. Do you remember me?"

"Simon?" The person behind the door pressed the door open wider and peered out.

Simon resisted the urge to embrace him, instead asking politely, "May we come in?" Herbert stepped aside and allowed Simon and Fletcher to enter the dim apartment. It was much the same as Simon remembered, the bookcases full of books, but it seemed barer somehow than before.

"Do you remember me?" Simon asked Herbert once they were inside.

Herbert shook Simon's hand. "Yes, yes of course, I do," he said. "Come in and sit down. It's been a while."

"Four years," Simon replied. It felt more like an eternity, Simon thought. He turned to Fletcher and introduced him. "This is my friend, Fletcher Brown."

Herbert shook Fletcher's hand. "Pleasure to meet you." He gestured for them to sit down on the sofa and Herbert sat down opposite them in an uncomfortable looking upright chair. Simon noticed that Herbert appeared haggard. Although some time had passed between them, Simon was eager to dispense with the formalities and get straight to the reason for his visit.

"Have you any news about my mother?" Simon asked.

"Your mother?" A look of bewilderment crossed Herbert's face. "Who? . . ."

"Tiffany Rose. Do you remember that you said you were going to look into it?"

Herbert sat quietly for a moment, staring down at his lap as though grasping for a transitory memory. "Are you all right, Herbert?" Simon asked, concerned now by his odd behavior. What could have happened in four years?

But then, like the clouds parting for the sun to come out, Herbert blinked, and from his slumped position he leaned forward in his chair to address Simon's question. "Oh my yes, yes," he said, clearing his throat, "Tiffany Rose, of course I remember."

Herbert placed his hand to his chin and sighed. "So much has happened since you and Imogen left," he said. "I apologize for my disorientation, but I haven't conversed with anyone in weeks. There are times I fear I've forgotten how to speak."

Simon decided it might be better to delay further questions about his mother for the time being.

"Herbert," he said, "we can discuss that later. Tell me what has been going on with you."

Having an audience seemed to ignite something in the once great orator and storyteller and former firebrand preacher and he began to speak.

"After you left, I had high hopes," he said, motioning with his hands like the old Herbert. "I wanted to take flying lessons, as you might recall." Simon smiled at that memory.

"I have always been fascinated by technology and invention and when Imogen described the many wonders of the future, I was inspired, but regrettably, I did something foolish. As you might remember, Georgia Bitgood, your former fiancé and I became friends.

It seems absurd now, but one day we struck up a conversation about women's corsets, of all things, and how uncomfortable they were to wear. Georgia mentioned that she had a friend who had invented a lightweight, soft "brassiere" and she encouraged me to invest in her new business enterprise. It began to take off and it looked like we had a winner." Herbert looked away and paused before confessing, "I am ashamed to admit what happened next, but Georgia and her friend fled, along with most of my life savings. I would never be that naïve, but I thought Georgia and I were friends. I trusted her. I did not believe she could do such a thing."

As he listened to Herbert's story with growing alarm Simon's lower lip had been slowly dropping down to his chin. To say he was shocked by the news of Georgia's betrayal, was an underestimation. It was so unlike her. He was speechless. "I have no words, Herbert," Simon said, shaking his head back and forth in disbelief. "She could be obstinate, certainly, and granted, she did have a bit of a mean streak, but I would never ever have imagined that she could carry out such an appalling deed."

"Was it a sexy bra though?" Fletcher interjected, trying unsuccessfully to lighten the mood. Simon lobbed a stern look in his direction. Fletcher shrugged and tried a more helpful tactic. "Who was the inventor?" he offered. "Maybe when we get back, we can dig up some information on her."

Fletcher's comments didn't seem to trouble or offend Herbert much. "It doesn't matter," Herbert said, defeated. "It's all gone downward from there anyway, not only for me, but for everyone. Despite our presidents' assurances of neutrality, I fear we are on a collision course for a war to end all wars," he said.

Knowing what Herbert only sensed, Simon and Fletcher nodded uneasily. History was already written—within the next few months Herbert's worst fears would come true.

"I do have some news to report," Herbert said, hoping to lift the gloom-and-doom bomb he had dropped on everyone in the room.

"I intended to notify you through the channels Imogen suggested, but with all that happened with regard to Georgia, I never got to it. You see, I ran into someone who had previously worked as an orderly at Crestview and he remembered your mother."

Simon perked up at this bit of positive news. "Yes? And?"

"I'm sorry to have to tell you this, but she was receiving shock treatments that weren't working. In fact, they had scheduled her for a lobotomy." Simon's face fell. "No!"

"However," Herbert interjected, "before that happened, apparently someone stepped in and helped her escape from the hospital."

"Escaped?" Simon gasped. He had not even entertained the

idea of something like this occurring. All this time, he had envisioned his mother locked up, alone and helpless, clearly forgetting about who she was, her resiliency, her drive and survival instinct. She had, after all, managed to survive being tossed into an unfamiliar time and place and spent years trying to be rescued, never giving up. So, of course, it made perfect sense that she would have latched on to any opportunity for escape and to anyone who would endeavor to help her in that undertaking.

"It is no wonder that we could not get any record of her," Herbert added. "Surely, the hospital would want to keep that information quiet. It wouldn't bode well for them to have the public aware that patients were escaping from their fortress."

With the mood substantially lightened, Simon invited Herbert out to dinner, a luxury he was certain his old friend had not been treated to in some time. And besides, Fletcher was eager to take in a bit more of 1917 before they returned.

"You are a card!" Herbert said laughing hard and clapping Fletcher on the back as they reentered Herbert's apartment. The two men had gotten on famously from the start. Over dinner they exchanged stories and jokes, even laughing a bit about the failed brassiere affair. During a lull in the conversation, Herbert, who was naturally curious about where Simon had been for four years, asked him directly, "Did you and Imogen go to the future?" Simon looked down at his hands and fidgeted. He knew he wasn't supposed to discuss the topic of time travel with someone in the past, then again, Herbert had witnessed he and Imogen's "magical" departure. He owed him some explanation.

"We went to the year 2019," Simon said.

"My oh my," Herbert said, shaking his head in amazement. "What is it like? Tell me everything!"

Rules be damned, Simon launched into a wondrous futuristic tale of inventions and books and airplanes, cars and appliances, computers and phones you could carry in your pocket. For an hour, the three of them drank scotch and laughed and joked while Simon and Fletcher entertained Herbert with amazing stories of a future he would never know.

And at the end of the evening, Simon secretly slipped the cash he had wisely brought along with him into his friend's coat pocket, knowing the generous amount would be a godsend for someone living well below the poverty line in 1917.

When they were preparing to depart, Fletcher shook Herbert's hand. "It was a pleasure meeting you, sir," he said enthusiastically.

"And vice versa," Herbert returned. "I hope we shall meet again."

"Oh, we will! We definitely will!" Fletcher said, grinning broadly at his new acquaintance.

Simon stepped up and embraced Herbert with a proper manly bear hug, clapping his broad shoulders and hoping that he didn't notice how emotional he felt.

When he let him go, Herbert's hand brushed against the lump in his coat. Reaching into his pocket he pulled out the wad of money.

"What is this?" he asked, genuinely surprised.

"Take care of yourself Herbert," Simon said, and before he could open his mouth to protest, Simon and Fletcher had locked their arms together, leaving Herbert as alone as he was before they had arrived.

23

The tires made crinkly, crunchy noises as they rolled over the profusion of small branches, pine needles, and wet leaves littering the dark road. From inside the car, Imogen could feel the impact of the wind as it howled outside, buffeting the car and causing the trees lining the street to bend to and fro in a frenzied dance. Normally, Imogen loved fall storms like this, but being out in this one, not so much. She was glad to be home and more than eager to get inside where it was warm. Emerging from the car, a sudden blast of wind propelled her forward, blowing her hoodie down. Soppy sideways drops of raindrops pelted her head as she rushed to reach the shelter of the porch. A twisting swaying line of wind chimes greeted her with a jarring symphony of chaotic notes. In the wind, the screen door made a loud clap-clap-clap noise and when Imogen reached out to open it a strong gust of wind suddenly whipped the flimsy door from its loosened hinges sending it sailing off into the front yard.

Startled now by the powerful gusts, she hurried to get out of the storm but was startled to discover that the front door was wide open. "What the . . . ?" she mumbled as she struggled against the wind's force to close it. She pushed it closed and it slammed shut with a thud. Inside, the house was dark and eerily quiet. Feeling along the wall for the light switch, she flicked it on and off, but the power had gone out. "Fletcher are you here?" she called out into the darkness. "Where is everyone?"

Using the flashlight on her phone she searched the house, guardedly entering each room—the kitchen, the bedrooms, the bathroom, but no one seemed to be around. She dialed Fletcher's number. She tried Simon. No one was answering their phone. Where could they have gone? More important, where was Dad? Outside the storm raged, rattling the windows and filling Imogen with growing anxiety and dread. When she heard the noise, a thump and a rattling coming from the hallway closet, she thought about leaving the house. Leaving would be the sensible thing to do, but there was a storm out there. It was probably nothing, a mouse, famous last words uttered in every horror movie she'd ever watched, right?

"Hello?" she said softly as she approached the closet, slowly turned the knob, and opened the door. Shining the light inside, she found not a mouse, but Niles, hunkered down on the floor in the corner of the closet, a blanket wrapped about his shoulders, shaking, his face wet with tears.

"Oh Daddy," Imogen said as she bent down and wrapped her arms around him. Niles still didn't seem to recognize her, but he didn't recoil when she helped him up, allowing her to lead him out of the closet.

As Simon feared, the return trip did not produce a smooth landing for Fletcher. When they arrived back in Teddy's apartment, he let loose of Fletcher's sweaty arms. He slid to the floor like melted butter and was immediately ferociously ill. All things considered, Simon didn't feel so great either, but he forced himself to go to the kitchen and return with a pot for Fletcher to vomit into. When he finished retching, Fletcher groaned and rolled over onto his back on the floor, not moving. "Are you okay?" Simon asked him.

"Do I look okay?" Fletcher managed to respond sarcastically.

"I knew it might be rough, but that was bumpier than I thought it would be," Simon noted.

"You're telling me," Fletcher said, weakly raising himself up and leaning over the pot, his stomach lurching again. "I think I'm going to be sick again," he wailed.

Perhaps his eyes were playing tricks on him, but off in the corner, Simon sensed movement. "Who's there?" he called out, hoping he was only imagining things.

Before he could react, two people dressed all in black in hoodies and wearing sunglasses that shielded their faces, sprung from the shadows. One of them seized Simon, roughly twisted his arm around his back, and stuck a knife to his neck. The other lifted Fletcher up by his shirt collar and held him in a vise grip.

Confused, sick, and drooling, Fletcher wailed, "What . . . what's happening? Who are you people?" Neither of the disguised figures spoke as they roughly hauled the two men downstairs and around the corner to the shop.

The pawn shop was in disarray again. Books and papers were scattered everywhere, and two other disguised men looked up when Simon and Fletcher were dragged into the room.

"Well, well, who do we have here?" one of them barked.

"Found them upstairs," said the one holding Fletcher. "This one's sick." He released his hold on him and Fletcher slid to the floor, too ill to put up any resistance.

The man, possibly the leader of the crew, addressed Simon. "Who are you? How'd you get in here?"

"I would ask you the same question," Simon said, mustering as much courage as a man can with a knife held dangerously close to his jugular.

"I'll ask the questions," the man shot back, approaching Simon and standing inches from him. Blowing hot air and bad breath into his face, he repeated the question, "Who are you?"

Just then, another man piped up. "He's the owner's boyfriend." Simon couldn't be sure, but he thought he recognized the voice. Only that Carl fellow who had been with Mimi Pinky at the lawyer's office the other day would know this.

"Is that you Carl?" Simon asked bravely, hoping to scare them off if they thought he knew who they were. Nervously, the would-be Carl, backed a step away.

The leader didn't seem fazed, however. "Tie them up," he growled, "we'll deal with them later, after we find the book."

Out of the closet and seated now on the couch, Niles seemed more relaxed after drinking the cup of tea Imogen had made for him. Calmer, yes, unchanged, no. And no matter how kind she was or how many times she addressed him as Dad, he either couldn't or wouldn't make the connection that she was his daughter. After losing him, believing he was dead, discovering that no, he's alive, finding him again only for him not to recognize her was more than she could bear. Watching him now, staring blankly past her like he was somewhere else was heartbreaking and upsetting and Imogen wanted to cry.

Where was Simon? Even more vexing, where was Fletcher? How could he have left Niles here all alone? How was she supposed to sit here like this, a bundle of sad and mad and worry? For the third time in the last hour, she tried calling both their numbers again. Neither picked up. That was her answer. If they wouldn't respond to her, she'd just have to go to them.

Bundling Niles up in boots, a knit hat, sweatshirt and jacket, she hustled him out into the storm and into the car. "We're going on an adventure," she explained, starting up the car. Niles stared straight ahead without responding.

The storm did not seem to be abating, and back on the road, Imogen began to question her decision to take her dad out in it. Even though Stambourg was only about 20 miles away, the wind continued and the rain, though intermittent, made it difficult at times to see the road. It was also getting dark. Other worries beyond the current situation began to seep into her thoughts. What if Niles never came around? she wondered. How would she take care of him? Would he have to go to a hospital? It was alarming how everything in her life was changing so quickly. Simon had been so angry with her. Was she losing him too?

They came around a turn and up ahead, looming in the darkness, was the familiar tunnel that burrowed through the mountain between home and Stambourg. The yellow lights and the rhythmic thump, thump, thump vibration of the tires always soothed her and, of course, always brought back silly memories of the game she and her dad used to play.

"We don't want to wake the nasty old troll that lives in this tunnel, so make sure you hold your breath all the way through honey," he'd say. He always made a big deal of it, counting down before they both sucked in their breath and held it in for the ride through to the other end, cracking themselves up when they let it out. Never in a million years did she think she'd ever again drive through a tunnel with her dad, yet here they were, together but not the same.

When she glanced over at him, he was unresponsive, perhaps unaware that they were even in a tunnel. With a heavy heart, she turned her eyes back on the road, but when they had cleared the tunnel, in the silence of the car she wasn't sure, but she thought she heard him exhale as if he'd been holding his breath. When she looked back over at him though, his expression was unchanged; he was still staring blankly in front of him, but for an instant, Imogen felt a tiny glimmer of hope.

By the time Imogen pulled up in front of the pawn shop, the wind had died down, the rain stopped. It was still storming but not nearly as treacherous.

"Stay here dad, I'll just be a minute," Imogen instructed, unbuckling her seat belt, and stepping out of the car. She wasn't sure how she felt about all the lights being on inside. That could mean only one thing—one or both were there, and neither were answering her calls. She didn't want to be angry, but damn it, yes, she was pissed. Before knocking on the door, she turned and took a quick glance of dad sitting in the car. He was the same, still looking straight ahead. He'd be okay for a few minutes.

Imogen knocked, waited, knocked again. Paused and then knocked again harder. Someone was in there, she knew. She could see their shadows moving around inside. She raised her fist to knock again when suddenly the door flung open. She had no time to react to the pair of hands that grabbed on to her and roughly yanked her inside. The next thing she knew she had been hurled, not gently, onto a sofa, and a man was pointing a gun in her face.

"Who are you?" he barked. Instinctively she lifted her hands in the air, but she was more than confused. She wasn't expecting this. Who were these guys? She could hear two or three other overlapping voices coming from another room. And then one voice that she knew. "Imogen, what are you doing here?" It was Simon. She snapped her head around in the direction of his voice. "Simon!" she screamed.

"Shut up," someone yelled, and another man rushed over and grabbed her again, this time leading her to a straight back chair, pushing her onto it and yanking her arms behind her, then roughly tying her hands up tight with rope. Imogen winced in pain. It hurt. Everything was happening so fast. She knew that Simon was nearby, but she couldn't see where he was until two more guys hauled both he and Fletcher in from the other room. Only Simon was tied up but both were noticeably bruised. It looked like they'd been roughed up, but Fletcher looked especially awful, as though he was very ill. One of the men shoved Simon into a chair, the other dropped Fletcher onto the floor where he laid unmoving like a lump of clay.

Without warning, the man who seemed to be in charge, stepped forward and sucker punched Simon. Buckled over in pain, he fell to his knees. "I take it you two know each other," he growled. "So maybe she knows where it is."

Stunned, Simon lifted his head weakly and looked at Imogen and was at once afraid for her. "She doesn't know anything," he managed to say even though he was gasping for air.

"What is he talking about Simon?" Imogen pleaded. "Where is what? What do you want? I don't know what's happening."

"Okay, hotshot," the man said to Simon. "She doesn't know

anything. I'll buy that. So how about this, either you tell me, right now, or we hurt her." He pointed the gun in Imogen's direction.

The other three men snorted, and a couple offered up suggestions of their own. "She looks like she likes it rough," one said.

"Yeah, maybe we should have a little fun with her before we kill her," another said as he made a few lewd thrusts in her direction.

Niles knew the lady had told him to stay in the car and he had been waiting patiently for a long time for her to come back, but his legs were starting to cramp from sitting so long. He pushed the passenger door open and got out of the car. Once outside on the sidewalk, he stretched his arms and legs, and looked around before turning the knob and opening the door to the shop.

"Enough joking you two. I'm tired of talking!" the leader roared before marching over to Imogen and with no hesitance punched her square in the face with his fist. Imogen's head flew backward in response, blood erupting from her nose and lip.

"Nooooo," Simon wailed as he tried in vain to get loose of the ropes that bound his wrists.

Standing in the doorway, Niles saw her, bloodied and hurt and something snapped inside his head. That wasn't just some nice lady, he suddenly realized, that was his daughter—that was Imogen!

Instinct or fear or both kicked in and Niles flew into urgent and immediate action. Their distraction with the boss inflicting pain on Imogen, gave Niles enough time to grab a brass floor lamp nearby. Putting all his weight behind it, he lifted it over his head and dispatched a direct hit to the gut of one of the men nearest to him. As he fell backward another guy scrambled toward him, but Niles was ready. He swung the light around a second time, the momentum knocking him out with a crushing blow to the head. The leader, the one who had hit Imogen was advancing on her again, likely hoping that by using her as a bargaining chip, he could regain the upper hand in the situation. But Niles was not about to let that happen. Pure adrenaline kicked in and fear had no name. That was his daughter, damn it, and he was not going to allow anyone to harm his little girl.

In a series of graceful, well-practiced karate moves, Niles pounced on him before he could land a blow and the two rolled together battling each other with fists and kicks and head butts.

Immobilized on the floor, Fletcher noticed it. Eastman's book. It must have fallen on the floor after he and Simon were reading it. They had forgotten to put it back in the safe, which was why the thugs, who had gotten to the safe and discovered that it wasn't there, were searching for it. Slowly, steadily Fletcher nudged the edge of the book with his foot hoping to push it farther under the sofa and out of sight, but his actions instead drew the attention of one of the men who was starting to get up from the floor.

Still reeling from Niles' brass lamp to the gut maneuver, he staggered over, stepping on Fletcher's hand, and before he could stop him, had snatched up the book and ran. Injured, but now in possession of the treasure, he limped out of the shop and disappeared down the wet street.

Fletcher dropped his head in defeat. "Oh shit!" he murmured under his breath. Yet, despite not being able to stop that guy from stealing the book, Fletcher did not intend to allow the rest of the hoodlums to get away, no matter how sick he was. Getting up was difficult. He was dizzy and disoriented but he managed to retrieve the two guns lying on the floor.

As soon as he heard the slow clicking sound of a handgun being cocked next to his ear, the man that had been fighting Niles ceased the struggle and raised his hands above his head in surrender. Fletcher handed the gun to Niles and trained it on the other two.

"Good work!" Fletcher said, pulling his phone out of his pocket and handing it to Niles. "Call the police."

After the police had handcuffed three of the four men involved in the robbery and assault, took a description of the one who had fled, and hauled them away, Fletcher joined Simon who, after being untied, had rushed to Imogen's aid. "I am so sorry, Imogen," he pleaded. "I never meant for this to happen or for you to be involved."

"It's okay Simon," she reassured him, giving him a weak hug.

Simon turned to Fletcher. "They got away with the book anyway."

Fletcher sighed. "Yeah, well at least we didn't die," he said dryly.

"That is true," Simon agreed.

Niles, who had been hanging back, hesitant to approach Imogen, finally joined the group. And when their eyes locked on each other, Imogen knew he was back. Rushing to him she flung her arms around him. "Oh Daddy," she sobbed. "Where have you been?" He gently patted his daughter and they clung to one another for a while, neither wanting to let go.

"I have so many questions," she said, adding, "but not now, not here. Let's go home."

"Uh, I have a question though," Fletcher said. "Where did you learn how to do all those sick ninja-karate moves?" he asked, making a comical attempt at emulating the movements with his hands and feet.

"Yeah, Dad," Imogen said.

With a modest grin, Niles responded, "There's a lot of things you don't know about me, Imogen."

24

Sensing her gaze on him, Niles looked up from his coffee cup. "What?" he said.

"Nothing," Imogen said, waving her hand dismissively in front of her. "I'm sorry, Niles . . . Dad . . . it's just . . . it's unnerving to me that you haven't aged.

A smile formed at the corners of his mouth. "I could say the same of you, turning into a grown woman. Where did my little girl go?" Imogen returned the smile.

"In my case," Niles added, "it may be the only positive quirk of getting stuck in a time loop for 25 years."

"I'm glad you still have a sense of humor," Imogen said, pouring herself another cup of coffee from the carafe on the kitchen table. "I'm not sure I would."

Niles pushed his mug forward for a refill.

"Can I ask you a question?" Imogen asked.

"Sure," he said.

"I know you don't want to talk about this, but I just have to know. Why didn't you hide your notebook at my house or in your studio instead of burying it in Jade's back yard? I might have found you sooner."

Niles pursed his lips and sighed. "I thought of doing that," he said, "but I was afraid to go home. I didn't know what I might be walking into if I did. And then after I looped back the first time, I found out that nothing I did in that first two months could be changed. Every time I tried to do something differently, it was like the universe pushed back and wouldn't let me."

"So, you're saying it wasn't like *Groundhog Day* then,"

Imogen said.

"*Groundhog Day*?" Niles asked.

"Yeah, the movie, where Bill Murray's character relived the same day over and over but changed things until it stopped."

Niles looked at Imogen and frowned. "No, not like *Groundhog Day*," he said. "Much . . . much worse."

Imogen regretted bringing it up now. "I'm sorry Daddy," she said.

"And I'm glad you're taking a vacation," Niles said, changing the subject.

"Simon suggested it," Imogen said, glad to move on. "And I guess he thought staying over at the pawn shop in Stambourg would give you and I a chance to catch up too."

Time to catch up, right, Imogen thought. Where to start on catching up? she wondered. Should she start at age nine and meander her way through her ridiculous adolescence straight to her complicated adult life, or focus on more immediate events? Sheesh, either way there was a lot of catching up to be done.

"Tell me about Simon," Niles said. "How did you two meet?"

Imogen sighed relieved, this was a more recent story, but still long and convoluted. She worried it might be too soon to tackle it. Telling him about Simon would predictably lead to talking about Teddy and Tiffany, and eventually, Francis. Was he ready for that? It had only been a week since the scene at the pawn shop and when they had returned home, naturally, she had to first break the news to him that his mother had died while he was gone. On top of that, that she could time travel and that Grammy had lied to her about their deaths.

Rationally, Niles seemed to accept the inevitable, that he'd been gone a long time and that Grammy was old, but it didn't make it any less of a shock. Imogen had left him alone to absorb the news and hoped he'd take whatever time he needed to properly grieve.

It seemed best not to dump too much on him all at once. They also had not discussed what he'd gone through while he was away, something he was understandably avoiding. But, he asked how they'd met, so why not? No time like the present, Imogen decided. Today was as good as any. Neither of them had anywhere to go.

Imogen began, "Simon and I met in 1912." Niles leaned in to listen, soon engrossed in Imogen's account of she and Simon's chance meeting and courtship, what happened to Tiffany, who as it turned out was Simon's mother, and how the dozens upon dozens of photographs she had left around as clues had led directly to Teddy; the awful truth that Teddy was Simon's father, and the worst part of all, that he was the one responsible for trapping Niles and Francis in the past.

Niles was silent for a moment after Imogen had finished her story, taking it in. Finally, he said, "Incredible. I always suspected that Teddy was a little off, but I had no idea how dangerous and savage he could be."

When Imogen described how Teddy met his end, Niles simply nodded, showing no visible emotion at all. "And Francis is still missing?" he asked.

"Yes."

"Do you know what year mom traveled to that day Dad?" Imogen asked.

"I don't," he admitted. "Francis held things in." He looked down at his hands and paused before saying, "The truth is Imogen, before I went looking for Jade, we were having some problems in our marriage. I think your mother was quite unhappy, and that she traveled to get away from us . . . well, from me.

Imogen was embarrassed to admit that she was already aware of her parent's problems. "I know, Dad. I read your journals."

"What? On the island? Bakunawa? You went there?"

Imogen nodded. "Yes, after Kansas . . . well, I had a bad experience in Kansas. It's a long story for some other day, but when I came back all I wanted to do was go someplace where I could decompress, and I remembered you and mom once talking about an island that you visited, and that when I was clearing out your studio I had filed a bunch of island pictures away. Niles was stunned. "But, but are you sure it was Bakunawa?"

Imogen realized why he was concerned. "Yes," she said, chuckling.

"I had envisioned myself lounging on the beach and drinking Manhattans at a tiki bar, so you can imagine my surprise when I got there!"

"The natives there are hostile, dangerous. They didn't harm you, did they?"

"No," she explained, "but yeah, they were pretty hostile at first, and I was ready to hightail it out of there until one of them, D'ar said your name, Niles, and he recognized that I was your daughter.

"Oh, my goodness, D'ar, my friend. You met D'ar." Niles said, delighted.

Imogen explained how they took her to a structure and that's where she had discovered Nile's belongings—his shoes, reading glasses, a notebook.

"I can't believe it's still there," he said, shaking his head in amazement. They spoke at length about the island and the common experiences they shared with the Native people—their music and food and a very potent drink called "quuntuhhun."

"It was a magical place," Imogen said. "I enjoyed every minute of it."

"Me too," Niles said, looking away, revisiting fond memories of his time on Bakunawa.

Interrupting his thoughts, Imogen asked candidly, "Do you think mom is alive after all this time?"

"Possibly, time moves so much slower, so she should be around the same age as me now."

"Would you ever consider going to look for her?"

Niles hesitated, searching for the right words. "I want to find her, Imogen" he said, "but I'm afraid. Not only of time travel—I'm certainly terrified of getting stuck somewhere again—but also scared of what I might find. Wherever . . . whenever she is, maybe she's happy now. I don't know. It's possible she doesn't want to see me at all."

Struck by the sadness on her father's face, Imogen rose from the table and flung her arms around him, breaking down. "I'm so sorry, Daddy," she said, tears streaming down her cheeks. "All of this is my fault," she sobbed. "If I hadn't been so dramatic after

Jade moved away, you might never have gone looking for her."

"Imogen," he said, cupping her chin in his hands. "You were nine. Of course, you were sad and dramatic. It's what children do when they lose a best friend."

"When I thought you were dead, the little girl in me died too," Imogen confessed as years of repressed sadness, confusion, emotions spilled out.

"I was so happy to have you back, but I couldn't stand that you didn't remember me," she said. "But when we were driving through the tunnel the other day, I saw you hold your breath and I knew you were still in there somewhere, keeping me safe from the trolls."

Niles smiled. "I don't remember *remembering* the tunnel, or the trolls," he said. "I'm not exactly sure what happened to me, but when I saw those men hurting you, something shifted, and for the first time since you were my little girl, I saw you."

Sitting down on his lap Imogen rested her head against her father's chest and was still, unburdened. A sense of quiet calm swept over her and for the first time in a very long time, she felt something close to content until her phone rang, breaking the spell. Imogen got up and took it out of her pocket. It was Simon.

"Imogen," he said.

"Simon, where are you?"

"I'm here at the shop in Stambourg," he said.

"When are you coming home?" she asked, trying not to sound too anxious. There was a pause. "Simon? Are you still there?"

"Yes, I am," he said. "I received a call from a gentleman who said he is from the Daguerreian Society. Have you heard of them?"

The name sounded familiar, but she wasn't sure. "I remember hearing about them, a long time ago. I think Grammy mentioned them. She said they knew stuff about time travel, or something."

"Yes, that's what he said too. They want to meet with us—you, me, and your father. He said they have important information to discuss, and they want to send someone out to your house this afternoon. Can we do that?"

"Hold on," Imogen said, glancing over at Niles. "Simon says someone from the Daguerreian Society wants to come talk to us this afternoon? . . ." she said raising her shoulders with a questioning shrug.

Niles nodded agreement. "Tell him they may come."

Simon had arrived and was just heading to the porch at Imogen's house when a black sedan pulled up to the curb. Two men dressed in dark suits and wearing mirrored sunglasses got out and walked across the lawn toward him. The first man removed his glasses and extended his arm for a handshake.

"Frank Metzger, Daguerreian Society," the man said, shaking Simon's hand firmly. He was older than Simon, his hair graying slightly at the temples. The second man, who looked to be in his twenties, stepped forward and vigorously shook Simon's hand enthusiastically introducing himself. "Kevin McCord, field operative II," he stated.

"So nice to finally meet you Mr. Elliot," he said, still pumping Simon's hand until Metzger frowned at him and he let go.

Simon smiled, despite enduring the younger man's slightly unpleasant sticky palmed handshake. "It's nice to meet you both," he said, in his characteristically courteous manner.

Simon led them to the porch and Imogen let them in."Hi Simon," she said, giving him a quick peck on the cheek. "Come in," she said ushering the other two men into the house.

"I'm Imogen Oliver and this is my dad Niles Oliver," she said. "Please, have a seat," she said motioning them toward the couch. "Can I get you anything? Coffee? Tea? Water?"

Metzger shook his head, "No, thank you," he said. After first looking at Metzger for direction, Kevin followed suit.

Imogen sat down and after one of those longish, awkward

silences where everyone looks around at one another waiting for someone to speak first, Metzger leaned forward, clearing his throat.

"I know you are all probably wondering why we are here today. You have a lot of questions, and we are here to try and provide some answers. As we pointed out to Mr. Elliot over the phone, we are agents of an organization called the Daguerreian Society. "My colleague Mr. McCord," he said turning to Kevin, "will first give you a brief overview of our organization."

Kevin McCord was nervous, this being his first in-person meeting with real time travelers since being promoted from data monitoring technician in the DTA to field operative II, but after poring over their case files, he felt like he already knew Imogen, Niles, and of course, Simon.

"Uh yes, of course," he spluttered, adjusting his tie and shifting uneasily on the couch, before launching into the exhaustive complexities of the daguerreotype photograph.

"The Daguerreian Society was formally established in 1988 as an organization for people with a shared interest in the art, history, and practice of the daguerreotype," he began.

" . . . In 1835, Louis Daguerre, proprietor of the diorama, discovered that exposing an iodized silver plate in a camera made a lasting image if the latent image on the plate was developed by exposure to fumes of mercury and then fixed by a solution of common salt. The result, a one-of-a-kind image on a highly polished, silver-plated sheet of copper . . ."

Glancing around the room and noting the bored expressions and the frown on Metzger's face, Kevin sensed he might be losing his audience. Determined to grab their attention, he continued.

"Then, in 1839, Daguerre introduced his process at the French Academy of Sciences in Paris and to the attendees the process seemed *m-a-g-i-c-a-l* . . ." he said, drawing out the word and lifting his voice for dramatic effect. It seemed to work because even though Metzger remained sullen, the others perked up—he had them in the palm of his hand.

Concluding, he said ". . . and when a handful of photographers discovered they could time travel naturally through photographs they established the Daguerreian Society to study the phenomenon, not unlike the Ministry of Magic in *Harry Potter*!"

Imogen laughed, clapping her hands together, delighted by his pop culture reference, while Niles and Simon only looked confused and stoic, not getting it on account of having never heard of Harry Potter. Metzger started to interject, but Kevin quickly added, "but it's all very sophisticated and scientific," he gushed proudly.

"Thank you for that, uh, interesting explanation of the organization Mr. McCord, but I'll take it from here," Metzger said.

"Despite my colleague's entertaining comparisons, there is nothing 'magical' about our work," Metzger clarified, making air quotes around the word "magical."

"We employ highly sensitive instruments to detect subtle changes occurring in the historical timeline and monitor the temporal journeys of time travelers and the time streams they are entering. The society's mission," he continued, "is threefold: maintain secrecy, educate, and study time travel. We also provide traveler assistance whenever possible. Our goal is not to interfere but to only intervene when absolutely necessary.

In essence, we have been monitoring each of you as well as the activities of a person who is no longer with us—Theodore Diamond. You probably know him as Teddy. As you may know, Mr. Diamond had a quite lucrative business model, buying and selling rare items acquired from his travels to the past. One such rarity was a book—*A Guide to Photographic Time Travel.*"

"Eastman's book!" Simon piped up.

"You are correct, Mr. Elliot. Although the methods outlined in the book are somewhat archaic and inconsequential, it is the mere existence of the book itself that is critical. It proves time travel," he stated.

"Why does that matter?" Niles asked.

Metzger launched into a rambling scientific explanation about the universe and how the society couldn't keep track of everyone and if everyone could travel through time it would be a disaster and the universe could potentially rip apart.

". . . and that is the reason we want to keep it from being widely distributed," he finished.

Imogen, Niles, and Simon stared blankly at Metzger.

Sensing that they weren't quite following, and that Metzger had muddied the message beyond repair, Kevin jumped in. "Excuse me, may I offer an analogy that might make things a bit clearer?" Metzger folded his arms together, incredulous, but willing to let his assistant give it a go.

"Think Avengers," Kevin said, looking directly at Imogen, knowing that she alone in this group would understand current cultural references and would be able to explain it to the others later.

"The Avengers?" she said smiling, but as puzzled right now as the others.

"Yes, so each team member in the Marvel universe has a certain power, right?" Imogen nodded.

"It can be a superpower, a superhuman power, or it can be an enhanced power. Ant-Man can make himself big or small and communicate with other ants. Wanda has reality and mental manipulation. Thor is a Norse God, and he has a very large and heavy hammer; the Hulk has superhuman rage. Tony Stark is human in a supercharged, enhanced Iron Man suit. Black Panther, magical resistance and a vibranium-assisted outfit. Well, you get the picture.

"The point is that any one of these 'heroes' could flip and use their special abilities to cause destruction or bring about world peace.

"And let us not forget, there are others in the universe that don't follow the same code of ethics, like Loki and Thanos, for instance, who are motivated by power and greed and jealousy. These are fictional examples, yes, but if you apply the Marvel universe to regular people, don't you think if someone could not time travel themselves, wouldn't it be possible they might find someone who could and manipulate that person into doing their bidding?

"Real life and fiction are not that far removed from each other. As it stands now, time travel has not been scientifically proven. It is a popular subject of fantasy novels and the fodder of supermarket tabloids and conspiracy theorists. The society would like to keep it that way."

Imogen nodded her head. "Great analogy. I totally get it," she said. Niles and Simon looked at each other, perplexed. "Do you get it," Niles said.

"Not really," said Simon.

"I'll explain it later," Imogen whispered.

Metzger, glanced over at his coworker and gave him a nod of newfound appreciation. "Thank you, Kevin," Metzger said. "Well put. I would add that there have indeed been several rips in time that have shut down entire regions because too many people were trying to manipulate too many things at once, but that is for a broader discussion of the universe at another time.

"We were all in danger of being killed over that book and one of the attackers got away with it anyway," Simon interjected. "Are we being called to task for this?"

"No Simon, not at all. We know that it wasn't your fault, and we have people working on correcting this problem."

Metzger continued, "In his book, Eastman also discusses the self-correcting universe, which brings me to you, Ms. Oliver. If something has been publicly documented, that history can be altered but the outcome cannot be changed, a hypothesis that we know you put to the test during your recent visit to Kansas, circa 1946." Imogen squirmed uneasily in her chair, reminded of the tragic events in Kansas.

"By no means are we here to castigate you. We know about the tragic train-car accident that killed the teenage sisters. We know that you tried to bring about a different, happier outcome. We felt a visit might help, to provide you with any information you might be missing."

Imogen held back the tears as long as she could. Damn it, why was she always crying or just about to cry? It was getting incredibly tedious. She was like a leaky faucet anymore. Covering her eyes with her hands she broke down. "I knew it was wrong," she sobbed, "but I just . . . I just wanted to change things for them, and for Harry. To die so young was too sad. I had to do something. I had to try!"

Simon touched her shoulder and drew her close to him. Niles abruptly got up and left the room returning from the bathroom with a box of tissues for Imogen, who grabbed a handful from the box and sniffled into Simon's shirt collar.

Kevin offered reassurance. "If I may, it's normal to be curious," he said. "Heck, I'm curious all the time about everything, but some things can't be changed no matter how much we want them to."

Imogen dabbed at her eyes and said, "I understand. I promise, I won't do that again . . . ever!"

"There's one more thing, Ms. Oliver," he continued. "Eastman talks about the Misery Index. I won't give you a long, detailed explanation of it, but in a nutshell, subtle alterations in the past perpetrated by travelers can change the course of people's lives in hidden ways. Even the smallest things that you do can significantly alter someone's entire path in life without us even realizing it. Most of the time it is minor, for example, any time you remove an item from circulation, as Theodore Diamond frequently did, it has the potential to alter lives, especially if that item is rare or valuable and could potentially change the prosperity of that person or their family. That's one part of the Misery Index, there are three.

The next involves passing knowledge along to someone in the past—knowledge that they perhaps should not be privy to." By the look Metzger was giving her, she knew she looked guilty.

"I may have told a couple of people," she admitted, quickly adding, "but only because it was absolutely necessary. I had to tell Herbert Doran and Georgia Bitgood because they had both seen with their own eyes, people vanish right in front of them, and I couldn't leave Adam Curry without knowing that he was sitting on a volcano that was going to erupt." Imogen winced before also confessing, "And yes, I may or may not have slipped D.B. Cooper a bit of inside information."

"Really?" Kevin piped up, barely able to contain his enthusiasm "D.B. Cooper, *the* D.B. Cooper? What was he like?"

Metzger silenced his overenthusiastic colleague with a withering look and turned to Imogen.

"I will repeat, it is never, under any circumstances, a good idea to give people information pertaining to the future. However, in the case of D.B. Cooper, there was no guarantee that he would be capable of mastering the skill, so no harm, no foul," Metzger said.

Imogen couldn't help but be curious. "Did he though?" she asked. "Did he ever show up as a blip on your anomaly catcher, or whatever it is?"

Metzger's answer was basically a non-answer. "As yet, no one has heard from the man since," he stated. She couldn't argue with that and nodded agreement.

"The point is, there can be consequences," he said. "Talking about future events or advanced technology can be disastrous if the information should fall into the wrong hands."

Imogen understood and readily admitted her error in judgment. "Of course," she said. "I'm fully culpable. I have been careless, made stupid mistakes. I won't do it again. I swear."

Satisfied with her response, Metzger moved on. "The third and final part of the Misery Index involves the effect your actions can have on the universe. The easiest way to explain this is for you to imagine a pond," he said.

"When you skip a pebble across it, it creates ripples. *You* are the pebble and each time you travel through time you send out ripples. The universe can handle a few gentle ripples and they eventually die down, but erratic behavior can make the ripples much, much larger causing them to 'bounce' off other ripples. The surface of the pond could potentially become so rough and agitated that those stones would no longer skip. Unless the cause is fixed, the massive ripples produce a feedback loop until the very fabric of time begins to rip.

We don't know what the end result of this occurring would be, however. Humankind might be harmed. Another theory is that the fissure would simply end time travel, essentially closing the door forever. We don't know."

Niles, Simon, and Imogen sat in silence absorbing Metzger's words. Niles and Imogen had never heard anything about 'ripples in the fabric of time,' and Simon was far too new at time travel.

"In fact," Metzger said, "a person you know, Tiffany Van Elder, caused huge ripples in the time fields up until about 1955."

Taken by complete surprise, Imogen twisted around in her seat to look at Simon. "Your mother is alive? Did you know this?"

"Yes, I only learned of it recently," Simon conceded. "Fletcher and I went back and spoke to Herbert. He told us that she had escaped the sanitarium."

Simon was most interested by what Metzger had said about ripples though. "How can that be, Mr. Metzger?" Simon asked. "My mother was not a time traveler. She was kidnapped and left in another time."

"That is correct," Mr. Elliot, "however, though not able to initiate time travel herself, she was a person '*out of time*,' meaning that she existed outside of the timeline of which she was born. For that reason, whenever she did something anachronistic, it caused a ripple."

"Fascinating," Simon said, the wheels turning in his head. "So, are you saying that through your technology you can pinpoint her whereabouts?"

"Well, no, not exactly," Metzger swiftly clarified, instantly deflating Simon's renewed hope of finding his mother.

"The science is not so precise, he said, "but what we do know is that she was rippling time into the 1950s and the disturbances were emanating from somewhere in Western Europe."

Simon appeared satisfied with this new information, but before he could ask a follow-up question, Niles, who had been listening silently throughout much of Metzger's discourse, spoke first.

"Sir, I have a question," he said.

"Yes, Mr. Oliver," Metzger answered.

"You spoke earlier of the Daguerreian Society's mission to maintain secrecy, educate, study time travel, and provide traveler assistance. Forgive me if I'm being disrespectful in asking, but why did the society not step in and assist me when I was trapped in a loop for 22 years?"

Simon leapt off the couch. "Yes!" he said angrily, "I'd like to know too, where was the society when Teddy dumped my mother in another century?"

Things were rapidly spiraling out of control. Niles and Simon were both standing now and all three glared at Ralph Metzger, who's confident demeanor was quickly evaporating before Kevin McCord's eyes.

Stepping forward and creating a wall between Metzger and the angry people, Kevin attempted to take control of the escalating situation.

"Folks, folks," he said, raising his hands in the air in a motion of surrender. "Look, I know you are upset, but if you would please sit down, I think I can explain this to your satisfaction."

Simon, Niles, and Imogen weren't convinced, but returned to their seats anyway willing to at least give him a chance to address their questions.

"Your questions are completely valid," he said, "but the point to understand here is that our work at the Daguerreian Society is not infallible."

Kevin was fully aware that it was against company policy to speak negatively about the society's methods and that he could get fired for what he was about to say if Metzger wanted to turn him in, but in this instance, it was a chance he had to take. He liked these people very much and he knew how much they had all suffered. Imogen losing her childhood, Niles nearly driven to insanity; the enduring pain Simon's mother must have experienced at the hands of Teddy Diamond, and Simon's loss of his mother to a mental institution. He couldn't change any of it, but at the very least, he owed them an explanation.

He took a deep breath and dived in. "Whatever I say, it will never make up for the pain all of you have endured," he began. He looked directly at Niles and Imogen. "I can never give you back the time you two missed with each other, and I can't spare your mother's pain either Simon, but time travel is risky business, as you well know. There are two words that underscore our mission to provide traveler assistance and those words are 'whenever possible.'"

Imogen rolled her eyes. Simon and Niles reacted similarly, shaking their heads. Kevin knew that what he was saying likely sounded like a huge cop-out, but he needed to be completely transparent with them.

"I know I bragged at the beginning about our sophisticated equipment, and it is, but it hasn't always been," he explained. "Yes, we are much better at detecting anomalies now, but even so we can't possibly monitor everyone all the time. And back in 1997, none of you were on our radar. Should we have detected a ripple when Teddy dumped Tiffany in 1895? Yes, probably. Did we miss that you were reliving the same two months over and over again Niles? Of course, we did. We are only as good as our data, but our data is improving. We are able to track travelers much better now, but at the same time, we are humans, not Time Gods, and we make human mistakes, just like you do. So 'whenever possible' may sound like a squishy excuse, but even though we failed you, we have successfully been able to help many other people."

It appeared that Kevin's explanation had resonated with them because Imogen, Niles, and Simon nodded at one another, and Niles addressed Kevin and Frank Metzger, who had been hanging back listening quietly.

"I . . . we, apologize," Niles said, tears threatening to spill from his eyes. "We have all been through a lot and for you to acknowledge that means a great deal. Thank you for your kindness and for making a special trip out to help us understand better." Overcome with emotion by Niles words, Kevin moved in for a group hug with Simon, Imogen, and Niles.

When after a minute or two Metzger cleared his throat and said, "There is one more thing," the group disengaged from the hug to listen.

"Much has been said here today by my colleague," Metzger said gesturing at Kevin, who braced himself, fearing the worst.

"And I commend him for his candor. It was right for him to disclose the society's efforts to improve the safety of those who travel." He acknowledged Kevin with a brief nod and what came dangerously close to a real smile before resuming.

"However," he continued, "the main purpose of our visit involves you, Mr. Elliot."

Simon was stunned. "Me?" All eyes turned to Simon.

"Yes, it seems you have a unique ability, one that the society has never encountered before."

"It has come to our attention that you are able to travel freely from one photo to another without having to return to your base portal. You first appeared on our radar when you traveled to 1970. Nothing unusual there, a seemingly normal leap in time, but then, when you 'jumped' from one location in 1946 to a completely different place in that same year, and then made a third jump from there to 1917 before returning to the present, it set off alarms."

"Oh man," Kevin reacted excitedly, "did it ever. Our instruments went friggin' crazy!"

Metzger maintained his serious stance. "Yes, thank you, Kevin," Metzger said before continuing. "The Daguerreian Society would like to learn more about this phenomenon and have given me authority to extend to you an invitation to visit our headquarters and participate in a six-month study."

"For six months?" Imogen asked, alarmed. "Why so long?"

"We need that length of time to examine Mr. Elliot and complete our tests," Metzger answered.

Imogen couldn't help noticing that Simon's cheeks were flushed, his pupils dilated. There was a hint of excitement on his face she had not seen since he had witnessed 21st century cars driving on paved roads for the first time.

Without thinking, Imogen blurted, "I'm afraid you aren't coming back!"

Of course, I'll come back," Simon reassured her, cupping her hand in his. "You heard them. They only want to 'examine' me, run some tests, find out what I can do." Imogen wasn't so sure.

25

"After you," Simon said, ushering Imogen through the familiar glass and brass revolving door into the lobby. Although the rooms had been updated and the decorative lift replaced with a modern elevator since they had been here together in 1913, the ornate lobby of the Benson Hotel with its rich walnut paneling and pillars, classical coffered ceilings, floor to ceiling fireplace, grand staircase, and elegant ballrooms, were mostly unchanged. Imogen looked over at Simon and from his expression she could tell that he was reminiscing too.

"It feels a bit like coming home, doesn't it?"

"Yes, it certainly does," Simon said as he glanced around the lobby taking it all in and reflecting on the abundance of poignant memories the place invoked.

Tomorrow morning, Imogen would drop Simon off at the airport for his six-month stay at Daguerrean Society headquarters in Chicago, but tonight to soften the sendoff, they would be spending the night at the Benson, in room 213, to be precise—the same room in this hotel they had inhabited for a short while more than a century ago in what seemed like another life.

Yet, as they approached the front desk to check in, both noticed how much this area had undergone change. Gone was the polished wood desk and the panel of wood slats along the facing wall that held the brass, heart-shaped skeleton room keys—that darn key that she always had to jiggle around to ever make work—and of course, no Marvin, the desk clerk, dispensing snarky unwanted advice either. Imogen accepted the room's passkey from the clerk and together they ascended the staircase, stopping to view the photographs on display in the now historic stairwell, of presidents and dignitaries who over the years had stayed at the hotel, including every US president since Taft.

"And to think we were one of the first guests," Imogen noted.

As they strolled along the hallway toward their room it was like being transported back in time.

"I don't think I'll ever forget racing down this hallway and pounding on the door, twice, missing your departure by mere minutes both times," Simon said.

"Or when we held hands and skipped down the hallway like children when I came back?" Imogen said, laughing at the happy memory. "Simon chuckled too. "I could never resist you, Imogen," he said.

When they arrived outside room 213 Imogen inserted the passkey into the slot, waited for the beep, and pushed open the door. The room was very nice and spacious with a king-sized luxury bed, a chaise lounge, a comfortable chair, and an executive desk, and out the window a sweeping, panoramic view of the city.

"This is nice, but I have to say I do miss the rose-patterned wallpaper and the claw-foot tub. Do you remember when you came up to my room the first time to help me with my injured ankle?"

"Indeed, I do, like it was yesterday," Simon said, setting their bags on the chair and sitting down on the large bed.

They had met briefly once before, but the second time they ran into each other at Herbert Duran's lecture a fire broke out and in the mad scramble to get out of the hall, Imogen had tripped on her dress and fallen, spraining her ankle. Simon had rescued her and brought her back to the hotel. He had gotten ice to put on it. The way he looked at her, his hands so gentle when he tended to her injured ankle, something had stirred within her even though she was sure at the time that he totally wasn't her type at all.

Bouncing up and down a few times on the bed, Simon declared it, "Comfy."

Simon tried to tamp down the thoughts and memories this room was triggering inside him as well, but the feelings were there, burbling right under the surface. While he pretended to check out the room they played back in his head like a movie—his heart beating out of his chest when he first saw Imogen waiting in the lobby after she had returned, sharing ice cream sundaes, her introduction to that new book smell at the bookstore, kissing her for the first time in the alleyway, the stimulating conversations they shared about literature and science, inventions and crossword puzzles and evolution, the indescribable electricity of their lovemaking—wild and wanton and powerful and passionate; lying together in bed, wrapped in each other's arms. Drying her tears and cradling her when her precious cat died.

He looked over at her as she rummaged through her suitcase.

Imogen looked up and caught Simon watching her. "What?" she asked, embarrassed by his gaze.

"Nothing," he said, smiling. "We'd better get downstairs for dinner. Our reservation is at 6:00."

Over dinner they kept the conversation light, sidestepping any relationship talk. Neither wanted to ruin it by talking about recent events. And besides they were both busy devouring their dinners, a huge Rib Eye for Simon, Alaskan Halibut for Imogen. For dessert, they shared a chocolate peanut butter mud cake.

"This reminds me of the sundaes we shared," Simon said, licking the spoon."

"At that ice cream parlor a few blocks down," Imogen remembered.

Simon nodded, "Yes."

"Do you remember the bookshop? And how I introduced you to "that new book smell?"

"It's funny that you bring that up. I was thinking about just that this very afternoon."

"It's this place," she said. "It holds so many great memories for us both. I wish we would have come back here sooner, before you were getting ready to leave, that is." Simon looked down at his napkin in pained distress.

"I'm sorry, Simon, I don't want to make you sad. Hey," she said, quickly changing the subject. "Did you know that they have a cigar lounge here?"

"No, I did not," Simon said, surprised.

"I thought you might like a nice after-dinner drink and a cigar."

Simon grinned. "Yes, please," he replied.

The cigar lounge was intimate and appealing with plush leather seating, dark wood, dim lighting. Imogen ordered a Manhattan and Simon had a scotch, accompanied by a La Aroma de Cuba, known for its smooth, seamless, and rich taste. Full of dinner and suitably relaxed, they left the lounge and headed back to the room.

"Tonight has been wonderful, Imogen," Simon said as they walked. "Coming here with you was brilliant, thank you."

"Thank *you*," she replied. "I think we both needed to get away."

"I agree," Simon said.

Letting go of his hand, Imogen slipped away, suddenly making a detour down another hall away from the staircase. "Where are you going?" Simon called out to her.

He found her standing outside one of the doors and giggling conspiratorially. "Should we sneak a peek?"

Simon recognized now where she had led him. "Oh yes, I definitely think we ought to," he agreed.

They opened the door on a dark room. Imogen felt around on the wall and found a light switch. The room, though empty, lit up and it was still as gorgeous as she remembered it. With its Austrian crystal chandeliers, cathedral windows, and ornate ceiling, it was the same enchanted space where nearly a century before they had glided across the marble floor together under the flickering glow of a hundred candles, dressed in their best finery, and where Simon had felt so overcome with emotion, he thought he'd burst. It was the place where he had professed his love for Imogen for the first time. If the lobby and room 213 weren't enough to summon a gazillion memories, the Crystal Ballroom would surely send them over the top.

Simon looked at Imogen and extended his hand. "Shall we?" he asked.

"Let's," she said as she kicked off her shoes. She could almost hear the orchestra playing as Simon swept her into his arms the same way he had so long ago and expertly guided her across the polished wood floor. Simon looked as debonair as he did that night, even without the tuxedo, he looked as fine and put together in his contemporary sports coat and slacks.

"That was quite the enchanted evening, wasn't it?" Imogen professed as they danced.

"It was," Simon countered, "until Georgia threw her shoe and hit me in the back of the head." Imogen chuckled at the memory. "She had a lot of power in that right arm. I wonder what became of her."

"I know what happened to her," Simon said. "She ran off with Herbert's life savings to invest in a *brassiere* company with some woman."

"No!" Imogen was shocked to hear this. "I can't believe Georgia would do such a thing."

Simon wasn't interested in discussing Georgia or Herbert, however. "mmmm, you smell good," he said as he burrowed his face in her neck and playfully nibbled along her earlobe, giving her goosebumps.

"Oh you," she said enjoying his flirtatious naughtiness. "Hold me close the way you held me that night," she whispered. Imogen began to hum the *Blue Danube Waltz* as they glided across the empty room.

Stopping in the center, Simon took Imogen's hands in his while they slow danced back and forth. "You are a vision of loveliness tonight, my love," Simon said. Imogen had forgotten how much she adored the way Simon spoke, his thoughtful touch. She had purposely worn this new dress—a beaded modern iteration from a bygone era—hoping that this hotel, the dress, the memories might renew the spark between them. It seemed to be working. "I love you in this dress," Simon said, admiring her with his eyes.

"I like the way it feels against my skin," she said rubbing her fingers sensuously along the seam, starting at her breasts and ending at her hips.

Simon laid his hands gently on each side of her neck, leaned in close, and whispered, "I like the way you feel against my skin."

Their lips met in a slow, soft, unforgettable kiss that quickly intensified into something more until he had backed her against the wall of the ballroom. Time and space vanished in the moment as they kissed, rekindling a passion that had been lost to months of avoidance and routines and misunderstandings.

Without a word, Simon stopped kissing her. Grabbing hold of her hand, he pulled her from the ballroom and out into the hallway, at first walking at a brisk pace up the stairs, then pausing on the landing like impatient teenagers, urgently kissing and caressing one another more before racing to room 213. Simon kissed up and down her neck while Imogen fumbled with the passkey, finally successfully opening the door where they dashed inside.

This time, there were no buttons and ties, no loosening of corsets and collars, only clothes falling away, and bodies filled with desire urgently meeting again as lovers. Alone, together. Locked in their private love nest far, far away from the world outside there were no other voices, no pressures, no distractions, the way it was in 1913.

"I'm so sorry Simon for taking you for granted," Imogen earnestly pleaded.

"It's all right Imogen," Simon said.

"I was so self-absorbed. I should have looked for your mother . . ."

Simon placed his finger on her lips and shooshed her. "Not

now Imogen," he said. He was overcome with unrestrained emotion. He wanted her in every possible way. Passion and inhibition collided as he scooped her up in his arms and carried her to the bed.

Something about this room. *Everything* was different and *nothing* was different. A passing century could not quash the lingering impressions that had been imprinted here. And when their bodies melded, it was the fluttering of hummingbird wings all over again, an unspoken urgency, seamless and collectively timeless.

Through the night, they breathlessly clung to one another as if each embrace was their last.

"You will always be my darling, Imogen," Simon said. "And I will love you forever."

Imogen sleepily rolled over and reached for her phone on the end table next to the bed to check the time. Seven-thirty, they still had plenty of time to get breakfast before heading to the airport but all she wanted to do was linger here in this bed, in this room, with Simon, forever.

"Everyone leaves. Everyone dies" used to be her mantra. Her father had been returned to her, but now Simon was leaving. Was it tit for tat with the fickle universe? Get something, return something? Was that how it worked? It wasn't fair.

Yet, last night had been exactly what they both needed. In between making love they had also taken the time to have that chat they should have had long ago to hash out a few issues between them—she profusely apologizing for neglecting their relationship, admitting that she put up barriers and pushed people away—he, acknowledging that he had been overwhelmed and preoccupied as well.

Lying in Simon's arms, Imogen confessed that for her, Kansas had been a major wake-up call. "I kept trying to talk to you, to find time to tell you what was going on in my head, but there always seemed to be a distraction," she admitted.

"Tell me now," Simon had said, inviting her to unburden herself.

Everything she had repressed came spilling out, how she'd tried to undo something that couldn't be undone, how she wanted to spare everyone the pain, but, of course, it didn't work, no matter how hard she tried. History would not be changed. They died anyway. "And you know me, I just had to know, had to test it,." she said.

She described how getting to know the people in the past on a personal level had been her biggest mistake of all. She'd learned that these were real people, not a statistic, not a memory, not just another name etched onto a gravestone. But mostly, it made her reconsider what she was doing, to question whether the business of time travel business was even right for her.

When it was Simon's turn, he confessed that he had been more overwhelmed by this new century than he'd let on.

"It was too much, too fast, Imogen," he said. "The airplanes, the inventions, cars zooming by on the freeways, the computer, the 24-hour news on television, so many options for everything—I thought I might explode from the sensory overload. There were times when all I wanted to do was go home, return to my own time where everything was slower and quieter, peaceful."

When he was finished, Imogen reminded them of a pact they'd made with each other.

"What pact?" Simon asked.

"*for love are in you am in i are in we,* remember?" she said, quoting a line from an e.e. cummings poem in the book he'd given to her."

"Ah yes, of course," Simon nodded, recalling the pact they'd made.

"And only one crazy person at a time allowed!" Imogen added. "Deal?"

Simon laughed. "Okay deal!" he said, reaching out to shake her hand and seal their pact for the second time.

Seated at a table for breakfast in another of the hotel's eateries, the Palm Court was a charming little lounge of a bygone era.

"Now that you know your mother might be out there somewhere, alive, will you try to find her," Imogen asked. They hadn't discussed all of their future plans last night.

"Yes," Simon nodded, "I certainly would like to pursue that when the society is finished with me."

An awkward silence followed, and Imogen looked away, staring intently at a potted fern in the corner before focusing on her coffee.

"A penny for your thoughts?" Simon asked.

Imogen looked up from stirring her coffee. "Don't you think it's weird that they won't let you call home while you're there?" she exclaimed.

Simon sighed. "We've been over this, Imogen. They don't want me to have any news from the outside world that might influence or otherwise denigrate the tests."

"I know," she said, sulking "but checking in with your partner is different. I mean, I don't see why they won't allow it."

"It'll be okay, you'll see," Simon said reassuringly. "This time apart will give you an opportunity to get reacquainted with your dad, spend quality time together, catch up. I think it will also be good for us, too Imogen. Six months is nothing. I'll be back home in no time."

Imogen wasn't convinced. Even after last night with all the promises made to each other, she couldn't shake the uneasy feeling that something wasn't right, that this might not just be a temporary interlude. How much did they *really* know about this Daguerrean Society anyway?

Reading the worry on Imogen's face, Simon weaved his fingers through hers. "You know that I love you Imogen. I traveled across time to be with you, but everything happened so fast. I wasn't prepared for it. Ever since I arrived here, I've felt out of place, out of time. It's difficult to explain. It's like everything in the world sped up but I didn't," he said. "Let's take it slow this time, see where we're at when I get back."

They lingered in their embrace for a while, neither one wanting to let the other go, delaying the moment they both dreaded.

"You'll call me when you get there?" Imogen asked, her head rested against Simon's shoulder.

"Yes, of course I will," Simon said.

She looked up at him. "They won't confiscate your phone right away, will they?"

"I don't think so, but if they try to, I promise, I'll insist that I be allowed to call my special person first," he said. "Don't worry, Gen, everything is going to be fine."

Not usually one for public displays of affection, Simon surprised her by reaching out and pulling her in for a long and lingering kiss that took her breath away. "Goodbye, my love," he said. He started to walk away, but stopped, turned, and dipped his head in typical polite Simon fashion. "I'll see you soon, darling."

Still unnerved by moving stairs he tripped a bit as Imogen watched him ride the escalator up. When he reached the top, he stepped off, did a half turn and waved at her once more before disappearing into the passenger terminal.

Imogen forced herself to wave back. "Goodbye Simon," she whispered.

EPILOGUE

Fidgeting in the uncomfortable chair beneath the stark humming fluorescent ceiling lights she flipped through the pages of an outdated issue of *PEOPLE* magazine pretending to be interested. The grayish-drab walls, somebody's idea of soothing, had the opposite effect on her and the assorted other mask-wearing women seated in the room who seemed mildly bored mixed with a tinge of anxiety. A pungent odor of burnt coffee permeated the small space making her feel puckish. Imogen hated doctor's office waiting rooms about as much as she hated being sick every morning.

The first time it happened, she brushed it aside—maybe she'd overdone the pale Pilsners the night before or eaten one too many street tacos from the food truck. But after several mornings of waking up and barely making it to the toilet to throw up, she knew something was seriously not right.

Following the instructions on the side of the box, she peed on the stick. And after taking the test three separate times and still getting a plus sign, there seemed no denying it. She was pregnant. She wasn't entirely sure how she felt about that, even now.

She had not heard from Simon in six weeks. As promised, he had called her when he first arrived at the society's Chicago headquarters. At the time, he had said that he would not be allowed anymore outside contact until they completed their tests, which was expected, but now, all things considered, she had other concerns, oh, like a global pandemic, for one.

Was he okay? Was he under quarantine like the rest of the world? Surely, they would allow him to call if he was ill, wouldn't they? It was maddening not knowing.

Yet, how ironic that here they were, sandwiched between two pandemics. Simon's journey from 1913 to the future with her had spared him of the Spanish flu pandemic of 1918 only to run smack up against another one roughly 100 years later. She wondered if he thought about things like that too. More importantly, was he thinking of her?

She was vigilant about washing her hands, masking up, and socially distancing, and she had stopped taking clients and time traveling, for the time being.

At least she had people now and for that she was grateful. Along with her dad and Fletcher the three of them had formed a sort of protective pod around themselves, spending ridiculous amounts of time playing board games, singing karaoke, learning to bake bread, and binge-watching TV together. With Simon gone, she leaned on their support more than ever.

Tossing the magazine back onto the cluttered end table, she searched around for something else to read to pass the time. To her amazement she noticed a book, but not just any book, *Winter of the Midnight Sun*, by Loretta Ross. Loretta, from Kansas. What were the odds?

At that moment, one of the doors swung open and a nurse's assistant loudly announced, "Imogen Oliver."

Imogen got up to go, but not before snatching up the paperback copy of her friend's novel and slipping it into her bag.

ACKNOWLEDGMENTS

First and foremost, love and appreciation to my husband and best friend Jeff Bolkan for encouraging me and allowing me to pick his big brain about the complexities of time travel.

Huge thanks to Gail Curtis, who as with the first book, graciously took the time to read and critique early drafts, providing me with spectacular feedback and advice.

Much gratitude to my family: My mother, Marian Nelson; sister Carol Niblett, and my kids Cory Huffman, Kaylee Crum, and Daniel Stoltey for their love and support; and my dad, Russ Nelson—for the memories.

Many thanks to countless friends, family, professors, and coworkers who, over the years, have shaped, influenced, or contributed in big and small ways to my life experiences.

More books from GladEye Press

The Time Tourists
Sharleen Nelson
Time-traveling PI Imogen Oliver recovers lost items and unearths the stories and secrets of friends and relatives from the past. In this first book in the series she travels to 1967 in search of a young runaway, and then later accepts a case in the early 20th century that will alter her life forever.

Tripping the Field: An Existential Crisis of Ungodly Proportions
Ian Jaydid
Empiricist scientist, Professor Michael Huxley tumbles, stumbles, strides, and crawls through the jungles of South America, the mountains of Tibet, and the backwoods of Colorado in search of enlightenment and the hope of saving the world from a religious cult that has discovered a dark shortcut to the power of quantum realities.

10 Takes: Pacific Northwest Writers Perspectives on Writing
Jennifer Roland
From novelists to poets to playwrights, Jennifer Roland interviews a variety of authors who have one thing in common—they have all chosen to make the Pacific Northwest their home.

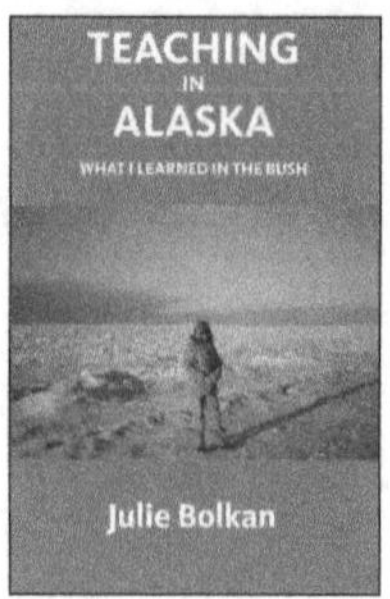

Teaching in Alaska What I Learned in the Bush
Julie Bolkan
Among the first outsiders to live and work with the Yup'ik in their small villages, this book tells Julie's story of how she survived culture clashes, isolation, weather, and struggles with honey buckets—a candid and often funny account of one *gussock* woman's 12 years in the Alaskan bush.

COMING SOON from

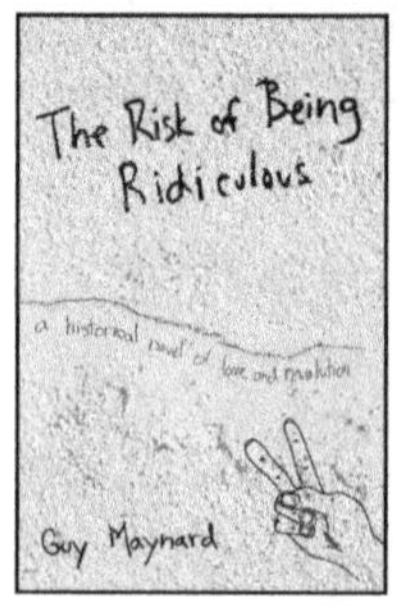

The Risk of Being Ridiculous: A Historical Novel of Love and Revolution
Guy Maynard
Join 19-year-old Ben Tucker for a passionate, lyrical six-week ride through confrontation and confusion, courts and cops, parties and politics, school and the streets, Weathermen and women's liberation, acid and activism, revolution and reaction.

Look for Maynard's second book coming soon.

Dying for Love
Patricia Brown
The fifth book in the Coastal Coffee Club Mystery series follows Eleanor as she investigates infidelity, murder, and long-buried secrets in the sleepy seaside town of Sand Beach.

Becoming Nancy
Camille Cole
Hop on the counterculture bus in this firsthand account of one woman's journey to find herself as she hobnobs with pranksters, hippy icons, colorful characters, and fellow travelers.

Visit www.gladeyepress.com for fantastic deals on all GladEye Press titles.

Follow us on Facebook: https://www.facebook.com/GladEyePress/

GladEye titles can be ordered from your local book store and Amazon.com.